Praise for *Without the Moon*

"Few people can match her extraordinary capacity to capture the atmosphere of louche, bygone London and the mood of its people. In *Without the Moon* she tackles the blitzed city of 1942 with the same unerring touch" Marcel Berlins, *The Times* (Crime Book of the Month)

"A classic noir novel in every way" *The Lady*

"What a fabulous piece of work this is. It practically out-Hamilton's Patrick Hamilton in its sense of menace and place, conducting a kind of séance with that bombed-out but brassy London of the war-torn '40s; on each page you can practically smell the cheap scent, powder, Brilliantine and black-market whisky" Travis Elborough

"Brilliant and brave, *Without the Moon* blends murder and magic to create a vision of London as a spiritual maze. Prostitutes, psychopaths, detectives, villains and psychics move through corridors, glimpsing heaven and hell in an atmosphere that is so charged it can almost be touched. Fact and fiction link as justice is demanded. The best work yet from a genuine, original talent" John King, author of *The Football Factory* and *Human Punk*

Praise for *Weirdo*

"A serious talent ... An unusually gifted writer of heartfelt noir ... she has brilliantly captured that desperate sense of teenage boredom, isolation, danger and mayhem" Henry Sutton, *Daily Mirror*

"An absorbing mystery, an extraordinarily powerful evocation of time and place and a cast of characters whose every breath feels real – Unsworth gets better with every book" Laura Wilson, *Guardian*

"The whole package works beautifully: memory traces, bad magic, sounds, smells … a great, page-turning read" Iain Sinclair

"Masterful … brilliant evocation of time and place, Unsworth adds astonishing and disturbing insight into the minds of disaffected youth who cannot find love and acceptance" Marcel Berlins, *The Times*

Praise for *Bad Penny Blues*

"The author has been compared to cult noirist Derek Raymond, but here she enters a pantheon of writers exploring London lowlife that extends from Patrick Hamilton and Colin MacInnes" Christopher Fowler, *Financial Times*

"There's something about the textured layers of Cathi Unsworth's third novel that effortlessly draws the reader into the dark and disturbing environment she creates … Unsworth lives up to her growing reputation as one of the UK's stars of noir crime fiction, combining hardboiled prose with vivid characters and a lucid sense of place" Yasmin Sulaiman, *The List*

Praise for *The Singer*

"A cracking page-turner that feels authentic, authoritative and evocative. And it's beautifully written. This is a bloody good book" Val McDermid

"Brilliantly paced, plotted and stylish crime novel from the hugely talented and highly original Cathi Unsworth" *Daily Mirror*

Praise for *The Not Knowing*

"Brilliantly executed with haunting religious imagery, interesting minor characters, great rock 'n' roll references and a spectacular ending. *The Not Knowing* is a cool and clever debut. Sleep on it at your peril" *Diva*

"Hugely entertaining debut from a future star of gritty urban crime literature" *Mirror*

CATHI
UNSWORTH
THAT OLD
BLACK MAGIC

Leabharlanna Poiblí Chathair Baile Átha Cliath
Dublin City Public Libraries

First published in Great Britain in 2018 by Serpent's Tail,
an imprint of Profile Books Ltd
3 Holford Yard
Bevin Way
London
WCIX 9HD
www.serpentstail.com

Copyright © 2018 by Cathi Unsworth

1 3 5 7 9 10 8 6 4 2

Typeset in Garamond by MacGuru Ltd
Printed and bound in Great Britain by Clays, St Ives plc

The moral right of the author has been asserted.

The characters and events in this book are fictitious. Any similarity to real
persons, dead or alive, is coincidental and not intended by the author

A CIP record for this book can
be obtained from the British Library

ISBN 978 1 78125 727 2
eISBN 978 1 78283 295 9

FSC
www.fsc.org
MIX
Paper from
responsible sources
FSC® C018072

For Ann Scanlon

If you go down in the woods today,
You'd better not go alone.
It's lovely down in the woods today,
But safer to stay at home...
Henry Hall, "Teddy Bear's Picnic"

PROLOGUE

Tuesday, 14 January 1941

London lay ghostly white beneath a fresh fall of snow, glowing in the thrall of a full moon. Despite the blackout, as Hannen Swaffer stepped from his cab, his view of the Holland Park thoroughfare, its stuccoed mansions and tall trees, was as clear as day. Humming to himself, he rattled across to 3 Lansdowne Road. Fine night for a séance, he thought.

Both as a reporter for the *Daily Herald* and a keen practitioner of spiritualism, Swaffer was delighted by the prospect of the night's gathering. A small circle had been invited by Miss Winifred Moyes, herself a former Fleet Street journalist, who now ran the Christian Spiritualist Greater World Association from this address. Since the onslaught of the Blitz, her mission had turned from spreading enlightenment to more practical matters, finding shelters and relief for the bombed-out women and children of the capital, and occasions such as this had become rare. Tonight was a special exception for the woman in the grey moiré gown who opened the door to Swaffer, and everyone else she had privileged with an invite. Tonight they would be sitting for one of the greatest mediums in the world.

"Miss Moyes," Swaffer doffed his stovepipe hat in greeting, unleashing a torrent of hair as white as his snowy surroundings.

"Mr Swaffer," she replied, a smile lighting up her rather mannish face. "Here you are. Please do give Mr Hillyard your coat and come through." With a sideways step, she revealed the short, stocky caretaker beside her, his blue boiler suit replacing the traditional butler's livery. With a few words of greeting, Swaffer divested himself of his outer layers and stepped into the room beyond, reporter's antennae bristling.

Chairs had been arranged in a semi-circle around a cabinet at the centre of the floor. Milling around it, sipping glasses of sherry and murmuring to each other, were four ladies in late middle age, dressed in their best costumes and fur capes. Swaffer's eyes strayed past their coiffured heads for the guest of honour and alighted on a couple, huddled together on a chaise longue behind the cabinet, in the furthest, darkest corner of the room.

Most of the space on the seat was taken up by a woman dressed entirely in black, with thick bobbed hair of the same raven hue. Her face was the image of the full moon against her dim surroundings, wreathes of smoke from her cigarette standing in for clouds. Her companion, a man in a dark suit, bit at the stem of a rosewood pipe, eyes darting around the room with an expression pitched somewhere between hostility and nervousness.

"Dear Mr Swaffer!" one of the ladies distracted him. Two companions fluttered after her, cooing greetings. The fourth, whose platinum curls, ostrich boa and diamond jewellery signified a greater wealth than all the others put together, stood exactly where she was. Self-made millionairess Olive Bracewell fixed Swaffer with a look of disdain.

"Care for a sherry, Mr Swaffer?" Mr Hillyard offered a tray of thimble-sized glasses.

"Most kind." Swaffer took a bracing sip as Miss Moyes approached.

"Are we all ready?" she asked. "Our guest is rather shy, as you may have gathered." She flicked her gaze towards the chaise longue and back. "To help her reach through the veil, she has requested that we say *The Lord's Prayer* and then sing for her the *23rd Psalm*. Mr Hillyard, would you do the honours, if everybody else would take their seats…"

The sitters fanned out around the semi-circle as the caretaker dimmed the lights, so that only a single red bulb, placed on a standard lamp behind the cabinet, remained to illuminate the room. Swaffer was aware of the long shadows that unfurled themselves into the absence of light; the ponderous ticking of the grandfather clock; the breathing of other sitters; and the shuffling of the caretaker's feet as he travelled across the carpeted floor to sit beside him.

"Now that we are all assembled," said Miss Moyes, "please welcome Mrs Helen Duncan and her husband, Henry, to the circle. They have come a long way to be with us." She began to clap, provoking an enthusiastic response from the others. In the twilight glow of the lamp, Swaffer found the Duncans' expressions even more unreadable.

He had first met this woman a decade ago, when he had written of her feats for the *Psychic Times*, a journal to which he frequently contributed. She hailed from Callander, a village in the Highlands, and had been blessed with the gifts of Prophecy and The Sight since childhood. As an adult, her copious manifestations had aroused both passionate devotion and virulent scepticism. Swaffer's first assignment with her had required him to put those powers to the strictest of tests devised and observed by magicians and medical men. She had passed each one with ease.

"Thank ye," the Scotswoman said. "I hope I'll no' disappoint you tonight." Nodding to her husband, she turned towards the cabinet and, with his assistance, lowered herself into the tall-backed chair inside it. Once she had settled, Henry murmured something to Miss Moyes and she turned back to her circle.

"Are we all ready?" she asked. At the nods of affirmation, she took her seat at the centre of the semi-circle. As the assembled began to intone the words of prayer, Mr Duncan drew the curtains around his wife. Swaffer caught a last glimpse of her head lolling onto her chest, her eyes closed. By the time they had said "Amen", the medium's breathing had grown heavier, and, in the brief pause before the beginning of the hymn, became the loudest sound in the room. Then the ladies began trilling "The Lord is My Shepherd", the reedy voices of the sopranos floating tremulously before the more forceful male baritones and Miss Bracewell's equally gusty alto.

Swaffer began to see a flickering of something pale beneath the curtains. Was this the ectoplasm that signalled the arrival of Mrs Duncan's spirit guides? His nostrils caught a faint aroma of brine, a sign that this was indeed the substance that linked the two planes of existence.

"*Goodness and mercy all my life, Shall surely follow me,*" he sang, teetering on the edge of his chair, straining his eyes as the thin line became more a substantial billowing, "*and in God's house for ever more, My dwelling place shall be.*"

Henry Duncan drew back the curtains. With a collective intake of breath, Miss Moyes' circle witnessed the vision of his wife sitting fully erect with ectoplasm streaming from each nostril, down onto the front of her dress and out into the room before them. Her eyes snapped open, two glittering black buttons that stared straight through the assembled as if seeing far beyond the confines of the room. Her laboured breathing stopped sharply. Swaffer felt the hairs rise on the back of his neck and his heart quicken.

"Oh, I say!" the lady to Swaffer's left gasped.

The spectre of a young woman rose from the cloudy mass surrounding the medium to float in the air in front of them. An enchanted creature, her head turned to one side, showing an aquiline profile surrounded by waves of hair that seemed to shimmer on the air, despite the absence of a breeze. She softly murmured a tune without any discernible words. For minutes, the seated watched in awed silence as she twisted languorously from left to right, performing a phantasmagoric fandango to the childlike melody she was fashioning, something between a nursery rhyme and the fragments of a dream.

"Spirit," Swaffer said, "what is your name?"

Slowly, the spectral head turned towards the mortal countenance of the journalist. The singing stopped and a different voice issued from the cabinet.

"You know what my name is, dearest."

It was a woman's voice, but not Helen's Highland brogue. She spoke clearly and precisely, like an actress projecting from a stage.

"And you were right, it *was* a fine night for it," she went on. She had a slight Midlands dialect, only she couldn't quite pronounce her 'w's. "Perfect, with this moon and the snow. You *are* clever. And this... Oh my... This..."

The vision undulated again, the features of the woman becoming less discernible, as if she was beginning to fade. Then a sob and the voice returned. "What is this? Why have you brought *me* here? This isn't what we agreed!"

The ladies looked around at each other in consternation. Mr Hillyard grunted.

"My dear, you are quite safe here," said Swaffer, "we only invite those to our circle who wish to be heard. Are you not known to anyone present?"

"No!" There was a sudden, abrupt choking sound and the vision fell sharply away, the ectoplasm seeming to collapse and vanish, so that afterwards, Swaffer was never sure if the expression of terror he witnessed had been upon the visage of the manifestation just before she disappeared, or was that of the woman who had brought the spirit forth.

"Noo!" Mrs Duncan's cry brought his eyes back to the cabinet. She was pulling at the neckline of her dress. "Help!" she gasped a wheezing rattle. "Help me!"

In two bounds he was beside her, shouting: "Put the lights on, Mr Hillyard! She's choking!"

Swaffer had received his medical training many years before, in a field hospital on the Western Front. Inside the cabinet was a heady reminder; a tight space so full of sweat and panic that he could barely fit himself in beside the heaving medium. His feet blundered on the fabric of her dress, but he managed to get his hands around her shoulders and propel her forward.

"Cough, Mrs Duncan!" he shouted. "Cough, if you can!" He gave a hefty thump to the centre of her back. Her wheezing worsened but she did as he said. A cough snapped across the room like thunder. Swaffer dealt a second blow and this time she spluttered something up, the vomiting noise she made was followed by a shuddering intake of breath. The floor moved under Swaffer's feet as she lurched, yanking the hem of her skirt away from under him. He caught hold of the back of the chair to stop himself from falling and, as he did so, the lights came on.

Henry Duncan knelt in front of his stricken wife,

murmuring: "It's all right, hen, you're safe now." Mrs Duncan's shoulders rose and fell dramatically, but thankfully Swaffer could hear her breath come in thick sobs. Beyond them, the ashen faces of Miss Moyes and her companions rose from their chairs, staring aghast.

"Don't panic," Swaffer advised, manoeuvring himself out of the cabinet, feeling more than a little disorientated. "We got to the problem in time, didn't we, Mr Duncan?"

Henry mopped his wife's face with his handkerchief. "Aye," he said, not moving his gaze from hers. "I think ye did, Mr Swaffer, I think ye did. Thank the Lord for that."

"How are you feeling now, Mrs Duncan?" Swaffer asked.

Her face was bright red and the fear still gleamed in her dilated pupils. She nodded, made a gesture to her throat with her left hand and coughed painfully.

"Of course, you shouldn't speak," he reprimanded himself. "Let me fetch you a glass of water. And a brandy, perhaps?"

"Should I call for an ambulance?" Miss Moyes' voice behind them strained with anxiety.

"No, no," Henry turned to speak to his hostess. "There's no need, Helen will be right enough in a minute. Eh, but the brandy's a good idea."

"Well, if you're sure," Miss Moyes looked doubtful. Mr Hillyard, meanwhile, had seized the initiative and pulled out an armchair for their guest to recline on. Each taking an arm, he and Henry helped guide her to it, while Swaffer returned with a glass of water in one hand and brandy in the other. Kneeling down to offer them to the medium, he felt a wave of light-headedness. He could still hear the spirit's lullaby-lament echoing through his mind.

"Take the water first," he said, steadying himself against

the arm of the chair. "Sip it slowly." She did as she was told, dabbing at the side of her mouth with Henry's handkerchief after each drop. The redness gradually faded from her cheeks.

"Mr Swaffer," she wheezed, "ah owe you." She put her hand on his arm and he noticed the delicacy of the white skin, her tapered fingers, the crescent moons on her neatly manicured nails.

"My dear lady," said Swaffer, "your good health is all that concerns me."

Helen shook her head slowly, her gaze becoming more intense. She pulled at his sleeve so that he had to lean in closer. "The lassie was being murdered."

Swaffer's eyes widened.

"Nearly took me with her, aye," Helen rasped on. "Tha's how she was gooin'," she put a hand back to her throat. "Chokin'" The movement caused her to start coughing again. "Please," Swaffer held out the tumbler she had emptied, "could somebody fetch some more water?" Another hand, belonging to Miss Moyes, took the glass from his.

Mrs Duncan's grip on Swaffer's arm tightened.

"She's lost out there, away in the woods, in the snow," she told him, black eyes seeing straight through him, to the other world she had witnessed from the inside of the cabinet.

"Clara," she said. "Her name is Clara."

PART ONE

THE SHADOW WALTZ

January – August 1941

1

NO MOON AT ALL

Friday, 31 January – Saturday, 1 February 1941

Karl Kohl had a bad feeling about his mission, long before he left Schiphol Airport on the moonless last night of January 1941. It had stolen up on him gradually, this sense of unease, this conviction that their carefully crafted scheme was going to end in disaster. At first, he had been exhilarated by the idea. His sudden selection from the backrooms of the meteorological division by the Abwehr, subsequent training in the arts of subterfuge and the daring nature of what he had been entrusted with, were all a confirmation of the powers he had been promised. Most of all, it meant he would be reunited with the owner of the face on the photograph he kept hidden, stitched inside the lining of his suit, the one who had made those vows to him.

Standing on the tarmac in front of the aircraft, he felt the last vestiges of confidence in his ability to carry out his orders draining away. The Heinkel HE 111 looked like a thing of nightmare. It had been painted black for its mission: to fly across the North Sea and drop Karl in the part of England that most resembled the land he was leaving, the marshy lowlands of East Anglia dug out of the swamp by Dutchmen three centuries before. Karl was to parachute, under the cover of darkness, to a co-ordinate on a map called Bury Fen. It was not a name that inspired confidence. He touched the amulet around his neck as he followed Captain Gartenfeld, head of the secret airborne division, up the steps and into the bowels of the sinister craft. He knew for sure now that, at heart, he was a coward. His fate had been written in darkness all along.

They were nearly two hours into their flight, himself and Gartenfeld in the gunner's gondola that hung below the fuse-lage, when the navigator's communication crackled over from the cockpit, announcing they had made it into enemy terri-tory. Gartenfeld slapped him on the back and relief coursed through Karl's veins. Throughout the whole, swaying, jud-dering journey, with the cold gradually seeping through the fur-lined flying suit he was wearing, the English-cut tweeds beneath that formed his disguise, to the very marrow of his bones, Karl had been expecting a burst of enemy fire; a desperate battle to stay airborne followed by the inevitable, sickening plunge into the North Sea.

The respite from that paranoia was short-lived. Now came the nausea-inducing prospect of the jump. Karl had never parachuted before and, despite the training he had received for the job he was about to do, a trial run was deemed out of the question. Although he had lived by his wits for most of his forty-three years, leaping from an aircraft thousands of feet over a strange and hostile land in the middle of the night was not the sort of test of nerve Karl would have willingly challenged himself to.

As if reading his mind, the captain turned towards him, the traces of a smile on his features that was not reflected in the cold blue of his eyes. Gartenfeld had had no say in the selection of this agent and it was obvious he resented it.

"About ten minutes until you make your jump, Kohl," he said. "Let's check through your kit once more, shall we? Make sure that everything is as it should be."

Karl had been issued with a compass, a set of maps and codes; a wallet stuffed with over £400 in English notes, a bogus ID card and ration book; a revolver and box of ammunition; a helmet, torch and spade and an attaché case containing a wireless set powerful enough to transmit over 500 miles, which he would use to make contact with his accomplice once he had safely landed.

"Now, let's make sure everything is secure," the officer continued, as if addressing a small child. Her face flashed through his mind again as Gartenfeld redid the straps binding his kitbag to the front of him, the parachute to his back. He pictured her sprawled out on black silk sheets, the glow of candles on her naked skin, smiling her gap-toothed smile and winking at him. He saw the flash of a ceremonial dagger, the smell of burning hair and herbs, the ceremony she had performed to bind them together for eternity, back in Hamburg, back before the war…

It was no time to be having such thoughts. He blinked rapidly, forcing her image away, as the aeroplane began to descend, taking his stomach with it.

"All is good," the captain nodded and consulted his watch. "Of course, you know what to do if you are captured, don't you?" His eyes narrowed.

Before Karl could answer, there was a crackle of static and the navigator's voice carried over the engines' roar: "Approaching target, sir. Get ready."

Gartenfeld moved swiftly to open the down-facing window. An icy blast rose up to meet them. As Karl knelt down before it, for the first time in many years, he found himself offering up a prayer to a god he had thought he had abandoned long ago and wondering if He had chosen to wash His hands of this sorrowful sinner now kneeling before Him. Karl could see nothing but blackness below.

"Now!" the captain commanded.

But Karl remained frozen to the spot, his gloved hands holding onto the bottom of the exit window for dear life. As if he had been expecting this, Gartenfeld gave him a hefty push. Karl lurched forward but managed to bend sideways, so that he was blocking the hole with the width of his own body. As he did so, his right foot caught against the side of the opening and twisted. A vicious stab of pain seized the joint and ran up his leg.

"*Dummkopf*!" the captain pushed again, forcing him to cleave into the gap while uttering increasingly vicious curses that were swept up by the wind roaring in Karl's ears and up his nose, knocking the breath out of him. Gravity, abetted by Gartenfeld, did its work and he pitched forward.

"Don't forget to pull the cord, Kohl," was the last thing he heard before the captain closed the hatch doors and Karl plummeted into the blackness.

"Clara!" he screamed into the void.

When Karl opened his eyes again, he thought he was in heaven, surrounded by a bright, white light. Then the pain in his ankle coursed like wildfire up his leg and torso, through his neck to the receptors in his brain and he realised that the pure white waves billowing around him were actually the silks of his unfurled parachute. He must have passed out the moment it opened, as he could remember nothing further than that point. It was only the kitbag strapped to his chest that was keeping his face from contact with the snow-topped furrow of hard earth on which he had landed.

Gingerly, he rolled onto his uninjured left side, trying to think what he should do next. His hands were stiff with cold but he could still move his fingers inside his gloves, so he set to the task of trying to unbuckle himself from the harnesses attached to his silk cocoon. In tight spots in the past he had found ways of blocking out pain when he had to, and so it was he began to murmur the words to *Ich bin von Kopf bis Fuß auf Liebe eingestellt* while he concentrated on this task. It wasn't until he had succeeded in freeing himself from his kitbag and the parachute that he remembered why he was singing it – the ballad she had been performing the first time he laid eyes on her. The realisation jolted him back to reality, and for a moment he thought he might pass out again with the pain. He shut his eyes, concentrating on his breathing, until he was back in control of himself.

Lifting his lids again, he tried to take stock of his surroundings. The yards of fabric were replaced by another layer of infinite whiteness – of snow-covered fields stretching into the wide, low horizon, broken only here and there by thin rows of trees and huddles of farm buildings. A red sun was beginning to emerge from behind that long line, winking its colour into the greyness of the sky. It was bitterly cold.

A skein of wild geese flew over him, their sudden caterwauling bringing a jolt of panic to his chest. The captain's words about being captured boomed back into his brain. He was a sitting target out here.

Gritting his teeth, he crawled onto all fours and tried to balance himself on his kitbag to see if he could stand. It was no good. Even if he could manage to get upright, there was no way he could walk on this ankle: a mere touch was agony. The best solution he could think of was to pack it with snow and see if that would numb it sufficiently so that he wouldn't feel it any more. But, by the time that happened, he would likely have died of cold.

A snowflake drifted down from the heavy clouds above and settled on his lashes. Karl made no move to cuff it away. Coming from the direction of the farmhouses to the east, he could hear a distant barking. As a second flake fell, and then a third and a fourth, he could discern the outlines of two figures coming his way.

He felt inside his coat for his revolver.

"He's found it," said Charlie Baldock, as the Jack Russell streaked down the lane in front of them, guttural curses flying from his canine throat.

"Whatever it be," replied Percy Clifton, the owner of Hollow Heap Farm, the collection of buildings that Karl had seen in the distance. Both he and his companion, from the neighbouring Froghall Farm, had been woken in the night by the alarm cries of cock pheasants echoing across the coppices that dotted the fens. Over the last six months they had come to recognise what this heralded. The pre-dawn chorus was a prelude to the throbbing *woom-woom* of Heinkel engines in the skies above.

The craft had passed over them without any attendant explosions, but that hadn't settled Percy's dog. At first light, the farmer and his neighbour strode off on reconnaissance, letting the terrier lead them to what had been worrying him.

"Oh, look at that," said Charlie, straightening the twelve-bore he had been carrying cocked over his elbow.

The dog had gone straight underneath the gate. As the two men stared out onto the field, they could see a dark lump in the middle of the furrows. Only with the snow falling so thickly, neither of them could quite work out what it was.

Until the gunshot rang out.

Karl fell backwards onto the snow, tears rolling down his cheeks. In the end, he hadn't had the courage to put the gun to his own head and had fired it instead into the air so that the people he could see coming towards him would have no chance at all of mistaking him. Perhaps what the British would do to him now would be worse than the quick dispatch the captain had demanded of him. The blood-curdling sounds emitting from the small, brown-and-white dog hurtling towards him suggested that it would. But mercifully, he had blacked out again before the creature's hot breath touched his face.

"What d'you reckon that is?" Percy held the whimpering terrier back by his collar.

"That's a German, in't it?" Charlie considered, prodding the inert form with the barrels of his gun. "Must have dropped him over here last night, Perce. Looks like he's gone and broke his leg and all. That in't half at a funny angle."

"What should I do then?" Percy considered. "Fetch the Home Guard?"

"That's right." Charlie nodded. "Go down Dovehouse and get Harry Godfrey. He'll know what to do. I'll keep an eye on him 'til you get back."

"D'you want to keep the dog?" offered Percy. "Case there's another one of 'em lurkin' about?"

Harry Godfrey telephoned the police station in Ramsey and gathered his First Aid kit before he set off. When he reached Charlie, he saw that his friend had used the parachute silk to insulate the German against the snow. Not that Charlie had any love for the enemy, of course, but he thought he'd better try to keep him alive in case he was on some kind of secret mission that the government needed to know about.

Harry congratulated his quick thinking and set about binding the man's bad leg into a splint, a process not made easy by the fact that his patient kept lapsing in and out of consciousness, writhing and muttering indecipherable things in his own language. Still, he had done a good enough job by the time Percy came back with his horse and cart for them to be able to hoist him up on a couple of planks and transport him, and the kitbag they had found with him, down to Ramsey police station.

Sergeant Ernie Pottle and Harry went through the German's belongings and found all the evidence they needed to call the spycatcher, Detective Sergeant Thomas Mills, of the Huntingdonshire County Constabulary. Then Sergeant Pottle called the local doctor.

The doctor found the prisoner's right leg to be broken at the ankle and gave him painkillers and a fresh dressing, with a proper splint, that would keep him as comfortable as possible until it could be set. The suspect was still slipping in and out of consciousness, but the doctor was able to tell the others that the language he was speaking appeared to be a mixture of French and German, so he thought perhaps he was Belgian.

DS Mills arrived as the doctor was leaving. He studied the maps found in the prisoner's kitbag and noticed that there were pencil rings drawn around a nearby large RAF station and its smaller satellite, situated close to the field where the prisoner had landed. Further to the west, he found another pencil ringed around the market town of Royston. Then he turned his attention to the attaché case. He found another item in there, previously overlooked. Half a German sausage wrapped inside waxed paper and placed in a sock.

The next time Karl woke up, he was lying on his cot in the Ramsey police station cells. DS Mills was sitting beside him.

"I hear you can speak French as well as German," the detective said. "How d'you fancy giving English a try? Only, I wouldn't mind having a chat."

Karl looked down from him to his newly dressed leg. The pain had subsided to little more than a dull ache. He was as warm and comfortable as it was possible to be in his condition. Things could, apparently, be worse than being captured by the British.

As if to confirm this, Mills took a cigarette case out of his jacket pocket, flicked it open and offered it across.

"What do you want to know?" said Karl.

Following their conversation, the detective went off to make a phone call and another policeman brought Karl something to eat – bully beef in two thick slices of farmhouse bread. Karl hadn't realised how ravenous he was until he bit into it. When Mills came back with a mug of tea and more cigarettes, he had rethought his situation. While he enjoyed these pleasures, the detective asked a few more questions about the marks on the maps and who he was to contact with the radio.

No longer delirious, Karl was deliberately vague in his replies. He felt the information he had to impart should only be heard by someone higher up, agreeable though this officer seemed to be. So he asked if he might be able to talk to someone from MI5. Mills went away again. When he came back, his expression was graver than before.

"I hope you're well enough rested," he said, "because I've now got to take you up to London."

"To speak with MI5?" asked Karl.

DS Mills nodded. "You've got your wish," he said.

2

HANDS ACROSS THE TABLE

Sunday, 9 February 1941

Detective Sergeant Ross Spooner stood on the west side of Hammersmith Bridge, staring upriver at the Thames. The wind on his back was bitter, scratching icy fingers through the woollen scarf around his neck, blowing his thick, red hair out of its brilliantined shape.

Icicles hung from the pointed parapets and heraldic castings of Joseph Bazalgette's elaborate green and gold construction; a fresh dusting of snow lay across the rooftops to his right and on the tree-lined pathway along the south bank of the river where a flotilla of barrage balloons listed against their tethers. Yet the sun was winking at him through a crack in the clouds and he couldn't keep the smile off his face.

Last night, he had received a telephone call from the Chief. Now he was back in London.

Spooner had spent the past five months working from the ancestral seat of the Prime Minister – albeit in one of three huts in the forecourt, rather than inside Blenheim Palace itself – deep in the Oxfordshire countryside. A far cry from the place where he had first encountered the man he was waiting for. But when he had first volunteered to do war work and been selected to transfer from Scotland Yard to MI5, the organisation had taken up residence at Wormwood Scrubs, the fortress-like Victorian prison that brooded over the ragged stretch of common from whence it took its cursed name.

Spooner had been working on files of subversives, suspected Nazi sympathisers, secret agents and potential fifth columnists, all of whom belonged to networks of often interconnecting secret societies. His job was to shadow them at meetings around the capital, where men dressed in jodhpurs and black shirts stood in front of black and red banners with lightning-flash designs and made shrill addresses bent on stirring up hatred. Spooner, cutting as forgettable a figure as possible, would listen into the conversations going on around him, join the dots between speakers and audience and assess how immediate a danger they posed. He was ideal for this task: he had always been a listener, rather than a talker, careful to blend in with the background with his slicked-down hair and habitual grey trilby and suit. The oval, wire-rimmed spectacles that sat across his nose further served the anonymity of his features.

The reports he made were forwarded to the upper echelons of the Secret Service, who would decide whether to detain the suspects he had been tailing. He never confronted one himself, or attended subsequent interrogations, lest his cover be blown. His apparent blandness was, in fact, his strength, enabling him to travel unnoticed through fraught and paranoid worlds. But the documents he prepared were the opposite, rich in detail.

Spooner hadn't been doing this work for very long before he was joined one afternoon in the former cell that served as his office by a very tall, well-built man in his late thirties, wearing a dark green Harris Tweed suit. His face was dominated by a bulbous nose and pale blue eyes, overhung by dark eyebrows that matched a thick head of hair. His lips were clamped around the stem of a large half-bent Billiard pipe. He carried a brown trilby in one hand and a thick grey folder in the other.

"Ross Spooner?" he enquired, in a baritone that completed his avuncular demeanour. "I gather you're the man to go to for Warlocks, Witches and Wizards?"

The subversives Spooner had been tasked to follow were those with occult and mystical leanings – of which there were many. The Nordic League was rife with worshippers of Wotan; the Right Club held gnostics and former members of the Golden Dawn; there were Pan's people within the Kibbo Kift, and interconnecting Venn diagrams full of White Russian exiles, bright young socialites and society grand dames for whom a nightly spin on the Ouija board was nothing out of the ordinary.

It turned out that his visitor had a keen interest in these Venn diagrams himself. He explained he was studying the links between the occult philosophies of the Nazis and their followers, then spent the next four hours getting Spooner to talk him through the most interesting Warlocks, Witches and Wizards – or Triple-Us, as he dubbed them – contained in the grey folder he carried. The air became so blue with smoke that, to anyone who had pulled back the hatch in Spooner's door and peered in, it would have looked as though there was a full-blown séance in progress, the air swirling with ectoplasm.

"Tell me," the older man asked, "how did you come to know so much about all these ancient texts and obscure deities? It's a most unusual repertoire for a Met detective."

This Spooner knew only too well. He shrugged. "Aye, I'll

no' deny it," he said. His formative years were not something he cared to discuss with his contemporaries at the Yard. But he felt no such restraint talking to a man of such obvious culture. "If you're ever up in Aberdeen, pay a visit to 84 Belmont Street and you'll find Spooner's Rare and Antiquarian Book Shop, Established 1910. That's where I was born and raised."

"Well, well," Spooner's visitor puffed on his pipe, eyeing the young man sitting across from him. He had an angular body that did not seem quite comfortable inside the grey flannel suit he was wearing. His hair was greased back off his forehead, heightening the angles of his cheekbones. Spooner's specs had earned him the nickname of "Prof" at the Yard, but when he took them off, there was a flinty quality to the hazel eyes behind them.

"A fine city, Aberdeen. And what enlightened parents you must have had to have let you run amok in such a wonderful classroom as that."

A frown passed across Spooner's countenance, like a cloud briefly obscuring the sun.

"My mother died not long after I was born. My dad had his work cut out running the business and keeping us afloat, so my grandma moved down from Shetland to take care of me. And that woman's head was full of more jigs and reels than even these things," he tapped his nearest filing cabinet with his toe, "could accommodate. That's who's to blame for me turning out the way I did."

The lips behind the pipe turned upwards. "I rather think I'd like to buy you a drink. What would you say to that?"

Several drams of whisky later, Spooner's new friend had given him a card and told him to please call each time an interesting new Triple-U came to his attention. It had a Chelsea phone number printed on it, but no name.

"For whom shall I ask?" Spooner enquired, realising that not once had this information yet been offered to him.

His companion smiled. "Just say that you'd like to speak with Mr King."

"OK, Chief," Spooner replied and from then on that was the name he bestowed to the distinguished gentleman of MI5. They continued to meet regularly. Many of the Triple-Us Spooner considered dangerous were tried and detained, and, while reporting on these, the Chief had subtly probed his protégé for potential willingness to step into an undercover role in the field. It was a prospect Spooner had agreed to and anticipated with equal degrees of trepidation and relish.

But after the air raid on the Scrubs last September led to their move into the country at Churchill's behest, communication from that quarter had ceased. Spooner's workload became heavier and less interesting, comprised mainly of accompanying a King's Counsel in sifting through the cases of hundreds of refugees from Europe on the look-out for secret agents. When he'd had time to wonder about anything, Spooner would ponder what the Chief was up to and whether he would hear from him again. He missed their conversations and the ideas they had sparked in him.

On Hammersmith Bridge he felt truly happy for the first time in five months.

"You're looking well, Ross. I expect they have a good veg plot at the Palace, but do they let you into the wine cellars? That's what I want to know..."

"Chief!" Spooner turned, beholding the man in the Simpsons overcoat who had appeared, bulldog at his side, with the affection of a real nephew. "No, no fear of that. They have us all barracked with civilians back in Woodstock – I'm sharing with a family of five. It's a nice enough place, don't get me wrong, but…"

"You must be itching to get out of there," the Chief surmised. "So here's what I propose. I like to do this little circuit on a Sunday morning," he pointed across to the south side of the river, "along to Barnes from here, over the bridge and back through Duke's Meadows to Hammersmith. I think you'll find the path delightful and remarkably quiet at this time of day. Which is just as well, for I have quite a story to impart… And there's a very good pub at the end of it. What would you say to that?"

"This time last week," said the Chief, as they walked beneath the plane trees that grew in a sheltering avenue along the footpath by the river, his bulldog Dorothy now off her lead and snuffling along ahead of them, "I was told a very intriguing story…"

Seven days previously, he had arrived at a tall white Georgian house on the outskirts of Ham Common, summoned by a colleague in MI5 who had taken a statement from Karl Kohl at Canon Row station the night before. At Camp 020, as this house was now known, he was shown all the items the agent had landed with, plus two personal belongings he had tried to conceal, before being taken to a cell where Kohl, his leg now properly set after a night in Brixton prison infirmary, waited to continue his confession.

"He was not, on first sight, an impressive storyteller."

The Chief observed a man with thick brown hair that defied the usual German military crop and sprouted in waves over his forehead, though this did not disguise the heavy lines and battered demeanour of a face that had already seen too much. His deep-set, dark brown eyes were bloodshot and fearful. Karl had not slept well in Brixton. Every time he shut his eyes he was falling from the plane again, pitching headlong into oblivion. Despite being given sedatives, he kept waking up screaming.

"A hapless German spy, sent on a mission to blow up two RAF stations near Peterborough, who broke his ankle jumping out of his plane and was captured by a couple of farmers. It was the first mission he'd ever been on and, despite the fact that the Abwehr furnished him with an impressive kit, they had never let him try parachuting before. He had very little going for him, except for the story he told to explain these discrepancies."

Karl asked for a cigarette the moment their interview began. The Chief passed over a packet, watched his subject break into it hungrily. The detective who had brought him up from Huntingdonshire had noted that Kohl reminded him of the sort of opportunist you'd find hanging about in billiard halls, wearing padded-shouldered pinstriped suits – a typical wide boy. But the suit he had been wearing was quality tweed and Kohl had not been happy to be parted from it. There was every reason to believe he had chosen it himself, as he had gone to the trouble of getting his tailor to sew something into the lining behind his inside jacket pocket.

The Chief glanced at the preliminary statement the prisoner had made the night before, stating that he had been working as a humble NCO in the meteorological department of the Wehrmacht before being selected to join Intelligence.

"Why do you think you were chosen to go on this mission?" he asked.

Karl smiled, partly in gratitude for the cigarette and partly because even he now found this question amusing. The change of expression made him look almost handsome.

"It wasn't Captain Gartenfeld who picked me," he said, "that's for sure."

"Captain Gartenfeld?" The Chief was familiar with the name of the Luftwaffe's expert on aerial reconnaissance.

"*Ja*," Karl nodded. "He was the one who dropped me off. He's running this new operation, didn't you know?" He ran his fingers through his hair, brushing it away from his forehead with a weary smile. "I could tell you a lot more about him, only I would need some kind of assurance first."

The Chief puffed on his pipe. "I hate to tell you, old man," he said, "but you don't appear to be holding a very strong hand."

Karl shook his head, reached for another cigarette and lit it with the butt of the previous one. "I'm not really asking for myself," he said, waving his hand. "The mission that I was supposed to carry out involved another agent, one who is already operating from somewhere in Britain unknown to you. If I was to divulge anything further about our mission and Captain Gartenfeld's operations, then I would want to make sure that *both* of us could rely on being able to turn our expertise over to helping you."

The Chief beamed his cosiest of smiles. "Then you'd better tell me something good," he said, "to convince me that the other agent isn't just a figment of your imagination. You were quite delirious when you were found, I understand?"

"OK," Karl shifted uncomfortably, his foot beneath the plaster alternately throbbing and itching, the nicotine he had been so desperate for not a strong enough distraction. "My fellow agent has already orchestrated many successful missions for the Luftwaffe. On aircraft and munitions factories in and around Birmingham last year."

The Chief's eyes narrowed. "Which factories, specifically?"

"The Spitfire factory at Castle Bromwich," said Karl. "The Austin factory at Longbridge. Another four armaments works – I cannot recall their exact names. And finally, that bicycle factory where all your Sten guns are made. That was the one they were most pleased about. Knocked it out completely, didn't they? Well, all the co-ordinates for these attacks came from my contact. The person who selected me for this mission."

His red-rimmed eyes burned with intensity and, involuntarily, he reached for the amulet around his neck. The Chief watched Karl's expression freeze as he realised it was no longer there.

"The Serpent and the Lion?" he said.

They had reached Barnes Bridge and the sun was high above them, banishing the clouds and sparkling off the freshly laid snow. Children were running about in Duke's Meadows, laughter ringing in the cold, clear air. Ducks bobbed about on the river. It was surreal, in such a setting, to think about the carnage Kohl had described.

"Did it all turn out to be true?" Spooner asked.

The Chief nodded. "And it gets much stranger yet. The reason I was specifically asked to interview Kohl was because, when he was asked to part with his clothes at Canon Row, he almost choked himself trying to swallow this. I think you'll recognise it…"

He opened his fist to reveal a silver pendant attached to a

thin chain. A circle enclosing a pentagram, within whose six points was depicted the face of a goat.

"A Baphomet," said Spooner and whistled. "Depending on who or what you believe, the God of the Knights Templar; or the Goat of Mendes, worshipped by witches."

"I remembered you telling me so when we discussed this symbolism before," said the Chief, putting the amulet back in his pocket. "Which is how I realised the importance of the next item Kohl had gone out of his way to conceal – and not from us, I might add, but from the very people who sent him." From another pocket he produced his next item of evidence. "This had been sewn into the lining of his suit."

It was a small black-and-white photograph of a striking looking woman, sitting curled up on an armchair. Her outfit looked expensive: a silk dress in what were probably two contrasting colours, with matching shoes and a fat string of pearls around her neck. She was laughing through the gap in her front teeth, eyebrows plucked like horizontal crescent moons rising in a sardonic, almost mocking expression. Spooner stared at her for a long minute before flipping the image over, suspecting there would be an inscription on the back. What surprised him was that it was written in English.

"*My Dear*," he read aloud, "*Our time is at hand. Our love is for ever. The Serpent and the Lion. Your Clara, July 1940.*"

"She is his contact," said the Chief. "According to Kohl, her real name is Clara Bauer and she's a German actress. But to the people of Birmingham, where she's been living on and off since the thirties, she is an English singer, popular in the music halls, where they know her as Clara Brown. To the Abwehr, she is Agent Belladonna. Kohl was supposed to have used his radio to contact her when he arrived and because he didn't, she may have been suspicious when our signals, using the call sign Kohl supplied, attempted to reach her. She didn't respond and all subsequent efforts have failed to rouse her."

Spooner felt a tingling sensation up his spine that had nothing to do with the weather. "So what happens now?" he asked.

The Chief put his arm around his protégé's shoulder. "This, my dear Ross, is the moment we have long spoken of. If you are still willing, you leave the Palace and go into the field in search of someone that might not even exist, except in Kohl's imagination. But if she does, she's a Witch more dangerous than any others you've recorded before. In short, I want you to try and find Clara and bring her to me."

3

THE ECHO OF A SONG

Saturday, 15 February 1941

"Witches, Warlocks and Wizards, you say? Interesting. I can give you Mesmerists, Memory Men and Magicians. See if you can work out the difference…"

The words rang through Spooner's mind as he reached the outskirts of Birmingham. They had first been spoken to him five days previously by the man who was to be his guide through a different world of smoke and mirrors: a theatrical agent by the name of Norris Denman. Norrie, as he preferred to be called, was an old friend of the Chief's. He was also part of the intricate network of independent agents recruited to the Department of Counter-Subversion that was the Chief's sole responsibility, an outfit so clandestine that many of his colleagues in MI5 knew nothing of its existence.

Most of these agents worked alone, so that, at times, there might be three or even four of the Chief's protégés reporting back to him on any one of the many organisations he had under surveillance. Somehow, he was able to keep track of all the threads he had woven into his great tapestry of subterfuge, and knew exactly where the next stitch should be placed. In this rare instance, he had considered it pertinent for two of them to work together. Therefore Spooner, ostensibly on leave from his work at Blenheim Palace, had spent most of the past week assisting Norrie and learning the sleight-of-hand ways of the world of pan-stick and paint.

Norrie was a fine tutor, a wily old silver fox, with a mane of hair that curled around his large ears and an exotic aroma of cologne that lingered long after he had made his customary greeting of kissing on both cheeks. Showbusiness – along with French brandy and the smoke of fine cigars – ran through his veins: he claimed to have been born backstage at the Grand Palais on Commercial Road and had been running his agency for over thirty years. He knew his counterparts in Birmingham well, so Spooner's mission had been choreographed to look like a routine visit that would take care of some outstanding business at the same time as giving him the opportunity to hunt for Clara.

He had just about got the hang of the car he had been given for this assignment. A highly polished maroon Rover 16, it had a flashy exterior but felt like a tank to handle. With a map splayed out on the passenger seat beside him, he maintained a steady pace and, judging by the clock on his dashboard, he would arrive before sunset. The thaw had helped, the snow now replaced by low clouds that merged with the thick smoke pouring from a thousand chimneys that was his first sighting of the second city.

As Spooner wove his cautious way towards its centre, he was able to see for himself the havoc that had been vested on the place: a vast pile of bricks and fallen beams surrounded by scorched arches that was the old market hall in the Bull Ring, set ablaze on the first air raid on the city centre last

August. An Edwardian shopping arcade reduced into twisted fingers of warped metal, pointing angrily up at the sky. And, as he drew closer to his destination, the mountain of rubble that was all that was left of the Empire, renowned as the best Variety House in Birmingham – which made one less place to look for Clara.

The city had been battered precisely because of its importance in the construction of the war machine, but this was a secret shared only by its citizens and the Luftwaffe. A government D-notice had been placed over the city, forbidding any reportage of the regular aerial attacks that testified to the deadly accuracy of Kohl's story. But, using his contacts in the House and various ministries and departments, the Chief had been able to match all the spy's claims to verifiable fact.

There had been an attempt to knock out the Spitfire factory at Castle Bromwich on 13 August the previous summer, eleven bombs hitting their target and causing severe damage, seven deaths and forty-one injured. Seven days later, more bombs had been dropped on a shadow Austin factory in Longbridge, where Fairey Battles, Hurricanes, Stirlings and Lancaster Bombers were being produced under the cover of car manufacturing. Attacks on the city centre between 15–25 October had included the Fisher and Ludlow factory where shell-casings, bombs and wings for Lancasters were made; the Reynold factory that made Spitfire wings; GEC, producers plastic components for aircraft; and SU Carburettors.

Most devastating of all was the 19 November attack Kohl had boasted of, on the Birmingham Small Arms factory at Small Heath, responsible for the manufacture of rifles, sten guns and anti-aircraft guns. Fifty-two people had been killed when the shop floor collapsed on shift workers who had ignored the sirens for too long to reach the company's air raid shelters and instead sought refuge in the basement. Only one man had been pulled out from inside that flaming hellhole alive.

Still the city continued to pound, smelt and manufacture without respite. Along the miles of canals that served as the ventricles of the city, tons of back diamonds from the North and South Staffs coalfields were drawn along in barges by heavy horses, to feed the insatiable pumping heart of foundries and factories. Spooner could hear their relentless tattoo, smell the vapours of hot metal and coal permeating each breath of air. Birmingham shook to a constant war dance.

He was headed for a slightly quieter area of the city, a warren of cobbled streets laid out at the end of the last century, where music halls and theatres had long been established and the performers who worked there preferred to socialise. Norrie had booked him into a bed-and-breakfast called High View on John Bright Street that was run by a couple of his old clients, Janet and Bob Howell.

"She sings and cooks like an angel," Norrie had informed him. "He spends his life in the pub down the street playing the piano and the black market. You'll thank me for this."

As Janet opened the door to him, Spooner could see how well she had absorbed the skills of stagecraft. Her hair was the colour of conkers, pinned up around a face illuminated by bright green eyes and a red smile. Though now in her forties, she had kept her figure and manicured fingernails, despite her daily grind of washing, polishing, sweeping and conjuring enough food for her guests.

The Ross Spooner she was expecting to receive was a talent scout, sent up from London by her former manager – which was what was proclaimed on the card Spooner proffered to her at just gone four o'clock that afternoon. Janet looked from this to the young man standing there. He wore green tweeds, flecked with orange and blue, a pale yellow shirt and burgundy waistcoat. A red Paisley bow tie, inexpertly fashioned, flopped around his collar and his glasses tilted over the bridge of his nose. His hair, set free from the grease that had previously confined it, sprouted up in corkscrew waves.

"Ah, hello, Mr Spooner." The smile with which she greeted him left no doubt that this transformation had passed muster. "I do hope you had a pleasant journey. Please, let me show you to your room."

Spooner followed her up the stairs, catching sight of himself in the mirror by the coat stand as he passed. Norrie had helped design this new look, which Spooner created from items rescued from the back of his wardrobe that had been given to him when he first left home. He looked like one of the self-styled aesthetes who gathered on the Occult floor of his father's bookshop. Some of them had worn smoking caps, others had a monocle to peer through, but none of them was a frequent visitor to the barber's shop. As a youngster, he had been almost as fascinated by them and their disregard for conventional attire as he had been by the books themselves and, as he blinked back at his reflection, he still couldn't believe it had been so simple to become one of them. Nor yet understand why it was that he felt so much more at home in this disguise.

The final part of it was a battered diary-cum-address book, which contained the details of all Triple-U's native to the Midlands who might know how to perform a Black Mass, alongside actual showbiz contacts supplied by Norrie. As a precaution, this tome had been prematurely aged in tea and roughed up at the edges until it resembled the sort of dog-earned *aide-memoire* anyone in his new profession might be expected to keep in their inside jacket pocket.

At the top of the stairs, Janet turned to him. "I've given you the best seat in the house, dear. Any friend of Norrie's…" She opened the door on a small but cosy room, with a sloping roof and a skylight that looked out over an undulating vista of roof tops; the green tiles, golden spires and red brick crenellations fashioned by the Victorians, and beyond, the tall chimneys and cooling towers that formed the sooty crown of the industrialists. A clean towel had been hung under the hand basin, there were coat hangers adorned with lavender bags inside the wardrobe and, on the bedside chest of drawers, stood a green reading lamp. There was a desk beneath the window with books lined up against the wall, and a tiny glass vase in which Mrs Howell had arranged a sprig of heather. The new Spooner drank in these creature comforts – lavish by the standards of his digs in Woodstock – and felt instantly at home.

"Now, will you have everything you need here?" his landlady enquired. "I spoke to Norrie about you using the telephone," she raised one eyebrow a fraction, "and you can take the private one in our office whenever you need to, you just let me know. Breakfast is between seven and eight. I'm afraid there's not much I can offer you, things being the way they are, but I can guarantee you'll have porridge, toast and marmalade."

"Sounds perfect," Spooner said. "Thank you very much, Mrs Howell. Oh, and—" he put his father's battered old leather briefcase down on the bed and extracted a small, beautifully wrapped package of French chocolates from it, "these are from Norrie."

The landlady took them from him with a gasp of delight. She smelled of lavender and even her floral work pinafore had been fashioned from a pattern in *Vogue*. This mixture of fastidiousness with lingering traces of glamour reminded Spooner of his grandma.

"Oh, do call me Janet, dear." She twinkled a smile. "Everyone I like does. Now, would you like a cup of tea after your long journey? You must be *dying* of thirst."

An hour later, he was still sitting in the lounge, on his third cup of tea and picking at the remains of a second cheese scone. Apart from the William Morris-style wallpaper, Staffordshire dogs and pots of aspidistras, his surroundings were not so different from those of his recent work experience: around the walls hung a rogue's gallery of framed publicity stills for all manner of performers, each of them signed to Janet and Bob.

Clara Brown was not among their number.

The Chief had given Spooner a copy of Kohl's photograph to take with him. Norrie had studied her with a frown; expressing his bewilderment that one so beautiful could have become involved in such a terrible thing.

Kohl told the Chief that Clara had been famous before the war. He first met her when she was fronting a popular orchestra in a prestigious café club in Hamburg, where he was living in the early thirties. They had fallen in love and taken an apartment together, despite the fact that Kohl was married; splitting himself between two worlds was nothing new for him and besides, they didn't get to spent too much time there together.

Clara spent long periods travelling, her engagements taking her all over Europe and into influential circles. It had been her idea that he should start learning English properly. Kohl was no longer sure if that had been part of a scheme to start a new life together in a different country or a forewarning of things to come. Clara had always known a lot of important people in the military, even before the war. It was she whom he credited for his surprising selection for the Abwehr, a feat she had been able to achieve only once she had firmly established her own importance to them.

Kohl had been transferred to Dulwich hospital after his interrogation at Camp 020, and the Chief continued to visit him. Though he had been treated for his broken ankle and the effects of exposure, he remained frail and his mind seemed to be deteriorating in pace with the news that signals to Clara continued to disappear into the ether without receiving a reply, as if he were fading along with his imagined lifeline.

Having not been present at any of the Chief's interviews, Spooner had assembled his own picture of the hapless spy from their briefings. He had learned that Kohl had been born to German parents in Luxembourg in 1898, the strange dialect the doctor in Ramsey had noted him speaking in his delirium being *Lëtzebuergesch,* a mixture of German, French and Dutch. He had served as a soldier in the First War, a horror he was not keen to revisit, and had begun the second in the much safer backrooms of the German meteorological service – perhaps another of Clara's string-pulling exercises to keep him out of harm's way until he could be parachuted back to her in England. Spooner wondered what their attraction had been and how it had kept them together for so long.

Part of it was down to the amulet he had worn around his

neck, the symbol of Baphomet. Kohl claimed that he and Clara had been bound together in a ritual marriage more powerful than the Christian vows he had made to the wife he had discarded. But Kohl's beliefs had been tested too far the moment he was hanging over the hatch of the Heinkel, when he had, he admitted, called upon his old God for mercy. He had convinced himself it was this moment of weakness that had doomed the pair of them.

The Chief was, however, dubious about Kohl's ability to tell the whole truth, even when his life depended on it. He had discovered that a large part of the lovers' estrangement in the thirties had been the three years Kohl had spent in a Swiss jail for dealing in counterfeit gold and fake passports.

"I don't know why it is," the Chief surmised, "but there are certain women that find this kind of shiftless bastard irresistible. Agent Belladonna would appear to be one of them."

"She's a pretty girl," Janet now added her tuppenny's worth. "But I'm afraid there's something I don't like about her. What kind of singer did you say she was? Oh!" the sound of the front door opening distracted her. "There's our Bob." She got to her feet as her husband, almost obscured by the amount of bulging brown paper sacks he was carrying, barrelled into the room.

"Bob, dear!" Janet cried delightedly. "Are these all for me?"

As she began the process of relieving him of his burdens, Bob was gradually revealed. He was an inch taller than his wife, with a barrel-shaped chest and long legs. When his arms were free enough for him to unwrap the large, hand-knitted scarf and take off his flat cap, there was a handsome face with high cheekbones, hardly marred by his glass left eye, the result of an industrial accident in his youth that, he had told Norrie, he considered a blessing as it had saved him from fighting in the First War.

"This is Ross," Janet introduced him, "Norrie's new scout, up from London. Why don't you two get acquainted while I take all this through to the kitchen? My word," she peered into the top of a package, "this must be my lucky day."

"Pleased to meet you," Bob smiled, removed a glove and offered his hand to shake. "Bob Howell, at your service, kid. Now, d'you reckon there's enough tea in that pot to stretch to a cup for this poor old devil?"

Having divested himself of his outer layers, Bob sat down in the seat that Janet had vacated. "Just a little bit of milk, please," he directed. "And two sugars. Now, who's this?" he picked up the picture of Clara his wife had left on the arm of the chair.

"Ach, she's one of the singers Norrie wanted me to take a look at on my trip, if I can find her," Spooner explained, stirring in the sugar and putting the cup down on the table in front of his host. "Clara Brown. She's supposed to be local."

"Is that right?" Bob frowned at the photograph. "Funny. The face *does* look familiar, but I don't think I could have told you her name. What kind of music we talking about?"

"I'm told she's a very strong jazz voice," said Spooner, repeating the spiel Norrie had formulated. "A distinctive style as well as a look. See, I'm trying to find some better singers for the dance bands that are playing the big hotels in London just now. There's a real demand for them, but it's hard to get it right – a lot of the musicians we're using have come from classical backgrounds and they're just too stiff. I'm looking for someone who can give it a bit more, well, swing. And I've been told she fits the bill."

Bob nodded. "Tell you what, I've got a regular spot Fridays, playing piano in the pub at the end of the road here. Why don't you pop in later and I'll help you ask around? Someone's bound to know her."

This was exactly what Spooner had been hoping to hear. "That's very kind of you," he said, glancing at the clock on the mantelpiece. He was now only half an hour away from his first appointment, at the Hippodrome on Hurst Street. Its exiled Cockney manager, Bertram Adams, was another old pal of Norrie's, who apparently kept a record of his signings that was the Rosetta Stone of show business. "What time are you on?"

"I start at eight," said Bob, "and after that, they can't stop me. I'll go on 'til they throw me out."

4

YOU AND THE NIGHT
AND THE MUSIC

Saturday, 15 February 1941

The manager of the Hippodrome was waiting on the bottom step of his establishment, built in 1895 and boasting a soaring Moorish tower that was currently more of a source of grief than pride to him. He was holding a torch so that it pooled enough light around him to render him visible, smoking a cigar and making routine glances up towards the sky.

"Ross Spooner, ain't it? Norrie's boy? Bertie Adams, pleased to meet ya," he offered his hand through the window Spooner had lowered to greet him. "Lovely motor you got there, son." He removed the cigar from his lips and caressed the paintwork with his gaze. "You want to put that round the back. Don't want her getting too many admiring glances, know what I mean?" He returned the cigar to his mouth and gave the street the same kind of penetrating glare he had been shooting up at the sky earlier. "Let me show you," he said, opening the passenger door and hopping in. "Just turn her right here," he said, pointing the torch out of the window, "next to the bombsite. That's it."

As he made the manoeuvre, Spooner saw that whatever had once stood next to the Hippodrome had been reduced to another pile of twisted metal, brick and ash.

"Must have been a close shave," he observed.

"Yerse. Tony's Ballroom, that was," Bertie nodded sanguinely. "Took a direct hit. We was luckier; an hour away from opening time when the raid started and all my staff was already in. I got everyone up on the roof and caught all them bleedin' little incendiaries they was dropping, put out every last one of 'em. Took all night and I had to sacrifice one of me best dress shirts to use as mittens. Still worries me every night, that bleedin' tower – it's a landmark for the Boche, ain't it? That's it, son, pull her in over here, next to me old Jag there."

Spooner parked beside a gleaming silver Roadster. "Perfect." Adams nodded. "You'll be safe here, son. Even if I have to go back up the bleedin' roof again to make sure of it." He gave a loud guffaw. "This way."

Spooner followed his host through a door and along a corridor that passed around the back of the stage. He could hear a comedian doing his patter and the oceanic roar of a full house showing their appreciation. Trotting ahead of him, Adams' stocky, bandy-legged frame was covered in a blue dogtooth suit, his black hair swept around his bullet-shaped head in artful waves. He looked every inch the ringmaster.

Opening his office door, Bertie cleared a sheaf of papers from a chair and pulled it out to face the one at his desk while Spooner stood staring. The room was chock-full of stage props: balsa wood palm trees, stuffed birds in ornate cages, fabric flowers and ostrich plumes, and framed playbills for entertainments stretching back into the last century. A crystal chandelier hung overhead and a ring of filing cabinets lined the walls. Everything was covered in a layer of fine dust and the musty smell of Adams' cigars.

"Now then," his host disappeared from view as he

rummaged in his desk drawers then emerged, triumphant, with a bottle of Scotch and two glasses. "Here we go. Now we can get down to business."

"To business," Spooner agreed, knocking back a slug. Though he would have preferred to be prudent, he didn't think his new alter ego would refuse such hospitality. Besides, it was good quality Scotch. "Now then," he opened his briefcase. He had more gifts to bestow and this time, besides the box of cigars, there was some legitimate business from Norrie: contracts and publicity photographs of new acts he was sending to Adams. In exchange, Adams went through a similar list for him, which included three musicians intended for the over-stretched hotel ballrooms of the Smoke. Two of them were performing on the bill that evening, so Spooner could judge for himself how good they were, the other was so well known to both parties they didn't need an audition, and would be on the first train the next morning.

This business talk and mutual contract signing took around half an hour, before the way was clear to Spooner's real purpose. Returning his signed papers to the briefcase, he brought Clara out to show his host. "I think Norrie mentioned that we were also trying to find this woman: Clara Brown. She's quite a memorable face, hasn't she?" he said hopefully.

"Yerse, Norrie did say there might be one for the old ledger," Bertie said, taking the photograph. To Spooner's relief, his expression suggested recognition. After Bob's response, Spooner had started to wonder if Clara might just have been a German hausfrau after all, her jazz-singer-spy persona either the product of Kohl's delirious ramblings or a desperate bid to keep himself from the firing squad. But that was a chance the Chief had not been prepared to take.

"That's one singular boat race, all right. And she does ring a few bells. But I can do one better than the Memory Man." Bertie tapped on the side of his nose and winked. Swivelling around in his chair, he opened the bottom drawer of a filing cabinet with a key kept on his fob chain, brought up a leather-bound tome and placed it on the table.

"I've kept this book over thirty years," he explained, "and I've been up 'ere in Brum for the last five of 'em. This is me Bible, son. If I ever booked this gel before, then she'll be in here." He rubbed his palms together and opened it up.

Inside was a list of names and numbers, arranged under colour-coded sections relating to the nature of the acts. Each entry included the dates they had been engaged and comments to remind Bertie about a performer's work and other qualities that might encourage him to book them again – or not. This minutiae was rendered in a special coded shorthand, so that, should the disaster ever occur that it fell into a rival's hands, it would appear incomprehensible.

"Clara Brown," he said, flicking through his list of singers. "Nothing under that name, but…" he trailed a nicotine-stained finger down the edge of the page, licked the end of it and turned the leaf over, "bear with me, son. I can feel something stirring." Without looking up, he poured them both another drink.

"Nah, nah," Bertie flicked through another page, showering the table with ash. "Not 'er, not 'er and *definitely* not 'er but, 'old on a minute," he bent forward, a smile spreading across his face, "'ere we go. *Spellbound*," he read, his finger travelling across his own tiny lettering. "*Female musical duo. Songs of theatre and music hall, folk tunes and murder ballads, performed on piano and violin. Clara Brown and Anna Hartley.* And look here," he studied the attendant cryptography. "Anna's a blonde, scrapes the catgut. Clara's a redhead, plays the Joanna. *Go down well with the table-tappers*, I've put here." He laughed, looking up. Then his focus shifted beyond Spooner, as the words kindled sparks of memory. "Yerse, that's right," he said. "I *do* remember this pair. They had a lot of ginger old songs about ghosts and witches. Folk songs they collected." His gaze returned to Spooner. "And that's the sort of fing you're after, is it? I thought Norrie wanted jazz singers?"

"Aye, well, it's me who has an interest for the folk songs," Spooner improvised. "I've been trying to persuade Norrie there's an audience for it."

"Course, I s'pose you would do, coming from Scotland," Bertie considered, scratching his blue, bristly chin. "The land of fings what go bump in the night. Well, I tell you what, son, you might be onto something. They went down well here. And they was both lookers, as I recall. The blonde one, especially…"

"Did you keep a number for them?" Spooner thought it best to cut this train of thought off before it had further time to develop. "Or do they have an agent?"

"Ah, yerse," Bertie looked back down at his book and the smile fell away from his face. "Ah, no. No agent listed. Just this number and an address in West Brom – most probably their digs. D'you want to take that down anyway?"

"Thanks," Spooner copied out the first new entry in his address book. "So they are local."

Bertie removed his cigar from his mouth, stuck out his lower lip and shrugged. "They *was*," he corrected. "But the last booking I took for 'em was back in November. You might not find 'em at the same place now. Might not even be standing if the bleedin' Boche had anyfink to do with it. But, you like that sort of fing, then I can make you plenty more recommendations…"

By the time Spooner was bumping his car back down John Bright Street, he was praying that this wasn't going to be the time he had to suddenly introduce himself to any of the local constabulary. The remaining half of Bertie's bottle of Scotch had all gone south in a stream of anecdote before they had left to watch the show. As a result, Spooner's driving was even more erratic and his address book was bulging with useless contacts for Midlands-based folk singers.

But none of that mattered compared to the one address and phone number that did. The proof that Clara really did exist and had been here in Birmingham – and the added twist that she had invented an entirely different act here from the one she could have been expected to replicate from her life on the continent.

"A lot of ginger old songs about ghosts and witches." Remembering Bertie's words caused the hairs to rise up on Spooner's neck the way they had done when he'd first heard them. Clearly, it was an act that reflected her interests and, presumably, those of her musical partner too. Anna Hartley was not a name that had come up on any of Spooner's Triple-U files, but the Chief had an even more comprehensive ledger even than Bertie's to go through. As he eased the Rover back into the High View car park, he shook his head at the thought of the man's prescience. If he could find this duo, then he could easily convince them of his love for their kind of music. Especially songs about ghosts and witches.

"D'you have your own crystal ball, Chief?" he mused aloud, turning the engine off.

Though it was tempting, he dismissed the idea of calling his boss now. They had prearranged twice daily when Spooner should call with reports for Norrie that would really be answered by the Chief. The first one was due after breakfast tomorrow. He had been given another number for use in an emergency, but this wasn't one. Neither did he think it worthwhile to try the number he had got for Clara and Anna. Everyone in their profession would already be out, either performing or carousing at this hour of the night. Better to try them first thing in the morning, when he'd be more likely to catch them bleary and unawares. Besides, he had another engagement to keep.

Taking his torch from his pocket, Spooner turned down the pavement towards the Victoria public house, wondering if Bob would have unearthed any promising leads by now. He could hear the raucous sounds of a piano being played and songs being sung long before he reached the front doors, which were entwined with elaborate ironwork foliage, like the gates to a fairy-tale castle.

Inside was every bit as ornate – dark wood panelling, corniced ceilings with plaster roses painted in shades of forest green, blood-red and gold. A long mahogany bar with a copper top dominated, facing into all of the rooms built around it: the saloon, public bar and snug. Rows of bottles glittered down from the top of its carved shelves, while the bevelled glass back panels reflected a scene of Hogarthian revelry. Friday night was in full swing.

Making his way through the throng to the bar, Spooner took mental snapshots of certain customers. A little man in a yellow suit who might have been a Munchkin escaped from Oz. An old fellow with a long white beard, holding a walking stick and nodding his head in time to the music while staring into the middle distance with the milky white eyes of the blind. A fat man with a round red face who looked like he'd had a good day at the races; his equally rotund female companion swathed in mink, her laugh like a donkey's bray. From the corner by the fireplace, a man with black hair as glossy as a raven's wing, a pencil moustache and a chalk-striped grey suit with shoulder pads shot him a searing glance.

Impressive though his flock was, the landlord was another spectacle entirely. Norman Johnson was an enormous great man, with a torso that resembled one of his beer barrels and a shining bald head. His skin was the colour of milky coffee and he was dressed in black from top to toe, shirt sleeves rolled up over biceps the size of hams. He had formerly been an all-in wrestler, who ruled the ring in the thirties under the moniker 'The Black Butcher' and his image, dressed in an apron splashed with theatrical blood, leered down from old fight posters on the walls. Yet despite his fearsome appearance, Norman greeted Spooner with an amiable nod.

"You must be Ross," he said. "Bob said I should look out for you."

Spooner was pleased. His change of image had at last rendered him memorable.

"Sounds like he's going great guns," he nodded to where the landlord was thundering through a rousing version of "Bye Bye Blackbird", assisted by a howl of enthusiastic singers all competing for a common key as they clustered around an old upright piano.

"Lucky for you, you've missed most of it," said Norman. "But show us that photo you got. I think I might know your mystery woman, even if he don't."

The pint looked small and fragile in the former Black Butcher's great paw.

"That's right," he said, nodding, "it is her. I thought it would be." He looked back at Spooner. "She's not one of me regulars, but she did come in here once and give us a song. Last November, it was – I recall it quite distinctly, 'cos it was the same night the BSA factory went up. She had another girl with her, a little blonde one, played the violin. They were bloody good and all…"

The scene unspooled before the landlord's mind's eye: the usual crowd clustered around the piano all flushed with booze and merriment; the red-haired woman's fingers dancing up the keyboard while her little companion twirled across the copper top like some kind of fairy fiddler. The red-haired woman's voice cutting across the smoke and the laughter, deep and raucous. Singing such a strange song, happy and sad at the same time…

Then someone called his name, breaking his reverie. Norman handed the pint back to Spooner, admonishing the thirsty punter to wait his turn. "Sorry about that," he said. "But you know what it's like Friday night. What can I get you, anyway?"

Spooner's eyes ran across the taps. Beer would be a safer option. "A pint of mild, please," he said, "and have one yourself."

Norman nodded. "Bob said you was a gent. So what else can I tell you?" he wondered. "Oh yes, them girls. Spellbound they said their name was. I would have had them back here again in a flash, but I don't think their boyfriends approved of the place."

He placed the pint on the counter.

"Boyfriends?" echoed Spooner.

"They was with a couple of fellas – hoity-toity types, the pair of them. One of them looked military. He wasn't wearing a uniform, but I'll bet you he was RAF. That lot always think themselves better than the rest."

Spooner didn't lift his pint in case a shaking hand gave him away. "Aye," he said, rummaging in his pocket for change instead. "That's right."

"Yeah, well, he didn't look too happy about it," Norman recalled. "He dragged her off after the one song. Probably didn't like other men looking at his girl, you know what I mean? Shame, that was, I would have let them play all night if they wanted to, they was like nothing else you'd ever heard before. I tell you what, if you manage to get hold of them, tell them they've got a booking here if they want it," he winked, nodded back towards Bob. "Anything's got to be better than that bloody racket, right?"

5

THERE ARE SUCH THINGS

Sunday, 16 February 1941

Karl's dream had changed since they moved him to the hospital. Now, each time he closed his eyes, he was back in the snow-covered fields of the fens. Only, he had made a successful jump, landing with no bones broken. In this white world, he was blissfully free from pain and couldn't even feel the cold. The sun was just coming up above the horizon, a red eye blinking at him, indicating the path he should take towards a copse of elms. His progress was easy, his feet gliding inches above the snow. What he had to do next was clear in his mind.

He selected the tallest tree and laid his attaché case out at the bottom of it. Though he had only been taught how to do this task three weeks previously, he remembered the drill clearly. He plugged his aerial into the back of the wireless set and then threw it high up into the branches. The tree obligingly caught it first time.

He selected the 6180 KC crystal that should provide adequate range and placed it vertically into the holes in the socket on the right-hand corner of the set. He turned the transmitter switch upright to the 5-8 position, the coupling switch to 1 and the transmitter receiver switch on. He breathed a sigh of relief as the set made a high-pitched whine and a small light bulb went on over the resonance switch, the needle on the RF meter starting to turn to the right. He had judged his requirements correctly.

"*Alles klar*," he said to himself, waiting for the bulb to become really bright before he adjusted the tuning knob to dim it sufficiently to begin his transmission.

Karl took his codebook from the inside pocket of his jacket, and laid it inside the lid of the attaché case. He unhooked the headphones, plugged them into the socket in his set and put them on. Finally, he began pressing down upon the key, tapping out his call sign in morse: ABRAXAS TO BELLA-DONNA. The bulb flashed alongside each movement. The set was working perfectly. Once he had relayed his call sign, he turned the transmitter switch over to receive. It was then he heard a strange swishing sound. He looked up to see the branches of the tree had begun to stir. He frowned. He could feel no wind. What could be causing this to happen?

Karl looked up at the tree. The branches whirled above him, a maniacal dervish, sending dried-up leaves, moss and twigs raining down on his head. The light flashed on his wireless set, a message incoming:

HELP ME HELP ME HELP ME

Karl woke up screaming.

The ringing in Spooner's ears jolted him upright. For a second, lost in dreams of burning factories and Stuka bombers dropping flaming trails of incendiaries, he thought he was in the middle of an air raid. His hands reached out in the darkness and landed on the alarm clock that was telling him it was six-thirty and time to get up. He fell back, head swirling, trying to separate his memories of what had really gone on the night before from the nightmare images that had twisted their way around them as he slept.

Then he sat back up. Despite being turned off, another was still ringing loudly in Spooner's head. *Clara had been seen with someone from the British military.* It was enough to propel him out of bed.

Luckily, the new Spooner didn't have to spend half as much time on his toilette as his fastidious former self. A quick wash over the basin and he was back into his velvet and tweeds and following his nose down to the dining room, in pursuit of an aroma that caused his stomach to growl noisily. Frying bacon. He could almost hear it sizzling away in the pan, along with the distant sounds of the news being read on the radio.

He hovered near a seat on a table that had been set for one with a checked placemat and another tiny vase, this one bearing snowdrops. Another memory surfaced, of himself and Bob coming home from the pub, the older man's hand on his arm, though who was steadying whom was a moot point. He remembered thinking that Bob had a sailor's walk, which must have come in handy for times like this when the earth was tilting sideways. He wondered how Bob's head was this morning. His own felt as if it was being used as a foundry.

"Ah, there you are!" Janet appeared through the kitchen door, bearing a tray full of pots, cups and saucers. "Can I tempt you with some of that bacon our Bob managed to scrounge for me yesterday?"

Spooner bounced from one foot to the other, his stomach, head and nerves all vying for the upper hand. "Aye," he said. "I'd love some." He had wanted to ask her about using the telephone, but this intention dissolved into the aroma wafting from the kitchen. He sat down, telling himself that he would think more clearly once he had eaten.

Janet regarded his pallor and uncomfortable expression and made her own deduction.

"Now, dear," she said, putting her tray down on another table and a comforting hand on his shoulder. "I do know what our Bob's like. I dare say he was leading you astray last night when you were supposed to be working. Shall I make you an Alka Seltzer?"

Spooner nodded with gratitude.

She brought for him, along with a pot of coffee, a doorstop bacon sandwich and a copy of the *Birmingham Post*. Before he got stuck in, Spooner said a silent prayer of thanks to Norrie for providing him with such a surrogate mother and made a plea for the wisdom not to let any of them down.

Two hours later, he had managed to find his way to West Bromwich. Before he left High View and after he had made his report to the Chief, he tried the number Bertie had provided. But the operator wasn't able to put him through. Now he knew why. What his map was telling him should be there had become a scene of utter desolation.

A blackened spire reaching up against the cloud-heavy sky and half its supporting wall were all that remained of the church that had once sat on the corner of two residential streets. There would be no more Sunday worship here. One of the piles of rubble that lay in the wasteland behind it contained the address that went along with Anna Hartley's number. Rain slanted across the windscreen as he turned the engine off. He decided he would have to make the rest of the journey on foot.

It was hard going, picking through broken bricks and splintered glass to the other side of the church. Spooner's eyes travelled three hundred and sixty degrees around the shattered landscape. Half of the road was a mess of tangled metal and charred beams, bricks turned to charcoal by the intensity of the heat they had endured. The other half just wasn't there any longer. A huge, muddy crater had taken its place into which a raw north-easterly wind threw a spiteful barrage of rain.

As he rounded the back of the church there was a shrill whoop and a small figure slipped out from under some floorboards that were still protruding from the wall. He was a child of no more than eight, with a raven's feather stuck to a bit of ribbon tied around his head, muddy and red in the face from his morning's play. But in his mind he was Chief Crazy Horse, on the lookout for General Custer. "Who goes there?" he demanded in a high-pitched voice.

Spooner stopped and regarded the little tyke. Beyond him, he could see a couple more pairs of eyes blinking out of the gloom from under the repositioned floorboards. There was probably a whole tribe in the ruined church.

"Good day to you," he said, doffing his trilby. "Mr Ross Spooner, at your service. To whom do I have the pleasure of addressing?"

"Me Big Chief," the child announced. His braves drew nearer, picking their way into the daylight. "Crazy Horse. This Sioux territory."

"Ah, I see," Spooner joined in with the game. "These are all your lands. Whereabouts are your wigwams?"

The boy nodded. "Over there." He pointed in the direction of the still-standing terrace on the other side of the church, where smoke was rising from the chimney pots.

Spooner looked back at him. "And what happened to cause all this mess?"

"An air raid, of course," he was informed, Crazy Horse slipping back into his real native accent. "We was all in our shelter when it happened. We've got a big shelter, we have, right in the middle of our garden. Can get our neighbours on both sides into it. Heard the bombs going down all night. It was bloomin' scary." He looked back at Spooner, fixing him with a beady eye. "You're not from round here, are you?"

"No," Spooner agreed. "I'm from a very long way away. But I'm looking for someone who used to live on this street, a friend of mine who was staying here."

"You're a bit late, aren't you?" another brave enquired.

"Why, when did it happen?" Spooner asked.

"Nineteenth of November," he was told.

"Ach," Spooner consulted his mental filing cabinet. That was the same night as Norman's last sighting of Clara and the raid on the BSA factory. "I've been away too long. Do you know what happened to all the people who were living here? I bet they'd no' got a shelter as big as yours, eh?"

Crazy Horse shook his head. "Most of them got killed," he said. "I heard the warden telling our dad about it. Twenty-eight of them, he said; or something like that." His expression softened. "I hope your friend wasn't one of them."

Spooner shook his head. Was this why Clara had been unable to reply to her signals? Why no one had seen her since the previous November? Had the Luftwaffe she had served so well wiped her out in return for her favours?

"Is the warden about, do you know?" he asked. "Could you take me to him?"

The boy cocked his head. "I could," he mused. "But how

do I know you're not a Jerry spy? Or General Custer planning a sneak attack?"

Despite the bleakness of the situation, his words made Spooner laugh. "Well, if I am, I'm handing myself in to you," he said, holding out his upturned palms as if to be handcuffed.

The little boy seemed to like this. He threw himself into the air, punching an arm out before him and yelling. "All right then, mister," he said, grabbing hold of Spooner's hand in his mucky paw. "Come with me. The rest of you, stay here – and keep yer eyes peeled for Custer."

The ARP warden was called Ted Hendricks and he ran a bicycle shop on Moor Street, though Spooner's small guide led him to the door of the place where he could be found on a Sunday morning – inside the saloon bar of The Leopard pub, where he was playing darts with a group of men that included the boy's father.

Spooner handed out some more of his cards, explained to them that he was a talent scout sent by a London agency to book some local musicians, among them two girls that had given an address on the now destroyed Richard South Street. The men quickly established that this would have been a boarding house run by a Queenie Simpkins, who was killed in the air raid along with her guests, despite the fact they'd been sheltering in the basement. But they didn't know if everyone who lived with Mrs Simpkins had been in that night. Some of them thought that one of the lodgers had been out in Brum and escaped the carnage. Though they couldn't agree on how many lodgers Mrs Simpkins had, nor who they all were.

After further discussion, which extended out to the rest of the pub, it was the barmaid who hit upon the solution – Spooner should go and talk to Mrs Smith, because Mrs Smith knew everything. Another murmur of dissent went up: it was approaching Sunday lunchtime and not perhaps the best time to call. But, countered another voice, Mr Spooner had come all the way from London – surely she would want to help him? Mr Smith, a small man quietly reading a newspaper in the furthest corner of the snug, was consulted. He shrugged and said that if Spooner thought he was a brave man, he didn't see why not.

Crazy Horse was whistled back by his father and told to show his new friend to the right house, in the middle of the terrace beyond the shops at the end of Moor Street. For his help, Spooner gave him sixpence and his young guide whooped even louder as he ran back in the direction of the bombsite, happy with his lot – which was more than could be said for Mrs Smith.

As the pub regulars had predicted, this formidable looking woman was not happy to be disturbed from the operations of her Sunday roast. However, when Spooner presented her with the card denoting his credentials, she brightened. Delegating all cooking chores to her daughter, she showed Spooner through to her sitting room where he was invited to rest on the chair usually reserved for Mr Smith.

Spooner found himself surrounded by lace doilies, china dogs, framed religious paintings and family photographs and more rambling pot plants than even Janet's dining room. Having shouted further instructions into the kitchen for roast potatoes to be turned, carrots to be put on to boil and tea to be made and brought forth, his hostess descended onto the settee.

"Do please call me Mavis," she instructed Spooner, in a

tone more refined than the one with which she had just been dispensing orders.

The Oracle of West Bromwich was in her late middle age, wore her black hair up in a bun and viewed her guest through penetrating green eyes. With her long, dark skirts and a knitted shawl around her shoulders, she gave off the impression of an imperious, if suburbanised, gypsy queen. Spooner noted the copies of the spiritualist journal *Two Worlds* lined up in the magazine rack by the fireplace and further envisioned his hostess at the centre of a circle in a darkened room, asking all present to join hands so they could partake in gossip from the Other Side.

Once her daughter had brought the tea in the best china and returned, red-faced and frazzle-haired, to the kitchen, Mrs Smith turned her attentions to the events leading up to the evening of the nineteenth of November.

"She was a tender-hearted woman, Queenie Simpkins," she said, holding her teacup with little finger aloft. "Went to school with her, I did, knew her over fifty years. Terrible to think of her passing the way she did."

"And you're sure I've the right address for her?" asked Spooner. "Where I would have found Anna Hartley and Clara Brown?" Putting his cup down, he went into his jacket pocket for the picture of the latter and handed it over. "I've only got the picture of Clara, I'm afraid. Have I got the right person?"

Mrs Smith wrinkled her nose as if a bad smell had passed beneath it. "No," she said, "it wasn't her that lived with Queenie, but she was friends with the one that did. Anna, did you say her name was? Yes, and a fine pair they made too. This one," she handed the print back to Spooner, "was all big and clod-hopping. That Anna looked like a little fairy next to her. I dare say she had some fairy in her. Played the fiddle, didn't she?"

"That's right," said Spooner. "Clara played the piano and they sang together as an act. Did you ever happen to see them?"

Mrs Smith's eyebrows rose almost to the top of her head. "I should think not, dear," she said. Then she caught herself, modified her tone. "Not my kind of thing, the music hall. But it's like I was saying, Queenie would listen to all the sob stories, take in all the waifs and strays. She lost her husband, you see, and once her eldest had wed, there was nothing left to keep her going until she cracked on to the idea of taking lodgers. Don't get me wrong, most of them were very respectable people. I'm just not sure your Anna was."

"Why do you say that, Mrs Smith?" Spooner asked. "I've been told she's very talented and it is a prestigious organisation I'm representing here."

Mrs Smith put her cup down. "Be that as it may, Mr Spooner," she said. "But once she gave that Anna houseroom, Queenie never had a moment's peace. There were supposed to be strict rules about guests, and about coming in at night at a reasonable hour." She rolled her eyes. "I know we live in trying times and it's not always easy to get about, especially after dark. But she had people coming at all hours. Not just that big-boned redhead, either," she curled her top lip. "There were men."

"Men?" Spooner echoed.

Mrs Smith nodded. "Men. Two of them. Their boyfriends, I suppose. One of them had a great big car he used to come and go in. Called himself an officer, if you can believe that anyone like that would be caught messing about with the likes of them. And the other one," Mrs Smith pulled her shawl closer around her and spoke her next words in a whisper, "said he was a *Dutchman*. Now what do you make of that, Mr Spooner?"

She watched Spooner's mouth open and close twice before she saved him the bother of replying. "That Anna told Queenie they'd worked together before, that he was some kind of entertainer. But I don't believe that either. What would a Dutchman be doing here, in West Bromwich, at a time like this?"

Spooner felt a trickle of sweat run down his back. Perhaps Mrs Smith really did know everything. But it wasn't a spy that his hostess took her mystery man for.

"They were confidence tricksters, you ask me," she rattled on. "Come from the circus, all of them, putting on an act the whole time. And there you are, you see. She did the vanishing act when she needed to, didn't she?"

Spooner clattered his cup back into his saucer. "On the night of the air raid?" he said.

Mrs Smith nodded. "Myrtle from over the road saw her. She turned up the next day, the Wednesday morning – well, it would have been more like lunchtime – in time to see the wardens pulling bodies out of the wreckage. Just stood there, in her glamorous frock from the night before and her violin case, with nothing to go back to. Myrtle's soft-hearted too. She took pity on her and got her George to take her to the Sally Army in Brum and she's not been back here since."

Spooner sensed he was being dismissed before he even realised a figure was hovering in the doorway – Mr Smith, back from the pub and ready for his Sunday lunch. "It's all right, Don, we've finished here," his wife said. "I'll show the gentleman out."

"Well, thank you for your time, Mrs Smith," said Spooner,

stepping out onto the street as everyone else was going indoors to be fed. "And for your tea."

"Go to the Sally Army on Corporation Street," were her final words. "I expect they've managed to find somewhere to put her."

The tribe had moved off from the bombsite now but, as he got back into his car, Spooner noticed another car parked across the street that hadn't been there before – a black Ford Anglia. He couldn't see anyone inside it. But when he drove off a few seconds later it followed him.

6

LITTLE LADY MAKE BELIEVE

Monday, 17 February 1941

"Anna?"

The woman in the Salvation Army uniform knocked gently on the door. Spooner crossed his fingers behind his back. There was a sound of a radio being silenced.

"Who is it?" another voice came through the door.

"There's a gentleman here to see you. He's come all the way from London, from one of the big talent agencies, looking for musicians to play in the bands down there, and he's been told how great you are." She turned to look at Spooner, her face anxious. "That's right, isn't it?" she whispered. He nodded.

The previous afternoon Spooner had decided to go straight from West Bromwich to the Citadel on Corporation Street, just stopping at High View to make another call to London. The black Ford Anglia had kept with him right into the city centre, but must have got tired of the circuitous attempts Spooner made navigating his way back to John Bright Street, as it lost interest in following him somewhere around the ruins of the old Bullring.

But once Spooner was there, Janet's offer of roast beef for lunch was as impossible to resist as her breakfast bacon. At three in the afternoon he arrived at the Citadel to find the building turned into a canteen for servicemen. Air raids had made it too dangerous to be used as a place of worship, he was told, so the Army had gone back to street preaching in daylight hours. But when he said he was searching for someone who had been bombed out in West Bromwich on the nineteenth of November, the officers went out of their way to be helpful.

They led him to the woman who was now knocking on her spare bedroom door. Judith Atherstone played trombone in the Salvation Army band and she had been out with them yesterday afternoon raising money. Spooner made a generous contribution to their funds on behalf of the Paramount Agency and Judith had told him her story. She had recently persuaded her elderly mother, with whom she lived in Edgbaston, to let her take in a young waif who was a fellow musician, a girl who had lost everything but her instrument and the clothes she stood up in during the raids of the nineteenth.

She didn't immediately volunteer her lodger's name because, she explained, the girl had been in such a state of shock and distress when she first came to live with them. Only by accompanying her with her music each day had she managed to calm the girl back down to relative normality. Though she had claimed to have no family or friends to turn to, Judith had got the impression her lodger was hiding from someone. She was terrified of going out and of unexpected rings on the doorbell.

"Perhaps what she needs is a fresh start," Spooner had suggested, outlining the sort of package Norrie offered musicians he wanted to hire, hoping that her shared passion would help Judith understand such an opportunity and let him in to talk to Anna – he was certain this had to be Anna. The only alternative to getting her story was to inform local CID there was a suspected spy at this address, something neither he nor his boss wanted to happen. Taking this course of action might send up a signal to Clara and these two mystery men that they'd been rumbled and give them the opportunity to flee.

Besides, neither he nor the Chief knew if Anna had any idea about Clara's real identity. The Chief wanted Spooner to proceed with his cover story in the hope that Anna would come back to London with him of her own free will. But Judith didn't think she would.

"I've tried to get her to come out and play with our band," she explained, "and sometimes, if we've had a good session, she'll be all for it. Then, as soon as the moment comes when I try to get her to leave the house, she just digs in her heels. I honestly think she's terrified of something – or someone – out there. She even asked for me to have a lock put on her bedroom door, which upset Ma, when she'd already been so kind to her."

"I understand," said Spooner. "But if she's the person I think she is, then you have a major talent locked away in your spare room. If she *is* Anna Hartley," he said, noting how Judith blinked and looked down when he said the name, an indication that she wanted to avoid both lying and giving her friend away. "The reason I want to bring her to London is that I'm convinced she'll have an audience. See, I'm a wee expert on folk tunes and she's collected a lot of rarities. Songs that might not have been heard for hundreds of years, but tell us about our history in ways that books don't. They're like heirlooms handed down the generations by the people who could play and remember them, usually the women." When he got to this point, Spooner realised it was his grandmother talking, and from the expression on Judith's face, her sudden possession of his words was turning the situation to his advantage. "They're important," he finished, "and it's a tradition I want to keep alive."

"If that's really what she's done," said Judith, "then I will try to help you convince her."

She suggested Spooner call round again tomorrow morning at ten o'clock, and to wait outside her door without knocking or ringing the bell until she let him in. Now, at the top of her stairs, he heard a sound of footsteps, of keys being turned in the lock. The door opened a fraction and Spooner found himself staring into a pair of wide, sea green eyes.

"Did you tell him who I am, Judith?" her voice had the cadences of birdsong, lilting between the West Midlands and somewhere else, but with an unmistakable ring of fear.

"No, dear," Judith said. "He's an expert on folk music and he knows all about you. He's been told how brilliant you are by the people here and he wants to bring you down to London – which I've got to admit, is better than you hiding away up here. You'll give him the chance to talk to you at least, won't you?"

The sea green eyes rolled between Judith and Spooner, finally resting on him. Spooner had already selected a song he hoped Anna would like, if it wasn't already in her repertoire. Instead of introducing himself, he began to sing.

"Sylvie, Sylvie, all on one day, She dressed herself in man's array, A sword and pistol all by her side, To meet her true love she did ride."

The sea green eyes widened, and so did the gap between their owner and the doorframe. A round face was revealed, framed by white-blonde hair that sprung out from around the headscarf she had tied around it. Her expression turned from serious to curious as he sang.

"*She met her true love all in the plain, 'Stand and deliver, kind sir,' she said, 'Stand and deliver, kind sir,' said she, 'Or else this moment you shall die!'*"

A smile slowly spread across Anna's face. She nodded her head and picked up the next lines herself, in a voice high and pure as mountain air.

"*Oh, when she'd robbed him of all his store,' she says, 'Kind sir, there's one thing more, A diamond ring which I know you have, deliver that, your sweet life to save.'*"

Then she put her hand to her mouth, looked across at Judith and started to laugh. Judith shook her head. "You're a dark horse, aren't you?" she said. "No wonder Mr Spooner's been looking so hard for you. Will you let him in now?"

Anna opened the door far enough to reveal all four foot ten inches of her, dressed not in the glamour Mrs Smith had described, but a pair of dungarees and jumper. She gave Spooner a shy smile.

"You've proved you know your music," she said, "so all right. But, Judith," she looked at her friend anxiously, "you won't be far, will you?"

"No, dear," said Judith. "I'll just be downstairs. I'll bring you up some tea."

"Come in then," Anna said to Spooner. "I'm afraid it's not exactly the Ritz." She stepped aside and let him enter. The room had the sort of irredeemable chill that came with high ceilings, despite being stuffed full of large, dark wood furniture – a wardrobe, dressing table, radiogram and bed, over which had been thrown a knitted Afghan, lending a splash of colour to the otherwise austere surroundings. A music stand was set up underneath the window, next to which, on a high chair, rested the violin case. Anna picked it up and placed it down on the bed as carefully as if it had been a child.

"Please," she said, "have a seat. And don't mind what's on the music stand. That's just something to please Judith. She's been so good to me."

As Spooner sat, he noted the score was for "Nearer, My God, To Thee".

"Apart from this," she continued, touching the violin case, "I don't own a thing. Even these clothes came from the neighbours. Outgrown by a twelve-year-old girl," she said. "So anyway," she sat down on the bed next to her precious remaining possession, "who was it told you about me?"

"Bertie Adams," said Spooner, "from the Hippodrome. He's an old friend of my boss, Norrie Denman – you'll have heard of him, I take it?"

Anna nodded, bit her bottom lip. "That's the Paramount Agency, isn't it?"

"Aye." Spooner nodded. "You might have heard that there's a shortage of jazz musicians in London right now. Every hotel wants its own dance band but there's not enough to go round who can actually play the music. Bertie put a few our way and while I was up to see them, I wanted to follow some ideas of my own. See, I'm sure you're good enough to sit in on any of these bands, but my own passion is for the folk songs and when Bertie told me you had a collection of them, I wanted to talk to you about it. If you don't mind me saying, it's quite unusual to find someone as young as yourself with such an interest."

"Oh well," said Anna, "that's because I was brought up by my grandma, an old Welsh woman from Tenby. She used to sit by the fire spinning her wool and singing them to me. And the grislier, the better."

Spooner shook his head. "Astonishing," he said. "That sounds exactly like my childhood. Except the old woman in my case came from Shetland. She kept hundreds of jigs and reels inside her head and I've tried desperately to remember them all since she passed away. It's a way of bringing her back, I suppose."

"Did she teach you 'The Lady Highwayman?'" Anna sat forward, her smile now completely genuine and lighting up the room better than any bulb or candle.

"Aye," said Spooner. "For some reason you made me think of her. Must have been the dungarees, eh?"

"Oh, what else do you have?" said Anna. "Let's see if I know any of them."

"Now then," Spooner consulted his mental song repository, "there's 'Barbara Allen', 'The Three Ravens', 'Miss Bailey's Ghost'..." Anna nodded along as he spoke. "... 'Down Among the Dead Men', 'Jack Hall' and ah, I know – how about 'The Witches Reel'?"

Anna clasped her hands together. "That's one I don't know," she said. "Please sing it for me and I'll try to join in." She opened her violin case.

"This was one of Granny's favourites," Spooner told her. "It's about the trial of Francis Stewart, the Earl of Bothwell, for using sorcery to try to kill King James VI. He was supposed to have had a coven of witches perform the reel on a cliff top one night when the King was sailing past, so that a storm would brew up and capsize him."

From within her case, Anna produced a very old, yellow-brown violin.

"That's the sort of song I want to learn," she said, tucking it under her chin and lifting up her bow. "Away you go, then."

Spooner remembered back to the fireside of his own youth, Granny's voice keening:

"Cummer gae ye before, cummer gae ye, Gin ye winna gae before, cummer let me, Ring-a-ring-a-widdershins, Linken lithely widdershins, Cummer carlin cron and queyn, Roun gae we!"

After the first verse, Anna joined in on her instrument. Her fingers were as light and deft as the cadences of her voice. She had each note almost before he had come to it himself.

"Cummer gae ye before, cummer gae ye, Gin ye winna gae before, cummer let me, Ring-a-ring-a-widdershins, Loupen' lightly widdershins, Kilted coats and fleein' hair, Three times three!"

"Oh!" Anna enthused. "It's brilliant!"

"There's one more verse," said Spooner and she started to dance around him as he sang it.

"Cummer gae ye before, cummer gae ye, Gin ye winna gae before, cummer let me, Ring-a-ring-a-widdershins, Whirlin', skirlin' widdershins, De'il tak the hindmost, Wha'er she be!"

Anna's face shone as she sat back on the bed, laughing. "Can you write it down for me? I can remember the tune, but the words are a bit hard to follow in your dialect." Laying her violin back in its case, she opened her bedside chest of drawers. "Have you got a pen?" she asked, producing a notebook and turning to a fresh page.

"Oh, aye," Spooner felt in his jacket pocket, trying not to look the way he felt: heady with the exhilaration of her accompaniment, almost as if he was drunk. He knew why the landlord of the Victoria had wanted so much for her to come back.

"You know how to do the reels as well," he said, taking the book from her.

"I just do what comes with the music," she said. "No one's ever taught me."

"Well, I never," Judith stood in the doorway with her tea tray. "Are you doing a concert together already?"

"Oh thank you, Judith," Anna sprang back up to take her offerings. "That's so kind. Mr Spooner was just teaching me a song I didn't know."

"Well, there aren't many of those, are there?" Judith said.

"I've tried to remember all the ones I lost," Anna said. "I've put them in that book you gave me. It's nearly full up now, but there's room for another, isn't there, Mr Spooner?"

"Well, I'm glad it's going so well," said Judith. She was amazed by the transformation in her lodger. Though she had been aware that music was the key to unlocking Anna's torment, she obviously hadn't been playing the right kind with her. "I'll leave you to it."

While Anna poured, Spooner flicked through the pages of her book. It was as she had said a huge collection of songs, a lot that he knew and many that he didn't, but all with a supernatural theme. It was time to risk treading a little further down this path. He waited until he heard Judith reach the bottom of the stairs.

"Bertie said you used to play as a duo with another woman," he said. Anna put down the teapot carefully, looked from one cup to another.

"Do you take sugar?" she asked, without looking at him.

"Aye," said Spooner, "I'll take a spoonful if you have it. And just a wee drop of milk."

She followed his instructions without replying and passed the cup over to him.

"Thanks," he said, wondering if he had smashed the fragile

trust he had just established. He took a sip. The tea was strong but not stewed, just the way he liked it. Anna poured a cup for herself and curled back up with it on the bed, blowing across the surface of the liquid.

"That's right," she finally said. "Clara." Her voice had returned to its former whisper. "But we're not friends any more. Nor are we likely to be ever again."

Spooner shrugged. "Ach, it makes no odds. You've talent enough for two people," he said, "and it doesn't affect the offer I'm making. I was just curious."

Anna looked at him. "No, I'm sure people will have told you how brilliant she is. I can't deny it, she's a far better singer than I am and the way she plays piano is perfect for your London bands, she has a jazz background, unlike me. It was my idea for us to do Spellbound, and I taught her nearly all my songs… But, she taught me a lot too." The sea green eyes washed over Spooner and travelled far away.

Quietly, he asked: "How long were you together?"

"Not long," Anna continued to stare into infinity, "about a year, I suppose. I met her at the old Empire, another thing that doesn't exist any more. We were part of the same bill: I was playing the violin for a tightrope walker and she was singing. I've been round this circuit for ten years now, since Nonna died and I left Tenby, but I'd never come across her before. She was what they call a mystery. Said she'd been working in London and she knew the music for all the latest shows. When I asked her why she'd come here she just shrugged and said she was trying to forget someone." Anna shook her head, blew again on her tea and took a sip before resuming.

"You know when we were playing just then? You felt something, didn't you?" Her eyes focussed on his again. "A connection. Words that didn't have to be spoken. Well I had that with Clara. Better than with anyone. It was the way she sang, but something else, this aura she brought with her. We only did two songs of hers but they always brought the house down. Brilliant, they were. A bit like gypsy music – I've played with some gypsies in my time – and a bit like Jewish music. Old, but so modern at the same time."

"Like nothing else you've ever heard before," Spooner remembered Norman's words. "That was what the landlord of the Victoria told me. If you don't want to come to London, he told me to say you've got a permanent invitation to play there."

Anna put her cup down shakily in her saucer. "The Victoria," she said. "Oh my. That was when it all went wrong. That night with her and the officer."

7

BEWITCHED, BOTHERED AND BEWILDERED

Monday, 17 February 1941

"The officer?" Spooner echoed. "Who's that?"

"Good question," said Anna. "And one that I don't think I have the answer to. He called himself Ralph Nicholson. I called him 'the officer' because he looked like one and he talked like one and he drove around in a big black Bentley. The original Mr Tall Dark and Handsome, he was. To Clara, anyway," a note of bitterness crept into her voice.

"Where'd he come from?"

"Another good question." Now that she had started on this subject she had bottled up for so long, Anna found herself unable to stop talking. "I'm not really sure. When I first met Clara, I was living in a hostel on Broad Street – it was cheap and a step up from some of the fleapit boarding houses like she was living in at the time. I got her a room and from then on, we did just about everything together. Except for when she went for her piano lessons. I can only think that she met him there."

"Really?" said Spooner. "Her piano teacher was given to matchmaking, was he?"

Anna scowled. "I don't know. I never met him and it was something she was quite mysterious about. She called him Professor De Vere and went on the train to meet him. He wasn't based in Brum, but somewhere out over Dudley way."

A siren went off in Spooner's mind. There was a Triple-U he had once shadowed called Simon De Vere, whose social life took in regular meetings of the British Union of Fascists and The Right Club, as well as visits to a bookshop near the British Museum that stocked highly expensive occult works. De Vere kept an account there and a townhouse in Chelsea, he was the son of an Earl with an ancestral pile in Worcestershire, an aristocrat whose blue blood could be traced back to the Norman Conquest, when his ancestors rode behind King William. Traces of his heritage lived on in the lines of his high forehead, its black tresses swept back from a widow's peak, the slim, aquiline nose and high cheekbones that guarded his deep blue eyes. Spooner had seen the charisma De Vere exuded through his cultured tones and those hypnotic orbs and always ended his reports pegging him as a fifth columnist. But, despite a big sweep in May 1940, in which all the leading figures of the organisations his suspect admired had been arrested and interned, Spooner had never learned of the same fate befalling De Vere.

"That was one world I was never invited into," Anna went on. "I thought it was because I didn't come from the right background. I mean, Clara was always as strapped as I am, but it was obvious she'd come from money. She had this steamer trunk that she'd sometimes get things from – a mink shawl or a string of pearls – and tell me they were heirlooms. Now, I've not had much to do with the upper classes. They slum it in the music halls when they fancy, but they don't mix beneath their station, that's one thing I do know. So, with him being a professor, that's what I thought it was – at first."

Anna put her cup aside and leaned forward, as entranced in her own mystery story as she had been with Spooner's song. "Then, I started to wonder if that was how she knew all those songs I was telling you about, that it was him teaching them to her. 'Cos she did like to make up stories, did Clara, and after a while I started to realise that. Even her calling him 'the professor' might have been some kind of private joke.

"So one night I followed her. I did what I often do to avoid being noticed," she hooked her thumb through one of the shoulder straps on her dungarees. "Dressed up as a boy. Pair of trousers, hair under a flat cap, and off I went. Sure enough, she took the train, all the way to Stourbridge, and when she got there, there was a big car waiting. A black Rolls-Royce Phantom, driven by a chauffeur. Now," she fixed Spooner with a knowing look, "when have you ever met a piano teacher that puts on that kind of service before?" Spooner shook his head.

"Thought not. So, of course, I couldn't follow her any further. But soon after that, the officer came to our next show, waving a bunch of red roses and a bottle of champagne for Clara. She started doing everything with him. Never had any time to practise, turned down bookings, spent all her time at his place. In the end, I had to go back to working with Nils – the tightrope walker – to earn enough to get by. Then it happened for the first time…" Anna's gaze slipped away from Spooner's.

"The hostel got hit in an air raid last October, the same one that did for the Empire. Luckily, neither of us was in at the time, and the damage wasn't too bad. Of course, Clara's boyfriend came to help us clear out what we could find. It was all covered in dust and rubble, but no one had been in and robbed the place, like what sometimes happens.

"When I was putting my bags into the boot of his car, I saw that Clara's trunk was already in there. And it wasn't all covered in dust, didn't have any dents or marks on it either – in fact, it didn't look like it had been touched, which did strike me as odd. But I wasn't really thinking clearly at the time, so I didn't say anything.

"The officer had a place for her at his flat, but, of course, there wasn't any room for me. He was generous enough to let me use his phone and ring around all the people I knew. I'd almost forgotten about Mrs Simpkins. She was an old friend of Nonna's, came to Tenby for her holidays every year, and I remembered then that she started taking in lodgers after her husband passed away," Anna gave a sad smile. "I looked her up and she was so pleased to hear from me, she said yes, of course I could have a room and to come right away. He drove me there, and that caused a sensation. From the time we stopped outside Mrs Simpkins' door and rang the bell to the time she answered it, just about every old biddy in that street had come out to stare at us. Though driving around West Brom in a Bentley with a redhead in a mink coat, I suppose that was inevitable." Spooner could picture Mrs Smith leading the race to the doorsteps.

"After that, Clara seemed more committed," Anna said. "I thought at the time it was because the air raid had got her what she wanted – she could move into his posh flat and keep me at arm's length in West Brom. And maybe she felt a bit guilty about that, 'cos for the next month, we did quite a lot of shows, including that one for your friend Bertie. I started to get my hopes up that night. There was a crowd of us who wanted to carry the party on to the Vic. You never think lightning's going to strike twice, do you?" She answered her own question with a shake of her head. "I got a lift with Nils so I didn't see it, but when we got to the pub, it was obvious Clara and her boyfriend had a tiff on the way and now she was doing her best to annoy him. That's why she asked the landlord if we could play some songs, and that's why she chose the one she did." Anna looked back up at Spooner, who nodded silently, not wanting to break her concentration.

"A song about drinking and charvering." Her voice turned harsh, along with her words. "She wanted to let him know that he was nothing special, there were plenty more where he came from. And I was so happy that she had fallen out with him that I joined right in." Anna smiled grimly, her eyes starting to shine. "She cast her glamour over both of us. He dragged her off the piano and out of the door and then the air raid sirens went off. I tried to follow them, but the bombs started dropping and everyone was panicking. By the time I got outside, his car was gone and the sky was bright red with flame. It was the BSA factory, burning."

A lone tear leaked from the corner of her eye and ran down her face. She rubbed it away with the back of her hand. "I didn't get back to West Brom until the morning. By then there was nothing left of dear Mrs Simpkins, or the house. Just those nasty old women, staring at me. Only one of them was kind enough to get her husband to bring me to the Citadel because she knew the Sally Army helped bombed-out women."

"Jesus. I'm sorry to hear that." Spooner shook his head. "But now you've said it, don't you think it makes sense to try and make a fresh start in London, away from all these bad memories? We've plenty of work and I'm sure I can find you somewhere to stay."

He wished he could cross his fingers behind his back as he said these words. He felt sure that once the Chief had spoken to Anna he would see what he could now – an innocent who had been ruthlessly used – and that he could persuade Norrie to give her work. He felt quite spellbound himself by her talents.

Anna rubbed her eye again. "It's very kind of you and I don't know what I've done to deserve it," she said. "But will you let me think about it first?"

"Of course," said Spooner. "I know it's a big decision. Only I've to be away back to London tomorrow afternoon," he gambled, hoping to speed up her contemplation, "so if you want to get a lift down there with me, you'll have to let me know by then."

She nodded. "Can you come back at the same time tomorrow?" she asked. "I just want to talk to Judith about it. You know," she tried her best to smile, but emotion kept tugging the corners of her mouth downwards, "she's been so good to me."

"That's fine," said Spooner, getting to his feet. "I'll leave you to it, then. Thank you for letting me in. I've no' seen anyone like you before and I really appreciate it. I hope we'll be able to work together." Leaving one of his business cards on her music stand, he offered his hand. Her fingers were as tiny as the rest of her, but her grip was firm.

"You don't know what this means to me either," she said, following him to the door. "Thank you and see you tomorrow."

Spooner's head was spinning as he stepped back on to the street outside. But it wasn't so full of this rich seam of new information and all its ramifications that he didn't notice the black Ford Anglia parked further down the street from him. Nor that, as he moved away, it waited only a few seconds before following. This time it stayed behind him all the way to John Bright Street and only as he turned into the car park did it sail past. He couldn't quite see the driver's face. He had a black fedora tilted down over his eyes.

Karl was dreaming again. It came to him every time he closed his eyes, though each time it was different and more disturbing than the last. Now the bark of the tree began to writhe before his eyes, forming itself into a face – Clara's face. Her eyes were knots and her mouth a pitch black hollow that filled him with the greatest sense of terror he had ever known – worse even than the drop from the plane. Now it was not just his radio that was flashing out her distress signal in morse. Now he could hear her screaming from a place he couldn't reach her: "*Help me! Help me! Help me!*"

This time when he woke up, the nurse had her hand on his arm, trying to shake him out of his torment. As he took in her concerned face and the curtains she had drawn around his bed, the safety of the hospital ward compared to the nightmare of his subconscious, he realised there was someone else standing behind her – the tall man with the piercing eyes who had introduced himself as Mr King.

"Herr Kohl," the man said, "I'm sorry you're still not feeling any better."

The nurse gently piled up pillows behind Karl's back so that he could sit up and face his inquisitor in a more dignified position. She wiped a cool cloth over his forehead and gave him a glass of water to sip. It was all he could do not to clasp hold of her wrist and demand that she stayed with him for as long as the man remained there.

The Chief sat down in the chair by his bedside. "I hope you're well enough to answer a few more questions," he said. "It would be of the greatest importance to yourself and Clara if you could."

Karl brushed his forelock out of his eyes. "I'll try my best," he muttered.

"Good," said the Chief. "First, tell me everything you know about Simon De Vere."

The prisoner's face registered incomprehension.

"The professor?" the Chief tried again. "Perhaps that's the name you know him by?"

Karl shook his head. "*Nein*. I have never heard of this person," he said.

"All right then, let's try Ralph Nicholson. A military man, an officer in the Air Force."

"No." Karl's free hand reached for the charm he once wore around his neck.

"Ah," said the Chief, "you're still missing it, then?" Reaching into his pocket, he produced the Baphomet, hanging its chain over his fingers, just out of reach, and letting it sway from side to side. "Perhaps we should have a chat about this instead. You're awfully fond of it, aren't you? What does it mean to you?"

Karl cleared his throat, which was parched, despite the water. "Clara gave it to me."

"When you had performed what you described to me as your marriage?" the Chief asked.

Karl nodded, trying not to flinch as those eyes came closer to his own. He feared that in his current state, they could easily penetrate his thoughts.

"*I believe in the Serpent and the Lion, Mystery of Mysteries, in His name Baphomet,*" the Chief quoted from the text he had been brushing up on. Karl had a mental flash of Clara standing in front of an altar draped in black satin, pinpoints of flames from the black candles surrounding her, a dagger in her hand. "Tell me more about this society that Clara introduced you to. Did it have a name?" Raising her arms, a cloak the colour of midnight parting to reveal she wore nothing below. "Were you followers of Eliphas Lévi or were you a witches' coven, serving the Goat of Mendes?" A black cock and a white hen, squabbling out their terror, the blade flashing in the candlelight, the scent of herbs and blood heavy in the air. "Was the Goat indeed present on the happy day?"

"Now I think you are mocking me," Karl croaked.

"On the contrary, I am deadly serious. You see, Clara has been a frequent visitor to this man De Vere, who has a home close to Birmingham and a keen interest in the Dark Arts. I imagined you had been part of the same coven, in your pre-war days in Hamburg. It seemed logical that De Vere helped Clara to become so at home in her adopted city."

The amulet swung from his fingers like a pendulum.

"Look," said Karl, "I went with Clara to these circles, made these rituals with her, because that was how she got what she wanted. To live well, to be recognised for her talents – and not to have to work like a dog for it, like most women do."

He could see the other members of the coven, kneeling before the altar in their black robes, the hoods down to reveal their identities: men of industry; men of commerce; men of war. There had, once, been an Englishman, brought by one of Clara's highest sources, the Ambassador. But while he faced this man, he must blank all that from his mind.

"*Ja*, so she called herself a witch and she was proud of those skills as much as all her others. There were powerful people at these meetings, as I have told you before, but you have to believe me – I only saw a small part of it. Only what she wanted me to see." Processing before the altar to sip at the bowl of crimson liquid proffered by their flame-haired High Priestess. "She never told me anything about these people in England, this professor and… what did you say the other one was called?"

"Ralph Nicholson," said the Chief. "But perhaps she wouldn't have wanted you to know."

"Why?" Karl was suddenly far from Clara's altar and back in the hospital room, where the groans came from the injured and the air smelled of antiseptic. "What do you mean?"

The Chief wrapped the amulet around his fingers and deposited it back in his pocket. "You trusted her, didn't you? Enough to jump out of a plane in the middle of the night for her. Well, I'm afraid to have to tell you but we have received information that Clara was intimate with this man – beyond what normally goes on at those ceremonies of yours. She was living with him in Birmingham."

Karl tried to swallow and found that he couldn't. He could no longer remember the right words to any of the spells of protection she had armed him with. Instead, he could only see the branches of the nightmare tree start to shake.

"I wonder what was going on in her mind?" the Chief went on. "Where you fitted into all her plans? Or perhaps you didn't. Perhaps you were never meant to make a successful landing. Has that thought ever crossed your mind?"

Clara's scream started to echo in Karl's mind and he was filled with impotent fury. He wanted to raise his drinking glass and smash it into the face of his tormentor. But the movement caused it to slip through his sweaty fingers and into the Chief's open palm.

"Steady, old man," he said, putting it back on the bedside cabinet.

Karl tried again. He grabbed the Chief's wrist with more force than he looked capable of. "Stop all of these games and just tell me where she is," he demanded.

"Where she is?" the Chief frowned. "How should I know where she is?"

"She is trapped, somewhere in the trees!" Karl hissed. "She is in danger! She comes into my dreams every time I shut my eyes to tell me so. You have to find her!"

As the volume of his cries rose, the nurse came back through the curtains. "What's happening? Is he delirious again?" she said, bending in closer to assess him.

"Or giving a good impression of it," said the Chief.

The nurse gently prised the prisoner's fingers away from his wrist. Karl murmured piteously at her touch, tears streaking down his cheeks. The Chief got to his feet.

"I'm beginning to lose faith in your abilities, Herr Kohl," he said, putting his trilby back over the threads of grey that ran through his mane. "Nonetheless, I shall return."

8

DIZZY SPELLS

Tuesday, 18 February 1941

Spooner stopped the car outside Judith's house and checked in the rear-view mirror. As far as he could see, there were no black Ford Anglias creeping up behind him. Perhaps the trick he had pulled yesterday had actually worked.

The idea had come to him in the High View car park. As he pulled in, fresh from his visit to Anna, Bob was cleaning his own car, a battered old Ford Eight. Seeing Spooner, he wandered over for a closer look at the Rover.

"What a beauty she is," he said, rubbing an imaginary speck off the wing with his chamois leather. "I would have loved one of these at your age. Wouldn't mind one now, truth be told. Can't you just picture our Jan sitting on the passenger seat, eh?" The longing behind his words was clear.

"Well, would you like to take her out for a spin in it?"

"Well, I…" Bob did his best to look as though he was flabbergasted by the suggestion, "I mean, that's very kind of you, kid. Are you sure? Have you got enough petrol?"

"Aye," said Spooner. Not knowing how long he would be needing them, Spooner had been issued with a wedge of petrol coupons before he left London. Producing his wallet, he handed a couple to Bob. "But I tell you what, I'd be grateful if you could fill her up for me while you're out. I'll be leaving tomorrow and I'd rather leave on a full tank."

Bob nodded furiously. "Of course, kid, of course. Christ," he said, examining the coupons, "I won't ask how he sorted these out, but Norrie's a marvel, isn't he?"

"The only other thing is," Spooner added a caveat, "would I be able borrow your car in return? See, I still need to make another trip this afternoon."

Bob scratched his head. "How far you going?" he asked.

"Over Stourbridge way," said Spooner. "Why, d'you not think she'll make it?"

"No, kid, with the right handling, I think she'll be fine. It's just that I don't know if there's as much in the tank as you'll be needing for the round trip."

"Ach," Spooner couldn't help but smile, "then I'll fill yours up in return, nae bother."

An hour later, Spooner was heading towards the rise of hills that marked the borders with Worcestershire. According to his map, the highest peak of the Clents was called Wychbury Hill and on top of that stood a stone obelisk which, against the bare winter fields and leafless trees, had been visible for the last few miles. This monument, the information from his Triple-U file on Simon De Vere reminded him, had been commissioned in the middle of the eighteenth century by his ancestor, Viscount Francis De Vere, who had embarked upon an ambitious project to rebuild his family seat in the then highly fashionable Picturesque style. Beneath this monument to his ambition, the estate of Hagley Hall stretched across the valley, surrounded by landscaped woodland.

Bob's car could only creep along at a fraction of the speed of the Rover, but the switch had been worth making. Out in the countryside with a long ribbon of empty road behind him, Spooner could be sure he hadn't been followed. He wanted some time and space to evaluate the events of the past few days and what better way to get that than to take a drive out to the ancestral home of the one suspect that had already been in his address book when he left London? Though it seemed unlikely that Simon De Vere could be the driver of such a common make of car as the one that had been pursuing him recently, the idea couldn't be entirely discounted.

There was a small lay-by halfway up the hill which he pulled into, running through Bob's hints for getting the car to start again if she were to prove reluctant before he switched off the motor. A path led him through a copse up to the open hillside, where the wind was strong. But there was another thing he could be thankful for – it was a clear and crisp day, the sun still just above eye-level in an almost cloudless sky. After the constant smog and noise of Birmingham it was exhilarating to smell air that was fresh with the scent of soil and grass, of nature still going about her business unhindered by the chaos thrown up by man. With the aid of his binoculars, he would be able to see for miles.

Spooner inspected the obelisk first. It was Greek in its line, with a square pedestal supporting a slender, tapered shaft and fashioned in sandstone the colour of a fox's pelt. But its glory days had long passed – part of the shaft had toppled away into the long grass that surrounded it and the base was thick with moss. Nonetheless, the sight of it and the view over which it presided were still awe-inspiring.

The valley beneath was thick with trees, between which

protruded more towers, spires and turrets in the same russet hues, buildings that had been created within the same epic vision as the obelisk. As he adjusted his lenses for a better look, Spooner ran through the details of the report he would be writing for the Chief later.

He had come away from his meeting with Anna convinced that she had been telling him the truth – everything Judith and Mrs Smith had said confirmed that the events of the nineteenth of November had turned the violinist against her former friend and led to the current state of fear under which she had hidden herself away. But, though she had told him more than he expected, he also divined there was another notion she'd kept in check. He thought she had tumbled what Clara was really up to.

It was the detail about the steamer trunk that made him think so: the fact that it had already been in the boot of her boyfriend's car when they were ostensibly both trying to retrieve their belongings from the blitzed hostel. The implication was that Clara had deliberately taken her belongings and gone before the raid, leaving Anna to her fate and then only pretending to help her afterwards and continued with the band to maintain that façade. The second raid on the BSA factory and West Bromwich on the same night had confirmed in Anna's mind what she hadn't allowed herself to process before: Clara knew where and when the bombs were going to fall and perhaps, in the second instance, even had some hand in where they had been directed. Which could only mean she was a spy.

If so, then it followed that her boyfriend was in on it too, a British officer turned traitor by her will – their public spat at the Victoria a play-act, an excuse to get away from the vicinity of the air raid before the bombs started falling. Anna's hunch about who had introduced them fitted with the Chief's conviction that a fifth column lurked in Britain – with members drawn from the elite of society – and his own about what Simon De Vere had been doing at those fascist gatherings in 1939.

Spooner's binoculars settled on the turrets of a ruined castle in the valley below, a folly fashioned to replicate the likes of those recorded by artists on the Grand Tour. A building designed to deceive, to present an idealised and romantic fiction to retreat to. Spooner doubted the romance between Clara and this Nicholson was anything but a façade too, a front for her to amass as much information on the munitions factories of Birmingham and the operations of the British military as was possible.

"*She cast her glamour over both of us,*" he recalled Anna saying. He wondered if, by this, she had been telling him that she was once in love with Clara too. That was the way it had sounded. He also wondered if he, in turn, hadn't fallen just a little in love with Anna.

Then there was this third man both Mrs Smith and Norman the landlord had mentioned: the Dutchman. Anna had talked about her friend Nils, the tightrope walker. That sounded like a Dutch name and if they had often worked together it would explain why his witnesses had taken them to be lovers. Or perhaps, he mused as he moved his sights across the valley, he was being overly romantic with the truth himself.

His sweep took in the soaring spire of a church and some other kind of construction, lower down the hillside from where he stood, which was largely obscured by trees. It was just as he had pictured it; as if he already knew what he would find waiting for him here. As a setting for a secretive coven practising pagan rites, the De Vere estate could hardly have been bettered in any work of fiction.

But in reality he wondered which of these people Anna was hiding from. When she said that Nicholson had a "posh flat" he wondered if Clara's boyfriend could possibly have lived close by to where she found herself now, Judith living on the fringes of Edgbaston, one of the best districts in Birmingham. It would make sense of Anna's fear of leaving the house if, by some quirk of fate, she had found sanctuary from her tormentors in the very place they were holed up. That was the explanation that made the most sense, he decided, as his gaze finally came to rest on the Hall itself.

The great Palladian construction basked in the centre of the parkland, its sandstone flanks glowing rich umber in the caress of the slowly sinking winter sun. A thin line of smoke drifted up from one of its chimneys, signifying that someone, if only one of the servants, was at home. Spooner studied the stable block and garages for signs of life, but was rewarded only by the lone figure of a gamekeeper, a rifle cocked over his arm and a string of rabbits slung over his shoulder, making his way across the lawn towards the kitchens, a springer spaniel trotting at his feet.

He knew the door would never be opened to him if he should call unannounced and besides, Spooner wanted to be able to get back to Birmingham within the hours of daylight. However, he found himself reluctant to leave. It wasn't just the beauty of the house and its surrounds that held him so in thrall, it was the notion that there was something he was missing. Perhaps it was his own unwillingness to go back to the deception he would need to continue with Anna tomorrow, the fact that, when her meeting with Norrie turned into a briefing with the Chief, she would be unlikely ever to hold him in any kind regard again. Chiding himself about the unworthiness of these thoughts, Spooner lowered his binoculars and turned back towards the car. He would never know if Anna would have trusted him more if he could have told her who he really was. But surely that was a price worth paying?

Spooner stepped out of the Rover minutes before the appointed hour. They were expecting him, so he didn't knock or ring the bell, but while he was waiting, he continued to reconnoitre the street. At exactly ten o'clock, the door opened and to Spooner's relief, Anna stood there with her violin case and a small travel bag, wearing a smart grey wool suit, a green overcoat with matching beret and a nervous smile. Judith stood behind her, a protective hand on her friend's shoulder.

"Well," Anna said, "as you can see, I've decided to take the plunge."

"She's got my blessing," Judith added.

"As well as half her possessions."

"Don't be daft," Judith said. "That's nothing and you know it. But I happen to think it's for the best. Just so long as you take good care of her, Mr Spooner."

"Aye," Spooner said. "Shall I take these for you?" he nodded towards Anna's luggage.

"You can take my case," Anna allowed. "But I never let anyone else touch the fiddle."

"Fair enough," he said. "I'll put it in the boot for you and let you say your goodbyes. Thank you," he said to Judith, "and I promise, I'll do my best for her." That at least was true. Spooner had no wish to intrude on their parting, so he made his way back towards the Rover. As he did, an engine started up a little further down the road behind him. Checking the wing mirror as he opened the boot, he saw a maroon Austin saloon nudging its way onto the street. Probably just a local resident going about his business, he reasoned. He put the case down next to his own bag and briefcase, turned and waited. Anna came out of the door without looking back, a big smile on her face. Judith stood behind her on the doorstep with a hanky in her hand.

As Anna walked down the pavement, the maroon Austin accelerated. She heard it and turned round. At the same time, out of the corner of his eye, Spooner saw a shape moving from across the road, a shadow becoming animated.

Anna turned back towards him, her mouth open and her eyes wide with fear. "It's…" she began but the rest of the sentence was lost in the sound of squealing brakes as the Austin veered towards them. Spooner put his body between Anna and the car, tried to push her back as it swerved to stop a hair's breadth away from him. He could see Judith's face turn white as she stood on her doorstep and the black shape from across the street getting closer, taking on the form of a running man who was wearing a fedora – like the driver of the Ford Anglia had been. Before he could turn his head to see who was driving the Austin he felt a blow between his shoulders. Spooner's knees buckled and everything went black.

When he came to, he was lying on the pavement to the side of the Rover. Everything seemed a little blurred, but he could make out Judith standing over him and beside her, the man in black kneeling at his side.

"He's coming round," he said. "Let's get him upright." Strong hands lifted him into a sitting position. Spooner's head was throbbing and there were stabs of pain from where his hands and knees had grazed the pavement. "It's all right," his aide went on. "You're safe, I don't think there's any bones broken. Just lean your head forward a bit. That was a nasty trick. All right, sit back up now, sir. How's your eyesight? I think he's probably got concussion." Large fingers, like a pair of sausages, danced in front of his face. "How many am I holding up?"

"Here," he heard Judith say, "I think he'll see better with these on."

"These your glasses? Lucky they didn't get broken." The same bulky digits replaced the spectacles across the bridge of Spooner's nose. "How's that?"

Spooner's pupils settled on a wide face, a pair of round blue eyes. The fedora was sitting on the pavement beside them but the man's hair was equally as black, slicked back in brilliantined waves, the scent of which made Spooner start to feel nauseous. He had a neat pencil moustache over his top lip and it was this which made Spooner realise where he had seen the face before, glowering at him from in front of the fireplace in the Victoria on his first night in Birmingham.

"I think I'd better get him to the hospital. Don't worry, either of you," the man continued, rummaging in his pocket, and producing a small document that Spooner recognised to his surprise to be a warrant card. "I'm a police officer. Here," he passed it to Judith. "You better read it to him, I'm not sure he can see straight."

"So you are," Judith sounded as surprised as Spooner felt. "Detective Sergeant William Houlston it says, Mr Spooner. What were you doing here, anyway?"

"Following the villain that just coshed him and made off

with your tenant," Houlston said. "We'll take my car, his will be safe enough to leave here, won't it?"

"I expect so," Judith sounded doubtful. "You don't think they'll come back, then?"

"I doubt it," DS Houlston said. "They've got what they wanted. For now."

"Oh my," Judith's voice started to waver. "Poor Anna. No wonder she was so scared."

"Don't you worry about her now, Mrs…?"

"It's Miss, actually. Miss Judith Atherstone. And why shouldn't I be worried after what I've just witnessed from my own front doorstep?"

"Because I'm going to sort it all out," Houlston assured her. "The best thing you can do is go back inside and write down everything you just saw and heard while it's still fresh in your mind. I'll be back to take your statement as soon as I've had this one looked over."

"Well," Judith drew in her bottom lip, "will you let me take Anna's bag from the car?"

"I dunno," said Houlston, looking back at Spooner. "What do you think?"

Spooner flapped his arm ineffectually. "Please," he said, his voice sounding thick and slurred. "Let her take it. And get my briefcase too, will you?"

"All right," said Houlston. "Have you still got your car keys?"

Spooner found that they were in his trouser pocket, where he must have stashed them by reflex as the Austin bore down on them. Houlston took them, let Judith retrieve Anna's case from the boot, put Spooner's briefcase down beside him and then locked the car up.

"I'll look after these 'til you're fit to drive," he said, putting the keys in his own pocket. Then he slid his hands underneath Spooner's armpits and helped him up to his feet.

His car was parked across the road. It was a grey Wolseley and not a black Ford Anglia.

"Are you sure this is correct procedure?" asked Spooner, as he slithered into the passenger seat, putting his briefcase down between his legs

Houlston rolled an eyeball. "You're a talent scout, aren't you Mr Spooner? How would you know what correct procedure is?"

Spooner put his throbbing head in his hands. "You don't look much like a policeman," he said, realising how lame that sounded.

Houlston gave the slowest wink Spooner had ever seen as he started up the engine. "Well, that's all right, then," he said, "'cos neither do you."

9

BETTER THINK TWICE

Tuesday, 18–Wednesday, 19 February 1941

"It was me following you," DS Houlston explained as he drove. "I've gotta hand it to you, you were pretty sharp trying to throw me off. That's why I switched motors today. Two can play at that game."

"But why?" Spooner continued to hold his head, not sure whether he had actually come round at all or whether this was all some sort of nightmare.

"Well, I don't know if it's coincidence or not, but your presence in Brum has flushed out some characters I've been after who had gone to ground – Miss Brown, Miss Hartley and their tightrope-walking friend, Mr Anders. What I'd like to know is, were you really trying to hire them to play the smart hotels in London? Or were you deliberately trying to attract attention to yourself to see what happened next?"

Spooner knew he wasn't dreaming. His subconscious could not come up with anything this precisely torturous. He had to start thinking clearly now. "Do you know who it was just coshed me?" seemed to be the most pertinent enquiry.

"You answer my question first," Houlston demanded, with an edge to his voice that cancelled any doubts Spooner might have entertained about breaking cover. He found his talent scout self took over from the dazed man in the passenger seat with surprising ease.

"Well, as you may have gathered, I was just about to take Miss Hartley to London with me. I've contracts in my brief-case made up for her to sign, if you want to see them. She said it would have been the first break she'd had since she was bombed out of her home in November last year – which was that pile of rubble in West Bromwich that you followed me to on Sunday, if you don't already know."

Houlston kept his eyes on the road. "I see," he said. "That's what she told you. And what about the other one. What did she say happened to Clara Brown? It was her you was really after, wasn't it?"

"Are you keen on music yourself, Detective Sergeant?" Spooner asked.

"Very," Houlston replied. "But what's that got to do with it?"

"If you were in my business and you'd heard Miss Hartley perform then you'd want to bring her to London too," said Spooner. "Aye, so it was Clara Brown my boss was tipped off about. But Anna's talent enough for the two of them, so I'm no' going away empty-handed… At least, I didn't think I was. Now, who was it just hit me?"

"Clara," said Houlston. "You never told me what happened to Clara."

"Anna doesn't know and I don't either. The last those two saw of each other was the same night she got bombed out. Unless that was Clara just now?"

Houlston said nothing, just stared ahead at the road until they reached the hospital. He continued to keep his tongue and his thoughts to himself until he stopped in the car park. Then, he gave a deep sigh and appeared to relent his harsh manner. "No, it wasn't Clara who hit you," he said. "I only wished that it was so I'd know she was still here and I had a chance of getting after her. But I'll tell you this for nothing – them three are rotten to the core. Maybe what happened today was a blessing in disguise. For you, anyway." He took the keys out of the ignition and turned to look at Spooner. "It was Nils Anders who hit you. The circus clown – I mean, the tightrope walker. I've not seen hide nor hair of him since January, when he fenced a load of phoney passports along with certain other items I've reason to believe he used his circus skills to acquire."

"You mean he's a burglar?"

Houlston's upper lip curled and his eyes brimmed with disdain. "At the least."

"So what do the other two have to do with it? Why would he attack me and drag Anna off the street like that?" Spooner asked.

"Did she tell you she was hiding from someone?" Houlston asked.

"No," said Spooner, but conceded what he knew Judith would later have to say. "But her landlady did and she'll tell you the same thing. Anna was too scared to leave the house, which was why she was wary of letting me in. You're not the only person round here who finds me suspicious."

"Well, you think yourself lucky I didn't just leave you on the pavement and go after them pair like I should have done. I've probably lost them again by now," Houlston opened his door. "But seeing as we're here, let's get you looked over. We can save the rest for later."

*

"I think I've blown it, Chief."

Spooner was back at High View by late afternoon, alone in Janet's office. His check-up at the hospital hadn't taken long, but the doctor had warned him not to risk a long-distance drive until he had taken a night's rest, adding that if his vision started to blur or he felt nauseous again, he must get medical help right away. Houlston had driven him back to his car via the police station, where he had obliged him to make a detailed statement of the morning's events, which he managed without divulging anything more of what he knew about Anders, Clara and Anna.

Fortunately, Janet was still pleased to see him. She hadn't made any kind of fuss that he needed to stay another night; it wasn't exactly high season. She gave him his room back, then left him in peace to make his calls. If she had noticed the fresh grazes on his knuckles, then she said nothing about it.

"I've lost Anna and now I've a CID officer on my case who looks like a gangster and talks like a Brummie Cockney – if such a thing is possible."

This at least made the Chief laugh. "Tell me all about it," he said, the voice coming down the line from London sounding not in the slightest bit put out. Spooner related the disastrous events of the morning, finishing with his own deductions about DS Houlston.

"I've a feeling we're both after the same thing," he said. "He said Anders had passed off a load of fake passports here in January and I remember you telling me that was one of your failed parachutist's special tricks. But he also said that was the least of Anders' misdemeanours and suggested all three of them were up to something much worse, without revealing why or what he knew. And I wasn't going to tell him anything either, so we reached stalemate. Though I did promise to let him know if I heard from Anna again. Don't suppose I will, though."

"We'll cross that bridge when we come to it," the Chief responded. "The main thing is, you got more from him about this Anders character than he got from you."

"Also," Spooner offered the last crumb of comfort he could take from the whole affair, "he seemed to know nothing about the officer. A bit surprising that he was the only person not to mention him, but there you go. He'd much more of a bee in his bonnet about Anders, who I'd wager he's been after some while."

"Well, I have better tidings for you on that subject," said the Chief. "I think I've located this officer chappie for you. The good news is that he's within driving distance of where you are now. The bad news is that he's in a psychiatric hospital, apparently raving mad."

"Are you sure it's him?" Spooner said, astounded. It went a long way to explaining why his boss sounded so genial, despite him losing Anna.

"Well, what would you make of this otherwise? A man called Nicholas Ralphe, working in Intelligence at RAF Abbots Bromley, turns up on the fifteenth of January this year, blabbering about double agents and witches. Tries to blow his brains out all over his CO's office, so they cart him off in a straitjacket. His home address in Edgbaston is searched and among the things they find there is a steamer trunk, German in origin, containing a fur coat, some expensive jewellery and a radio hidden inside an attaché case that's the double of the one that fell out of the sky with our friend. Thankfully, they took these items away with them, because after they'd left, the flat was burgled, stripped of its contents from top to toe."

"Anders?" Spooner gasped, feeling faint again.

"Sounds like it, doesn't it? You did just say the last time your friendly local detective had sight of him was January, didn't you?"

"Aye," Spooner tried to corral his spiralling thoughts. "And Norman was spot on too. He said the guy looked like he was in the RAF."

"Well, you can buy him a drink later, if you like, but before you do, I've made arrangements for you to visit the unfortunate Mr Ralphe, if you think you can manage it. He's being treated at the RAF hospital in Lincolnshire, not so far from where our friend crash-landed, ironically enough. A draught of Belladonna seems to have turned both her beaux into invalids. You're to show them that official card of yours when you get there and ask for a Dr Bishop, who will allow you to interview the patient if he thinks the man is up to it. Your ETA is fifteen hundred hours and you can at least congratulate yourself on saving a bit on petrol by staying where you are for an extra night. Then you can report back to me in London, I don't think it would be prudent for you to stay in Birmingham any longer. You still have adequate coupons, I take it?"

"Yes, sir," Spooner said quickly.

"And your thoughts on Anna Hartley?" the Chief's tone darkened. "Have you altered them at all since the last time we spoke?"

Spooner felt his knuckles start to throb again as his insides churned. "I thought it was music lessons I could do with taking from her," he admitted. "But perhaps it was the acting she was best at."

*

Despite his protestations, Spooner decided against accompanying Bob for "just the one" at the Victoria. He was still feeling his injuries – and he didn't want to risk running into Houlston again if he could possibly avoid it. Better to get a good night's rest, as the doctor had prescribed, time to write his next report and go through everything he knew, or thought he knew, about Clara and Anna, so as to arm himself for what lay ahead – his meeting with the madman.

He felt sorry to say goodbye to the Howells the next morning. Janet had made him some sandwiches for the journey, that sat next to his map on the passenger seat, wrapped in wax paper and giving off a faint aura of her lavender perfume. He thought he'd save them for the journey back to London. He just had one last stop to make before he left Birmingham.

Judith took a while to answer her doorbell, and while he stood there, checking for black Anglias, grey Wolseleys and maroon Austins down the street, Spooner wondered if she had changed her mind about seeing him, despite the assurances she had made on the telephone earlier. When she finally opened up, she looked so worn out that he immediately wanted to apologise. But she got there first.

"I'm so sorry, Mr Spooner. Mother had a dreadful night after everything that happened. She's worried sick about where Anna is and what sort of people will come knocking for her next. That awful policeman yesterday frightened the life out of her, telling her she'd given houseroom to a suspected criminal. Now I feel terrible for bringing so much trouble to our door. All I was doing was trying to help. I just can't bring myself to believe Anna was a bad sort, can you?"

Spooner shook his head. "No, me neither," he agreed. Despite all the evidence that had piled up around the violinist, he couldn't quite come to terms with the idea that she had knowingly consorted with Nazi spies. "I've met all sorts of strange people in my life," he told Judith, "and usually, you've an instinct for the ones who are going to be trouble. Not Anna. I was just as taken in by her as you were. It was probably something to do with the music, you know, it's a bond we both thought we shared with her. But you shouldn't be so hard on yourself. What sort of a person would you be if you hadn't wanted to take in a bombed-out orphan with no one else to turn to in the world?"

Judith put her hand up to her heart. "Bless you for saying that, Mr Spooner," she said. "Will you come in for a cup of tea? I've got mother to settle now. We'll be able to talk in peace."

She led him through to her kitchen. "I thought I'd never get rid of that policeman," Judith said as she lit a gas ring. "He was round here for hours, asking about everything we'd ever talked about. Then he turned her room upside down. I told him she left with only what she'd arrived in, but he wouldn't believe me." She placed the kettle over the flame, and turned her attention to a big red teapot. "How d'you like it?"

"The way you made it the other day was perfect," said Spooner.

Judith nodded, measuring tea leaves. "I've learned to be quite an expert," she said.

Spooner understood in that moment that for Judith, Anna hadn't just been someone to save. She had been a friend who had taken her out of an existence of drudgery, someone to talk to, rather than take orders from.

"She's not rung or anything," Judith went on, wiping her eye with the back of her hand. "God knows what they've done to her, those so-called friends of hers." She looked ready to crumple. "I wonder if I'll ever see her again."

"Why don't you sit down and let me make the tea for a change?" Spooner offered, getting to his feet. "You need to put your feet up a minute, hen. My grandma taught me well enough, I know what to do. Come on now."

"D'you know," she replied, "I didn't realise how tired I was until now."

"I'm sure you didn't," Spooner said. "You've been too busy putting everyone else first. What happened yesterday was quite a shock."

Judith nodded, her gaze drifting out of the window. There were a few moments' silence, during which time, her expression subtly altered to one of resolve. "I did manage to save something for her," she said.

Spooner frowned. "What do you mean?" he asked.

Judith put her cup down. Looking him square in the eye, she raised her right index finger to her lips. "Stay there," she said and left the room. He had scarcely had time to scratch his head before she was back. In her hands was Anna's book of songs.

"She'd left this in her luggage, hadn't she?" Judith's voice was a whisper. "That bag he gave back to me before he took you off to the hospital. I knew I had to keep it safe for her; I couldn't let him take it. It was the closest thing to her heart, besides that violin."

She put it down on the table between them.

"What did you do with it?" asked Spooner, his admiration for Judith rising.

"Put it under a cushion on mother's bath chair. She didn't know it was there either, but she was sitting on it the whole time he was searching the house. Oh, you have got a nice smile, Mr Spooner."

"My hat off to you, Judith, that was exceptionally cunning," he said. "You're going to keep it for her until she comes back?"

"Well…" Judith frowned. "I'm not sure. I think it might be better if you were to take it. See, it's Ma. If anyone else were to come looking for it, any of those undesirables we were warned about yesterday…" She shivered, wrapping her cardigan tighter around her. "I wouldn't want to risk exposing her to anything like that. And I wouldn't want them to take it either. I think it'll be safer coming with you to London. And, if she *does* come back, then all she has to do is find you there. Like she was going to anyway."

Following the directions given to him by the Chief, Spooner drove the Rover east, away from the chimneys and cooling towers, through the suburbs and into a landscape of rolling fields and wooded ridges that grew flatter and wider by the mile, until he was deep in the farmlands of the fens.

Rauceby hospital was an imposing Victorian structure of towers and turrets, the former county lunatic asylum. Its sinister exterior was partially obscured by the elms and lime trees that formed an avenue down to the iron gates, now manned by sentries. Spooner wondered if the trees had been planted originally to give the inmates something peaceful to look at, or to hide them away from the world.

He showed the man on the gate his warrant card as ordered, but otherwise Spooner had decided to maintain his aesthete's appearance. Though he had allowed time enough to change along the way, when he had pulled in at a roadhouse and examined himself in the mirror, he hadn't been able to bring himself to plaster his hair back the way he used to. He had chosen a more sober green shirt and tie beneath his tweeds, but he was now so much more at home in this get-up he felt that to go back to his old habits would undermine his ability to carry out the next part of the operation properly. He had become a different person on his journey to and from Birmingham, one who was no longer content to lurk in the shadows, on the fringe of things. And perhaps he needed a bit of his grandma's old Shetland magic woven into the tweeds to help with all that.

He drove up the avenue of trees towards the hospital.

10

THE MOON GOT IN MY EYES

Wednesday, 19 February 1941

"I've had a few patients who've been driven out of their mind by what they've seen up there," Dr Bishop sat across his office table from Spooner. Like the chairs on which they rested, it was made from whitewashed steel and had its legs screwed into the floorboards, reminding Spooner of his former office in Wormwood Scrubs. "Pilots and air crew, who've been caught in heavy flak and forced to bail or had their planes come down in the sea and been cast adrift for days. We've also got plenty of men here with serious burns and other such injuries that will prevent them from ever living the sort of lives they had before the war. But I have seldom before seen anything like that which possesses Nicholas Ralphe."

"Possesses him?" Spooner echoed, taking stock of the man doing the talking. He was of medium height, with angular features, penetrating brown eyes and dark hair receding away from his furrowed forehead. Strong, capable hands gripped a clipboard on which rested the patient's notes. He didn't seem the fanciful type.

"Exactly so." Dr Bishop nodded. "Ralphe believes himself to be under psychic attack from the Devil. Your CO asked me to investigate one such case with him before, some years ago, and since it was he who sent you to see me, I was led to believe you understood the situation."

"Forgive me," said Spooner. "Perhaps I wasn't expecting you to speak so freely."

"I do so because of your CO," the psychiatrist stated. "So there's no need to pussyfoot around. I gather you know most of the facts, but I'll briefly run through the story he's been telling me. Ralphe tried to kill himself because he had been lured into handing over sensitive material to an enemy agent, which he believes enabled the Luftwaffe to pinpoint crucial munitions targets in Birmingham on several bombing raids last year. He believes that this agent is a witch, who enchanted him using magical rites over several meetings he had with her at the house of a man whom he says is a Magister Templi – a high-ranking Black magician, intent on assisting the Nazis to take power in Britain. Ralphe was supposed to be investigating this man, but it seems that he and his associates turned the tables on him. After a ceremony that he was obliged to take part in on Hallowe'en last year, they had him in their power and from then on, he was the permanent consort of this woman. Only when she was called away for two weeks between December and January did he manage to pull himself out of their control, and set a trap for her upon her return."

"He managed to catch her?" this much of the story was news to Spooner.

Dr Bishop's nod was slower this time. "So he says. But what he refuses to divulge is what he did with her subsequently. You had better come and see him for yourself and I'll attempt to get him to speak to you. Perhaps the fact that you are working to the same ends as he was supposed to be will prompt him to tell you. But you must be very gentle with him. In his current state of mind, he supposes that anyone who comes to see him could be a demon in disguise, sent to trick him by the infernal master he was made to pledge his unfortunate allegiance to."

"Do you believe what he says about the witch and the Magister Templi?" Spooner asked.

"Yes, I'm afraid I do," Dr Bishop said. "Ralphe was entrusted to my care because he is a high-ranking officer of impeccable background. I don't doubt that these people have managed to destroy what was once a very fine mind. There is a logic to everything he says that is not present in the usual delusions of the patients I see and I do not, therefore, consider him insane. Though all I can do for him in his current state is help him attempt to ease his distress. Come, see for yourself."

Dr Bishop led Spooner to the upper floor of the hospital where he had been able to make special accommodation for Ralphe, as far away from the rest of the population as possible, in a secure cell that, barring a small spyhole on the submarine-style metal door, had no windows through which the entities that troubled his mind could find easier access to him. The psychiatrist took out a heavy chain of keys, unlocking the door while calling out to reassure his patient of who he was. He told Spooner to wait outside while he attempted to grant him an audience.

It took ten unnerving minutes, during which time Spooner tried to tune out the sounds that permeated the corridor in strange clanks, echoes and cries, the overriding smell of disinfectant doing battle with bodily fluids. Tried not to let the residual fears and torments of so many patients over so many years seep into his own consciousness. Whatever its original intention, he felt this was a place to inspire, rather than recover from, a nervous breakdown.

Eventually Dr Bishop opened the door and stepped into the corridor beside him.

"I've managed to convince him of your corporeal status," he said, "and who it is you are working for. But please be careful when you go in. Don't cross into his pentagram or upset any of the special arrangements I've allowed him to have in there. Just sit down on the floor in front of the door and show him your open palms. He won't be any danger to you, it's what he could do to himself I'm worried about. I'll be watching through the spyhole here, so if I see anything that concerns me, I'll come straight in."

"Right you are," said Spooner, hoping he looked more prepared than he actually felt.

Stepping through the doorway, he could see at once the "special arrangements". It was hardly standard hospital treatment. Though the room was spotlessly clean, the patient was not reclining in a bed or chair, but instead sitting cross-legged, wrapped in white pyjamas and a blue dressing gown, in the centre of a pentagram that had been drawn out across the floor in lines of salt. At every point of the star was placed a white candle, a sprig of sage and a phial of what Spooner took to be holy water. The smell of the herbs hung heavily on the air.

The "Original Mr Tall Dark and Handsome", as Anna had put it, looked up at Spooner through hollow, ravaged eyes. Thick streaks of his formerly black hair, from the centre of his crown outwards, had turned completely white and his complexion was the sallow grey of ashes. He looked at least ten years older than the thirty written on his medical form.

Spooner lowered himself into the position he had been instructed to adopt, resting both his hands on his knees so his empty palms lay uppermost.

"Mr Spooner," said Ralphe, his voice crackling like an off-station radio, "you have come to hear my confession?" His eyes were searching, but devoid of the gleam of madness. As he leaned forward, Spooner could see he wore rosary beads around his neck.

"Thank you for seeing me, sir," Spooner said. "I hope it's not too much of an imposition. But I'd like to know what happened to Clara Bauer, or Clara Brown as she was known."

"You mean the Witch?" Ralphe said. "That's what she really is. Not just any old storybook hag either. She is the Queen of her kind."

"Aye," Spooner nodded. "I believe you. We have another of her order in custody back in London. A German agent, caught not far from here, carrying a map with two air bases ringed on it and a radio transmitter hidden in an attaché case, the same as the one she had. It was a mission she herself had planned, he told us; only he went and broke his ankle on the way down, so he never got the chance to carry it out. Now he's trying to plead his way out of the firing squad by claiming he can get her to work for us. Only trouble is, he doesn't know where to find her."

Ralphe's pupils widened. "This is precisely why I did what I had to do," he said. "There are always going to be more of them, using their tricks and devilry the way they used me. It will never end until it is cut off at the source." He shook his head. "Please be assured, I have put her in a place from where she can never again exert this evil. The Queen of the Witches is powerless now. But, of course, there will be many others who seek to carry on her work. The Prince of Darkness never tires."

Spooner felt cold chills run down his spine as the man spoke. There was fervour in Ralphe's voice, but it was only, he felt, the overwhelming desire to be taken seriously.

"Believe me, I'm very thankful to you," Spooner said. "But can you not tell me what it was you did to assure our safety? Once I can be certain there is no point in me continuing to search for her, then I can report back to London and make sure that this associate of hers is rendered equally as harmless."

Ralphe raised his left hand and then made a chopping motion against the wrist with the side of his right hand.

"The Hand of Glory, have you never heard of it?"

Spooner shook his head.

"It's an ancient white ritual, practised for centuries in Britain and I learned of it from an adept. It is the only thing that can keep the country truly safe from her. Because of that, I cannot tell you where she is. If she is disturbed, then the spell of protection I have placed around her will be broken and her spirit may again be able to roam free. You must believe me, Spooner, I know what I am talking about. Why else do you think that you find me here, in this pitiful state?"

"Why else?" Spooner shook his head. "Is there someone else in Birmingham that you're still frightened of? Is that why you've had to make all these defences here? I can help you with that too, if you let me. We're both working for the same objective, after all."

Ralphe closed his eyes. His body was trembling, and a line of sweat had broken out across his forehead. "It is Lucifer himself I am afraid of," he said, so softly as to be barely audible. "Can you imagine what that's like? He can see me anywhere, get to me anyhow he pleases. These puny defences are laughable compared to his power, but they are the only recourse I have. Listen to me, Spooner," he leaned forward from the waist, the rosary swinging out of the neck of his dressing gown. "You don't have to search for the Witch any more. I have trapped her for you, somewhere that, God willing, she will never get away from. So go back to London and make sure that follower of hers is dealt with. If you want to help me, if you want to protect our country, then that's the best thing you can do. The *only* thing. Don't get drawn in any further, don't get mixed up with these people to the point that I did. Otherwise you'll be putting your very soul in peril."

"You really don't believe there is anything else I can do?" asked Spooner.

Ralphe shook his head. "Isn't that enough? I know I have done a terrible thing but please, don't ask any more of me." He bowed his head, closing his eyes and reaching for the crucifix on the end of his beads.

"What about Simon De Vere?" asked Spooner, his mind flashing temples and obelisks, hidden within the swells and trees of the Clent Hills. "What does he have to do with it? That was who you were originally sent to investigate, wasn't it?"

Ralphe's eyes flashed open. "I know no one of that name," he said. "Now, kindly leave me alone. I have said all that I can say to you." He made the sign of the cross and started to pray: "I believe in God, the Father Almighty, Creator of Heaven and Earth; and in Jesus Christ, His only Son…"

The door behind Spooner opened. "I think that's enough," said Dr Bishop, putting his hand beneath Spooner's elbow, propelling him upwards to his feet and out into the corridor.

"Kindly wait outside for me." He closed the door between them before Spooner could offer a word of protest.

Back in the corridor, he put his hand up to the point between his shoulders where Anders had hit him with the cosh. It was still sore and Dr Bishop's sudden method of eviction had reignited a stabbing pain there. But he knew trying to rub it away would do no good. Instead, he lifted the catch over the spyhole and peered in.

The psychiatrist had entered the pentagram to be with his patient and was kneeling beside him, his hand on the distressed man's shoulder. Ralphe was clutching the crucifix on his rosary beads, mouthing the words of prayer. Then his face creased and his mouth opened in a silent scream. His hand reached for the top of his left arm, with a strength that broke the chain of beads and sent them scattering over the floor. Dr Bishop sprang to his feet, hitting a switch on the wall that activated an alarm, then crouched down to where Ralphe had fallen, face-first, rolling him over and pulling his dressing gown away from his chest.

Spooner could only watch in horror as the doctor tried to revive his patient, before the sound of running feet and voices echoed down the corridor behind him. He was swept out of the way by white-coated medics racing a trolley towards Ralphe's cell and shouting at him to get out of the way. He stood aside; sweat trickling in a clammy trail down his back.

The last he saw of the officer was of a man being carted away, eyes closed, Dr Bishop by his side. He shouted over his shoulder, "You had better leave now, Spooner. I will keep your CO informed."

The sun was sinking down towards the flat horizon when he drove back down the avenue of trees, a fireball of red making silhouettes of the turrets and towers reflected in the wing mirror so it appeared the whole hospital was being consumed by flames. Whether the man would survive or not, there was only one conclusion Spooner could draw from his interview. Ralphe must have killed Clara Bauer.

11

I'M LOST

Friday, 15 August 1941

Since his court martial, Karl's dream had altered again. Perhaps it was the ordeal of reliving his painful descent and capture, to see again the faces of those farmers who had found him, the detective sergeant who had driven him to London. Having to relive every step of his failure, knowing there was only one outcome.

The man from MI5 had continued to visit him and Karl came to wonder if some form of white magic had been used upon him during these interrogations about his life with Clara. For it was then that he could remember it all with such clarity.

In the past six months, Karl's memories had begun to unravel, along with his nerves. Long hours with nothing to do except play cards or attempt to stumble his way through the simplest books in the hospital library had provided no distraction from his limbo. He knew he was now a man with no future. But this did not incline him to revisit his past and ponder on what might have been. He knew that way was signposted madness and he wanted to keep what shreds of his sanity he still possessed for as long as he could.

Instead, each time he closed his eyes he visited the snowy fields. His journey across them was now made with weighted feet across clinging mud. He knew he must get to the trees to attempt communication with Clara, but his path lay in darkness, with no moon to guide him at all. When he opened his attaché case, he found it empty, the radio gone. Alone in the dark, unable to communicate – it took him a while for the significance to sink in.

It was because Clara was no longer there.

He hadn't wanted to believe his interrogator when he first came to tell him, back in the middle of February, that he had put a halt to the search for Clara because he had reason to believe that she was dead. But as the listless weeks dragged on, and his visits, which at least provided intellectual stimulus, became fewer, the possibility that he was being told the truth grew more persuasive. On his last night in Wandsworth prison, where he had been held since the court martial, he had a final caller.

"Here," his visitor said, "I thought I should return this to you. It may give you some comfort." He placed the Baphomet on the table between them. "Though my own feelings are that it would be better for you to renounce it, so that you may face whatever is to come next with the hope of God's mercy."

Karl stared at his former talisman without reaching for it. "What are you trying to say?"

"You once told me that when you faced the prospect of jumping out of that aeroplane you were so terrified that you began to pray," said the Chief. "You called upon God for His mercy."

"*Ja*," said Karl, "and what mercy did He show me?" He looked around the cell walls, the barred window with the sentry outside it and back to his visitor. "Is this what you would call it? Being shot at dawn is a sign of His mercy?"

"Tomorrow you will face a far greater peril than the firing squad," said the Chief. "Once you have passed from this world, what will you have to face on the other side? Are you willing to let Satan take your soul for all eternity?"

"You seriously believe that?" Karl said. Images rushed through his mind unbidden, as vivid as if he were watching a lurid film of his life. He remembered the taste of the sacrament Clara had baptised him with: a mixture of urine, blood and bitter herbs. The visions he had seen afterwards, the couplings before the altar, those men of power and commerce fornicating like the Goat they worshipped. Then, in stark contrast, he saw his church wedding, before the First War, when he was young and life was full of promise. He saw the wife he had long ago abandoned in white silk, holding the single stem of a lily as she stood at the altar, a smile on her face that was like a shaft of pure sunlight against the crimson hues of all those previous recollections.

"I'm afraid that I do," his interrogator's face was sombre. "I speak only with your interests at heart. Your time here is nearly up, but you will have all eternity to find out if I am wrong. There is a chaplain here who I can call upon to assist you, if you should wish to cleanse yourself before your ordeal. You only have to say the word."

Hot tears sprung from Karl's eyes without him being able to control them. He pushed the Baphomet back across the table and bowed his head. "Fetch him," he said.

Spooner was dreaming of Rauceby hospital for the first time since he had driven away from it, six months earlier. It was sunset, the turrets stark against the flat horizon and a red and gold sky that looked like the whole world was aflame. He was staring up at the top windows, where he knew Nicholas Ralphe was imprisoned in his pentagram. All around him he could hear the rustling of the trees that surrounded the hospital, the sighing of wind through the leaves, which gradually altered into the whine of a long-wave radio being tuned in, the crackling of static as the station was picked up.

"*This is Germany calling, Germany calling,*" a voice travelling though the airwaves, clipped, aristocratic tones that Spooner had heard before, in smoky London clubrooms in 1939. "*This is our first news bulletin of the day from the Führer's headquarters in Berlin.*" A voice that had begun to be heard across the land since the beginning of March, on nighttime broadcasts timed to co-ordinate with a fresh campaign of bombing in London, outlining forthcoming acts of terror between sessions from an in-house dance band. Now it was invading Spooner's subconscious.

In his dream, he felt the branches of the trees scratch at his face, tendrils reaching towards his feet to try to trip him. Peals of girlish laughter floated through the air as the sky darkened, laying a silvery trail through the woods.

"Spooner!" Ralphe's voice called out. "Don't listen! They're all trying to trick you!"

Spooner looked back up. Through the window he could see Ralphe's ravaged eyes pleading with him. Then his ankle turned on a gnarled root and he found himself falling. His eyes opened, before he landed, on the wallpaper of another boarding house room.

Spooner pushed himself up. He was covered in sweat, his feet tangled around a sheet he had kicked half off in the night, which must have given him the sensation of tripping, but his heart was hammering as if he really had just been for a run through the woods. He glanced at the bedside table where his glasses rested on top of the book he had been reading before he fell asleep, *The Witch Cult in Western Europe* by Professor Margot Melvin, a tome that had no doubt inspired some of his nightmare. Within it was a description of the ritual known as the Hand of Glory.

The alarm clock told him it was six-fifteen. As he slid out of bed to pull up the blackout, Spooner was well aware what his subconscious had been alluding to. Having been found guilty of an offence against the Treachery Act 1940, in precisely an hour's time, Karl Kohl would be facing a firing squad at the Tower of London. Then both of Belladonna's Beaux, as the Chief liked to call them, would be no more.

Poor Nicholas Ralphe had died before Spooner had even finished his journey to London. He had heard the rest of the story from the Chief a week later, in the living room of his flat in Dolphin Square, where he had been welcomed back from Birmingham for a fireside debriefing over a bottle of Talisker.

"I'm sorry to have to tell you that he suffered a massive heart attack, and passed away probably no more than ten minutes after you last saw him. A man who had scored As for fitness at his RAF medical only the year before, frightened out of his wits and then his life."

Spooner put down his glass, the peaty aroma of mountain air floating in his nostrils. "That's astonishing," he said. "All of it. I mean, the man I saw didn't look as if he could possibly be only thirty. Most of his hair had turned white and he'd the face of an old man. How could they do that to him in such a short space of time?"

The Chief rolled his tumbler in his hand as he regarded Spooner. "Dr Bishop told you that we had reason to work together once before on a similar case, years ago," he said.

"Aye," Spooner nodded. "He seemed a bit taken aback by my ignorance on the subject."

The Chief shook his head. "Brusque is his usual setting, it helps to be as pragmatic as possible in his profession. But I should like to explain a bit more to you. It will help you to understand more clearly, perhaps. I regret to say that, on consideration, I may have sent you out into the field without adequate ammunition for all you have faced out there."

Spooner felt the colour rising in his cheeks. Instead of a cosy fireside chat, he had been expecting to be hauled over the coals for losing Anna and tangling with Houlston. He lifted his glass for another drop of courage, in case this was the prelude to a roasting.

"A few years after the First War," said the Chief, "I began employing an unusual young man to infiltrate a group I considered dangerous, who were meeting in the East End. It was an area he had a great deal of knowledge about, despite being a resident of Hampstead with a private income, because he was an enthusiast of both Oscar Wilde and sailors, something that he was at no pains to hide."

Spooner took a larger gulp than he had been intending. At the same time as it hit the back of his throat, the Chief's bulldog, Dorothy, who had been sleeping peacefully at his feet, gave a loud grunt, as if commenting on her master's words.

"Indeed," he went on, "not many of my colleagues would have had truck with such a person, but he had a genius for

the work, which is all that mattered to me. He twined his way around secret societies like bindweed, sinuously and with an unnerving grip, showing nothing but the pretty flower until they were firmly in his grasp. That was, until the summer of 1923, when he appeared to vanish.

"He had been dealing with some dangerous people and, given the way he disported himself, this was perhaps an inevitable consequence. His interests had recently taken him away from the rough pastures of Aldgate and Soho and into the rather more refined setting of St John's Wood, where he had fallen in with a group of White Russians. He had always been fascinated with magic and witchcraft and, as an understandably lapsed Catholic, had taken some pleasure in mocking the church he had grown up in. But what these people got up to went a little beyond absinthe tea parties. Because he was such a social chameleon and so good at making the right impression, he was rapidly promoted through their ranks and chosen to assist a Magister Templi in performing a serious ritual.

"News of this came back to me through various sources, and I couldn't help but blame myself for putting him in such peril. I sought out experts in white magic, who convinced me to look closer to home for the missing man and indeed, when I finally tracked him down, it was to his own house. He had boarded himself up in the attic in similar circumstances to those in which you found the unfortunate Ralphe. There was nothing I could say to convince him to come out of his pentangle, so, as Dr Bishop was, and still is, the best psychiatrist I know, I asked him if he could help try to restore this young man's sanity. In doing so, we learned the full extent of what he had been through. Believe it or not, he claimed to have seen a demon conjured up in St John's Wood."

The Chief noted Spooner's expression and leaned forward to refresh his empty glass.

"The ritual he described to us was very similar in its detail to the ordeal Ralphe was made to go through last Hallowe'en – or Samhain, as the followers of Satan would call it."

Spooner put his glass down carefully. "You mean, Ralphe said he saw a demon too?"

The Chief's blue eyes held Spooner's in an unwavering gaze. "Ralphe said he saw the Goat of Mendes manifest in a temple in the grounds of a house on the Worcestershire borders which you and I both believe to be Hagley Hall."

"But Ralphe told me didn't know De Vere. That was when he started to get really agitated and…" Spooner began.

"I know," his companion cut him off. "Which tallies with my previous experience. After undergoing such an ordeal, the victim finds himself unable to speak of the person who put him through it. It may be that is part of the enchantment they believe they have been placed under, or, more likely, orders they have received while under a state of hypnosis. What he saw could have been the work of a trained magician. As Norrie no doubt told you, such masters of illusion can fool hundreds of people that they are seeing an elephant disappear in front of their eyes, so to conjure up a demon in circumstances over which they had complete control is entirely possible. In both cases, Dr Bishop assisted in trying to break the spell by having them renounce Satan, the fear of whom was the root cause of any messages, subliminal or otherwise, that had been planted in their minds. And in both cases, the shock of doing so was what caused the premature ageing that you witnessed in Ralphe. The only explanation I can offer you is that the mental trauma they have endured is the equivalent to severe physical torture."

"What happened to your other man?" Spooner trusted himself to raise his glass again.

"He survived, and has since become a priest," the Chief replied. "Though, of course, only the Church of England would have him." At his feet, Dorothy gave another loud grunt.

"So what happens now?" asked Spooner. "Will you be questioning De Vere?"

The Chief put his glass down. "Would that I could," he said. "But I've not had any luck locating him. He's not to be found at his Chelsea residence nor Hagley Hall, and though his parents, the Earl and Countess, took themselves off to stay with friends in New Hampshire before Christmas, he didn't join them there."

"This past Christmas?" said Spooner. "The same time that Clara went back to Germany?"

"Yes," said the Chief, staring into the fire. A shadow stole across his face, making him look older and more wearied than he had only moments before. "That is a rather chilling coincidence, isn't it?" He looked back at Spooner. "Look, if all this puts you off undertaking any further work for my department, I will fully understand and return you to your previous duties with my commendation."

Spooner shook his head. "It's a lot to take in," he admitted. "But d'you really think I did a good enough job back there? Make no bones about it, Chief, did I no' botch the whole thing up letting Anna go?"

The older man smiled. "Not a bit of it, Ross. You returned every bit of faith I had in your adaptability. And I see you have kept this new look of yours."

Spooner looked down at his tweeds. "Maybe it's something

I picked up from Norrie's world, a bit of stagecraft, but I feel more at home like this. Can you understand that?"

"I have an inkling," said the Chief. "How did you like working with Norrie?"

Spooner frowned. "I enjoyed it all right. But I don't think it's quite right for me," he said. "See, there was another thing occurred to me in Birmingham. All the best pieces of information came my way from women. I don't know if this get-up makes me more approachable, but I got on better with the fairer sex than I ever have before." He swirled the whisky in his glass. "I think women are the key to this work. They've their own secret networks, away from the world of men. I think they let me in on some of that because I didn't look like authority to them. And I've an idea of where I might continue to do this work a little less conspicuously. Somewhere I think I'd blend in and be privy to more information that could be of interest. In fact," he saw again the magazine rack by Mrs Smith's fireplace, "it was a woman I met in West Bromwich gave me the idea…"

Spooner pulled up the blackout. Dawn was bathing the terraced roofs of Ancoats in sunlight. These digs were not as nice as High View and neither was the landlady a patch on Janet; but they were still better than what he'd left in Woodstock. From here, it was just a short tram ride to the city centre, where he had recently begun his new job as Assistant Editor on the spiritualist publication taken by Mrs Smith and hundreds more like her across the land: *Two Worlds* magazine.

Spooner had begun submitting articles to the editor, Ernest Oaten, shortly after his debriefing with the Chief. Short pieces drew on the subject he had discussed with Anna: his knowledge of folklore and traditional songs and how heartening it was to remember these during the current conflict. Oaten had enjoyed them enough to offer him a regular column and invited Spooner to visit his office, at the Spiritualists' National Union building on 18 Corporation Street, where he ran a frugal operation with the help of one elderly secretary and the typesetter and press operator in the union print shop below.

During the course of a long conversation there, and subsequently at Oaten's club on Deansgate, Spooner had expounded on his bookish background and occult interests. From then on, his contributions to the magazine and visits to Manchester became more frequent, until he had persuaded Oaten to give him a job. In return for learning how to run a publication, Spooner had offered his services free, getting paid only for his articles. So far, it had proved interesting and enjoyable, a beneficial arrangement to all concerned.

On a day that, for him, was still so full of promise, he felt a strange kind of sadness as he looked out – a day which Karl Kohl would see very little more of. After all, it was only Kohl's bad luck that had brought him here.

The last glimpse Karl had this morning, as he was escorted the short distance between the armoured car and the long, narrow wooden building that was his final destination, was of 900-year-old battlements, two rounded towers between walls fifteen-feet thick and ninety-feet high. Beyond that, the gothic spires of Tower Bridge glinted in the sunlight, carrying traffic to and fro across the water, unheeding of his fate. He breathed in his last few lungfuls of fresh air – although, being London air, it was suffused with smoke, sulphur and the watery miasmas of the Thames. Surrounded by soldiers of the Scots Guards, only the ravens and the gulls that wheeled overhead witnessed his progress into the miniature rifle range between the Bowyer Tower and the Flint Tower.

Once inside this sinister hangar, smells of wood and sawdust filled his nostrils, and something else lingering there: a combination of fear and death waiting, a potent aroma he recognised at once from the trenches. At the end of the range, he could see the marks previous firing squads had made on the brick walls.

Because of his broken ankle, Karl was not tied to a post like previous men in his position had been. Instead, a sturdy brown Windsor chair awaited him. The men who tied him to it did not look at Karl's face, but one pressed a hand on his shoulder for a moment before he moved away, and another placed a canvas hood over Karl's head in order that he could see no more, before pinning a target to his chest. He could only hear their departing feet, the click of their rifles as they loaded their ammunition.

A song began to drift through his mind, a siren's voice calling to him through the veils of time, place and memory. Karl had made his peace with the world last night. He had written a long letter to his wife, apologising for all the harm he had done her, and the Father promised to make sure she would get it. In doing so, Karl felt he had unchained himself from all the regrets of his past and had no need to burden the kindly priest any further with confession. Funny that the man from MI5 had been so concerned in the end, but the path Karl had taken had been entirely of his own choosing. It was a brutal, unjust world and he had seen enough of Hell here on Earth – but at least he had had one good dance before the curtain came down.

Beneath his hood, Karl smiled as a vision filled his mind. A goddess with jewels in her red hair, standing in the golden scalloped footlights of the Café Ette, holding her arms out towards him as she sang:

Männer umschwirr'n mich,
Wie Motten um das Licht.
Und wenn sie verbrennen,
Ja dafür kann ich nicht.
Ich bin von Kopf bis Fuß
Auf Liebe eingestellt
Ich kann halt lieben nur…

Gunshots rang out in a volley. The seated figure slumped in his chair.

PART TWO

WE THREE (MY SHADOW, MY ECHO AND ME)

December 1941–February 1942

12

JUST AS THOUGH
YOU WERE HERE

Tuesday, 2 December 1941

To get to the Master Temple Psychic Centre on Copnor Road in Portsmouth, it was necessary to go through the chemist's shop beneath it. Fortunately, Mr Grenville Shadwell and his wife, Gladys, were the proprietors of both establishments. So when the shutters came down on one half of their business, they could usher members of their local spiritualist society through the lotions, salves, pills and potions that helped ease their passage through this world, to the staircase behind the apothecary that led upwards to enlightenment. The Shadwells' living room, kitted out with an upright pedal organ, played by Gladys, a specially constructed cabinet for mediums and seating for up to twenty, acted as the main atrium of the Temple.

On the second of December, a full house was anticipated for the arrival of a special guest, the renowned materialisation medium, Helen Duncan. In the home of the Royal Navy, rumour was always rife among those who had loved ones at sea and, in recent weeks, it had run to speculation over the fate of a vessel that had failed to return to base two weeks previously.

Many of the men and women taking the pilgrimage up the Shadwell staircase that evening held high, yet nervous expectations that Mrs Duncan might be able to lift the veil enough to glimpse what could have become of this ship.

Such was the demand for tickets that Grenville had managed to fit in some extra seats and allowed in at a reduced rate a further five men who were prepared to stand at the back of the room. Perhaps it was auspicious that a full moon hung over the city that night. Though it was barely discernible through the fog that had rolled in off the channel, it was certain to help to guide the vibrations – or so Gladys Shadwell thought.

Having witnessed Mrs Duncan's powers before at spiritualist gatherings, Gladys was beside herself when the famous medium had granted her written request, made through the offices of the *Psychic Times*, to appear at their humble abode. She had been preparing for weeks, filling her days with baking and organising, making sure that all her regulars had seats and reserving those closest to the front for her most generous patrons.

When the Duncans arrived, she was ready with a selection of meat and fish paste sandwiches, cut into fingers, a Victoria sponge and a pot of tea, all served on her best rosebud china. Unlike some mediums, who preferred to fast before a sitting, Helen made it clear that she needed to keep her strength up. She also – and Gladys hoped she hadn't let her annoyance at this show too clearly – chain-smoked between mouthfuls of her lavish buffet.

To distract herself from the ash fluttering from Helen's fingers onto her best tablecloth, Gladys helped prepare the medium to tune into the atmosphere by outlining some of the concerns of her congregation and the wider local community.

While the women chatted, Henry Duncan assisted Grenville on fixing the appropriate lighting, another matter that was of the utmost importance in assisting a smooth passage between his wife and her spirit guides. Three different coloured bulbs were required: red, white and green, to direct the flow of energies between the Sun, Moon and Earth that they represented.

To ensure that everything was above board, before the sitting Mrs Duncan allowed an inspection by an independent authority, in this case, a friend of Grenville's who was on the local council. It was a routine that she endured with the stoicism born of many hundreds of previous requests, continuing to smoke and take sips of tea even when she was down to her undergarments. Councillor Roberts was equally business-like, also being an old hand at this ritual, and decreed that he had found no spurious objects hidden either around the room or on the medium's person. After he signed a document to that effect which could be displayed on the door, the Temple was opened to the public.

By five minutes past seven, the final guest had been ushered in and, despite the freezing fog, inside the blacked-out room had become warm with the number of excited bodies packed into it. The women seated in front of the cabinet whispered to each other from behind their handkerchiefs. The men standing at the back, none of them regulars, studied the rest of the room intently and silently, shooting glances of appraisal at each other when they thought they wouldn't be noticed.

In the light cast by the three bulbs, Grenville made the introductions. As was traditional at Temple gatherings, Gladys played "For Those in Peril on the Sea" on her organ while Henry Duncan helped his wife into the cabinet. Once she had settled, he closed the curtains around her and, bowing their heads, those assembled recited *The Lord's Prayer*. Grenville then led the congregation through the medium's favourite hymn, "The Lord is My Shepherd", with accompanying notes polished to perfection by Gladys.

While they were still singing the last verse, the ladies closest to the front started to hear faint groans emanating from behind the curtains, and, with widening eyes, gradually became aware of a white, wispy substance pooling around the bottom of the cabinet. It was as if the fog had stolen in from under the blackout and crept up through the floorboards, bringing the faint aroma of the sea with it.

Henry Duncan moved from behind the cabinet to pull the curtains open, revealing his wife seated on what appeared to be the crest of a wave, with others roiling around her. Her head was tilted backwards and her eyes were clamped shut, her fingers gripping tightly to the sides of the chair.

"There's voices, so many voices, all calling out to me at the same time," the medium's voice trembled as she spoke. "I cannae bring you through like this, please, just one at a time." She cocked her head to one side, and as if she was trying to discern a lone signal from many, cupped her ear in her hand. "That's right," she said, her voice becoming calmer, lower in pitch. "That's right." The waves dipped and then rose again around her.

"There is someone here who is missing a son." Helen stretched out her right arm. "A lady in this room, who has heard nothing of her boy for the past two weeks. She fears he may be lost at sea." Her hand made a large circle around the right side of the room until one of the audience, urged on by her friends, rose bashfully and fearfully to her feet.

"I… er, I mean, my son is away at sea at the moment and I was expecting to hear from him sooner… It couldn't possibly be for me, could it?" The woman clutched a handkerchief tightly in her shaking right hand.

The medium nodded slowly. "It's Davey, isnae?" she said, cocking her head to one side again, so that the unseen presence could speak directly into her ear.

There were collective coos from the other women assembled around the one standing. "That's right," she confirmed.

"And you're Mrs…" Helen began.

"Mrs Walker, that's right," in her eagerness, the woman finished the medium's sentence for her. Mrs Walker's eyes flashed, as round as saucers in the dim light. Her hair was escaping from the bun she had pinned it up in; fuzzy tendrils caught in the glow of the red lamp framing her stricken face. "Oh my, oh my – then it *is* for me, is it?"

"Your Davey was on board this ship…" as Helen spoke the waves of ectoplasm started to undulate and fashion themselves into a recognisably human form. The gasps from the congregation grew louder and the men standing at the back craned their necks over the heads of those seated as the figure of a sailor in uniform manifested before their eyes.

The five men at the back all pulled out notepads and began furiously scribbling in them.

"Ma!" the sailor's voice floated across the assembly. "Ma, don't be afraid!"

Mrs Walker's eyes brimmed with tears as the ghostly figure rippled in front of her. His flickering image gave her the strange feeling that she was standing on the edge of the quay, looking down at her son who was floating beneath the water.

"And don't be sad now neither," he said, as if divining her

thoughts. "There's a lot of the lads here with me now and we're all safe, we're all happy, ain't we? And because you're here, they let me be the spokesman for us all. Now, ain't that an honour, Ma?"

"Oh Davey." The tears welling in Mrs Walker's eyes started to flow freely down her cheeks. Heads turned all around her, as the implications of this message sank in.

"I just don't want you to feel you're all alone, Ma," the apparition went on, and perhaps it was because her vision was blurred by weeping, but Mrs Walker thought that she could see him smiling, thought that she could feel his love radiating through the veil. "'Cos you never will be, you know. Wherever you are, I'll be by your side, looking out for you. Waiting for the day we can be properly reunited."

"My son," Mrs Walker reached her hand up to try to touch the vision. Davey shimmered in front of her, just out of reach.

"I love you Ma," he said. "Remember that, won't you? Always…" Then, with one last bow of his head, he dissolved back into the phantasmagoric foam he had emerged from.

Mrs Walker fainted, slipping to the floor as quietly and gracefully as her spectral visitor had departed. The women around her immediately formed a circle, like a brood of mother hens, lifting her back to her seat and pressing smelling salts to her nose.

The men at the back, all clutching their notebooks, made a dash for the stairs.

Hannen Swaffer, labouring over the review of a new play he had not found to his taste, was still at his typewriter in his *Daily Herald* eyrie at ten to eight, when the phone by his elbow started ringing. Glad to be distracted, he snatched it out of the cradle.

"Swaff? Maurice here," came a familiar voice down the line. Maurice Barbanell was the editor of the *Psychic Times* and host of the spiritualist home circle Swaffer belonged to, an old and trusted comrade.

"My dear Maurice, a delight as ever to hear your voice!" Swaffer replied, sending a shower of cigarette ash over his keyboard as he reached for his ashtray.

"Are you alone?" asked Barbanell.

"Well," Swaffer peered through the glass panel on his door to the crowded newsroom in front of him, in which journalists were typing, phoning and smoking furiously, piles of discarded paper at their feet, while above their heads, messages in cardboard tubes shot along on wires. "One is never entirely alone in Fleet Street, although…" None of them, as far as he could see, was paying any particular attention to his office. "I am being ignored for the moment. But what could make you sound so mysterious, Maurice?"

Barbanell's voice was unusually strained. "I've just had someone call from Portsmouth," he said, lowering his voice to a whisper, even though he was alone in his own office, "with a report that would, I believe, cause a sensation if it could be verified."

"Go on," Swaffer urged. "Go on!"

"Are you sure your phones aren't being tapped?" Barbanell asked.

"Are you being serious?" Swaffer spat out a fag end and scrambled around his paper-strewn desk for a fresh supply of smokes.

"Deadly," came the reply. "I'll only tell you if you swear no one else is listening in."

"On this plane at least," Swaffer, having located the errant packet, fired up his Ronson and inhaled gratefully, "we are perfectly alone, I assure you."

"Good, well…" Barbanell hardly knew where to start. "Have you ever heard of the Master Temple Psychic Centre? No," he answered his own question, "you won't have, it's a small affair, run by a husband and wife named Shadwell, they're subscribers and she's a regular correspondent. Anyhow, they had a special guest tonight: Helen Duncan."

"Helen Duncan!" Swaffer echoed, opening his shorthand pad. He had not seen the Scotswoman since he'd prevented her from choking on that dramatic night at Miss Moyes', getting on for a year ago now. Nor had he ever found any reports of a woman named Clara being strangled or otherwise asphyxiated on that night in January anywhere in Britain, which still troubled him. In his mind, it was still a file marked "open".

"Yes, I had one of my stringers down there report on it for me," Barbanell continued. "Almost immediately, she manifested a young sailor very recently passed over. He identified himself as Davey Walker and his mother was in the audience. He told her he'd gone down with his ship along with a lot of others. And he was wearing his cap in spirit, which clearly identified the vessel…" Barbanell paused. Scribbling at his notes, Swaffer had shifted so far towards the edge of his chair that he nearly fell off it.

"Don't stop there, Maurice, for Christ's sake! Do you know the name of the ship?"

"I do," Maurice said. "Only, the reason I'm stalling is that Helen wasn't the only special guest at the Master Temple tonight. Along with my stringer, there were four other men standing at the back of the room when the séance took place, all of whom made a rush for the public phone boxes outside the moment the sailor went back to spirit. My man says he recognised a plainclothes policeman and a reporter from the *Portsmouth Evening News* but that the other two were strangers, wearing identical dark blue suits. He thinks they were Naval Intelligence."

"Does he know for sure?" Swaffer paused this time.

"No, but it's a reasonable assumption," said Barbanell. "We already know there are people within that organisation on the other side of the river who have been bearing down on spiritualist activity since the start of the war, using national security as the excuse for it. Anyway, he's going to try and follow them, see where they go next. But I'd back his hunch with gelt. I am always getting warnings of such things."

"You're right," said Swaffer, looking back up through the door into the newsroom. He could see a healthy discussion taking place out there, the managing editor waving his hands, face turning a shade of vermillion. Soon the presses would be starting up on the floors beneath and it was that poor soul's job to get the paper to bed on time – which meant very soon he'd be headed Swaffer's way, in search of his missing review.

"Maybe we ought to continue this conversation elsewhere," he said, turning back to his typewriter. "Shall I come over to you? Good, just give me ten minutes…"

Spooner had also been working late, making himself useful to Ernest Oaten and his secretary, Miss Josser, a lady who spent most of her working hours compiling piles of letters into those worth publishing, responding to, or just quietly filing away. She had gone home at her usual time of five o'clock nearly three hours ago, while Oaten retired to his club for supper.

Spooner was alone in the office, but for the radiogram, tuned into longwave in order to catch the nightly propaganda broadcast from Berlin that both he and the Chief believed to be voiced by De Vere. Although his identity had yet to be revealed to the British public, the press had dubbed him Lord Lucifer and his arch commentaries, designed to pour scorn on the British war effort, attracted more listeners each night. Spooner barely noticed the customary musical prelude. He was ostensibly devising a more efficient filing system for Miss Josser, while searching the reams of correspondence for anything that could possibly lead him back to Birmingham. When the telephone on his editor's desk began to ring, he thought it would be Oaten, with something he'd forgotten to say earlier.

"*Two Worlds*, Ross Spooner speaking," he said.

"And how's my ace reporter?" came the voice of the Chief instead.

"Chief! Good to hear from you. How's tricks?"

"Interesting," came the reply. "Are you able to talk?"

"Oh, aye," Spooner's heart beat more quickly, "have you a new lead on Birmingham?"

"No, but this is something that I think you'll find stimulating. What do you know of a medium called Helen Duncan? She's Scottish, I believe."

Spooner swallowed his disappointment and eyed up the paperwork he had been burrowing through, myriad reports of sittings and sightings that took on a slightly anaesthetic quality after a few hours of reading. He hadn't been seeking her out, but Helen Duncan was a name that came up often – and not always favourably.

"I'm aware of her," he said. "Our readers spend a lot of time discussing her."

"Good," said the Chief. "Start digging, Ross. Let me know everything you can find out about her."

"She seems a bit of a controversial figure," Spooner offered.

"It appears so," the Chief confirmed. "From what I'm hearing, it's possible we could have another witch on our hands…"

From the radiogram in the room behind Spooner, a familiar voice crackled over the airwaves: "*Germany calling, this is Germany calling…*" Spooner's eyes scanned Oaten's bookshelves. "Leave it with me," he said.

13

SEEIN' IS BELIEVIN'

Thursday, 4 December 1941

"I told you that woman was dangerous," said Brigadier Rory Firebrace.

The Chief's counterpart in Scotland was a regular séance-goer who had shared information with him on Helen Duncan before. Which was why he had thought it prudent to bring him in on the debriefing of the men from D-Division, Naval Intelligence, who had attended the Master Temple. It was Firebrace's suggestion that officers Forshaw and Miles should be interviewed separately. He anticipated their reports might contain crucial differences.

Officer Forshaw described what he had seen as "a large-scale puppet show". To his mind, the Duncans had used a mixture of deliberately dim lighting and clear prior information to create an illusion, fashioning a sailor out of wood and a length of gauze and topping their apparition with a cap that read BARHAM for good measure. Forshaw believed the Temple's workings to be an opportunist façade, an opinion given further weight by his knowledge that the councillor who had inspected Helen beforehand was a member of the same Masonic lodge as the chemist Grenville Shadwell.

Officer Miles, on the other hand and to his own great embarrassment, thought he had seen a ghost. Unlike Forshaw, he had clearly discerned the features of a young man, dressed in a midshipman's uniform but minus the cap, who appeared before his mother. The words he had heard him speak were delivered in an authentic Pompey accent, rather than the Scots-inflected tones Forshaw reported. And where Forshaw had seen strategically draped cloth, Miles had seen the ephemeral mist of ectoplasm.

The only point they agreed on was that the men sharing the back of the room with them had been a plainclothes policeman, Detective Inspector Frederick Fraser from the local constabulary, and Richard Lexy, a reporter on the *Portsmouth Evening News*. The third man they pegged as a reporter too, as he had made an amateur attempt to trail them after they left the premises. Forshaw reckoned he was from the *News of the World*; Miles' money was on *Psychic Times*. On this last point, the Chief was with Miles.

When in London, the brigadier was fond of dining at Rules in Covent Garden, so the Chief booked a private room for lunch. The capital's oldest restaurant had been fortified by a thick outer layer of planking since the war began, but inside it was comfortingly reminiscent of the Firebrace ancestral game lodge, the menu offering copious rabbit, grouse and pheasant that remained beyond the ration, as well as its celebrated seafood. This menu, along with its dining rooms and closeted booths, made the place very popular with the organisation both men worked for, meaning that they were able to eat well and talk for the next two hours without risk of being interrupted or overheard.

Once the waiter had left them to their potted shrimp, the

brigadier set forth his opinion of Helen. This was not the first time he had known her speak of the sinking of a battleship – that was with his own ears, during a private séance in Edinburgh last May. There had been no manifestation that time, but, while in a trance, Helen had predicted that a disaster was imminent and a ship of great reknown was about to be destroyed. She could see the fires of Hell rising up from the icy waters of the Atlantic.

Days later, the brigadier learned of the nightmarish fate of HMS *Hood*, sunk during an exchange of salvoes with the German battleship *Bismark* from their main guns in the Denmark Strait. Having taken a direct hit to her own magazines, the vessel was ripped in two and exploded in a ball of flame, sinking in three minutes flat, her bow nearly vertical in the water. Out of 1418 men aboard, only three sailors had survived. By Firebrace's calculations, these events took place at the same time Helen had fallen into her trance at the Edinburgh sitting.

"What do you think explains the discrepancies?" was what the Chief wanted to know.

The brigadier shook out his napkin and tucked it under his chin. He lifted his fork, peering at his pot and assessing his aim before he spoke. "I should have thought that was obvious," he said, spearing shrimps. "Miles is more sensitive than Forshaw. More tuned into the vibrations, you know."

"Like a radio, you mean?" The Chief rolled his own fork around in his fingers.

The brigadier nodded, chewed and swallowed. "That's about the size of it."

The Chief had heard this analogy before from spiritualists. That every living being was a collection of molecules, vibrating at a speed that kept their corporeal form together, on a frequency like a radio wave. Death was merely the switching of a dial. That same force field of energy that made a person still continued to exist, it was just operating on a different wavelength. Mediums were the operators between the two worlds, able to intercept these lines of communication and share them with their intended recipients.

All very fascinating, but it still didn't explain why Forshaw claimed he was seeing a magic trick in the Temple while Miles – despite not wanting to believe it – perceived an actual spirit. Though one thing was clear. Unlike either Forshaw or, say, Mrs Vera Martin of Torquay, who had recently written to *Two Worlds* to complain about the trustworthiness of Mrs Duncan, the brigadier was not of the opinion that the medium was a charlatan, preying on the vulnerable naval families of Portsmouth. Nor, like the leader writers in the *Daily Sketch* and other, more informed sources in Intelligence circles, did he think it likely that enemy agents had infiltrated the spiritualists, using séances to spread disinformation. No, the brigadier firmly believed that Helen Duncan possessed terrifying supernatural powers.

"Well, what do you think we should do about her?" asked the Chief.

The brigadier chewed on for a while. "I should like to get her out of the way for the duration. Safer that way, don't you think?"

Alone in his office, Maurice Barbanell was looking over dummy front covers for his next issue. From a reporter's point of view, there was one clear winner: the copy that his journalist in Portsmouth had filed, illustrated by a striking, though not particularly recent, photograph of Helen. In it, she had a short, marcel-waved black bob and was wearing a drop-waist wool and satin pleated dress, redolent of the era around a decade ago when she had known her greatest celebrity, giving private readings to society ladies able to fund this style of upmarket dressing. The portrait had been staged to give the impression of further mystique; a length of gauze had been draped in folds before the lens, so that it appeared the sitter was staring out from beyond the veil.

The attendant headline spelled out the scoop: SAILORS FROM STRICKEN SHIP SPEAK! Beneath, the standfirst expounded: HELEN DUNCAN PASSES ON MESSAGES FROM CREW OF HMS *BARHAM* AT PORTSMOUTH SÉANCE.

Its competitor was a much less eye-catching report on a recent Spiritualists National Union convention and the speech the *Psychic Times'* editor had delivered for the occasion, illustrated with a photograph of himself at the lectern: a small, slight man with a receding hairline, thick-rimmed spectacles and a neatly clipped moustache. He could have been a geography teacher delivering a lecture, or a leftwing novelist declaiming from his latest masterpiece.

However, as the sole proprietor of a small newspaper with no great magnate to form a protective financial wall around him, Barbanell was very nervous about running the Duncan story. For a start, he still didn't even know if the HMS *Barham* had actually been sunk at all. It was something he and Swaffer had been trying to ascertain over the past two days. And, if she had, that would then present him with a further conundrum: was it in the public interest to break the news?

The telephone on his desk started to ring.

"Hello, Maurice, Godfrey here," the voice on the other end

of the line spoke in the hushed tones of one who didn't want to be overheard, and for good reason. Godfrey Heath was a civil servant at the Ministry of Transport as well as being, like Swaffer, a member of both Barbanell's home circle and the SNU. "Don't know if this is good news or bad," he went on. "But I've had it confirmed."

"You have?" Barbanell swivelled around in his chair. It was dark now, the blackout drawn three hours previously shielding him from the busy Holborn thoroughfare outside. But still the editor couldn't shake off the feeling he was being watched.

"I have," his confidant confirmed. "It happened two weeks ago. But I wouldn't advise you to disclose the fact. It's been placed under a D-notice, not considered to be in the public interest. Only the families of the deceased are to know."

Barbanell felt his palm go slick against the receiver as he stared at his dummy.

"Thank you, Godfrey," his own voice sounded faint to his ears. "I shall take your advice."

"I rather think it's best that you do, old chap. Well, TTFN."

Barbanell was left wondering if ripping the alternative cover into a thousand pieces would provide safety enough. He had only just returned the receiver to its cradle when the telephone rang again. It was his secretary, and she too seemed to have caught the whispering bug. "There's a man here to see you, he says he's…"

Barbanell looked up and saw a shape outside the opaque glass panel in his door, the long shadow cast by a very tall man wearing a Simpson's overcoat and a trilby hat.

14

WHISTLING IN THE DARK

Friday, 5 December 1941

Copnor Road ran down the centre of Portsmouth, a long, wide thoroughfare crisscrossed by tramlines, with parades of shops, pubs and garages between houses that had mainly been built in the preceding two decades. The chemist's at number 301 was less than ten years old, but the bay window over the shop front was designed on Tudorbethan lines.

Below the eye of the Master Temple, on each side of the front door, advertising hoardings promoted the merits of Vaseline and Virol, though the glass frontage that once displayed wares had been boarded over since the previous August when the first wave of German bombers had begun unleashing their cargo on the city.

It was a very humdrum looking place, thought Spooner, as he walked towards it. Not a likely setting for the scene of such great intrigue. He hadn't had to wait long to discover why his boss in London had taken an interest in Helen Duncan. The day after he had taken that call, his boss in Manchester was unusually uncommunicative, withdrawing into his office and closing the door for most of the morning. It wasn't until Miss Josser made her afternoon dash to the post office that he beckoned Spooner to join him in the inner sanctum, closing the door behind them.

"Have you ever seen this before?" he enquired. He slid a journal across his desk.

BULLETIN 1 of the NATIONAL LABORATORY of PSYCHICAL RESEARCH, Spooner read. *Regurgitation and the Duncan Mediumship by Harry Price. With 44 Illustrations.*

"No," said Spooner. Though he had found recent correspondence concerning the medium to pass onto the Chief, including that of the aggrieved Mrs Martin from Torquay, he had yet to discover anything more substantial in Miss Josser's files, nor on Oaten's shelves. This publication was dated 1931 – quite a relic – and he could see from the foxed corners it had been consulted many times over the past decade. Perhaps his editor kept it at home.

"May I?" he asked.

Oaten nodded. "Take a good look at it," he advised. "It's a record of the sittings Mrs Duncan willingly gave in Price's Laboratory to prove her legitimacy ten years ago. He has been using it to persecute her ever since."

Spooner lifted the document. Plates showed the medium dressed from head to foot in what looked like black sateen pyjamas, bound at the hands and feet and seated in a chair at the centre of a cabinet. The most striking element of the photographs was not merely the image of Helen trussed up, it was the stream of white material emanating from her nose.

"*Two Worlds* has always defended Mrs Duncan from the attacks of that man," Oaten continued. "But I fear she may soon be coming under a renewed assault."

"Oh?" Spooner dragged his gaze up to meet his editor's eye. A dapper, white-haired man in his mid-fifties, Oaten could easily have been mistaken for a prosperous wool or steel merchant. But today he looked less than safe and content; his face was etched with worry.

"And from more powerful quarters than that sinister one-man band," he continued.

"What do you mean?" asked Spooner.

Oaten gave him an outline of the story he had been given that morning, down the phone from London, by Maurice Barbanell. Two days ago, Mrs Duncan held a séance in Portsmouth, in which a sailor came through from a sunken ship, with a message for his mother in the audience. One of Barbanell's stringers witnessed it – along with a reporter from the local paper, a detective and two other men, believed to be Naval Intelligence. Barbanell had his journalist file the story while he sought verification on the ship. Just as he'd had it reliably confirmed that the *Barham* had been torpedoed two weeks ago, he received a visit from a man from "over the river" who told him that on no account was he to publish anything about the goings on in Portsmouth, otherwise he would find himself in court.

Barbanell passed the story on as a warning to Oaten, and also because he wondered if they should let Helen know that she had come to the attention of the security services. What, Oaten asked, did Spooner think would be the best course of action?

Spooner already knew who Barbanell's visitor had been and what he wanted him to do. The suggestion he made, he hoped, would please both men, while letting neither of their confidences in his abilities down.

"Why don't I take a trip down to Portsmouth?" he suggested. "Not to write a story, but to gather information that could come in handy if things do start to look bad for Mrs Duncan. Get some testimonials from the people who were there – the sailor's mother and the couple that run the Temple, for a start. Speak to this local reporter and see what he intends doing with his copy, or whether he's had a visit the same as Mr Barbanell. And see if I can't have a word with this detective, find out what his story is."

"Then what would we do with this information?" Oaten wanted to know. "Why do you think it would come in useful for Helen?"

"In case Mr Barbanell's visitor decides to charge her," said Spooner. "We'd have some contemporaneous eye-witness statements she could use in her defence."

Oaten wiped his handkerchief across his brow. "Do you think it might come to that?"

"Isn't that why you asked?"

The bell above the chemist's door tinkled as Spooner crossed the threshold. The chemist, in his whites, was handing one lady customer a brown bag containing her prescription, while three more, in their winter coats and hats, waited in a line behind her and another, in an overall and hairnet, worked the till. They were all so busy talking that not one head turned, leaving Spooner to peruse at his leisure the corn plasters and moth balls, camomile lotion and cod liver oil.

Around the walls, posters advised customers to *Take Beecham's Pills for Active Service!* or try *Bile Beans for Radiant Health and a Lovely Figure*. Spooner's eye was drawn from these sophisticated adverts to a cork noticeboard promoting local attractions. There was a dance at a church hall and a smudged handbill for an act called The Two Magicians, but most prominent was a poster informing customers about the activities of the Master Temple. That very night, at 7pm, he could witness *Voices from the Other World*, channelled via the *Amazing Mrs Violet Adams* for 15s – about 10s more than most sittings advertised in *Two Worlds*.

"Can I be of any help to you?" an accent thick with the coal dust of the Rhondda floated his way. Spooner turned his head. The woman at the till smiled. Her face was dominated by round, tortoiseshell-rimmed bifocal glasses, which magnified her dark brown eyes.

He opened the door for the departing customer then walked towards her, extracting one of his business cards.

"I was just checking I'd come to the right place," he said, proffering it. "My editor said I should drop in on you." He watched her eyeballs grow wider still as she read the words *Assistant Editor, Two Worlds*. "He's heard great things about your work here."

He could have acted like a journalist and telephoned earlier to announce himself, but the detective in Spooner wanted the Shadwells to meet him unprepared.

"Well, I never! Grenville," she hurried to her husband, making up another prescription in the back of the shop. "You're never going to believe it…" They were an odd looking pair, even with their backs turned, Mr Shadwell standing over a foot taller than his wife, with long, thin limbs and hair that looked like iron filings. After a few moments of muttered conversation, Mrs Shadwell returned, beaming. "My husband said, would you like to come up for a cup of tea when we close? We've only got ten minutes, if you can wait that long?"

"Of course," Spooner smiled first at her, then at the remaining three ladies at the counter, now staring at him with expressions that ranged from the enquiring to the downright hostile. "Though, I'll not keep you from serving the ladies, please go ahead."

Gossip time was over. Seven minutes later, Mrs Shadwell had got everyone out and put the CLOSED sign across the front door. "Come this way, Mr Spooner," she put one hand on his arm, while the other motioned the way up the staircase at the back of the shop. Like Officers Forshaw and Miles before him, Spooner experienced the strange sensation of going from the realm of science, with its lingering aroma of Friars' Balsam, into the parlour of the supernatural. In a few short steps, 301 Copnor Road ceased to be quite so ordinary.

"This is where we hold the meetings," he was informed by his hostess as she flicked on the light. Spooner peered past rows of chairs towards a Woolworth's print of *The Last Supper* hanging over an unlit electric fire. In front of that stood a sideboard on which was placed a crocheted mat and a plain wooden cross. To the left of this makeshift altar was a compact organ and piano stool, but it was to the contraption on the right that Spooner's attention was diverted.

"And this is our cabinet," Mrs Shadwell read his gaze as one of admiration. "Would you like to take a closer look? We've nothing to hide, you know." She gave a little laugh.

"Thank you," said Spooner, moving towards it.

Mr Shadwell, who had been clearing away downstairs, appeared in the doorway behind them. "Made that myself," he said, with more than a hint of pride. Hearing him clearly for the first time, Spooner turned round. For a moment, he could have sworn he was listening to Bob Howell, back at the High View guesthouse in Birmingham. Grenville walked up beside him. "Good, solid walnut," he said, running his hands down a panel.

"But it's this," he drew back chocolate-brown curtains to reveal the Jacobean armchair within, "is the pièce de résistance. Over two hundred years old, this is. That's what gives the mediums such a good reception here – they've all said as much."

"Extraordinary," said Spooner, rubbing his chin. "Where did you come across it?"

"It's an heirloom," Grenville said. "I had a rich ancestor, once, on me mother's side."

"And where is it you're from?" Spooner couldn't help but enquire.

"Pelsall," said Grenville. "Just north of Birmingham, if you don't know it, and I don't see why you should. It's just a small place really, a pit town. Only, there's been a lot of my family got themselves killed in that profession, which is why I trained as a chemist. We've that in common, me and Gladys: both of us come from mining folk."

"How did you meet your wife?" Spooner was curious to know.

"At the seaside. Llandudno. I was on holiday when Gladys was playing in the orchestra on the end of the pier. She's very talented musically, as you'll no doubt hear later. Given our backgrounds, we've both a love of being in the fresh air, near the sea. That's why we've ended up here…"

"Are you still talking, Grenville?" Having emerged from the kitchen where she had shed her hairnet and housecoat, Gladys had plumped up her hair, dabbed on a spot of red lipstick and flung her best turquoise cardigan around her shoulders while the kettle was boiling. She wasn't sure whether this fellow from *Two Worlds* would be wanting to take her picture or not, but she wasn't taking any chances. "I've made us some tea," she said, smiling at Spooner. "Won't you come through?"

"Go ahead, kid," said Grenville, sounding even more like Bob. "We can answer any questions you'd like to ask us. Only I'll have to leave you two to it by half-past – I've got Councillor Roberts coming then to make the usual checks."

"Oh?" Spooner followed him through to a smaller room, where a dining table and chairs, a settee, a radiogram and two armchairs vied for space. Every available surface contained ornaments: costume dolls, china animals, replica Blackpool towers, vases, ashtrays and plates commemorating the many seaside towns the couple had visited. By the fireplace, a brass coal scuttle and guard sat next to a pot of aspidistras and a rack of *Two Worlds* magazines, turned proudly outwards to face him and completing the resemblance to Mrs Smith's parlour in West Bromwich.

"Councillor Roberts always checks the room before a service and the mediums when they arrive, to make sure we're not being taken for a ride," Grenville explained. "'Cos you do read about fraudulent mediums in the papers, and we don't want to be getting that sort of reputation. Then we put the certificate on the door, so folks know it's all above board."

"I see," said Spooner, taking his seat. "That's very conscientious of you, Mr Shadwell."

"Well, you can't be too careful now, can you?" Gladys narrowed her eyes. "Shall I pour?"

"Thank you, Mrs Shadwell," said Spooner.

"Oh, call me Gladys, please," she said. "Milk and sugar?"

"Thanks," said Spooner, noting the piles of rock cakes arranged on a stand and divining he was getting star treatment.

"Is Mrs Adams a local woman?" he said. "One of your regulars?"

"She was one of the first to make contact with us when

we set up the Temple, five years ago, now. She's been a rock, has Violet. Especially since the bombing started last January. You'll know how badly we got hit, I'm sure, but there were thousands lost their lives and their homes. We do our best to bring them consolation."

"You must be a close-knit community," said Spooner.

Gladys nodded. "We have to be. We're up against it here; the navy makes us a sitting target. But people know they can bring their troubles here and leave with a lighter heart, sure in the knowledge there's always someone watching over them."

"So many who've been recently bereaved," Spooner said, "and many more who are waiting to hear from their loved ones. It must be a relief for people to be able to just get together and talk about it, eh? Share each other's troubles."

"It's that, all right," said Grenville. "It's the not knowing, isn't it, that gets you?"

"Aye," Spooner agreed. "And apart from Violet, who would you say have been your most reliable mediums?"

Husband and wife exchanged glances, smiles forming on their faces. "We had the honour of having Mrs Helen Duncan here only last Saturday," said Gladys. "She gave the most wonderful sitting, oh, it was ever so moving. This lady, Mrs Walker, was brought by one of our regulars because she was so worried; she'd not heard from her son, Davey, in weeks. He was a midshipman on a battleship, you know."

Spooner shook his head. "Was?" he echoed.

"Well," Gladys's eyes seemed to get larger still behind their lenses, their stare more intense. "Davey came straight through for her as soon as Mrs Duncan was here. He was wearing his uniform and everything, there was no mistake about it. The ship he was on…"

"The HMS *Barham*," put in Grenville.

"… had gone down at sea," continued Gladys. "Terribly sad for her, of course. But he had a message, you see. He told his dear mam that the rest of the crew had asked him to be their spokesman and to tell everyone not to worry, they were all well and happy on the Other Side. Now, isn't that glorious?"

"Stunning," said Spooner, almost tripping over his shorthand to get it all down. "So," he said, looking back at Gladys, "what was Mrs Walker's reaction to the news?"

"She fainted," said Grenville.

The corners of his wife's mouth twitched downwards. "The poor love, she was quite overcome. Well, you would be, wouldn't you? But she was very grateful to have her friends around her at such a time."

"I'm sure she was," said Spooner, looking down at his pad, thankful for the excuse not to keep staring into the forcefield of those eyes. "I know it's still very fresh, very personal," he said, "but is there any chance she'd talk to me about it, d'you think?"

"That I don't know," said Gladys. "She's gone to stay with her sister in the country. To have a little rest and get over her loss."

"Of course," said Spooner. "I wouldn't want to intrude on her grief. I was only thinking what a story it would make. What a tribute to Mrs Duncan's abilities."

"Hmmm," Gladys pursed her lips. The ringing of the doorbell cut through her thoughts.

"That'll be the councillor," said Grenville, getting to his feet. "I'd better not keep him."

"Do stay for another cup, Mr Spooner," offered Gladys. "Violet will be along any minute. I'm sure you'll want to talk to her too, won't you? And naturally, you'll stay for the service?" She began pouring without waiting for an answer.

Spooner prepared himself for a long night.

15

THEY DIDN'T BELIEVE ME

Friday, 5 December 1941

Three hours later, Spooner made his way back along Copnor Road towards the corner of Stubbington Avenue, where he had been told he would find the Star and Garter public house. Even in the unfamiliar terrain, the size of the establishment, built to serve the raft of new houses that had gone up in the last decade, was hard to miss.

Like the row of shops that housed the Master Temple, attempts had been made by the architects to cast a carapace of Olde England about the place. Stretched out before Spooner as he entered the saloon bar was a baronial world of dark wood panelling and an enormous Devonshire fireplace clad in Portland stone. Above this hung the azure shield bearing the gold star and crescent of the Portsmouth coat of arms.

The room was two-thirds full, with a clientele of middle-aged couples and elderly, naval types. Though it was screened off with more panelling and bevelled glass, the noise from the public bar indicated a roaring Saturday night trade.

Spooner was greeted by a young barmaid with red lips and a tower of peroxide curls, whose ringed fingers glinted as she poured his pint. He was just fishing in his pocket for change when a voice behind him said: "I'll get that, thank you, Betty. And can you do me a gin-and-it while you're at it, love?"

Reflected in the glass behind her, a dapper young man winked. He was wearing a sports jacket and flannels, as if he'd just come off the golf course; he had a round, dimpled face and hair a shade darker than Spooner's, swept into a side parting.

"Richard Lexy?" he presumed.

"Call me Dick," came the reply, along with an outstretched hand. "You found everything all right then?"

"Oh, aye," said Spooner, shaking. "Your directions were spot on, thanks."

Lexy winked. "Good show. Here you go, Betty, love," he handed her some coins. "There's one for yourself in there too," he added as she started to count. Spooner saw her face light up with pleasure as she thanked him.

"I've a seat over in the nook there," Lexy indicated with his little finger to where two jutting partitions had made a small annexe at the far end of the room. "You can see everything without being overheard. Not that I really expect any of the Shadwells' regulars to turn up here, but you can never be too certain, can you?"

"I'm not certain of anything after what I've just witnessed," said Spooner, following him.

"You weren't entirely convinced by them, then?" there was a droll irony in Lexy's tone. They arrived at the nook, which was furnished with its own coat stand. Spooner took off his mac and scarf and hung them next to a camel hair and silk paisley combination he took to be Lexy's, then sat down opposite the reporter.

Unlike his previous interviewees, Spooner had taken the

trouble to locate this witness to the Duncan séance via the offices of the *Portsmouth Evening News* before he'd left Manchester, introducing himself as the assistant editor of *Two Worlds*. He told Lexy they had recently received a lot of correspondence concerning the Master Temple that his editor wanted him to investigate. He intimated that some of these stories were critical of the Shadwells and Lexy had responded as if this was music to his ears. It was his suggestion that Spooner should turn up for the regular Friday night "doings", as he called it, then meet up with him afterwards. He had even given Spooner the details of a decent hotel nearby that took guests off-season.

Norrie's first words to him were on the tip of Spooner's tongue by way of reply. What he'd seen in the Temple tonight was in the realm of magicians, mesmerists and perhaps most of all, memory men – or women, in the case of Violet Adams. "I have some concerns," was how he put it.

"Oh, go on," Lexy leaned across the table, his eyes sparkling "What sort of performance did they put on this time? Did Mrs Adams have her sheet on or off?"

Spooner couldn't help but chuckle. "On," he said, "while she was in the cabinet, at least."

Violet Adams had turned up not long after Councillor Roberts. The Shadwells had insisted Spooner witness the councillor searching the room, in particular, the cabinet, and then the medium, who dutifully stripped down to her corset and stockings without batting a heavily mascaraed eyelid. Mrs Adams was in her late forties, with a hairstyle only slightly less complex than the Star and Garter barmaid's and underwear so solid that it could have been welded in the local dockyard, giving a battleship finish to both her prow and stern.

However, in front of her congregation, Mrs Adams became considerably more demure. She conducted her conversations with the Spirit World from beneath a white sheet, while sitting in Grenville's ancestral chair, the curtains of the cabinet open and the dim light bulb bathing the scene in a flickering glow.

"She said her spirit guide preferred her to be shrouded," he told Lexy. "But you'll no doubt be reassured to learn that I was privy to Councillor Roberts' examination of the premises and Mrs Adams herself before they let the public in." Spooner lifted his pint. He was sure the medium had winked at him while in the middle of disrobing.

"Good old Councillor Roberts," said Lexy, raising his own glass to clink with Spooner's. "It was he who led me to the Shadwells in the first place." Lexy raised an eyebrow. "So don't tell me – she did the old moaning and groaning under the sheet for a while, then she brought through Mrs Dowson's budgie, old Mr Markham's kid brother who died when he was six, and Miss Foxley's young man Harry who was lost in the last war but waits for her still in Paradise?"

Spooner put his drink down, nodding. "That's about the size of it," he agreed. "How many times have you seen her do it, then?"

"Oh, four or five," said Lexy. "The people who come on Saturday nights are nearly always the same, so I think the sheet comes on if there's someone she's not sure about in the audience – I got it the first time I went and obviously on this occasion it was for you. Did she manage to bring anyone through for you, after all that effort?"

"Not as such," said Spooner. "Though she did tell me that a woman I was seeking would come back into my life unexpectedly, only to disappear again."

Lexy whistled. "Astonishing stuff in the middle of a war, when people go missing all the time, don't you think? No, sorry old chap, it's not as good as what was on offer last week. They really got their money's worth when they brought in this old battleaxe Helen Duncan." He leaned forward, dropping the volume of his voice. "She actually got a sailor from a torpedoed ship who came through to speak to his mother."

"Mrs Shadwell told me about it, aye," said Spooner. "And you were there?"

"Luckily, yes," said Lexy. "Which is why I thought I should take the trouble to talk to you. What they got up to that night would be pretty impressive if you didn't know too much about the navy, had never learned any amateur magic and were from out of town, or preferably all three. See, the general public doesn't know the HMS *Barham*'s been sunk, but of course the Admiralty do, and they'd already started making house calls to the relatives. I don't know how they missed poor Mrs Walker off their list or if they just hadn't got round to visiting her, but people here were talking. Add to that Mr Shadwell's membership of a certain society of stone-cutters, which he shares with Councillor Roberts and most of the naval top brass, and I have no doubt the Shadwells knew about it before Helen Duncan arrived. And I'm doubly certain that the old bag was filled in with all the gossip the moment she arrived."

"You don't like her much, do you?" said Spooner. "What makes you so sure?"

"The cap," said Lexy. "The spirit – which I assumed was Mr Duncan under a sheet not unlike the one you saw earlier – was wearing a cap that identified his vessel. The navy stopped that practice as soon as war was declared and *that's* what proves to me it was a set-up. They must have rustled it up before the séance, then Mrs Shadwell, who does the seating arrangements, would have pointed out where her mark was going to sit and after that…" He scanned Spooner's face for a reaction. "Sorry if it goes against your editorial line," he said, "but I happen to think it's really not on."

"Actually," said Spooner, "I agree with you. It's my editor who won't see it that way. He's a big supporter of Mrs Duncan, so he'll want me to run with a story that shows her in the best possible light." He drained the remains of his pint. "Get you another?"

"Yes please," said Lexy, looking thoughtful. "Gin-and-it, if you would be so kind."

Spooner watched him in the glass behind the bar while Betty was serving. It was the only angle that, through the reflection of other mirrors placed around the room, afforded a glimpse into his well-chosen nook. Lexy was flicking through his notepad. In the time it took Spooner to return with fresh drinks, he had found the relevant page and lit up another cigarette with an American Zippo lighter.

"Thanks," he said as Spooner placed the drink in front of him. "I've something that might be helpful if you wanted to put your editor off. I've been burrowing into the history of the Shadwells. They came here five years ago, led by a friend from her hometown who plies a similar trade. He's called Llewellyn Jones and he used to perform what he called 'healings'. He washed up six months ahead of the Shadwells and it took another two after that before he got himself nicked for laying his hands on places they weren't wanted." Lexy consulted his notebook and looked back at Spooner. "He had form for molesting very young women – girls, really – stretching back to the twenties. I've a list of previous convictions here, if you want to see." He laid the open pad in front of Spooner.

"Ach." Spooner shook his head. "That's terrible. And is he still part of their circle?"

"Thankfully not," said Lexy. "He's currently residing in another seaside location: HMP Portland," he raised his glass towards the fireplace, "where I hope they're putting his hands to better work chiselling out a load more of that stuff."

Spooner's eyes scanned down a list of seaside towns, from Blackpool, through to Llandudno, Tenby, Minehead, Padstow, Penzance, Falmouth, Torquay, Plymouth, Bournemouth… all the travels he had seen recorded via Gladys Shadwell's knick-knacks. For a second, *Tenby* flashed louder than all the other names: the place where Anna was brought up by her grandmother: a parallel world of seaside B&Bs catering for lonely old ladies with an interest in the supernatural. He could see other links too.

"Gladys used to play the piano in a band, her husband told me," he said as he copied Lexy's information. "What are they then, all part of some travelling circus?"

"Used to be the Variety circuit, before the war," said Lexy. "Now all the beaches are full of mines and barbed wire. The people who're left there aren't having a good time any more. Vulnerable to Jerry attack from the sea *and* where the Luft-waffe get rid of all their unused bombs on their way home. Easy prey for spook racketeers."

"What about the rest of those sort of music hall people?" Spooner's mind returned to Birmingham. "Do you have much in the way of entertainment here these days?"

"You mean, do we have anywhere for them to perform after Jerry's finished?" said Lexy. "There's not much of the city centre left, you know. There's a few tea dances and bingo at some of the church halls, a handful of picture houses. But that's another thing that makes the Master Temple so appealing to bored, lonely, frightened people. Gives them something to do and something to talk about on these long winter's nights."

Spooner finished note-taking. "Thanks," he said, putting his pad and pen back into his pocket. "So, what about you? Are you aiming to cover any of this for your paper?"

Lexy reached for his notebook, exhaling a large smoke ring that wobbled up towards the ceiling. "Like I said, Councillor Roberts led me to the Shadwells. He's the big fish I'm pursuing; they're just the small, yet fascinatingly ugly fry he brought up in his wake. I don't want the councillor to be alerted to my presence in his world at this stage of the game. Because he never actually attends any of these séances he certifies he has yet to clock my presence at the Master Temple. I need to keep it that way for the time being."

Spooner frowned. "So what's he doing it for?"

Lexy tapped his finger on the side of his nose. "That's confidential information, old chap," he said and winked. "Now, I should also mention that there's someone else been keeping tabs on the Shadwells – Detective Inspector Freddie Fraser. He was at the Duncan séance too. Looked a bit red in the face afterwards. Don't think he was best pleased."

"Detective Inspector?" said Spooner. "So he's quite high up, then? My editor might be right in thinking that powerful forces are amassing against Mrs Duncan."

"Well, I wouldn't go that far," said Lexy. "But he's not a particularly pleasant chap. I doubt you'd enjoy actually having a conversation with him."

Spooner wondered whether this was a veiled threat

– whether he was being told to keep his nose out or being given sound advice. He pushed his spectacles back up his nose, hoping to convey a lack of ambition for fighting. "I'll bear that in mind, Mr Lexy."

"It's Dick, remember?" The journalist grinned. "Well," he checked his wristwatch, "I'd better push off. Will you be all right finding your way back to the hotel?"

"I'll be fine," said Spooner, getting to his feet to offer his hand. "Thanks for everything, erm, Dick. You've been a great help. If it puts your mind at rest, I'm pretty sure I can persuade my editor what's the wisest thing to do."

"Good man," said Lexy. His palm was noticeably warmer than when they had first met at the bar. "And thanks for the drink. I'm glad to discover it isn't true what they say about mean Scotsmen." He winked, blew another smoke ring and disappeared behind it.

16

WHILE A CIGARETTE
WAS BURNING

Saturday, 6 December 1941

"Who's there?" Spooner jerked upright in bed. He didn't know if it was the creak of a floorboard that had woken him or the tickling sensation against his cheek, as if someone had been leaning over him, trailing hair in his face – but someone had got into his hotel room. He could feel another presence in the unfamiliar darkness, smell the aroma that came with it: an incongruous stench of wet animal. He lurched towards the bedside table, groping for his glasses. Clumsy fingers instead sent the things that had been resting there spilling to the floor – his spectacles in their case, his bedside reading matter and the alarm clock.

Spooner swore, trying to kick his way out of the sheets that had wound around his lower limbs. Starting to panic, he reached out, aiming for the light switch. This time his fingers closed over their target and he pushed it down. But no illumination was forthcoming. He pressed it up and down again, three times in succession. The room remained in darkness.

A low, guttural chuckle beside him brought his flailing to a halt. It sounded barely human. The animal smell grew more pungent and he felt the tingling sensation again on his cheek, forming in his mind the horrible idea that a great, greasy goat was standing at his bedside, tickling him with its whiskery chin.

At the same time, from somewhere else in the darkness of the room, a radiogram switched itself on. There was a crackle and hiss, the sound of jazz music fading into the clipped tones of an upper class voice: "*Germany calling, this is Germany calling...*"

Icy terror surged through Spooner's veins and he lashed out, breaking through the surface of the dream and sending a second wave of objects sliding down the counterpane to land on the floorboards with a thud.

This time he was really awake. He threw back the bed-clothes, shot out of bed and made for the light switch, which was, he now remembered, by the side of the door and not above his head. A click and a pool of yellow light banished the shades of his imagination back to the darkness that had spawned them. Before him stood only the rumpled bed, the table with his glasses case and alarm clock still on it, an arm-chair on which he'd placed his briefcase, and a wardrobe. The air was chill with the damp of early morning but the musky smell of Capricorn had vanished along with the nightmare.

Spooner thought of Nicholas Ralphe and the rosary beads he had worn around his neck.

"Is this what they did to you?" Spooner wondered aloud. "Had you dreaming of goats?"

His eyes dropped to the floor. What had actually woken him were the volumes he had been consulting before he'd fallen asleep. One of them was Anna's songbook, the other was Professor Margot Melvin's second treatise on The Old

Ways, entitled *The God of Witches*. On its cover was a painting of a coven in full flight, dancing around their Horned God – a gigantic goat, rearing up on his hind legs.

He stooped to pick them up, shaking his head with a nervous chuckle. "Ach, you can only blame yourself," he decided, moving towards his briefcase to put them back in. All the same, he took an instinctive look behind him before he opened it. The feeling of being watched hadn't quite evaporated.

Once there was enough daylight to drive by, Spooner was ready to leave. He wanted to make a call first, but the telephone booth in the hotel reception was occupied. Spooner lingered there a while, the tremors of his dream still prickling through his blood as he perused the noticeboard to the side of it. Another bill for the same act he had seen at the Shadwells' was pinned up there. It was only when he saw it that his mind flashed back to his bedside reading and the revelation that had lain within it – there was a song in Anna's book that was also called "The Two Magicians".

He caught his breath as he surreptitiously removed the drawing pin and took it down for a closer look. This had come off the press better than the one in the chemist's and he could see the duo of a man and a woman, whose show he had missed by a week. An icy-looking blonde and a man in a top hat with a curly black moustache. Although he had no idea what her funambulist friend looked like, the woman didn't resemble Anna in the slightest. Perhaps it was just coincidence, made to seem more like by the links he'd made between the Shadwells and the old Variety circuit. Still, it would be worth asking Norrie if he knew anything about the pair.

He folded the bill and put it in his pocket as a man came out of the telephone booth. He was middle-aged, thickset, with the florid complexion of the habitual drinker. Though he held the door open for Spooner, there was something about his sardonic expression, coupled with the gabardine mac folded over his arm and battered trilby in his free hand, that brought to mind Lexy's words about DI Fraser. Spooner smiled as they passed. He stayed in the booth until he heard the front door close behind its former incumbent. Then he replaced the receiver in its cradle and went on his way. It would be better, he decided, to call London after he'd put a distance between himself and the naval city.

It was a decision he felt more sure of with each passing mile. Spooner was glad to see Portsmouth in his rear-view mirror and the weather appeared to agree with him. Once he had left the city, still swathed in the chill Channel fog, and taken the road up into the South Downs, the sun made a rare appearance to illuminate his journey over the ancient chalk landscape. In the skies above his head, the Battle of Britain had taken place over the summer of the previous year. But today Spooner had the rolling hills between Portsmouth and Guildford to himself, but for a couple of skittering partridges that broke from a hedgerow to run wildly across the road in front of him, and a kestrel, hovering above. As he drove, Spooner mulled over the events of his short stay in Portsmouth.

While he suspected Lexy might have been laying it on a bit thick about his local detective, it was also possible that DI Fraser was in touch with other agencies interested in the activities of Helen Duncan, who would keep a contact on the local force. The reporter didn't know that Spooner had no intention of writing a word about the medium that could ever be published. Not that he hadn't carried out the interviews he had promised Oaten.

Before meeting with Lexy, he had lingered at the Master Temple after the last hymn had been sung and prayer said, chatting to the regulars. He had found them just as Lexy would go on to describe – lonely old folk, frightened out of their wits by the blitzing of their city and without anyone able to offer them an alternative to staying there, coming together to seek some form of comfort. He had been particularly touched by the elderly Mr Markham, bent up with arthritis, the elegant Miss Foxley, who smelled of the same lavender perfume Janet had worn and had kept herself just as fastidiously, so that she resembled the twilight-faded ghost of a young woman waiting for her fiancé to return from Ypres.

To see Mr Markham's rheumy eyes light up when he received his message and Miss Foxley's papery hand reach up to touch the locket that contained a photograph of her beloved Harry, as she was told she looked beautiful and he couldn't wait for them to be reunited, was to witness the only happiness they might have known throughout a dark, uncertain week. For the service the medium was providing, Spooner could see no harm – other than the unnecessarily greedy demands the Shadwells made on their pensions.

It was the matronly Mrs Dowson, she with the spirit budgerigar, who had provided the most interesting information. She had brought her friend Mrs Walker to the séance at which her Davey came through. Though she wasn't able to describe what she had witnessed with very much clarity, she told Spooner there had been no doubt in her friend's mind that she had seen her son that night. As they were leaving, Mrs Dowson slipped into his hand the telephone number of

Mrs Walker's sister in Dorset. She knew it was a long way for Spooner to go, but in case he wanted to, she didn't think her friend would mind talking about her experience. In fact, she felt sure that she would like to.

The congregation of the Master Temple last night had not been anywhere near as large as that which had turned out for Helen. The handful of people he had met there were not thrill seekers, just normal, everyday folk. Spooner didn't consider them to be stupid. He had, after all, once been one of them himself.

When Spooner was a teenager, he had started finding his way into the homes of people in Aberdeen who held their own séances. These included a couple of friends from school whose parents dabbled with Ouija boards and the more serious students of the occult he started talking to at the shop. Unlike many of his contemporaries, who were brought up strict Calvinists, his family had little fear he would come to any harm in these places, and indeed he hadn't. Instead, he had witnessed many strange and wondrous things.

Rooms lit by Aladdin lamps where white, spectral shapes floated across the room, always emerging from and then retreating back into the curtains of various homemade cabinets. Trumpets and tambourines dancing in thin air by flickering fire- and candlelight. Victorian coins materialising onto the tops of tables while the sitters all held hands. Spirit guides from different continents and centuries, speaking in Greek, Arabic and Hindustani. He was often told he had a gift for contacting the spirits, so many of them made a bee-line for him at sittings. But never once had he ever had confirmation of the one thing he had entered this shadow realm to seek – an apparition of, or a message from, his own departed mother.

As he had confessed to Lexy the night before, he did not consider what he had seen at the Master Temple to be genuine psychic phenomena. Spooner was unsurprised by neither the reporter's cynicism nor the Shadwells' apparent opportunism. But this did not mean he entirely ceased to believe such things were possible, nor that some of these spectacles he had been privy to, in the darkened parlours of Aberdeen and at other places since, could always be explained away as conjurers' tricks.

Helen Duncan seemed to inhabit a murky world somewhere between his Triple-Us and the Three-M's of Norrie's world: magicians, mesmerists and memory men. If Lexy was right and the Shadwells were using theatrical trickery to extract money from the vulnerable then it actually put Helen in the clear of the theory that she might be an agent. It was local gossip they were using to weave an illusion, not information received from Germany, though Spooner now had a number for someone who would testify differently again, should the matter ever get that far.

The person he really wanted to talk to next was the man who had spent a lifetime pursuing the paranormal, including taking those photographs of Helen that Oaten had shown him. What he had begun to learn about Harry Price was interesting indeed.

Spooner had reached the highest point of the Downs now, the road leading into a densely wooded valley below. His map told him that Guildford would soon be in sight. At least there was one thing he could be pleased about. He had covered a lot of miles in the past few days and he had obviously chosen a good car to make the journey. The black Ford Anglia he'd bought secondhand before he moved to Manchester had yet to let him down.

*

Hannen Swaffer emerged from the front door of his house on St Martin's Place. It was a clear, crisp morning and Mrs Swaffer had furnished him with an excellent breakfast while he perused the morning papers. With a freshly lit cigarette dangling from his lips, he strode down onto the Strand with a sense of purpose.

Maurice Barbanell had summoned him to a rendezvous late the previous night. Swaffer knew it was going to concern Helen Duncan by the way his friend behaved, as if he had started taking lessons from that man at MI5 who had struck such fear into him – talking in vague allusions on the telephone, arranging to meet in the open air, preferably by the river, so they could say what they really wanted without fear of being overheard.

Thus he found himself slipping down the steps to Villiers Street and into Embankment Gardens which, on such an unexpectedly delightful morning, was already full of people strolling, sitting and turning their faces to the winter sun with expressions of happiness. He found his friend standing underneath the statue of John Stuart Mill. As usual, Barbanell wasn't smiling. He greeted Swaffer by raising one eyebrow and stalking off in the direction of the Thames. "Have you ever heard," he said, "of anyone by the name of Ross Spooner?"

Swaffer tried to summon a face that went with this name. "I'm not sure," was the best he could do. "Why do you ask?"

"I was speaking to Oaten again last night," said Barbanell. "He said he's just sent his assistant editor down to Portsmouth. I was quite alarmed – I did warn him what happened to me, but apparently he was convinced to do so by this chap, Spooner."

"Oh?" said Swaffer, feeling the stirrings of a memory tapping somewhere at the back of his mind. "And where did he appear from?"

"Aberdeen," said Barbanell. "His father runs a rare and occult bookshop there. I know of it myself; it has a sound reputation. According to Oaten, he's a very personable and knowledgeable chap – so personable that he's been giving Ernest his services for free while still managing to be able to afford digs in Manchester."

"Is that so strange?" Swaffer asked. "Perhaps his father's giving him an allowance. He probably considers it good background for taking over the business…" Another possibility crossed his mind. "Or is he a draft dodger, do you think?"

"He told Ernest he'd failed the medical. Flat feet and bad eyesight, I shouldn't wonder." Barbanell snorted.

"Well," Swaffer said, "good for Ernest if he's got someone young and keen to help him."

"I would have agreed with you," said Barbanell, "if it wasn't for the way he explained Spooner's reason for going to Portsmouth. He said that it would be in Helen's interests to get some eye-witness testimony in case she is ever taken to court."

The editor came to a sudden stop and wheeled to face Swaffer. "Now, excuse me if I'm wildly off the mark," he said, "but doesn't that sound like a policeman talking? It's been gnawing away at me all night, Swaff. Weren't some of the Heavy Mob seconded to that bunch over the river at the start of the war? And aren't they all exempt from the call up?"

That tapping in Swaffer's mind became the knocking on a door which now began to open. It was three years ago, before the war, and at the office of his firmest friend in the Flying Squad, DCI Edward Greenaway. The detective had just raided a brothel on Dover Street run by a remarkable Jamaican dominatrix and reputed to have some interesting clients. Greenaway had been courteous enough to carry out his search during daylight hours and Swaffer had been trying to chivvy some finer details to little avail, when the knocking came. It was no more than a brief interlude – another detective coming in with some paperwork Greenaway had requested, a pale looking chap with plastered down hair and glasses, the sort of face that slid evasively from recall – but Swaffer thought the DCI had said: "Cheers, Spooner," to the man.

He looked at his friend with renewed respect. "You know, Maurice, you might have something there..."

"Harry Price," said the Chief, lifting the cover of the booklet. "A name to conjure with?"

"Quite literally." Spooner watched the expression on the other man's face as he studied the photographs taken in 1931. He had saved what he thought was the best bit of his report for last. "An initiate of the Magic Circle, President of the Ghost Club and founder of the National Laboratory of Psychical Research. He's been carrying out experiments on mediums for decades. My editor roundly despises him."

It wasn't Ernest Oaten's copy of the first NLPR Bulletin that turned beneath his boss's fingers. That would have been far too much of a risk to remove from the *Two Worlds*' office. But Spooner's father had managed to track one down for him, as well as a wealth of other information on this man who was Triple-U and Three-M all rolled into one.

"These are quite extraordinary," the Chief said, looking back up.

"If there was to be a prosecution of Mrs Duncan, then I think he's the guy the Crown would want on the case. But there's another reason I'm keen to meet up with him."

Spooner rolled his glass of whisky around in his hand. After he had telephoned from Guildford, the Chief had invited Spooner back to the flat in Dolphin Square to talk over his findings, even offering him a bed for the night. Spooner was grateful for this thoughtfulness; he had been expecting to have to find another cheap hotel.

"I asked my dad what he knew about him," he went on, "and it turns out to be quite a lot. Price is a big collector of rare magical texts, some of which are connected to giant figures of literature. And I don't know if he's fallen on hard times, but word is he's prepared to make some of them available, if the price is right."

"Now you do interest me," the Chief said. "Tell me more."

"Well, for a start, he claims to have the copy of Scot's *The Discoverie of Witchcraft* that Shakespeare consulted to write *Macbeth*. But there's another thing that's even more interesting – to us, anyway. Back in the thirties, Price acquired a transcript of a fifteenth-century grimoire known as *The High German Black Book*. He tried out one of the spells in the summer of 1932, up in the Harz Mountains, a region he says is the most pagan in all Germany. He was supposed to turn a goat into 'a youth of surpassing beauty', though, needless to say, it didn't work."

"Fond of Germany, is he?" the Chief tapped out his pipe and reached for fresh tobacco. "Under what auspices did he carry out this ceremony?"

"It was Goethe's centenary," said Spooner, "and Price says this was the text he consulted when he wrote the

Walpurgisnacht scene in *Faust*. Those literary allusions, you see. He was invited over as part of the celebrations hosted by the local newspaper and he wrote it all up in another book Dad sent me, *Confessions of a Ghost Hunter*, from 1936."

"How much is this grimoire worth?" the Chief pressed tobacco into the bowl of his pipe.

"It's one of those things that, if you have to ask, you can't afford it," said Spooner. "We know someone who could." His mind's eye caught a flash of russet-coloured stone, a temple hidden within Hagley Woods. "Word among the collectors goes that Himmler was seeking to buy it."

"Ah," the Chief's eyes sparked in the flame of his lighter. "Now you're getting to it. With help from a certain Mr De Vere, you think?"

"That's what I'd like to try and find out," said Spooner. "Though, I'm sure I'll have to be slightly more circumspect than just asking him outright."

The Chief puffed hard on his pipe. "And how are you going to run the idea of interviewing him past your editor, if he's so against the man?" he enquired.

"I'm not," Spooner said. "I'm running it past you. I think Price will be amused enough by the idea of a *Two Worlds'* journalist asking to grant me an interview, he's not exactly publicity-shy. Then, when I let him know my connections in the book trade, I might get to find out more about subjects other than Helen Duncan. If you're happy for me to try, then I'll write to him. I just wasn't sure…"

"Don't let me stop you," said the Chief. "Where is this lab of his, anyway?"

"Roland Gardens," said Spooner, "in South Kensington. Just off Old Brompton Road."

"Roland Gardens!" The Chief put down his pipe. "Extraordinary!" Before he could explain why, the telephone began to ring and his expression changed abruptly. "Excuse me, Ross," he said. "I'll need to take this."

Spooner nodded and moved away from the desk, wandering over to the fireplace at the furthest end of the room so that he couldn't overhear. Though the electric fire was on, the Chief's bulldog was not lying in front of it today, making him wonder if this was actually his boss's home, or perhaps a flat provided by his job. He began to scan the bookshelves. The subject of angling dominated, suggesting he was right, and his mind soon drifted back to Wychbury Hill. This possible connection between Price and the one link to Clara who would be interested and rich enough to afford a copy of *The High German Black Book* had sparked fresh hope that he might yet pick up the loose ends of his previous case, a situation that never stopped gnawing at him.

Spooner had taken out subscriptions to all of the Birmingham papers, which he scoured daily for stories that might indicate Houlston had at last caught up with Anna and her Dutchman, so far, to no avail. He revisited his talent scout persona in the music halls and pubs of Manchester, attending any bill that looked like it might feature either or both of them. But, while he had seen a lot of good acts to tip Norrie about, he had not caught so much as a whiff of a fairy tune nor a high-wire act.

Neither had Anna contacted the Paramount office in search of her songbook, which remained Spooner's sole consolation, the one link he felt sure would bring her back – if she was still alive, of course. He felt in his pocket, touching the bill for The Two Magicians, making sure it was still there and not just a dream masquerading as memory.

The Chief put down the phone and stood up.

"I'm afraid I'm going to have to leave you," he said. "Do, please, make yourself at home here and help yourself to anything you want. I'll leave the keys on the desk, just post them back through the letterbox when you leave."

"OK, Chief," said Spooner. "Is it anything I can ask you about?"

The Chief began gathering up his belongings. "I'm sure you'll hear all about it if you turn the wireless on later – the Japanese have just bombed America into the war."

17

WHAT A LITTLE MOONLIGHT CAN DO

Friday, 19–Saturday, 20 December 1941

"That cheesecloth," said Harry Price, "was eight feet long and thirty inches wide and it reeked of ripe Gorgonzola. Have you ever smelled such a thing, Mr Spooner?"

Two weeks and a flurry of correspondence later, Spooner had at last entered the lair of the Ghost Hunter. Though the man who greeted Spooner at the door of 13d Roland Gardens was not quite as he had imagined. Price looked older, stouter than he had in the photographs that accompanied his book of adventures in the Harz Mountains the previous decade; and the onset of angina meant that he now walked with the aid of a cane.

He still dressed like a film director's idea of how a Ghost Hunter should – in a thick grey worsted suit, double-fronted watch chain and starched collar, which perfectly offset the craggy contours of his face, receding hairline and black eyebrows that frowned across the bridge of his nose like two angry caterpillars. A pair of saucer-shaped eyes the colour of his suit stared from underneath in an only slightly less startling manner.

Spooner had chosen his words carefully in his letter of introduction, hinting, as he had done with Lexy, that he was not following his editor's line on Helen Duncan, but that a recent spate of complaining letters compelled him to begin making his own enquiries about the medium. He added that he was impressed by the methods Price had employed to ascertain whether the mediums he had tested in his laboratory were fraudulent or not. There were a couple of them whom Price believed to have been genuine: a young nurse he had met on a train in the 1920s known as Stella C; and the Irishwoman Eileen Garrett, whom he had engaged to attempt to make contact with Sir Arthur Conan Doyle upon his death in 1930. Garrett had instead brought through the pilot of an airship that had crashed in France two days before, describing the terrain and descent of that final flight in precise detail, when Price checked it with the RAF.

In contrast, his experiences with Helen Duncan still filled him with an icy rage.

Upon his arrival, Spooner was shown to the laboratory and given an account of the photographic equipment developed for the sittings with mediums and a run-through of each technique deployed with Helen. Then he was taken to the séance room, with its curtained-off cabinet, and matching blood-red velvet sofa and armchair, where Helen had been pictured, bound and blindfolded, releasing her ectoplasmic emissions. Panelled with bookshelves, it would have made the perfect stage set for a tale of the supernatural. There he had been shown a sample of the material Price had found on Helen – an inch square of it, preserved under glass, which made it impossible to assess any lingering aromas.

In the study where they retired to conduct the interview,

photographs from the Duncan sittings joined those of other charlatans unmasked by Price. These were arranged over the fireplace and, at the centre of them all, a portrait of the legendary magician and debunker of psychics Harry Houdini frowned accusingly down.

Under the forbidding double gaze of these two men, Spooner had to admit to Price that he had never come across a ripe Gorgonzola himself. "But," he said, "some of these reports about Mrs Duncan have mentioned a curious odour at her sittings."

Price allowed himself a smile. "What do you think that could have been?" he asked.

"Gastric acid?" Spooner suggested. He knew from the *NLPR Bulletin* that Price had conducted four sittings with Helen, in which he had whittled down the possibilities of where she could have concealed lengths of cheesecloth about her person. Every orifice having been medically explored – and more rigorously than the desultory examination he had witnessed Councillor Roberts performing on Violet Adams back in Portsmouth – Price had come to the conclusion that Helen stored her ectoplasm in her stomach and regurgitated it when called upon to produce phenomena.

"Not a common trick, but not unheard of," he opined. "A talent more likely to be deployed in the freak shows of America than the parlours of Kensington or Hampstead. That's what I think makes it so hard for her supporters to – swallow."

Price leaned back in his chair, assessing Spooner. This young man was a familiar sort of presence to those who routinely sought him out at the Ghost Club: an ardent pursuer of esoteric knowledge, with one brogue-shod foot entrenched in the study of the arcane and the other striding determinedly towards new worlds. But he wasn't the usual type to have come from the spiritualist press. He was much more attentive to the detail of Price's experiments, jotting it all down in his notebook and asking for clarification on anything he didn't grasp. Much less inclined to argue than the old man who employed him. Price was more than aware of the regard in which Ernest Oaten held him.

The *Two Worlds* editor had been present in the Edinburgh courtroom where Helen had been successfully prosecuted for fraud in 1933, and afterwards in print had described Price's pivotal appearance for the prosecution as "sinister". Vitriolic correspondence had flowed between the pair over the years which left him in no doubt that Oaten would not have sanctioned this interview. He flicked his glance from his guest to Houdini on the wall and back again.

"That was my contention," he said, "but as you know, Mrs Duncan refused to be x-rayed. Instead, she had a fit of hysterics, punched her husband in the face and ran out into the street, still wearing that outfit you see her pictured in up there," he nodded towards a framed depiction of the medium in her black pyjamas, "screaming blue murder. Mrs Duncan is not a temperate woman, Mr Spooner. Can you imagine the scene she caused? It wasn't long before the police arrived. Thankfully, they believed me rather than the mob that had begun forming on my doorstep. And," he tapped his finger on the table, "lest anyone forget, the Duncans had the temerity to charge the NLPR fifty pounds, payable in cash up front, for the privilege of working with her."

Spooner shook his head. "Each time?" He whistled, "that's expensive."

Price nodded. "That's the hazard of not being recognised

as a legitimate scientist, you see. Everything you see here was built from hard toil and dedication. Unfortunately, I have yet to find a magic spell that achieves the same effect without the effort."

Spooner put down his pen. "It's quite a responsibility you have, Mr Price, keeping all of this going."

Price's eyebrows twitched. "It's a vocation," he said, his expression grave. "One I don't imagine myself ever retiring from. Whatever it might take out of me."

"Of course not," said Spooner, "how could you ever let a subject like this go?"

Price's gaze became more intense. "Mr Spooner, do I detect some ulterior motive to your visit?" Spooner's stomach jolted at the man's perception. He tried to hide it with a bashful smile.

"You're not about to start offering me your services, are you?" Price went on. "I can see what a keen student you are, and how you must have impressed your editor, despite his own judgements about Mrs Duncan."

"No, no," Spooner shook his head, feeling his cheeks colour. It was from relief, but to Price, it made him look more innocent. "I wouldn't dare to presume any such thing. It's just that…" Deciding now was the time, he reached inside his jacket for his father's card, "as a collector yourself, you might have heard of my father."

Spooner's Rare and Antiquarian Book Shop, Price read, *84 Belmont Street, Aberdeen.*

"When I told him you'd granted me an interview, he got a wee bit excited. He'd heard rumours that you were thinking of selling some of your collection. Of course, I'm sure rumours are probably all they are, so I hope I'll no' offend you passing on a message. He wanted me to let you know that, if it's true, he would be very interested in talking to you."

Price turned the card over in his fingers. "Ah," he said, "now it becomes clear." He looked back up at the picture of Houdini, where his gaze remained. "Does he mean the entire collection, or any specific folios?"

Spooner couldn't judge whether Price was about to kick him out or show him treasure.

"Well," he said, "he's interested in anything that you would have here. A lot of his business is in rare esoteric works and he's the only bookseller in the region who deals in such things, so he's a long list of collectors always after the unobtainable."

Price's eyes returned to Spooner's and he nodded, lacing his fingers together. "I see," he said. "And you have learned much from your father's professional interests yourself."

"Aye," Spooner gauged that remark meant he was safe, so pressed on. "Though, there's one edition he's had more enquiries about than any other – *The High German Black Book*."

"Now that *is* interesting," said Price, his eyes becoming a shade greyer. "Well, Mr Spooner, thank you for bringing it to my attention and let your father know I will give it due consideration. But for now, I'm afraid, the time I have put by to talk to you has just about run out. Will you allow me to see you to the door?"

"Of course," Spooner hurriedly gathered his belongings. "It was good of you to see me."

"This way," Price showed him back through the séance room, where he stopped before one of the bookshelves. "I thought I caught you staring at these earlier. Now I understand." He smiled and slipped a volume off the shelf. "Here.

Why don't you give this a try? It might look simple, but it's where I began my work. You'll never be able to catch a fraud until you learn all of their little tricks."

He passed Spooner a dog-eared copy of a children's book, *Magic for Beginners*.

"Gosh," said Spooner, turning it over in his hands, still unsure if he was being mocked or encouraged. Lexy's words about amateur magic echoed in his mind. "Thanks, Mr Price."

Price smiled fully, showing pointed teeth.

At the doorstep, the Ghost Hunter reached over to Spooner's top pocket. With a magician's flourish, he extracted the bookshop's card Spooner had given him earlier, turning it round to show it to his departing guest. "I think I'll take this after all," he said. "And you, keep up your studies. Next time I see you, I'll expect you to be able to do the same to me."

Spooner had again been offered the flat in Dolphin Square, although his boss met him there only briefly to hear his report before he was wanted elsewhere. Spooner thought that Price's swift, dismissive reaction to his enquiry about *The High German Black Book* indicated that their theories about De Vere could be right. He assessed that he had managed to convince Price he was angling for a job within the NLPR and that the passing on of his book on stage magic had been a challenge: Spooner's homework, to be tested on the next time they met. The fact that the old man had kept the bookshop's card indicated that Spooner would be hearing from the Ghost Hunter again.

The Chief was pleased; all of this was what he wanted to hear. After firing off a volley of further questions about the Ghost Club, he left Spooner with a bottle of malt whisky he declared as a Christmas present, and one further seasonal offering. "Before you leave tomorrow, nip in and see Norrie. He's got something for you too."

While Spooner settled down for the night with his new book and festive lubrication, across the blacked-out city in Archer Street, Hannen Swaffer was leaving a club called the *Entre Nous* in good humour. He had managed to track down DCI Ted Greenaway, recently transferred to the Murder Squad. Though unable to furnish Swaffer with more details than that they had once worked in the same department, he had confirmed that there had been a detective called Ross Spooner at Scotland Yard and furthermore, he was one of those transferred to work for MI5 in Wormwood Scrubs in 1939.

Swaffer knew of only one man within that organisation who did not hold ordinary Met detectives in such lowly esteem as the rest of his colleagues, on the basis that they all, like him, ran their own networks of snouts. Funnily enough, it was the same person he had been angling for information about when he interviewed Greenaway about the raid on Dover Street. He was given to believe that the Chief of Counter-Subversion was a man of many unusual tastes.

Greenaway claimed to know nothing about that either, not that Swaffer had expected him to say any different. But he was exhilarated with his discovery. Especially as his next destination was to the Christian Spiritualist Greater World Association in Holland Park, where he was due to deliver a lecture. It seemed an auspicious day.

As his taxi pulled up, Swaffer put the final touches to his plan. He was going to ask Miss Moyes to invite Helen Duncan back – and see if Spooner didn't turn up to see her. That way, he might find out if the detective and the journalist were, in fact, the same person.

The Paramount Agency was situated at the top of a narrow staircase, above a restaurant in Dean Street. In daylight hours, its grimy, diamond-paned windows looked down on the Soho street below, where trade in food, drink and other good times went on, oblivious to wartime restrictions. It was only a few doors down from the York Minster, known as the French pub, or merely Berlemont's, after its owner Gaston, who had brought the exiled French community together with a louche bunch of writers, actors, artists and agents to jostle for attention at his bar. Norrie liked to spread his business between the two locations according to licensing hours.

Before visiting his former mentor, Spooner stopped off at Fox in St James to buy one of Norrie's favourite cigars. There was an excitement in the London air about the imminent arrival of American forces, though the news hadn't come without a certain measure of umbrage at them for taking so long about it.

"Do them good to find out what's really going on," he heard more than one voice on the street opine, "'stead of pretending like it's none of their business."

The talk in the York Minster, where Norrie was polishing off bread and cheese with a glass of red wine, was more concerned with the runners at White City dog track that evening. But that changed when Spooner appeared. Dusting crumbs from his fingers and slipping a note into his bookmaker's top pocket, Norrie steered them back to his office.

"About time you turned up, my boy. I've got something to show you," he promised, leading the way up the creaking, ill-lit stairs, which smelled headily of the onions frying in the restaurant below. He opened the door at the top, ushering Spooner inside.

"Take a seat," said Norrie. "Any seat." Spooner tried to locate one, under the piles of paperwork and publicity stills that rested on every surface.

"Me and Bertie got to talking," Norrie explained as he unlocked a filing cabinet, "about that Clara of yours and some of the German acts we used to know before the war. We had good relations in them days, if you can Adam and Eve it. A lot of them were Jewish, like we are. Obviously not her, but all the same, I wondered if she might have found her way over here with one of the circus troupes or big orchestras. Now then…" He lifted a cardboard tube out of the top drawer, from which he carefully extracted a large sheet of rolled-up paper. "At the death, it wasn't her we found. But look who we did turn up…"

Norrie unfurled it across the desk – a 1936 poster advertising *The Talk of Berlin: Goldschmidt Brothers Circus*, appearing at the Holborn Empire. "Now look at this," he dropped a paperweight over the top left-hand corner of the bill. "*Nils Anders,*" he read aloud, "*the mad-cap whirlwind of the mid-air.* There's even a picture of him."

It was a beautiful, full-colour artwork, featuring a top-hatted ringmaster, lions and tigers on each side, a trapeze artist flying by one ear and the tightrope walker prancing across the trajectory of the other. Spooner honed in on the latter, took in blond, marcel-waved hair and blue eyes fringed by long lashes, a red grin and rouged cheeks. Anders was dressed as a sailor, dancing the hornpipe on his tightrope. There was something strangely familiar about him.

"So, at least you know roughly what your flying Dutchman looks like, if he ever shows up again." Norrie scratched behind his ear. "That's a funny thing with them acts. I've known a fair few of them to drag up as women. On and off the wire."

"That's quite some talent to have," said Spooner, realising what Norrie's words could mean as he said it. "Especially if you wanted to disappear without trace."

"What, tightrope-walking?" said Norrie. "I s'pose…"

"No, passing yourself off as a woman when you're being sought as a man," said Spooner, mental images slotting into place. "Norrie, you're a genius." He delved inside his briefcase to retrieve the first of his offerings.

"Well, I brought you up all right, didn't I?" Norrie tucked the cigar into his top pocket.

"Now look at this," Spooner fetched the handbill he had found in Portsmouth. He placed the inky image of the blonde woman next to the full-colour drawing of Anders. "I think there's a resemblance," he said. "What d'you make of it? Ever heard them?"

"No," said Norrie, squinting at one image, then the other. "But I see why you arsk. Let me look into it for you. D'you want to take this with you?"

"Won't Bertie mind?" asked Spooner.

"He knows you'll look after it," said Norrie. "You can bring it back to him next time you're in Brum. Maybe he can help you track down this pair, eh? Seeing as there seems to be a local connection…"

18

BECAUSE OF ONCE
UPON A TIME

Saturday, 20 December 1941

Morning was about to break as the Chief entered Ashburn
Gardens, though a blanket of fog muffled its arrival, along
with the tops of the giant plane trees he passed as he strode
down the middle of the South Kensington garden square. The
only sound besides the clack of his feet as he climbed up the
black-and-white tiled steps to a white, mid-terrace house was
the twittering of birds. Relishing the conspiracy of nature's
cover, he put his index finger to the doorbell of the garden
flat.

He didn't get an answer immediately and had to press the
device again at two more five-minute intervals until he finally
heard the sound of footsteps approaching. He spent the time
identifying the birdsong he could hear, while smiling at the
Judas hatch in the door from where he knew the occupant
would take their first look at him.

When that portal eventually swung open it was to reveal
the scowling visage of a tall, ramrod-thin woman, wearing
a padded peach silk dressing gown, feather trimmed, high-
heeled slippers and a face all but obscured by cold cream.

Only two blue eyes and a pinched pair of lips stared accusingly at him through this protective outer layer, blonde hair swept up by a silk scarf tied into a turban.

"Lady Wynter, how delightful to see you. Did you know you have at least seven different types of garden birds living in that square out there?"

"What is the meaning of this?" the woman demanded.

The Chief gave her his most avuncular smile. "Unfinished business. Mind if I come in?"

"I certainly do," she snapped, but took a step backwards all the same. "Have you a search warrant this time?"

"Why ever should I need one of those?" asked the Chief. "I only want to have a friendly chat, about a subject dear to your heart. I'm sure we needn't disturb the admiral with it."

"You've disturbed us enough already, ringing the bell at this hour," she retorted, the skin beneath the cream turning a shade of puce. "But," gathering the neckline of her gown together in one hand, she opened the door a degree further, eyes darting along the street for any watching neighbours, "you had better come in."

The Chief closed the door behind them and followed her down the thickly carpeted hall, through the fire door and down the stairs to her spacious garden flat. Though he had been here before, he trod carefully, for Lady Mirabelle Wynter, the wife of a retired British admiral and a former suffragette turned fascist, was one of the most slippery characters he had encountered in his long and strange career.

By rights, she should have been interned by now, along with the rest of her friends that he had scooped up in the May of 1940: Oswald Mosley of the British Union of Fascists, Captain Archibald Ramsay of the Right Club and the fashion designer Olga Wolkov, whose parents ran the Russian Tea Rooms just around the corner on Roland Gardens. It was Wolkov who had been the focus of that operation and was duly convicted for passing on sensitive messages between Churchill and Roosevelt stolen from the US Embassy by her American lover, Taylor Preston, himself now a resident of HMP Camp Hill on the Isle of Wight. But, despite what the Director of Public Prosecutions had considered watertight evidence against her, Mirabelle had been acquitted of assisting her Nazi needlesmith when it came to her turn in the dock.

It hadn't helped that the Americans, on the directions of their ambassador, had not allowed the Chief to show his evidence, a Top Secret message between the Prime Minister and the President copied out in Lady Wynter's hand, to the jury. But, despite the paucity of her testimony, it seemed they had found it impossible to believe that a titled, educated woman – a former doctor and an admiral's wife, to boot – was capable of such treachery. The Chief knew it was the admiral himself who had introduced her to the Wolkovs and that the pair of them shared views more common to the ruling elite – that the working class were subhumans deserving of no form of advancement and that Britain could only be great again after it had been scoured of Jews – than to the representatives of the lesser orders who had weighed up her case in court. It was to his bitter regret that they had believed her lies.

What he hadn't known then was that Lady Wynter had another passion: for the supernatural. Going back to the watchers he had sent to shadow her and Wolkov before their arrests, he learned that Mirabelle boasted of psychic talents, claiming to have once seen the shades of duelling knights on the lawn of the ancient Hampshire pile owned by her husband's family. The Chief had not infiltrated the Ghost Club before and, with Spooner's own enquiries ongoing, didn't want its president to suspect he was coming under any scrutiny from spooks of a different nature from those that he studied. But one of his friends, a writer of thrillers who was given to throwing a good party, had been a member for years.

The Chief asked if he wouldn't mind inviting over a few of his Ghost Club friends for a soirée one evening, so that he could be introduced to them as a fellow writer engaged in researching a biography of their most illustrious former member, Charles Dickens. He hit gold with the Club's secretary, Mrs Pamela Joyce. Pam, as she soon asked him to call her, was a Dickens devotee and most keen on the idea that the Chief might rekindle knowledge of his interest in the Club.

It became evident from their conversation that, while Harry Price was the flamboyant figurehead, it was Pam who was the keeper of the Ghost Club crypt, taking care of most of the arrangements, correspondence and all of the records, from its beginnings at Trinity College Cambridge to its closure in 1936 and subsequent revival eighteen months later – both of which had been instigated by Price. In the time of Dickens and up until the First War, the Club's members had actively investigated supernatural phenomena. But these days, it was more of a supper club, meeting to hear talks given by psychic researchers – another ring to the Price circus that attracted curious socialites like the Chief's writer friend, who could be relied on to pay their subs.

The Chief offered to take Pam for lunch at Rules in return for a look at the hallowed archives. She happily agreed. Not only that, she was decorous enough to leave him in solitude to make his search – which was when he found an entry in the visitors book for 1940. At a lantern-slide talk "Behind the Scenes with the Mediums" given by Mr William Marmolt at the Hall of India Overseas House on 7 June, Lady Mirabelle Wynter (Member) had attended with two male guests – neither of whom had been her husband.

Though the Chief was well aware that she would do her utmost to deceive him about her relationships with these men, he was also certain that she would not want to risk another day in court with him. Which was why he had come early and without warning, employing the psychology of the regime on the continent that she was so keen on. Mirabelle was a drinker; she would not be at her best at 6am.

Dropping curses under her breath, she ushered him into her lounge and bade him sit on an uncomfortable looking metal chair. She perched herself opposite on a chaise longue.

"Well," she said, eyes flashing. "What is it this time?"

"A few items of interest have cropped up," said the Chief. "Could you tell me how you came to be friendly with Harry Price?"

Mirabelle plucked a tissue from a dispenser on the coffee table between them and began to slowly wipe the cream from her face. It was a good distraction technique, he thought, enabling her to obscure her features while she took the time to form a reply.

"Harry Price?" she repeated. "From the Ghost Club?"

"That's right. You're a member, aren't you?"

She shrugged. "He works around the corner from here," she said, "I couldn't help but notice. He used to be in the papers the whole time, investigating poltergeists at Borley Rectory." She crumpled the tissue, dropping it into the waste paper basket and reaching for another. "I'm interested in such things."

"You had many things in common with him, then?" the Chief enquired. "I gather he's rather fond of Germany too. Has a lot of friends over there, to the point he was even in negotiations to move his operations to Bonn University, just before the war."

"He's a very cultured man, as well as being highly intelligent. Of course he would converse with his academic counterparts around the world, their work is ground-breaking – or it was, before all this nonsense," she curled her upper lip into a sneer, "intervened."

"What a great pity for him," said the Chief. "I'm told such a deal would have given him the ongoing financial assistance he's so sorely lacking at the moment. Tell me, do you have much of an occult library yourself?"

Her sneer turned into a pout. "I have signed first editions of all Harry's books, naturally."

"But you're not a serious collector? I mean, as much as you are interested, you wouldn't go as far as some of the more arcane works that he has in his own collection? Spellbooks," he paused to smile, "and suchlike?"

The blue eyes narrowed and she dropped the second tissue into the waste paper basket, staring at him down the planes of cheekbones that needed no real adornment. "You're not seriously suggesting that I'm a witch, are you?"

"Well, you do continue to surprise me," the Chief admitted. "Had I known about your involvement in the Ghost Club the last time we met, then I might have learned about your relationship with our absent friend—" he paused, studying her face as intently as he had been listening to the wildlife, "De Vere."

For just a second, a tiny muscle twitched underneath her

left eye. Then she waved her hand dismissively. "De Vere?" she said. "I don't know who you mean."

"Then your memory must be very poor," said the Chief. "Can't it even reach as far back as the Ghost Club's June gathering in 1940? Mr Price's secretary Mrs Joyce signed you in, and she distinctly remembered seeing you, Lady Wynter, because you were in such dashing company that night – both De Vere and that handsome friend of his from the RAF, what was his name?" The Chief leaned forward. "Ralph Nicholson. You knew De Vere from the Right Club, of course," he said. "But I wonder if you knew Flight Lieutenant Nicholson as well?"

With a glare, Mirabelle reached for the cigarette box. Her hand wobbled as she lit herself up. The Chief wondered if it was delirium tremens or if he'd managed to get to her.

"The man you were introduced to as Ralph Nicholson was an RAF Intelligence officer, whose mission was to monitor De Vere on suspicion that he was assisting the enemy. I've checked the reports he made to his CO and he provides a detailed account of the evening that he spent in your company. It wasn't just Mr Marmolt's anecdotes about Conan Doyle that he found fascinating. It was the mentions you made of your mutual acquaintances – Mosley, Captain Ramsay and that dear friend of yours and your husband's, the former Ambassador Von Ribbentrop. Though, what De Vere was most interested in talking about that evening was Harry Price's book collection. There was one manuscript in particular for which he was prepared to pay an extortionate sum – and you made an introduction for him."

Mirabelle exhaled a line of smoke from between her pursed lips. She broke eye contact, glaring out of the French doors to the garden beyond. "I somehow don't recall any of this," she said, outright denial continuing to be her favoured method of defence. She tried to keep her tone low and calm, but the pitch of her voice was beginning to rise, as it had done under questioning in court.

"You are a terrible liar, my dear," the Chief pointed out.

That brought her gaze back to him in an instant. "Don't you 'dear' me!" she snapped.

The corners of his mouth turned in grim parody of a smile. "I have the testimony of a senior RAF officer to take to court with me this time, and no helpful Ambassador Kennedy to direct that it should be withdrawn as evidence. They will be much stronger charges this time, Lady Wynter: Accessory to Murder and Treason, the latter, of course, being a capital offence…"

This time, real fear bloomed in her irises and the twitching beneath was more of a spasm. "What are you talking about?" she said, her voice louder, the pitch higher. "How dare you imply…"

"Ralph Nicholson is dead," the Chief cut her off. "And you supplied his killer with the weapon. *The High German Black Book* was what De Vere was after, wasn't it? And you brokered the deal with Price for him that night at the Ghost Club. Did you know at the time what he wanted to use it for?"

"Why don't you ask him?" her voice was shrill now. "Why are you hounding me?"

"You know as well as I do," said the Chief, "that De Vere is no longer in England." His eyes travelled across the room to the radiogram beside the cocktail cabinet. "I expect you listen into his nightly broadcasts from Berlin like the rest of the country – only unlike the neighbours, you are aware of who Lord Lucifer really is. And how he managed to book his passage, bringing gifts of the highest value to Himmler

– Price's book and the scalp of one of our top agents. It's not Borley Rectory the Ghost Hunter needs to investigate," he added. "There are more skeletons in your own closet."

"I say!" Behind them, the lounge door banged open and the admiral stood there in his dressing gown and slippers, eyes flashing wildly around the room, the remaining strands of his grey, frizzled hair standing on end like exclamation marks. "What's going on here?"

The admiral was a drinker too, but twenty years older than his wife, he was less able to deal with its ravages. Mirabelle sprang to her feet. "It's all right, dear," she said. "Go back to bed, I won't be much longer."

But his bleary eyes had focussed on her unwelcome guest. "You, sir!" he bellowed. "What are you doing in my house?"

The Chief got to his feet. "I'm giving your wife advance warning that I mean to see her in court again," he said, "and this time the evidence will be irrefutable. I'll see myself out, Lady Wynter, it's a shame all this nonsense has left you without the staff."

As he walked towards the door, this final allusion to her innate snobbery hit its target more surely than any threat of imminent prosecution.

"Simon left last Christmas, it's true!" she screamed at his departing back. "He went right from under your nose to where you'll never find him again! Never!"

The glass ashtray she threw after him hit the rim of the closing door and shattered. He waited behind it for a moment before he opened it again.

"If you want to avoid spending tonight behind bars," he said, "then you'd better tell me exactly what you know about it."

*

The Chief took a taxi to his next destination, stopping on the Embankment so he could walk the last stretch over Lambeth Bridge towards the stark modernist building on the other side. He entered a foyer lined with shops through a stone portico, taking the lift up to the top floor, which was listed as the premises of the Texas Oil Company Ltd. The doors opened onto an anteroom, through which his footsteps echoed as he walked towards the much quieter, linoleum-floored offices of MI5.

He had been summoned by his own CO, a lithe little man who might have been mistaken for a trader of second-hand cars on Warren Street with his receding hairline, pencil moustache and camouflaging cloud of cigarette smoke. He certainly shared a similar sense of humour with traders of that nature, perhaps equally as essential to his work.

Another man was already present in the wood-panelled office, one whose round glasses and charcoal grey suit signalled another profession that could hardly be mistaken.

"May I introduce Cecil Forbes-Dixon, assistant undersecretary to the Home Office, C-Division?" the CO said. Both men rose to their feet and everyone shook hands.

"The Duncan situation," the CO came straight to the point. "I'm not convinced that we should proceed. There are some in Fleet Street reading this situation as a potential martyrdom, and I must confess I share their concerns. It's my feeling that any move to prosecute now might serve to legitimise what she was supposed to have done in Portsmouth and give Hannen Swaffer and his friends a heroine to champion in court."

The Chief raised his eyebrows. "Yes," he said, "the thought had crossed my mind."

"Furthermore," the CO went on, "Cecil here has been

talking to the Assistant DPP about the likelihood of securing a prosecution under the Vagrancy Act, and neither of them is convinced this is the right way to proceed, either. Cecil?"

The civil servant nodded, opening a yellow folder he had brought with him. "Given the limited evidence that we have against her at this stage, we felt that a charge of Conspiracy to Defraud might have more chance of securing a conviction," he said, consulting his notes. "We've been looking at the transcripts sent from Edinburgh CID about her prosecution under a similar charge in 1933."

"She was fined £10 that time," the Chief recalled. "While I'm sure that would have hurt, it's not really the result Brigadier Firebrace is after."

"Exactly," said the CO. "We need to take a different approach. I would like Mrs Duncan's supporters to think that we have lost interest and leave her to get on with it in Portsmouth, where DI Fraser is amassing evidence about the Master Temple. I'm happy for him to go on, liaising with Cecil, until such time the DPP judges we have sufficient evidence to bring about an actual custodial sentence."

"Makes sense," agreed the Chief. "Do you want me to continue any lines of enquiry?"

"Not if they are likely to stir up trouble from across the river," said the CO, glancing over at the civil servant, who nodded his agreement. "Thank you, Cecil." The CO dismissed the civil servant, waiting until he had closed the door behind him before continuing.

"Will you do me one more favour?" he asked. "Break the news to Firebrace for me?"

"I'll take him to Rules," agreed the Chief. "That'll soften the blow."

"Good," said the CO. "Now, about this other matter. You have news on De Vere?"

"Not good. I've been speaking to our old friend Lady Wynter. It seems she was consorting with him at the Ghost Club, along with our dead agent Nicholas Ralphe, in order to help him get his hands on a book of German black magic sought by SS High Command. When I threatened to make her an accessory to murder and treason she got angry enough to admit she knew De Vere left last Christmas. Which ties up one matter, at least."

"Yes?" The CO raised his eyebrows.

"Well, according to both Ralphe and Kohl, that was the same time Belladonna was summoned back to Germany. The timeframe fits as well as the company he was keeping. I'll wager it was she who got him to Berlin."

19

IT'S BAD FOR ME

Friday, 20 February 1942

Now this, thought Spooner, gazing up at the white mansion, *is the sort of place you want to go to for a séance*. A brass plaque beside the gate informed him he had arrived at the Christian Spiritualist Greater World Association. Tonight, in more notable surrounds than the Master Temple on Copnor Road, he was finally going to see Helen Duncan in action.

It was his editor who had insisted that he should go, saying that this was the perfect opportunity for Spooner to see what *Two Worlds* would be fighting for, should any harm come Helen's way. He thought it might make a pleasant excursion, a reward for all the hard work Spooner had put into investigating events in Portsmouth, the eye-witness statements he had so diligently prepared, now deposited in Oaten's solicitor's safe.

Spooner didn't need to be asked twice. The past couple of months had moved frustratingly slowly and no one else had called him to London on other business.

Miss Moyes greeted him at the door, resplendent in her best grey moiré. By her side, Mr Hillyard had for once left his boiler suit on the peg and instead wore a black suit and bowtie. "Mr Spooner, so wonderful to meet you," she said, taking his hand. "Ernest has told me so much about you. Please, let Mr Hillyard take your coat."

Spooner did as he was asked, only just stopping himself from gawping when he realised that one of the caretaker's outstretched hands was made out of wood.

"Do come through." Miss Moyes led Spooner into a lounge that, in any lesser residence, would have seemed more akin to a ballroom. She steered him through the throng to a table of drinks and directed him to help himself to a glass thimble of sherry.

"Now, who can I find to take care of you?" She scanned the sea of heads until her eyes rested on the copper curls of one of her regular circle. She crooked her little finger in the woman's direction. Spooner followed her gaze. The woman – short in stature and probably in her early forties, immaculately dressed and coiffured and looking back at them with penetrating green eyes – was somehow familiar. As she made her way towards them, he realised why.

Back in 1938, his then DCI Ted Greenaway had organised a raid on a brothel on Dover Street. It had been a delicate operation – the premises were not any common or garden knocking shop, but a specialist "House of Correction", known to be frequented by MPs from both sides of the House, a couple of famous QCs and, rumour had it, some of their own superiors. Therefore Greenaway carried out his operation in the middle of the day, when the House was sitting, the Old Bailey was in session and he was least likely to embarrass any prominent members by sweeping them into his dragnet.

Instead, he had brought in the six-foot-tall Jamaican madam, still wearing her thigh-high leather boots, three other women who had been playing poker in the kitchen, and the rumoured brains behind the operation, the copper-haired, green-eyed maid. The same woman who was just about to offer him her hand.

"This is Mr Ross Spooner. He's a journalist from *Two Worlds* magazine," he heard his hostess inform her. They had called her the Duchess because she looked so regal. She still did. He, however, had altered considerably from the last time they would have laid eyes on each other from opposing sides of a cell door.

"A pleasure to meet you," Spooner said, taking her slim, cool palm into his own. Her eyes appraised him with interest. Was there any recognition there?

"A journalist?" she said. She spoke very carefully, finessing her vowels to cover any traces of the Cockney that lurked beneath. "How interesting. Have you been writing for the magazine for long?"

With a nod, Miss Moyes turned back towards the hallway to greet her remaining guests. Spooner played the innocent. "Tell you the truth, it's the first time I've been trusted to do a lead story," he said. "I hope I don't make a hash of it."

"And it's Mrs Duncan you'll be writing about?" she enquired. A smile danced across her lips. He remembered how she had infuriated DCI Greenaway. Got right under his skin.

"Aye, that's right," said Spooner. "She's quite a fearsome reputation with the ectoplasm, hasn't she?"

The Duchess raised her perfectly plucked eyebrows. "I don't doubt she's full of it," she said. Then she lowered her voice conspiratorially. "Do you know of her from Scotland, then? I'm afraid to say I'm not so familiar with her talents myself. I'm only really what you could call a dabbler, you see."

"Oh aye, yes, well," Spooner tried not to reveal his amusement at this last comment. His cheeks flushed with the effort. "Mrs Duncan's from Callander, she's a Highland lassie, whereas I'm from Aberdeen. We've no' actually met before, but I have been taking a keen interest in her career for a wee while now."

She looked disappointed. "Well, I'm sure your story will turn out fine," she said, her glance moving over his shoulder. "It's a shame Mr Swaffer isn't here," she added. "He would have been able to give you some tips on getting a scoop, no doubt."

Hannen Swaffer. Spooner flashed back to the white-haired old reporter sitting opposite Greenaway in his office when he was bringing in the files on the Dover Street women. Though the others had left long paper trails and many different aliases, this one had never so much as stepped into a magistrate's court. Had Swaffer clocked him on that occasion? Greenaway's Fleet Street pet was famous for his uncanny fact-collecting abilities. In fact, he was famous, full stop. He had better seem suitably awed.

"Mr Swaffer?" he jerked his hand upright, spilling drops of his sherry down the front of his waistcoat. "Hannen Swaffer, you mean? *The* Hannen Swaffer?"

"That's right." His companion's eyes continued to scan the room, settling somewhere over his left shoulder. "Though, we have got another of his protégées with us – that lady there," she pointed, "Daphne Maitland her name is. She does the in-house magazine for Miss Moyes. Puts the whole thing together and then prints it in the basement here. Would you like to meet her?"

Spooner saw a willowy woman in a dove-grey suit leaning

over a man in a bath chair who was holding up an ear trumpet for her to talk into. Although the room contained a lot of clearly well-off people, the simple lines of her outfit and the sleek cut of her hair made the shows of diamonds and furs of some of the older matrons look cheap by comparison. He wondered what had brought her here.

"Oh, aye," he said, shooting a quick glance back at his companion. Was she starting to slip into a procuress role here, he wondered? He cleared his throat. "I mean, yes, please."

"I'm not really a journalist," Daphne Maitland seemed embarrassed by the suggestion. "It's just a few skills I learned with a friend of mine, who sadly passed away recently."

"She was murdered," the Duchess put in bluntly, traces of the Cockney surfacing. "Swaff brought Daphne here to help her recover, didn't he? Where's he got to tonight, Daph? I thought he'd have been the first through the door."

Daphne did a good job of turning a wince into a smile. "I'm afraid he's not going to be able to attend," she said. "He's been called away on urgent newspaper business."

"Aw, that's a shame," the Duchess pouted.

"He's been very kind to me," Daphne looked at Spooner with sincere, oval-shaped eyes, the same colour as her suit and shaded very subtly with violet. "It was Mr Swaffer's suggestion that I might turn my grief towards helping others by coming to work for Miss Moyes. I'm sure you are aware of all the good she does with her night shelters for bombed-out women and children. So, what I mainly do is try and find donors to keep the work going, via this small news-sheet I design and print for her each week."

"She's good at that and all," her companion added, craning

her neck to see what else was going on in the room. Daphne ignored her.

"Swaff always contributes. It is such a shame you won't get to meet him, he was particularly keen on seeing Helen Duncan again. I gather she was here once before, last January, and it was all rather dramatic…"

Daphne was cut off by the tinkling of a bell. Miss Moyes was about to begin the séance.

"Would everybody please take their seats?" she asked. "Our special guest is ready."

"This way," the Duchess took Spooner's arm, propelling him to the front row. "You'll be wanting the best seat in the house to write your article, won't you?"

"Ach, er, thanks," was all Spooner managed to say before she plonked him right down in the middle, facing the cabinet – which was also a much grander affair than the one in the Master Temple, fashioned from mahogany and velvet curtains, like the one in Harry Price's lab. Daphne sat down on the other side of him. From behind, Mr Hillyard turned off all the lights, but for a single red bulb beside the cabinet.

Standing directly in front of them, Miss Moyes spoke. "I can't tell you how happy we are to welcome Mrs Duncan, and her husband Henry, back to our circle. Some of you were privileged enough to see her last time she was good enough to visit us, and will feel especially grateful that she has returned. For all of us, this is an honour."

She turned towards the medium, who had made her way from the back of the room, resting her hand on her husband's arm. Even in the dim light, Spooner could see that time had not been kind to Helen. The woman in the black satin pyjamas photographed by Harry Price was a slip of a girl compared to this black-clad behemoth, shuffling along in her long dress and Paisley shawl. It seemed that, as for her nemesis Harry Price, even the act of walking had become a troublesome thing for the medium. Her husband strode carefully by her side, his eyes darting from left to right, seeking out obstacles to their progress.

"Thank ye," she said, when she finally arrived at Miss Moyes' side. "I hope to bring ye happier tidings this time." Her voice wheezed with exertion.

"To assist Mrs Duncan in finding the right vibrations, if we could all now say *The Lord's Prayer* and then sing the *23rd Psalm*," Miss Moyes instructed. The assembled bowed their heads and began to intone the words to the prayer. Spooner kept his eyes on the cabinet. Henry Duncan tucked his wife's skirts underneath her and offered her one last drag on his cigarette before he closed the curtains around her.

From some distant corner of the darkened room, piano notes tinkled out. All around Spooner, voices tackled the singing with varying degrees of aptitude and he joined in, noting the tones of Daphne's alto and that the Duchess didn't sing along at all.

As the last notes faded away, Henry Duncan pulled back the curtains. His wife sat slumped, her head on her chest and her eyes closed, her arms lolling over those of the chair. She began groaning, softly at first and then louder as a pale substance began to form around her mouth. With the emergence of the ectoplasm came that smell that Spooner had heard so much about, which must have hit his non-singing neighbour's nostrils as swiftly as it did his own, as she coughed and wrinkled her nose.

"Is this how it normally goes?" he hissed in her ear.

"No," she whispered back, "I can't say I've ever seen it done quite this way before. Leastways, not here."

The medium's head was surrounded by a cloud of the filmy material, which bulged and trembled as it hovered, then cascaded down the front of her, causing startled exclamations around the room. Then, just as dramatically, it began to rise up, fashioning itself into what looked like human form. A headless human form.

"What a pleasure it is to see so many of you gathered here." The voice of the apparition was not the same as the voice Helen had used to introduce herself. If anything, Spooner thought, it sounded *more* female, the words pronounced in an icy English accent. He stared, trying to work out how this was being worked if it was, as Harry Price had said, merely a length of cheesecloth. And which of the Duncans was so good at throwing their voice? As if wanting to give him a better look too, the spectre drifted towards him.

"Some have travelled far to be here, seeking answers to their woes." He caught some inflection in the way the last word had been spoken – a "w" pronounced as a "v". He broke out in a cold sweat. *Of course she's speaking carefully,* a voice in his head told him, *she's trying to hide the fact that she's German.*

As he had the thought, something tapped him hard on the knee. He jumped and heard laughter – from the Duchess to his right and from the thing hovering in front of him. For one instant, he clearly saw the form of Clara there, her body swathed in flowing silks and her hair a mass of curls, eyes staring straight into him. "You are on the right path," she spoke directly to him. "And you will have your answer, soon enough."

A hacking cough barked out from the cabinet. At this, the

vision trembled and, like a picture turning to snow on a television screen, slipped away before Spooner's eyes. To his left, Miss Moyes got to her feet, hoping that history was not about to repeat itself with the medium choking again. She was just about to call for Mr Hillyard when the coughing ceased as abruptly as it had begun.

The ectoplasm rose up from the floor and once more began to undulate. Gradually, the pale outline of a child could be discerned and a soft crooning replaced the voice that had spoken to Spooner. It sounded like a little girl, singing the first verse of "Loch Lomond". Knowing this was Peggy, one of Helen's principal spirit guides, a relieved Miss Moyes sat back down.

But it was all Spooner could do to stay put in his chair. The spot where he had been touched still felt icy cold and the hairs all down his spine were standing as upright as those on his head, as if he had just suffered an electric shock.

When the spirit had spoken to him, he tried to reason, he must have mentally replaced its absent head with the face of Clara he knew so well from the photograph he kept, so that for one terrifying instant, it had seemed it was she who was talking to him. Like everybody else in the room, it was his subconscious desperation to hear from a soul departed that had brought him here and, therefore, his mind was playing tricks on him. That part of him which was susceptible to such things had taken a willing role in this game of illusion, on which it was so easy to project one's needs and desires...

But the spirit's mocking laughter still rang in his ears. His heart was beating so quickly he felt it might burst – nothing like this had ever happened to him at a séance before. He downed the remainder of his sherry, wishing it was something stronger. In an attempt to pull himself together, he bowed his head and closed his eyes.

When he opened them again, the ectoplasm had moved away, across to the other side of the room, and Helen was addressing the old man in the bath chair, saying that she had his sister with her, who had recently passed away. The old man was nodding, acknowledging the indistinct form before him as if he recognised it. Spooner took off his spectacles, breathed on them and gave them a polish with his handkerchief. Replacing them, he stared hard at the phantom. It looked altogether more like a man in a cheesecloth shroud. Could he have fallen asleep once the lights had dimmed and dreamt the entire Clara episode?

Beside him, the Duchess was wafting her fan. The motion distracted him and he looked over. Her eyes were bright and she was biting her bottom lip, trying to stop herself from laughing – perhaps it was only her outpouring of mirth that he had heard? She noticed him and put her fan on her lap, reaching down to fetch something from her handbag. "Here," she hissed, "have some of this."

It was a silver hipflask, full of brandy. He took a deep slug then passed it back gratefully, returning to his senses as if he really was waking up from a dream. Around him was laughter; Mr Hillyard had said something that had amused the rest of the room.

The séance was drawing towards its conclusion and, if it had started with drama, it ended in farce. The last spirits to emerge were departed pets – a parrot, a cat and a rabbit. They all appeared as oblong blobs and while the parrot managed to squawk a quick "Pretty Polly!" its companion spirits kept silent. There was, however, a worsening wheezing noise coming from within the cabinet. Then, in a flurry of swirling skirts and scuffling heels, Helen came lurching out of her confinement.

"Henry!" she gasped, crashing into the arms of her husband.

Within moments, the lights were on and the stricken medium was surrounded by people, first among them Miss Moyes and Mr Hillyard, who had been preparing themselves for such a situation all night. Dazed by the sudden brightening of the scene, Spooner got to his feet at the same time as his companions. Daphne put a restraining hand on his arm.

"There's been this trouble with Mrs Duncan before apparently," she whispered. "As I was about to tell you, the last time she was here she nearly choked to death."

A great babble of noise broke out around them as, blinking in the intrusion of the light, people began to move in their seats, standing up and asking what was happening. Miss Moyes' schoolmarm's tones cut through the hubbub.

"It's all right, everybody," she said. "Mrs Duncan is quite safe, she just exerted herself a little too much and needs a bit of air and some quiet to recover. If you could make your way to the back of the room where there are still plenty of drinks…"

Keeping a smile on her face, she turned back to where Helen was sprawled on a chair, sucking hard on a cigarette. It was nicotine, it seemed, that she really needed to aid her recovery.

"I reckon you could do with a stiff one," the Duchess took Spooner's arm, looking up at him with those shrewd, green eyes. "You saw something, didn't you?"

Spooner avoided the question and her gaze, taking out his fob watch from his waistcoat pocket and consulting that instead. It threw up yet another surprise. "Is that really the time?" he said. "Nine o'clock? It can't be."

"It is," said Daphne. "She's been at it for a good hour. No wonder she exhausted herself."

"But…" Spooner was about to say that was impossible, it had only seemed like ten minutes to him, but bit the words back. The two women both gave him a concerned look.

"Come on. Let's get that drink," said the Duchess firmly.

20

SERENADE IN THE NIGHT

Saturday, 21 February 1942

Spooner was dreaming of deep, dark woods that moved around him as he trod a path illuminated by a shaft of moonlight. Gnarled branches cast grotesque shapes, brushing at his face with bony twigs of fingers and extending their roots to trip him – as if they were no longer trees but a coven of witches, a wood of hags, squatting over a steep hillside on the borders of Worcestershire.

Before him stood a Doric temple, pinpoints of light flickering between the six columns of the portico. A soft breeze brought the smell of burning herbs to his nostrils and he stopped, hairs rising on the back of his neck. He became aware of every sound around him: the scurrying of midnight's creatures through the fallen leaves, the crack and thump of a pine cone dropping from a branch, the distant hoot of an owl. He knew he had to stay silent, otherwise whoever was in the temple would hear him and stop him from getting to the open hillside, to catch the Queen of the Witches gliding down from the sky, using the full moon and the obelisk as her guide.

Taking a deep breath, he put one foot forward – and felt something snap around his leg with an iron grip. A silent scream welled up in his throat as he looked down and saw it – not a mantrap set by the gamekeeper, but a hand reaching out of the brambles and the leaves, white in the moonlight, fingers clamped around his ankle…

He jerked upright, breaking through the surface of the dream and into a Paddington guesthouse bedroom, the scream still halfway up his throat. Heart hammering, Spooner fell back on the single bed, listening to the loud ticking of the clock by his right ear and looking at the edge of the frayed blackout, allowing the first milky light of the new day to steal into the room. Desperate to expunge the lingering tendrils of his nightmare, he sifted his memories of the night before.

When the lights had gone up, the former Duchess of Dover Street had led him over to the drinks tray and plied him with several more thimbles of sherry. Standing apart from the other guests, he listened as she and Daphne dissected the evening's events, his sense of dread growing with each new revelation. It seemed that, from the moment the spirit of Clara – or whatever mental aberration that had really been – had departed, he had blanked out every manifestation the women were discussing, only coming back into full consciousness for the final croak of Helen's spirit parrot.

The joke he could vaguely recall Mr Hillyard making was apparently a communication between him and his brother Geoffrey in spirit. Geoffrey, a Yorkshireman, opined that he didn't think much of the medium; she was too fat. Mr Hillyard said that proved it was his brother who was "always mithering".

"Good job he thought so," was the Duchess's opinion. "Didn't think much of the accent myself." She winked at

Spooner as she said it. He managed to smile, but there was worse to come.

"And what about poor Miriam?" said Daphne, nodding towards a woman in a dark blue suit who, surrounded by a group of concerned friends, was dabbing her eyes with a hanky. "Do you think it could be true? I mean, I know her boy was sent to Singapore and he was with the Eighteenth…"

"Well," said the Duchess, waving her fan in such a way that no one could have read her lips, "it's not likely to be good news, is it? Chances are he's either been captured or killed. Even if she's got it wrong, how long will it be before Miriam hears otherwise? That one," she shot a cynical glance towards the back of the room, "will be long gone."

"I never met Miriam's son, did you?" Daphne followed her friend's gaze. Staggering along together, with Miss Moyes at their side, the Duncans were beating a retreat to where the adjoining kitchen door would allow them to make an exit unnoticed by the rest of the room.

"No, can't say I have," her friend admitted. "Still, I'm willing to bet, being as he's London born and bred, he might have sounded slightly less Scottish than his spirit did."

A smile twitched on Daphne's lips, but she managed to suppress it. "Strange, isn't it," she said instead, "that Swaff was so keen on her? I can't quite see…"

"Here," the Duchess nudged her. "Don't put our friend off. I think Mr Spooner might have seen things differently to us."

Spooner raised his empty glass. "I think I might have had too much to drink," was all he could find to say. It certainly provoked amusement, allowing him to make his excuses and return to the room he had booked for the night without shattering the illusion he had been hoping to cast of himself as a bumbling eccentric. Nothing like the dour detective Hannen Swaffer might have thought he remembered, were they to drop his name in conversation with the journalist.

But, sleep-deprived and with a headache gnawing, he was no longer certain he had convinced anyone, least of all himself. He reached over to pick up the alarm clock, but his hand fell on a small square of card. On it was Daphne Maitland's telephone number.

"Have you ever been reunited with a loved one at a séance?" asked Spooner.

Daphne looked up from where she had been arranging sorts and slugs on her composing stick, down in the basement of 3 Lansdowne Road. It was a moment before she answered.

She had offered to give him a tour of her small print shop as he was leaving the night before, another memory that had evaded him until his hand landed on her card. He rang after breakfast, hoping that he hadn't done anything else he couldn't remember that might have since made her want to retract the offer.

"Oh, I am so glad you called," she had said, the warmth in her voice taking him by surprise. "I thought we might have put you off entirely last night." Without directly mentioning her copper-haired companion, she went on to assure him that, apart from the usual staff, volunteers and women in need, there would be no one to bother them today.

They met at ten o'clock outside Holland Park tube station. Spooner parked on a backstreet half an hour earlier and spent the time reading Hannen Swaffer's paper, the *Daily Herald*, soon finding out what had detained the journalist the night before. Swaffer had been sent to Brixton prison, from where a woman named Olive Bracewell, leader of the Campaign against Capital Punishment, was orchestrating an attempt to save the recently captured Blackout Ripper from the death penalty. Trainee RAF officer Gordon Cummins had attacked six women, murdering four, over the space of the previous week, in a nightmarish frenzy that had only just been brought to a halt by Spooner's former boss, DCI Greenaway, now head of the Murder Squad.

Despite the terrible things Cummins had done to his victims – strangling them with their underwear and carving them up with knives – Mrs Bracewell was moved to defend his life with a hired orchestra and as many people as she could pay in beer and chips to parade up and down outside the prison walls, according to Swaffer's copy.

Spooner shook his head as he took it in. It was the sort of thing that had made him volunteer for filing cabinet duty in the first place. Still, there was plenty there to keep Swaffer occupied for the present; Mrs Bracewell planned to continue her protest today.

Daphne appeared at the dot of ten, seemingly delighted to see him and to show him around her small set-up. She had an old platen jobbing press acquired by Miss Moyes the previous decade from her former employers at the *Telegraph* and kept in perfect order. They managed to skirt around the events of the night before while Daphne filled Spooner in on her work and how Mr Hillyard lost his arm in the Battle of the Somme. When there was a pause in the conversation he found himself asking her that question.

Daphne eyed him sadly. "Not yet," she said. "Though, to be perfectly honest, that was the reason I sought Swaff out in the first place. That friend of mine we talked about last night, she *was* murdered and by that awful man they have up at Brixton prison now. I'm sure you read about it in the papers this morning."

"Oh, God," said Spooner. "I'm so sorry. I never would have asked if I thought…"

"No, don't be. I'm sure it's much the same reason everyone finds themselves in a place like this, isn't it?" She smiled, her eyes becoming more luminous. "Wasn't it something similar that led you along this path in the first place?"

"Aye, of course. My mother died when I was just a bairn. I don't have one memory of her; all I know is from photographs and what the rest of the family have told me. Don't get me wrong, I had a great upbringing," he considered, "but I've always felt her absence. I started going to the table tappers as soon as I knew that they existed."

"And have you ever…?"

He shook his head. "Not from her, no," he said, seeing the hope that was still so evident in his new friend's face. "But that's not to say I haven't experienced some powerful things in these places."

"Like last night?" Daphne said. "I must admit, I was hoping that Mrs Duncan might bring a message through for me. Swaff was *so* adamant about how good she was."

"That's right," Spooner recalled, "you were telling me something happened the last time she was here. Did you say she nearly choked to death?"

Daphne nodded. "Swaff saved her life, he managed to dislodge something that had got stuck in her throat."

Spooner thought of Harry Price's cheesecloth. "What was it, do you know?"

"This spirit she had brought through," Daphne said, "a

woman who was out walking in the woods somewhere and got strangled. Swaff said Mrs Duncan must have gone into her trance exactly as it happened – she was feeling the same sensations as this poor woman."

Daphne raised her hand to her throat. Her friend had been killed in much the same way.

"Awful to think about it, isn't it? I had no idea it could be so dangerous. Luckily, Swaff knew what to do and she recovered all right. But I know it's troubled him ever since. He's yet to find a news report that matches the circumstances. We thought perhaps those woods she was in were so isolated she hasn't yet been found."

Her fingers continued to circle her neck. Spooner tried to quell his unease as he watched.

"Mrs Duncan did tell him her name. What was it? Claire? *Clair de Lune…*" She began to hum the melody as she tried to catch the evasive memory. Then she snapped her fingers.

"No, not Claire – Clara. That's it. She said her name was Clara."

Spooner was early for their meeting, but the Chief was already waiting on Hammersmith Bridge. Spooner could still recall the exhilaration he had felt the last time they had met on this spot, how proud he had been to be chosen to search for Clara. It was almost a year to the day, yet it seemed an aeon ago. Today the Chief looked as haunted as Spooner felt.

"How went the séance?" The Chief turned towards Spooner with a frown. Dorothy, the bulldog, scrabbled to her feet with a disgruntled whine.

"Not what I expected," Spooner admitted. He had decided that honesty had to be the only policy. The Chief could send him back to Blenheim if he thought he had outlived his purpose and, at that moment, he wondered if he wouldn't be glad of it.

"Shall we walk?"

Inside the avenue of trees along the Mortlake side of the Thames, Spooner told the Chief about Clara and Helen, the Duchess and Daphne, and Hannen Swaffer's part in the tale.

"I'm not sure he would have recognised me if he had been there last night," he concluded. "But I wouldn't underestimate the chances."

The Chief, who had made no comment all the time Spooner had been talking, came to a halt beside an old stump and tapped his pipe out on the side of it.

"Neither would I," he agreed. "Just as well this Blackout Ripper business has given him something else to think about." His eyes swept in a circle around them. It was a raw February afternoon from which the last dregs of light would soon begin to drain. The threat of snow lay so heavily on the air that no other walkers had been tempted to wander the path, only blackbirds rustling as they picked through the undergrowth of dried brambles for snails. "It would seem we have come to an impasse, Ross."

Spooner's gaze fell towards the river, the onward rush of the grey-green waters so indifferent to their cares. Dorothy's panting became the loudest noise as the Chief refilled his pipe and lit his tobacco. "As you know, I have my own chief to answer to," he said, "and rather frustratingly, in view of what you've just told me, he has decided to lay the hounds off Hellish Nell. He feels, quite understandably, that if we were to make a move now, it might legitimise what happened in

Portsmouth and turn her into a martyr for people like Swaffer and your editor. So he wants me to sit on my hands and do nothing more, for now."

"Ah," Spooner's gaze followed a piece of driftwood carried by the tide, powerless to control where the stronger forces that encircled it would whirl it to next. "So…"

"So I suggest you return to Manchester and give her the glowing report your editor wants. Base it on what those women told you about the soldier in Singapore and the care-taker's commendable brother – I'm sure you can embellish – and omit your personal experience entirely. Then put your head down and continue to be as helpful as you have always been without taking any assignments that might bring you into contact with that tricky old man from Fleet Street. With his heroine out of danger, his anxieties will fade and no doubt there'll be other matters to concern him before he thinks of you again. Besides, if you were to disappear now, then it might justify any suspicions he has."

Spooner looked back at his companion. The relief he felt on hearing these words brought all his convictions back into focus. How could he have considered walking away?

"I know it's frustrating," the Chief went on, "but such is the manner of the game we are embarked on. And, while we appear to have gone up one blind alley, another avenue has opened – and all down to you. You were right about the Ghost Hunter, Ross. Come on."

The Chief put a toe under Dorothy's hindquarters. While they had been talking, she had gradually slumped back into a sitting position. "There's a reason your father won't have heard from him since your meeting," he said, as they resumed their walk. "He no longer has that grimoire to sell. De Vere bought it from him in June 1940. I think he used it for the ritual they performed on Nicholas Ralphe."

Spooner's eyes widened. "How d'you find out?"

"I drew another lead," the Chief said, "independent of Price. It was Ralphe himself who left testimony of his visit to the Ghost Club, where the deal that sealed his fate was brokered by a woman who should, by rights, have already been in jail. Another one of my failures."

Spooner looked across sharply. "What do you mean?" he said.

"Not you, Ross," the Chief shook his head. "De Vere. There is something more about him I need to tell you, although it will do me no credit and it might change your mind about carrying on with this work. Before the war, De Vere was one of my agents."

This was enough to bring Spooner to a halt. "No," he said, feeling his stomach drop.

The Chief scowled, his own gaze now drawn towards the river. The tide was high, the river a ferment of angry grey. Dorothy pushed her nose against his leg. "I met him at a party, years ago," he said, reaching down to stroke her. "I found him charismatic and unusual, a high intellectual capacity driven by the impulse to rebel. Perhaps a more sober evaluation would be that of a psychopath. But when Hitler took power, I saw him as a perfect plant – so many in the Reich harbour a soft spot for the aristocracy, not least the former Ambassador, von Ribbentrop, with whom he was already acquainted. I imagined he would be able to put devastating information my way."

The Chief straightened up. "I lost contact with him in October 1940. Nicholas Ralphe had been shadowing him independently, both of them believing the other to be an enemy agent, but filed no further reports than the middle of December with his CO… and you know what happened to him then. So when Karl Kohl landed in the fens with his tales about Belladonna, I felt this could be the missing link… or should I say, the link to the missing."

"And you sent me to Birmingham to prove it?" Spooner's face reflected his shock.

"You were the only person with enough knowledge of their esoteric pursuits to work it all out," the Chief said, "and work it out you did. De Vere's passage to Germany was paid for by Price's grimoire and Ralphe's life. Belladonna got him there and, after what you witnessed last night, you may have reason to believe Ralphe had a good point when he warned you off any further entanglements with her and her kind."

The Chief's blue eyes bored into Spooner.

"Do you think she's come back for your soul too?"

PART THREE

SATAN TAKES A HOLIDAY

April 1943–April 1944

21

IT STARTED ALL OVER AGAIN

Sunday, 18 April 1943

It was such a lovely day for it to have to happen, that's what Terry Jenkins couldn't get over. A warm spring evening, the sunlight slanting through the trees onto swathes of bluebells, the air alive with birdsong and promise, as the four friends foraged their way through Hagley Woods, on the lookout for nests to raid and rabbits that might have been snared before the gamekeeper made his rounds at dusk.

They shouldn't have been on the De Vere estate in the first place, but that was all part of the adventure. Danny Shepherd was the oldest of the group of four boys, fourteen years old and wise to routes into the lands that fringed Wollescote, the village where they lived, on the outskirts of Stourbridge. It was he who had lured them from a neighbourly game of football on the rec to a poaching mission, saying that he had found a way in and promising them that untold delights lay beyond that perimeter.

Terry, although tall for his age, was, at twelve, the youngest of the group, happy to go along with Danny and the two older lads, Bob Hodder and Frank Osbourne. Terry loved being out, exploring tracks through the Clent Hills, though he had never before strayed onto land that he knew was private. Like the others, he had confidence that Danny knew what he was doing. And so it seemed that he did, confidently leading them from the village up the path that wound its way beside the fields and into the undergrowth, through a gap in the hedge easy enough to crawl through, and into the Arcadia beyond.

Danny showed them where he had found animal traps and snares on his previous reconnaissance, although it seemed the gamekeeper might already have made his rounds that day. His friend might not have been right about rabbit stew for dinner, but as far as Terry was concerned, it was bliss enough to be out in the sun and the wilds that day.

Until they came to the tree.

It was the tree that had him waking up screaming later that night, which brought his parents running into his room and provoked the tearful confession that led to the police being called. Sitting with his pa by the fire with a cup of strictly rationed cocoa in his hands, Terry could not stop shaking as he stumblingly related his story to the kindly looking Detective Inspector Woodhead, who kept reassuring him he would not be imprisoned for trespassing by passing his story on.

It was like something from a nightmare itself, that tree. A monster of an elm, so heavily coppiced that its myriad branches protruded in a spiral like some vast crown of thorns around a thickset bole smothered in ivy. His first sighting of it had been enough to make Terry take a few steps backwards. "What's that?" he asked.

"That's the scariest tree I've ever seen," Bob, who had also stopped in his tracks, seemed to agree with him.

But Danny had clearly seen something different in it.

"Look!" he proclaimed, pointing a finger to a hollow just visible in the trunk. "There's a nest up there!"

Quick as you like, he had ferreted his way up through the ivy, his light frame and deft sense of balance aiding what would have been, for the others, a more daunting task. But as he drew level with the flash of white he had perceived in the hollow, even Danny's confident smile inverted to a puzzled frown.

"What's that?" he unconsciously echoed the words of Terry down below.

The tree smelled dank and earthy as it held him in its verdant embrace. In contrast, the white bone gleamed in the rays of the setting sun, stark against the forest green of the ivy. He thought at first it could be an animal skull, a small collection of which he kept in his pa's potting shed. He reached out for it before his brain caught up with the notion that he had never seen anything this size before, not even a badger's head was that big, and that, with its two hollow eye sockets and protruding teeth, it looked just like…

"What you got there, our Dan?" Frank's shrill voice keened up from below. Terry and Bob exchanged glances, neither wanting to move any further forward.

Danny's fingers curled around the object and he pulled it clear of the ivy. As he did so, his stomach tilted. There was still hair and skin stuck to the side of what really *was* a human skull, and a little white maggot reared up from the tangled mass in a writhing dance of annoyance as Danny interrupted it from its labours.

"Ugh!" With an involuntary shriek, he dropped it, screwing his eyes shut and clinging to the tree as a tremor of nauseating fear passed through him, slicking his palms with cold sweat. The smell of death crept up to rest inside his nostrils.

Frank ran forward to where Danny's bounty had landed on the thick grass below him, then skidded to a halt. Cautiously, he knelt down beside it, prodding it tentatively with a stick as he gradually took in what it was he was seeing.

"Bloody 'ell!" was the summation of his findings. Terry and Bob edged towards him, holding their breath. Frank looked up at Danny. "It's real, isn't it?" he said.

Danny forced his eyes open. "Looks like it," he admitted.

"What's real?" Bob was brave enough to venture.

"It's a skull," Frank's voice, which was on the verge of breaking, veered up a few octaves. "A human skull. Still got some hair stuck to it and everything…"

"Shurrup, our Frank!" looking down at the three faces, eyes round and mouths in perfect O's, Danny pulled himself together. It was up to him to be leader in a crisis.

"But worra we gonna do with it?" Frank wanted to know. "It can't be right, finding it up a tree like that. Shouldn't we tell the police?"

"We can't do that!" Danny warned. "We're trespassing as it is. If the gamekeeper finds us he'll shoot us, or take us to the earl and have us skinned alive. No," he shook his head, "we're gonna put it back in the tree and then we're gonna get out of here as fast as we bloody well can."

Frank's jaw sagged. "Put it back?" he repeated.

"That's right." Danny checked his footholds. "You pass it back to me, our Frank, and I'll put it back where I found it. C'mon," he encouraged, "don't be a baby."

Frank cleared his throat. "Orlright," he said, colour spreading across his cheeks. He didn't want to touch the thing, and at first attempted to lift it up with the end of his stick.

"Don't!" Danny shouted. "You'll break it if you do that."

He could feel his heart hammering but he had to try to stay calm, push away the thought that the skull might just have belonged to the last kid to go birds' nesting without permission on Earl De Vere's estate. "Just pick it up and give it here."

Frank reached in his pockets for his handkerchief. It wouldn't be so bad, perhaps, if he didn't actually touch it…

With the cloth wrapped around his fingers, Frank lifted the skull, being careful not to take hold of the part that still had a hideous clump of matted hair attached to it. Terry and Bob merely watched, horror having rendered the pair of them mute. Bob looked away, into the trees, back to the path they had been following, trying to get his mind back to that earlier place. But Terry found himself unable to stop staring at the grotesque object as Danny lifted it from Frank's wobbling grip and put it back into the hollow of the tree.

It seemed to Terry afterwards that, as the exchange was made, all the birdsong stopped and the sun, so bright only moments before, dipped behind the hills, taking all its warmth with it. When Danny dropped back down from the elm, it was suddenly twilight, their way back through the woods darkening fast. The lads followed their leader without a word, their hearts in their throats, for every snapping twig, every scurrying of an animal or beating of birds' wings, was perhaps the sound of a vengeful gamekeeper creeping up on them with both barrels raised… Or worse still – the phantom that inhabited that terrible tree seeking out those who dared disturb its remains…

Once they were safely out of the woods and back onto the lane, Danny pulled them all into a huddle, looking at them through huge, serious eyes, pale-faced in the gloaming.

"We don't tell anyone, right?" he demanded. "This is our

secret and it's gotta stay that way, OK? Otherwise…" He made a cutting motion across his neck.

The other three nodded their assent.

"Good." Danny nodded. Then, with the fear of the devil inside them, all four ran full pelt back home.

With the help of the De Veres' gamekeeper, DI Woodhead found his way to the coppiced elm directly after he had left the Jenkins' residence. He stood guard beside it while as many officers as the local force could muster cordoned off the rest of the estate. While he kept his ominous watch, the weather took a turn from the long, mild spring they had been enjoying since March. A spiteful north-easterly wind blew up, bringing stinging flecks of rain. Standing in this gloom before a crime scene that could have come straight from the pens of the Brothers Grimm, DI Woodhead knew why his young witness was so terrified.

There was something about this place, with its little follies scattered around the wooded valley, that had always seemed forbidding to those who had grown up near it, as DI Woodhead himself had. He was not surprised that someone could have committed a murder in such surroundings. Nor that, if not for Terry Jenkins and his friends, the body might have remained there undiscovered, until the day the tree rotted and fell.

Spooner was pottering in his Manchester lodging room, making himself a cocoa on his one-ring stove. It had taken him a few moves from various digs around the city centre before he had finally settled into a place where the landlady didn't mind him paying for a private phone line to put into his room and, so long as he continued to cough up his rent punctually each Friday, left him pretty much to his own devices.

The room was at the top of the house and looked out over the canal, which, along with the attendant chimneys and cooling towers of the district, reminded him of Birmingham. Most of the space within it had been taken up with a gradually encroaching library of books on subjects he had been studying, and stacks of box files containing articles he had written and research he was undertaking, all colour-coded for easy reference. Apart from the bed and kitchenette – a sink with a cupboard underneath that served as a pantry and a rack over the draining board, placed next to the one-ring stove – it more closely resembled his former office in Wormwood Scrubs than a cosy bedsitter.

Filing had taken over his world again. In the *Two Worlds* office, this had made him very popular with Miss Josser, who returned the favour in tins of cake, eked from her ration. He, in turn, had learned everything there was to putting out a magazine, from an editor who had begun to look upon Spooner as if he were his own son. There were times, within the cocoon of the office and this little room, when it was easy to forget he wasn't just what they thought him to be.

As the Chief had suspected, his employer's worries about Helen Duncan had abated. Over the past eleven months, there had been no further sightings of men in blue suits in Copnor Road, nor similar visitations to Maurice Barbanell's office. The report Spooner filed on the Holland Park séance, a work that had called upon all the literary skills of fiction he didn't realise he possessed, seemed to have shored up his standing with his editor, as well as serving to allay any doubts that Barbanell may have whispered into Oaten's ear. It went down well with the readers, too – up to a point.

The national mood was altering. Despite the arrival of the Americans, the German surrender in Stalingrad and the headway made by British forces in North Africa, there still seemed no end in sight to the war and, the longer hostilities raged, so the comfort civilians had once derived from a visit to the spiritualists was ebbing. It wasn't just cynical Fleet Street and the shadowy figures of the Intelligence agencies pointing the finger of doubt any longer. Public opinion, according to the letters Spooner kept seeing, was turning against mediums seen to be taking advantage of the bereaved, including Helen and the Shadwells, who were virtually her sole patrons these days.

This catalogue of misgivings he duly copied and sent to the Chief, who had him follow up certain characters when they passed through the city, reporting on spiritualist gatherings the way he had spent the early part of the war at fascist meetings, to assess for infiltrators. Though the DPP might have advised his boss against its use, other magistrates had started to charge fraudulent mediums under the Vagrancy Act. There had been three successful prosecutions this year, in Cardiff, Birmingham and Great Yarmouth.

Other trails remained cold. Norrie had yet to trace The Two Magicians, and if the Chief had made any use of the information that Nils Anders had first landed in Britain as part of a German circus, he was keeping it to himself. Spooner still read the Birmingham papers and made the odd foray into pubs in search of elusive entertainment, but when he had nothing more substantial to work on, he spent his evenings studying his magic books.

He had been intending to continue when the telephone

started up at exactly the same time as the milk for his cocoa came to the boil. The jerk of his hand splashed enough of the boiling liquid to burn his thumb. Wincing, he cursed at the appliance – it never rang unless he'd made a prior arrangement for it to do so – then put both mug and pan down carefully before lifting the receiver.

"Sorry to disturb you," came a familiar voice. "But I've just had some very interesting news. How long do you think it would take you to drive to Worcestershire?"

Spooner forgot all about his thumb. "Oh my word," he said, "what's happened?"

"Some young boys out birds' nesting this afternoon have found human remains in Hagley Woods," said the Chief. "The local police have cordoned off the site until the pathologist can get to it in daylight, which I think gives us both the chance to join him as he gets there, if we leave now. Think you can manage that?"

"From here?" said Spooner. "It'll probably take about three or four hours." The black Ford Anglia was now parked in his landlady's otherwise empty garage. He hadn't used it much lately, so it still had close to a full tank of petrol, and there was an illicit jerry can in the boot. On the tail of that came a more troubling notion. What if DS Houlston was among the police at the scene? Surely he would be, the moment he caught wind of it?

Spooner ran a hand through his hair. There was an old pot of brilliantine, along with his grey suit, languishing at the back of the wardrobe. Maybe if he looked more like a real policeman, then Houlston wouldn't recognise him.

"You know this place better than I do," the Chief went on. "Is there a landmark where we can rendezvous?"

Spooner's mind had scarcely left the ideal place since he had. "Wychbury Hill," he said. "It's right on top of the estate, the highest point of the Clent Hills. And just so you can't miss it, even in the dark, it's got a bloody great obelisk on the top of it."

Spooner arrived just after five o'clock, pulled into the layby and stared through the windscreen up at the hill. An almost completely full moon had been his guide from Manchester, sailing huge and ghostly above the grey tendrils of the clouds. It shed its silvery light across the hills and their protective trees, back to their full foliage now. The air was damp with the chill of the darkest hour and he was loath to turn off the engine, knowing the warmth it generated would soon evaporate. He had worn as many layers as possible, brought a blanket and a Thermos of ersatz coffee, to help him stave off both the temperature and tiredness – although he had not felt any inklings of fatigue so far.

He had stopped by the office on the way, to put a letter through the door explaining to Oaten he'd had a summons to attend urgent family business in Scotland. That would be enough to buy him a few days' leave, if he followed it up with reassuring phone calls. He still couldn't quite believe he was here…

Like the moon above him, Clara's spectral form floated in his mind's eye.

Spooner reached into the rucksack he had placed on the passenger seat. It contained the Thermos of coffee, ginger cake baked by Miss Josser, a torch, a map of the Clent Hills and a book sent to him by his father, which he thought might help to pass the time while he waited for the Chief. It was a collection of stories written by a Victorian clergyman, called *The Ingoldsby Legends*. In it were directions for the making of a Hand of Glory. Written as a pastiche poem, they were considerably more humorous than other tomes he had consulted on the subject, not least that of Professor Margot Melvin.

The sound of a motor brought him out of his literary reverie about an hour later. Spooner looked up as the Chief's Bentley glided in beside him. The sky was now a pale grey, streaked with the first smudges of pink. He wound down his window. "Found it all right then?" he said.

The Chief nodded. "It's a good spot. I see you've made yourself at home."

Spooner put his book back in his rucksack and began unwinding himself from his blanket, folding it up and putting it on the back seat, while gathering everything he thought he would need for their day's work.

"You've changed," his boss noticed, as he emerged from the Anglia.

"Aye," Spooner touched his now solid hair cautiously. "It's in case we run into my old friend from Birmingham CID. Remember DS Houlston?" He glanced back at his motor. "D'you think it might be better if we took your car from here?"

"I was hoping you'd say that. I've had a good run but I wouldn't mind you navigating from here." The Chief glanced down at his wristwatch. "We should be on time. I've arranged to meet two officers at the site: Detective Superintendent Roy Haslett of the Worcestershire constabulary and Professor Nigel Willis, the Home Office pathologist."

"It's her, isn't it?" Spooner settled himself into the passenger seat.

The Chief's eyes narrowed as he pulled out of the layby. "I wouldn't have come all this way if I wasn't ninety-nine per cent sure. It's strange, but when he was delirious in hospital, Karl Kohl told me Belladonna was trapped in the trees."

Spooner swallowed. "You've never told me that before," he said.

"No?" his companion went on. "Well anyway, it's Haslett's case and while we're in his company, we're going to have to be circumspect. They don't know what our interest in this business is and probably won't appreciate us joining them, there's just not much they can do about it. But it's essential we don't divulge any part of what we know or think we know – even if these remains do turn out to be who we think it is. Understood?"

"Loud and clear," said Spooner, watching his car disappear in the rear-view mirror as they drove down into the valley.

22

I'VE FOUND THE RIGHT GIRL

Monday, 19 April 1943

"Good," the Chief nodded. "Now all we need to do is find the entrance for this place. Are you sure we're going the right way?"

"Aye," Spooner peered through the windscreen. Patches of mist hung in the lower valley as they drove towards the Hall, making it look different from his first recce of the place. Revisiting both his memories and notes on a regular basis had kept the layout of the De Veres' estate fresh in his mind, so that he didn't really need to consult the map he had spread on his lap. "Turn left and go on about another hundred yards. We'll be at the gates before you know it."

"Ah yes," said the Chief, "and they've laid on a reception committee."

He wound down his window as they reached the two uniformed constables who'd been placed on sentry duty and produced his identification to the one that stepped forward.

"Go straight ahead, sir," the PC instructed as he handed it back. "Past the Hall and along the road about three hundred yards until it veers to the left and leads you into the woods. You'll find the others parked and you'll be able to follow your nose from then on."

His fellow sentry opened one of the gates and they drove on, past the slumbering house and deep into the valley. The road twisted through verdant foliage, allowing flashes of some of the sights Spooner had noted before and some that had been hidden – a waterfall tumbling into a stream around one bend, the ruined castle through another. With bluebells and anemones spread in knolls across the woodland floor, it seemed even more like a fairy-tale kingdom – except for the feeling of dread that pulsed inside him.

They came to a cluster of parked cars opposite Wychbury Hill. From this angle, Spooner could see the one building that had been almost completely obscured by trees during his previous surveillance: six sandstone columns rising out of the mist and the trees, halfway down the slope from the obelisk. That icy finger tapped on his memory: it was exactly like the temple he had dreamt of on the night of the Duncan séance.

"Wait here while I introduce myself to the superintendent." The Chief brought the Bentley to a halt beside the other vehicles. There was no black Anglia among them, though that did little to abate the pinpricks of unease dancing down Spooner's spine. It was as if Clara was somehow with him, directing him to the places she wanted him to see.

"Actually, is it all right if I take a wee look at that 'til you're ready?" he asked, nodding up at the folly, wondering if he could prove his subconscious wrong.

The Chief followed his gaze. "Good idea. See if you can find what they've been worshipping up there."

Spooner knelt down beside the dark stain, bringing his penknife out of his pocket to chip a little of it away for analysis, although he was pretty sure of what had caused it – dripping wax from black candles. He dropped the crumbling flakes into a sample bag and put it back in his rucksack. There was nothing else visible to the naked eye that might suggest what the building may have been used for, but a faint odour lingered in the sodden molecules of air, the odour of aromatic herbs burned within these walls. Rue, he could identify as the most overpowering of these. It took a minute before he realised that the Chief was calling his name from across the valley.

He stepped out, the smells of earth and flora replacing the mysteries of the temple. But Spooner still felt like he was walking through a dream as he headed back down the slope and into the woods, past the tent that the pathologist had just finished erecting, towards the group that huddled around the site where human remains had been found.

Was this then where Nicholas Ralphe had hidden the Witch Queen?

Nothing he could have projected from his subconscious could have matched the true horror of the gateway into the next world that stood before him when he reached it: its gnarled old bole like the distended stomach of a hag with dried-up ivy for veins and its spindly crown of branches her tangled green hair. Spooner drew in a sharp breath. Had Clara become part of the tree, or had the tree become part of her?

Ahead of him, the pathologist had climbed the ladder placed against the trunk to give him access to the hollow and found what Terry Jenkins and his gang had recently disturbed from its clandestine embrace. Carefully, Professor Willis retraced his steps downwards, holding a pale object in his gloved hand.

"It's a woman's skull," he said. "Look," he pointed, "you can see there's still some flesh and hair attached. It can't have been here too long."

"A redhead," the Chief noted, looking across at Spooner.

Spooner's stomach turned a somersault. "I wonder if there's anything else of her in there?" he said, looking past the grisly remains to its place of interment. "Do you think it's possible to fit a woman into that tree?"

"I should say so, provided you had only just killed her," the professor considered. "Before rigor mortis set in. Let's take a look, shall we?"

Four hours later she was laid out on a tarpaulin inside the pathologist's tent. There had been most of a woman hidden inside the hollow of the tree, but she had decayed to a skeleton now, rotted like her crêpe-soled shoes and the remains of her clothing, over the two-year period the professor estimated she had been there. It was a part of her attire that had been used to kill her, he further opined, though he would obviously give a more authoritative account after he'd taken her back to his lab and examined her properly. A ripped portion of material was wedged into the top of her throat, on which she had likely choked. More strangely still, she was missing her left hand.

That was when Spooner knew for sure that he was finally looking at Clara – and the deed that had sent Ralphe to the asylum. He had to be careful now that he wasn't the next person to be put in a straitjacket. Taking the Chief aside, he chose his words with care.

"I think I know where to find her hand. I think that was what was going on in the temple back there. Can we take a recce, without making it seem too obvious?"

The Chief looked ahead of them, at the superintendent in conference with his officers. He spoke out of the side of his mouth. "Go back over there now and if you find anything, call me over."

Letting go of logic for the moment, Spooner found a path through the woods that came to the temple at an angle recognisable from how the building had appeared in his dream. Then he knelt down and began to search systematically through the undergrowth with gloved fingers, finding himself drawn towards a patch of brambles less than a yard away from the portico, which matched the co-ordinates of his vision of a hand coming up through the earth. A cold sweat broke out on his forehead as he cleared the barbed runners away from a slightly raised mound of earth at their centre. His throat was so dry he could hardly call out.

The now skeletal hand was laid upright in a clay pot, clutching a black candle and wrapped in black cloth, stems of verbena and fern fronds. This was roughly what Spooner had expected, although the specifications of the spell varied from source to source. What he hadn't anticipated was the gold wedding ring still nestled around the third finger.

Who, he wondered, had given it to her? It didn't seem likely this was a token of the binding ceremony Karl Kohl had spoken of to the Chief. Could it have been a gift from the infatuated Ralphe instead, another secret he had hoped to bury with her?

It was the second of Belladonna's beaux who dominated Spooner's thoughts as he watched the pathologist add the contents of the vessel to his grim haul and begin to pack everything away. He tried to imagine what had happened from Ralphe's perspective: first murdering the woman he had once been so in love with, choking her in the manner Helen

Duncan appeared to have experienced, by stuffing something down her throat. Then sawing off her left hand before dropping the rest of her body into that ghastly tree. Finally, having put himself through all of that, preparing his dark ritual and burying the severed hand where he thought it would never be disturbed again.

Had he done it all in one night? He surely wouldn't have risked any of these feats by daylight? Or had his sanity so completely evaporated by then that it made no difference?

Spooner would never know the answer to that. Nor how Ralphe would feel now if he knew the protection spell he had so believed in could have been broken in an instant by a bunch of high-spirited boys.

As quickly as they had gathered, now everyone seemed to be leaving the woods. The pathologist was driving Clara away, back to his lab at Birmingham University. The superintendent had the unpleasant task of relaying the news of their discovery to the inhabitants at the Hall. The mass of officers who had guarded the site and helped with the searches all started going their separate ways, mainly on bicycles, some on foot, and with seemingly no Houlston among them.

The Chief put his hand on Spooner's shoulder, led him back in the direction of the temple and away from the ears of any remaining policemen. "I know it's been a lot to take in today. But, before we leave, show me what else you found in here."

Spooner stopped on the threshold, too overcome with fatigue and the overlapping in his mind of memory, dream and imagination to want to go any further. Instead, he propped himself up against the wall and watched the tall man with the large nose stalk his way across the floor, nodding to himself as he perambulated between the wax patterns.

"Well, well," he said. "I wonder if anybody else has made note of this."

Spooner shrugged. "This is where Ralphe made the Hand of Glory. You can still smell some of the herbs that he burned for the ritual. I just don't want to think what was going through his mind when he did it." He looked back out through the portico at the departing cars travelling through the gathering shadows.

"What happens next?" he asked.

"The superintendent must lead his murder enquiry," said the Chief, "and do everything he can to ascertain the identity of the unfortunate victim. It won't be easy for him, seeing as she isn't exactly local. We're going to let him get on with that and not interfere in any way, including offering our opinions on who that grim collection of bones might once have been, nor who laid them to rest. I doubt they will ever be able to ID her, but, from our point of view, there is just a tiny chance that news of this might flush out some of the other players in this game who are still missing in action."

Spooner frowned. "What about Houlston? I think he knows as well as we do who that pile of bones used to be and I can't see him keeping quiet about it."

The Chief raised his eyebrows. "I think you are over-estimating his influence. Even if he was somewhere here today, there is still slim chance of him being able to make a positive identity on someone for whom no one in this country holds either dental or medical records. And he's not going to get a rush of concerned friends coming forward to say they knew her. Everyone who did is either dead or absent, aren't they?"

Spooner shook his head. "Even so..." he began.

"You would have heard if he had ever caught up with either

of the others," the Chief said. "Don't concern yourself with him any longer. Now," he held up the arm with his wristwatch on it to the fading light, "shall we get back to Birmingham for the night? I don't think I'm fit to drive all the way back to London. But I do know of an hotel there where I don't think they'll recognise you and perhaps you'll allow me to give you the best dinner you'll have had in some time?"

The hotel was near to New Street station. It had been built at the height of the city's prosperity at the turn of the century, although its finery was now largely obscured behind taped-up windows, blackout curtains and scaffolding poles supporting areas that had had previous brushes with the Luftwaffe. Inside, however, life appeared to be going on much as it had since its Edwardian inception. As they passed through the lobby on the way to the lifts, Spooner could hear an orchestra playing "Moonlight Serenade" above the clinking of glassware and china in the ballroom beyond.

Whatever the musical talent on offer, the Chief wasn't moved by the idea of dining in public. He had obtained adjoining suites where a meal could be sent up and they could talk in private, though he made a thorough job of taking all the telephones off the hook, searching behind each mirror and in every light socket. As a final precaution against snoopers, he kept the radiogram on in the background while they ate.

He waited until they had enjoyed their tomato soup and roast beef and had moved on to the port and cheese before he began to discuss the day's events. "The patterns we observed in the temple today, those marks left on the floor in wax, to what would you attribute them?"

Spooner's knife hung in mid-air, a sliver of Cheddar on the

side of it. There had been the option of trying Gorgonzola on the hotel's rarefied menu, but somehow, he wasn't keen.

"It looked like a Black Mass to me," he said. "Thirteen candles burned around a circle, at the centre of which would have been a pentagram. The wax smelled quite strongly of sulphur, I expect the lab will find that was an element in their making…"

The Chief frowned. "I only counted twelve," he said.

"The thirteenth would have been the one found in the pot with the hand." Spooner put his knife down, no longer so keen on the Cheddar. He lit a cigarette instead. "See what the chaps at the lab come up with, but I'm sure there'll be a match. Also, they burned a lot of herbs in there, you could still smell that too. Rue leaves the strongest trace, it smells disgusting."

"What would be the aim of that?" the Chief enquired.

"To dull the senses while at the same time stimulating the imagination, triggering hallucinations. The sort of thing that made people in the seventeenth century believe that witches could fly. Your actual belladonna would be another one they'd use."

"All of which would be compatible with one of the spells from Price's grimoire?"

"Aye," Spooner took a sip of his port, "I would think so."

"I wonder," the Chief's expression darkened, "what Hannen Swaffer might make of this news of a body in the tree when he hears it. Whether he might want to call upon Helen Duncan for another séance, in order to try and contact the dead woman?"

Spooner raised his eyebrows, "From what Daphne Maitland told me, that's a possibility. I'll let you know if I hear anything to that effect."

The Chief nodded. "I think it might be prudent for me to reawaken some official interest in her. And you've just given me an idea. To have people start believing in seventeenth-century witchcraft again…"

The concert on the radio came to an end, with the sound of German voices. Spooner realised that the Chief had tuned into long wave, summoning forth the nightly broadcast from the scion of Hagley Hall. His clipped tones carried over the remains of their dinner.

"Germany calling, this is Germany calling…"

23

THE HOUSE IS HAUNTED (BY THE ECHO OF YOUR LAST GOODBYE)

Saturday, 18 December 1943

It didn't take Naval Intelligence Agent Forshaw long to catch up with Lieutenant Stanley Worthington in the Portsmouth Royal Navy Volunteer Reserve mess. His target's appearance was distinctive: thin and lanky, his hair nearly gone at the age of twenty-five and, at the end of his nose, the spectacles that had barred his way to the career of admiral he had dreamt of as a boy. It was Stanley's skill at navigation that had instead earned him a place as a reservist, serving at the shore-leave establishment in his home city.

The pair was already acquainted from regular night patrols on the little gunboats that stalked the enemy along the Channel, looking for submerged U-boats and mine-laying E-boats lurking in the dark. Forshaw was able to fall in beside Stanley with a few amiable words of greeting and join him in the eating of lunch, over which he made a casual enquiry as to the lieutenant's mother's health.

"Oh, she's been much better lately," Stanley was delighted that his colleague had asked. His mother was one of his favourite subjects, as Forshaw had discovered over long nights in the Channel, "since she started going out with Mrs Dowson from next door. There's a social club she belongs to, something to do with the church." Stanley and his mother were Methodists whose allegiance to the Pledge had largely been inspired by his late drunkard of a father. "I expect they spend most of their time playing rummy and talking about the best way to set jam. But it's really taken her out of herself. There's a woman there called Gladys who plays the piano, Mother says she's marvellous."

Forshaw raised an eyebrow. "Gladys Shadwell?"

"Yes, that's it," Stanley said. "Do you know her?"

Forshaw frowned. "Not personally," he said, lowering his voice, "but a friend of mine had a funny experience with her. Is it the Master Temple your mother's been going to?"

Stanley nodded, the smile fading from his face.

"Then, well, I don't mean to worry you," said Forshaw, "but they don't go there to swap recipes and play cards of a Friday night. They go there to contact the dead."

"Contact the dead?" Stanley echoed.

"They call themselves spiritualists," Forshaw informed him. "They hire mediums and charge women like your mother a pretty penny to sit in a darkened room listening for messages from the Great Beyond. My friend was there when they had this Scottish woman in called Helen Duncan... Have you ever heard of her?"

Stanley shook his head, his expression now completely grave. "No," he said. "Tell me..."

So it was that two weeks later Forshaw returned to the Temple with Stanley, for the first time since the *Barham* séance. The lieutenant had already escorted his mother on the previous weekend, to see for himself what the Shadwells got up to and purchase tickets for Helen's next appearance, which Gladys was selling for a premium of 20s each. The experience had galvanised him. Forbidding his crestfallen mater to ever step foot in the place again, he formed a further plan of action to keep her out of the Shadwells' clutches should she think of disobeying him while he was at sea. Grateful to have been alerted to the danger she was in, he asked if Forshaw could help. Forshaw was happy to oblige.

Like the last time the Naval Intelligence officer had set foot in the place, the room above the chemist's was packed to capacity. As well as displaying his certification from Councillor Roberts on the door, Granville was asking everybody to leave their blackout torches with him before they crossed the threshold and found the seat they had been allocated. There could be no changes made to these seating arrangements.

"I'm pretty sure I know what this means," Forshaw whispered to Stanley as they took their chairs. An hour later they were at the police station, reporting on what they had just witnessed to DI Freddie Fraser.

"I've worked out how they do it," Forshaw expounded. "Duncan gets her information about the people in her audience from the Shadwells, who have made it their business to find out what there is to know. She'll have been informed of all the recently bereaved, those who lost someone young and even—" he shot a glance at his companion, "those who are still missing their pet budgerigars. The Shadwells work out the seating plan so that Duncan can learn her lines accordingly. Nothing is left to chance."

DI Fraser cracked his knuckles, a sound like anti-aircraft

fire. "And how d'you reckon they work the spirits?" he enquired.

"Well," said Stanley, "for a start, Mr Shadwell takes away everyone's torches at the door and the lights are so dim in there you can barely make out your hand in front of your face."

"That cabinet they use is their prop cupboard," added Forshaw. "They've got a length of material, something like cheesecloth, and a couple of puppets that act as her spirit guides. Henry Duncan works them while she provides the distraction with all her moaning…"

"And singing," Stanley recalled the version of "Loch Lomond" that had closed the night's proceedings with a shudder.

"All you need to do," said Forshaw, "is smuggle a torch in there and shine it into the cabinet as soon as all the nonsense starts. Then you'll have her bang to rights."

Fraser lifted a heavy black eyebrow. "When does she make her next appearance?" he asked.

"January," said Stanley. "Wednesday the nineteenth."

Fraser nodded. "I'll put it in my diary. If you don't mind, give us a bell the day before, so we can discuss tactics." He passed over his card. "I think I know how we should handle Mrs Duncan."

Once he had closed the door behind them, Fraser reached for the phone. "Get me the Home Office," he said. "Cecil Forbes-Dixon."

An hour later, DI Fraser met with reporter Richard Lexy in his usual spot – the saloon bar of the Star and Garter. Lexy got special treatment from the barmaid there, who believed she was his steady girlfriend. In fact, Lexy had set his sights a little higher, on the daughter of the retired major he cultivated at the golf club. DI Fraser prided himself on this knowledge, which he intended to use as a future bargaining chip in the information exchange the pair of them shared.

Fraser didn't order anything at the bar, just made his way over to the nook in the corner which Lexy had made his second office. The barmaid, Betty, was leaning over him, clearing away his supper plates.

"A word in your shell-like, Dickie." Fraser pulled out the chair opposite the journalist. "Get us a pint of mild, will you, Betty?" he directed at her, enjoying the way her face flushed to almost the exact same colour as her dress. Lexy seemed to find it charming too, pressing change into her hand and then patting her behind as she went on her way, saying: "Thanks, love, put one in there for me too."

"Freddie," Lexy reluctantly turned his attention to the detective. "What can I do you for?"

"That slightly less attractive woman you're keen on," said Fraser, "the fat old Scottish one. She's been back over the chemist's and I've just had two naval officers come in to my office to make a complaint about her."

He took the cigarette Lexy proffered and allowed him to light them both up. "They're not stupid, neither. They worked out how they pull the con exactly like you told me. I was quite impressed. Now the thing is, I don't think this pair's going to go away any time soon, nor be satisfied with the usual old flannel about keeping an eye on things until the time is right. They've asked me to accompany them the next time the old boot makes an appearance."

Lexy exhaled smoke rings. "I see. And when's that going to be?"

"The nineteenth of January," replied Fraser. "Reckon you'll have your scoop ready by then?"

"Looks like I'll have to," said Lexy, raising his eyebrows as Betty plonked their drinks down in front of them with a wink in his direction and wiggled her way back to the bar.

"Things are changing all round," Fraser continued, once she was out of earshot. "This time, I fully intend to do the lot of them. Cheers." He lifted his pint and drained half of it, studying the expression on Lexy's face while he did so. As usual, the reporter's countenance radiated nothing but nonchalant bonhomie, made all the more plausible by his round schoolboy's face and wide eyes.

"Shouldn't be a problem, old man," Lexy said, blowing more smoke rings towards the ceiling. "Not for me. Though I don't envy your task, bringing that rabble in quietly."

It was Fraser's turn to wink. "That's my speciality," he said. "And you're welcome to come and report on me in action." He finished his ale in one further gulp. "D'you ever hear back from that bloke you met?" he asked, getting to his feet. "The reporter from the *Psychic Times* who was digging around?"

"*Two Worlds*," corrected Lexy. "Ross Spooner. No I haven't, as a matter of fact. Not a peep from him. He never wrote his article up either, although I did look out for it." He almost looked surprised by this.

"Well," said Fraser, putting his trilby on his head, "once he gets a sniff of this you might hear from him again. Be a good chap and let me know if you do."

Spooner had been expecting to be halfway back to Aberdeen by now, en route to a long overdue Christmas reunion with his family. Instead, he found himself standing halfway up a hill, on a farm track that led from Wollescote towards the road that marked the boundary of the De Vere estate. Spooner didn't realise it, as he framed his first photograph, but the barn he was aiming his lens towards stood beside the same pathway that Terry Jenkins and his friends had traversed on that fateful day in April.

Ernest Oaten had seen the bare bones of the story when it had come in on a Reuters newswire yesterday evening, before Spooner had a chance to get home to his nightly perusal of the papers. He thought it looked interesting, he said, as he placed it on Spooner's desk, something to look into after he came back from his holidays, perhaps?

Spooner had to agree that it did.

There were more details in the *Birmingham Evening Post*, where an enterprising reporter speculated about the as-yet-unsolved murder of a woman found inside a tree in Hagley Woods nine months before. As well as providing a recap of the case, his copy noted that all the efforts made by the police to identify the victim had so far been in vain.

After investigation in his laboratory, Professor Willis had been able to say that the woman had been five feet tall and was aged around thirty. She had reddish-brown hair and irregular teeth on her lower jaw, one molar having been removed some years since. She had not been suffering from any kind of disease at the time of her death, which the professor ascertained had been caused by asphyxiation, due to the portion of material stuffed down her throat. He judged that she was pushed into the hollow of the tree immediately after her death, as rigor mortis would have prevented her body from fitting inside the entrance to the hollow, which was barely twenty inches in diameter. She had remained interred for nearly two years.

At the inquest, in Stourbridge on 28th April, the coroner had accepted a verdict of Murder by Person or Persons Unknown.

Professor Willis was able to provide a pictorial reconstruction of the woman for the police to use, with which Spooner was already familiar. But for the absence of that knowing smile, it was similar to the photograph once owned by Karl Kohl. For months, detectives had been contacting every dentist in the land to try to find a match for the distinctive teeth in her lower jaw, had trawled through every Missing Persons report to eliminate matches, and even traced the identity of the buyers of all but six pairs of shoes identical to those found with the body, sold from a market stall in Dudley. Still, the woman in the tree continued to be neither known nor missed. Until now.

Spooner had had to make some rapid readjustments to his schedule to get here, but he had managed to arrive at midday. Luckily, there had been no rain overnight and the spectacle he had come to record was still intact and in situ.

The words had been written in chalk, in letters three feet high. They had first been spotted by a dog walker on his usual circuit around the fields at eight o'clock on Friday morning. The farmer who the land belonged to had told the intrepid reporter from the *Post* that the barn had been clean as he passed by it the evening before.

WHO PUT BELLA DOWN THE WYCH ELM?

Spooner's finger pressed down on the button and the shutter clicked. He wound the film on and walked a few steps back down the hill to take a second shot that revealed more of the setting that this stark question has been posed on – the old, red brick barn, the hard, furrowed earth of the field surrounding it and the pale, cloudy sky behind, through which weak shafts of sunlight were trying to break.

The journalist from the *Post* ended his piece by positing a theory. Was there somebody who had known the woman in the tree by this name? And, if so, had they left these words as a clue for the police, or to taunt them for their inability to solve the case?

To Spooner, the communication meant only one thing: Anna wasn't dead. She was out here somewhere and she wanted him to know it.

24

MOONLIGHT BECOMES YOU

Wednesday, 19 January 1944

"Professor Melvin," Spooner said, "thank you for seeing me."

The dainty hand that took his might easily have belonged to a sprite, an impression enhanced by the silk scarves swathed around the head and neck of its owner and the tinkling of silver bells suspended from her necklace. A tiny woman, Margot Melvin made real the image he had constructed for Anna's fortune-telling grandma and was just the sort of lady who used to come to tea with his own.

She was actually one of the country's most renowned historians, having assisted the Egyptologist Flinders Petrie on his greatest digs in Egypt and Petra and held positions at the British Museum and Cambridge as an authority on antiquity. Then, in the 1920s, she had joined the Folklore Society and developed an interest in a different kind of ancient world – one inhabited by witches, fairies and Horned Gods.

It was in her 1921 treatise, *The Witch-Cult in Western Europe*, which laid out her theory that witchcraft was the ancient native religion of the continent, where Spooner had first read about the Hand of Glory, a protection spell made from the eponymous severed limb of a murderer. This work had proved controversial on publication, damaging Melvin's academic reputation, though it had nonetheless been seized upon by less high-minded readers eager to believe. She had responded with the further, still more populist tome *The God of the Witches* a decade later, in which she had described the pagan worship of a Horned God that had been mistaken for Devil-worship and led to the persecution of witches. In this book, Professor Melvin stated her belief that a coven had laid a curse on the Earl of Bothwell, the source of Spooner's favourite "Witches Reel". He had come to seek her expertise on behalf of his editor, in an attempt to explain the most perplexing part of the story that had gripped the *Two Worlds*' readers since December.

The day after Spooner had taken his photographs in the fields around Wollescote, another message appeared on the surviving wall of a bombed-out terrace in West Bromwich, apparently penned by the same hand and using the same material. Perhaps in response to the article in the *Post*, this time it had been more specific: HAGLEY WOODS BELLA it had said. There were more to come over Christmas, appearing by nightfall in locations across Birmingham and the surrounding countryside, usually on bombed-out buildings where, it was to be presumed, their mysterious author would not be disturbed during composition. The next variation was the one that would go on being repeated, bestowing the mystery woman with a name that, by the New Year of 1944, even the police were using: WHO PUT BELLA IN THE WYCH ELM?

By the time Spooner returned to the *Two Worlds*' office after his shortened Christmas break, Miss Josser had an overflowing post-bag, the national press had joined the regionals with coverage and Oaten was eager for answers.

"In all of this," he said, indicating the small mountain on his letter spike, "there's not one coherent thread to be spun. Most of them have come from sitters claiming this Clarabella, Lubella or just plain Bella came through to them – but not one of them is able to say who she was or what she were doing in them woods. Neither can any of them offer an explanation as to what happened to her hand – and that's what I think's the key to it."

Spooner's thumb paused over a pile of cuttings. "How do you mean?" he said.

"Well," said Oaten, "I'm sure you'll agree that stuffing a woman inside a tree is a funny enough thing to do in first place. But perhaps, if you were the murderer and you had the local knowledge, you could have planned that part out. After all, it were remote enough to hide her away for nigh on two year – perhaps for ever, if it weren't for them poor lads that found her. But that still doesn't explain why you would first want to cut her hand off and bury it, does it?"

"No," Spooner agreed. A thoughtful expression crossed his features. "You've a point there. I think there is maybe someone we could talk to about this…"

He hadn't wanted Oaten to take the risk of publishing the notion he was about to propose until he had ascertained the whereabouts and availability of the expert he thought could back him up. Nor, of course, before he had the Chief's permission to spread her opinions across his front page, in the hope that others would pick up on the theory. It was his boss in London who had provided the information on the current whereabouts of Professor Melvin who, having moved from London to the relative safety of Cambridge in 1940, was now working for a volunteer group teaching military personnel and researching a history of the area. She had responded immediately to his letter.

Professor Melvin had a first-floor flat on Market Street from which the spires of Caius College could be seen through leaded windows. Inside it was decorated in an exotic mixture of Persian rugs and oak furniture and a multitude of icons. Gods, goddesses and amulets from every continent of the ancient world peered down on them from the shelves and tables, a more educated echo of the parlours of the Smiths and Shadwells who had previously entertained him, but with the same aesthetic principles. Spooner sat on a Tudor chair while the professor poured tea from Japanese porcelain, breathing in air suffused with the scent of jasmine.

"I'm so glad you brought this to my attention," she said. "I think you're absolutely right in your reading of this extraordinary situation as an indication of the Old Ways…"

Forshaw and Stanley were fifteen minutes into the packed Helen Duncan séance at the Master Temple. So far, the medium had brought forth two manifestations and the third, a beefy looking woman in white, was making her way towards her bereaved son with outstretched arms.

The two men exchanged glances and Stanley got to his feet. Pushing past the couple in front of him, he lunged towards the cabinet with startled protests ringing in his ears. As Stanley reached his destination, Forshaw stood up and turned on the beam of the torch he had concealed in his pocket. For a moment, the seated figure of Helen was illuminated, a vision in black satin and white cheesecloth, staring in startled incomprehension. In that second of advantage, Stanley managed to grab hold of the length of white fabric that trailed from her lap.

There were shouts of "What's going on?" and the sounds of chair legs scraping against the floor as people got up. Then a cry of pain from Forshaw as an unseen presence kicked him in the shin, causing him to drop the torch.

In the darkness that now consumed them, Stanley was put at a disadvantage. Grappling to keep hold of the fabric, he was rabbit-punched from behind. Stanley let go of his evidence.

"It's gone into the audience!" he cried, crashing into the side of the cabinet. Forshaw, though, had recovered his torch from under the heels of those milling around him. He staggered back to his feet and aimed his weapon in Helen's direction. The torch beam picked out her near-murderous expression.

"Doctor!" she yelled at the top of her lungs. "Get me a doctor! Ah'm dyin' up here!"

But Stanley had one more trick left to play. The whistle DI Fraser had given him cut through the clamour. He blew hard on it three times – the signal for the plainclothes officer who had been lurking at the back while the séance was in progress, to turn on the light and open the door to Fraser and three more detectives, waiting on the stairs below.

"Everybody stay where you are!" Fraser's eyes travelled around the room, taking in fallen chairs, panicked faces and furtive expressions. The detective who had let them in secured the door behind him, while one of his colleagues rounded on Granville, another took Henry Duncan and the third, a female officer, made her way to Helen. The medium had slumped back into the chair inside the cabinet, where another woman was holding a handkerchief to her brow. The DI held up a Magistrate's Warrant to the furious face of the organist, who barrelled her way towards him, goggle eyes flashing.

"Gladys Shadwell, I am arresting you," he said, "your

husband Grenville and Helen and Henry Duncan on suspicion of contravening the Vagrancy Act of 1824, by pretending to hold communication with the deceased. You do not have to say anything…"

Gladys put her hand to her heart, her eyes rolling upwards, in almost as dramatic a performance as the one given by Helen, who had gone into a full swoon, blocking entry to the cabinet. Her attendant, who said she was a nurse, demanded they call an ambulance.

In contrast, Grenville and Henry stood with their heads down, saying nothing.

"This is how they treated Jesus!" Gladys cried. "Pontius Pilate and the Romans – this is how they made Our Lord suffer!"

"I can add a charge of blasphemy to that, if you want?" offered Fraser.

The eyes snapped open. "You'll never get away with this," she said.

"I hope you're not threatening me, Mrs Shadwell," said Fraser.

"I have friends in higher places than you know."

"Don't you believe it." The DI couldn't wait for her to see who else was holed up in the cells that evening. Councillor Roberts had been disturbed from taking his tea at home two hours before the séance began, in connection with the thousands of pounds missing from the ship scaler's company he had employed for the city, revealed after an unscheduled visit from the admiralty's accountant. It appeared that taking a cut from Grenville's business was one of the more minor infringements of the public's trust that Lexy's industrious beaverings had brought to light.

"Councillor Roberts never showed up to sign your certificate for you tonight, did he?"

"Sir," the female policewoman broke in between Fraser and Mrs Shadwell, "we'd better get our surgeon up here, I don't know how we're going to move her otherwise."

Lexy waited outside the Master Temple with his photographer as the parade of offenders made its descent from the Temple to the station. The first flashbulb to pop illuminated a suitably stern-looking Fraser escorting a pursed-lipped Gladys. The second caught Grenville trying to cover his face with his hat, the third a scowling Henry and finally Helen, looking pale and afraid, on the arm of the police surgeon who had just certified that she was well enough to spend the rest of the evening in the cells.

A bewildered Stanley was the last person left in the Master Temple. Neither he nor anyone else had yet to recover the cheesecloth.

"There's been some arrests tonight," the Chief said as he opened the door. He ushered Spooner into the lounge before he went on. "Both the Duncans and the Shadwells."

Spooner sat down in his usual chair beside the fire. Dorothy raised her head and grunted a bulldog greeting before returning to her slumbers. "That was fast work," he said. "Do you mind if I ask how it happened?"

The Chief smiled. "From what I've been hearing, a naval reservist took objection to his mother being taken for a ride and asked DI Fraser to investigate." He poured them both a drink. "When he explained the situation to the Home Office, they agreed it was time something was finally done."

"You must be pleased," said Spooner, lifting his glass.

"I am," agreed the Chief, clinking with him. "Though I'm afraid the news of it could knock your story off the front page."

"Might not be such a bad thing," Spooner shrugged. "Professor Melvin has given me some good copy, but only so much that's fit to print. In her opinion, this is a definite case of Black magic; but then she also thinks that Joan of Arc was an earthly manifestation of the Witch God who was burned in a ritual sacrifice at the height of her powers. It could be that if other journalists speak to her, she could quite easily discredit the theory we want her to prove by appearing too, shall we say, eccentric."

"I see," said the Chief. "And who, in her opinion, is the sort of person the police should be looking for?"

"This is where she did come up with the goods," said Spooner. "She knows of a Black magic coven operating in Birmingham. She received some correspondence from them in the winter of 1940, asking her about her sources for the Hand of Glory ritual. The letters were forwarded to her from her publisher, whose address she used when she replied. They were all typewritten, came without an address and were signed '*A Follower*' – but there is another form of identification on them, so I got her to lend them to me. Here," he dug into his briefcase, "you'll see they all came with an Edgbaston postmark."

"Edgbaston?" The Chief took the letters. "That's where you found the girl Anna."

"Aye," said Spooner. "And where Clara was living with Nicholas Ralphe in 1940."

The Chief sifted through the envelopes. "Three of them."

"The contents of which get yet more intriguing," said Spooner. "When Professor Melvin wrote back, she mentioned she was preparing a history of the Cambridge area. Our left-hander writes by return of post to see if she knows anything about a cave under a crossroads between two Roman roads, in the town of Royston. She replies that she believes it was a repository for the treasures of the Knights Templar, who worshipped the same god as Joan of Arc, which is represented by the artwork on the walls and the circular, recessed altar at its centre which has places for twelve disciples and one witch. His final reply is brief, but he thanks her for confirming that and says he will make sure to visit. Now, I looked up Royston and it's not a million miles from where Kohl made his landing in the fens."

"Well, well," said the Chief. "Who do you think it was writing to her?"

"I'd like a second opinion on that," Spooner said. "There's a subtle, but major difference between the first letter and the other two. Ralphe did tell me he'd learned the ritual from an adept, and I doubt there could be anyone more qualified to tell him about it than Professor Melvin. I'm certain the first one is from him, but not so much about the others, which is why I got her to lend them to me. I can't remember if you said Air Force Intelligence took a typewriter from Ralphe's room or whether it was one of the things that got spirited away?"

"I can't remember either, but I'll look into it." The Chief put the letters down.

"There's something else I need to show you," Spooner went on. "I took the opportunity to do some more digging in Birmingham when the Bella messages started appearing. Every one of them was put in a place that Anna had either mentioned to me, or marked a path towards the tree. I'm sure they're from her and they're meant for me."

"Then why," the Chief's eyes narrowed, "is she using the name Bella?"

"Only one reason," said Spooner. "She knows who Clara really was and she's using her codename. In one instance, she called her Clarabella, as if to make doubly sure."

"If that's the case, then doesn't it suggest she's worked out what you are really up to?"

Spooner swallowed a mouthful of the amber liquid from his glass. "It might," he said. "And if it does, I mean to rise to the bait. This business with Helen couldn't have come at a better time. It'll keep Ernest occupied while I go back to Brum."

"Yes," said the Chief, "the State could really take advantage of Helen at a time like this. As perhaps your leading article will go on to say. What will you do in Birmingham?"

"Pick up another trail that came back to life at the same time as the Bella messages began," Spooner said. "Norrie's friend Bertie, who works at the Hippodrome, is booking an act for me. The Two Magicians, they call themselves."

This time, he took from his briefcase Anna's songbook and from within that, the bill he had taken from the Portsmouth hotel lobby.

"Strangely enough, if it wasn't for Helen, I might have missed this. Though, I wasn't sure about it until Norrie showed me that circus poster."

The Chief took in the faces of the two performers: a man with a top hat and curly moustache and the woman who was presumably his assistant. The woman grabbed his attention, with her blonde marcel-waved bob, high cheekbones and penetrating gaze.

"And," Spooner continued, "he happened to mention that tightrope walkers have a thing about dressing up as women."

The Chief looked again. The contours of that face would sit more easily on a man. The part of the throat where an Adam's apple would be found was obscured by ropes of pearls. Shaking his head, he looked across at the man.

"Anna herself told me that, when she wanted to go incognito, she dressed as a boy."

The Chief saw that the curly moustache was painted on, along with the pointed sideburns. But the way the brim of the top hat rested over one eye, throwing shadow across the face, distracted from an initial noticing.

"And finally," Spooner opened the songbook on its very last entry. The title of the ballad scored there was "The Two Magicians". "I don't know if she knows I have this, nor why it's taken all this time for them to show up again either. But Bertie has finally found a booking address for them – and it's in Edgbaston. It would seem that in all these years she's never actually been very far away…"

25

SHAKE DOWN THE STARS

Thursday, 20 January 1944

"Maurice," the voice that came down Barbanell's office phone line spoke in a whisper, "have you heard the news about Helen?"

Barbanell had only just got to his desk. It was nine o'clock and all the news he had heard so far this morning had concerned the Allies' advance on Rome.

"Godfrey?" he said. "Is that you?"

"Yes," his correspondent from the Ministry of Transport confirmed.

"I'm having trouble hearing you. Did you say something about Helen? Helen Duncan?"

"That's right." Godfrey cleared his throat and became slightly more audible. "She was arrested last night in Portsmouth, hauled before the magistrate this morning without representation and is currently on her way to Holloway prison."

"Good God! But why now? And what's the charge?"

"The Vagrancy Act. Pretending to hold communication with the deceased."

The implications sunk in. "But this is monstrous!"

"Yes." Since the last time he had called Barbanell about

the news of the sinking of the *Barham*, Godfrey Heath had risen up the SNU ranks to become President of the London District Council. It was within his power to appoint legal representation for stricken members. "I think we'll need a barrister," he went on. "Have you a recommendation?"

"Ernest," Barbanell's next call was to Oaten. "Have you heard the news about Helen?"

"Yes." The *Two Worlds* editor was already hard at work on his front page. "I got a tip-off last night from my lad Spooner," he said.

Barbanell bridled at the mention of the name. "How did he find out?" he wanted to know.

"From that journalist he met in Portsmouth," said Oaten. "Richard Lexy."

Spooner was looking at the previous evening's *Portsmouth Evening News*, brought to him at a roadside café on the outskirts of the city, by the reporter who had penned the two stories that split the front cover of the paper.

WHERE'S THE CASH, COUNCILLOR? went head-to-head with GHOST GRABBED BY POLICE! Illustrated by caught-in-the-act photographs of Councillor Roberts on his front doorstep and DI Fraser hauling Gladys out of the Temple, both promised to divulge SHOCKING THINGS.

"Good, eh?" Lexy's eyes twinkled. "What you might call the perfect scoop." He tapped his finger down on Fraser's visage. "I had to give him top billing, of course."

"Oh aye?" It had come as a surprise to Spooner when, phoning in his story on Professor Melvin to Oaten after his meeting with the Chief, he was informed that he'd missed an earlier call from Portsmouth – Lexy tipping him off about the raid on the Temple.

"Well, just between you and me, old chap, I might never have got some important details about the councillor if it wasn't for Freddie," the reporter revealed. "He was my insider at the Lodge."

Spooner recalled the man in the Portsmouth hotel lobby, holding open the door to the phone booth. There was quite a resemblance between him and the detective in the photograph. "Is that so?"

Lexy blew a string of smoke rings. "Yes, and he's definitely suspicious of the spiritualist press, he said as much last time I saw him. That's why I thought I should let you know about last night, give you a bit of a warning. And," he raised his eyebrows, "ask your opinion on something I've never been sure of."

"And what might that be?" Spooner asked.

"Well," Lexy rubbed his hands together, "Freddie has been itching to bust the Temple apart for years, but something's always stopped him. Then, just before Christmas, he called to tell me things have changed and he's going to raid the place on the nineteenth of January, the next time the Duncans are in town. So can I have all my outstanding business on this," he tapped Councillor Roberts' image, "finished by then? Of course, I can see the possibilities, so I make sure I've got everything ready to spring on Roberts and still have my copy filed before events unfurl at the Temple. But still it leaves me wondering—" another smoke ring floated towards the ceiling. "Why did Freddie finally get let off his lead?" Lexy lowered his voice to a whisper, although the roadhouse was virtually deserted. "Someone's controlling him – but who?"

Spooner's expression remained blank. "Who do you suspect?" he asked.

"The way I see it, there's two possibilities," Lexy opined. "MI5 or the navy. Either way, it doesn't look good for the Duncans, does it?"

"No." Spooner shook his head. "I'll give you that."

"So," Lexy pressed on, "I thought we might pool our resources. You might hear something from the Duncans' defence team; I might pick up something else from the Admiralty or the less cerebral officers at Freddie's station. Something that might be of use to all of us…"

Spooner stood up, folded the newspaper and tucked it under his arm. "Thanks for the paper and the tip, Mr Lexy," he said, fishing in his pockets and dropping enough coins on the table to pay for what they'd ordered. "But I'd best be on my way."

"But you don't understand," Lexy pushed back his chair. "We can help each other out here. And you might need it, Spooner. Freddie will be gunning for you and your magazine when this goes to trial and, whoever his real paymasters are, they'll be giving him all the ammo he needs. Why not gun for him first?"

Spooner held out his hand. "I'm obliged, Mr Lexy, honestly. But I don't need your help."

He left the journalist standing there, for the moment lost for words.

Spooner couldn't afford to spend any more time in the environs of Portsmouth. He had another interview promised to Oaten and Lexy's warnings only strengthened his urge to get it done quickly. The years that had elapsed since he had been given the contact details meant the testimony might not be as powerful as if he had pursued it back then. When he had finally dialled the Dorset number the night before, he was prepared for the voice on the other end of it to turn him down flat.

But as Mrs Dowson had suggested, back when she slipped him her details, Davey Walker's mother welcomed the idea of sharing her story. She had heard of the arrests from her friend in Portsmouth who had been at the séance when they happened. Sounding less frail than he had anticipated, she gave him instructions for finding her sister's farm.

Spooner was glad of them. Without any road signs, he might easily have got lost along the narrow lanes that twisted through this undulating landscape, banked by towering hedges that gave him the feeling he was travelling through a bramble and hawthorn maze towards his location, between three villages at the bottom of a river valley.

As the black Anglia finally bumped its way into the courtyard, he was greeted by a small figure, dressed in tweeds and gumboots, her hair pinned up into a bun from which tendrils were busily trying to escape. Spooner ran his eyes across the limestone farmhouse and its huddle of barns and outbuildings. "You're well hidden here," he said.

"Which has its compensations," she broke into a smile. "Will you come in, Mr Spooner?"

He had to stoop to avoid knocking his head on the lintel as he followed her through the door and into the kitchen. Built around a central chimney, it was a large room with a range, flagstone floor adorned with rag mats and an oak table with Windsor chairs, all of which was kept cosy from the fire being so close to the ceiling, evidenced by the tabby cat sleeping on an armchair. A practical room, uncluttered by ornamentation, save for the horse brasses tacked around the fireplace and the bright yellow curtains.

"I don't think I would have got over what happened to Davey if I hadn't been able to come back here," Mrs Walker admitted. Wrapping a tea towel around her hands, she reached a copper kettle off the hob. "But I was born into this life and it has always sustained me in times of need."

As she prepared tea, his hostess explained how she and her sister had grown up on the farm, the third generation of the family to own it. She wanted a career and went to train as a nurse in Portsmouth, where she met her husband, a captain in the navy. Her sister married a farmer's son, taking over the place from their parents. They had two lads of their own, both now serving with the 43rd Wessex in France. Two volunteers from the Women's Land Army were working with them now.

"The girls are a great help," Mrs Walker said. "They fill the place up and keep things lively, including making those curtains. Does me good to be around young people. When my husband was taken in the last war, I came up here with Davey and stayed until he was old enough to go to school. It meant he was never lonely." She returned her attentions to the teapot. "But it's the same with June – Mrs Dowson – and a lot of our friends. Our husbands were in the navy and so our sons wanted to follow them, even though they hadn't got a father to remember. You can't stop them, can you?"

She set the teapot, mugs and a bowl of sugar down on the table, went into the pantry for a jug of milk and a tin of biscuits. Her motions stirred the cat, who jumped down and began to twine a path between her feet, mewling for attention.

"Get away, Tiggy," she chided. "Here," she said, arranging

the china in front of Spooner and taking the lid off the tin, "dig in."

Spooner did as he was told. Mrs Walker observed his enjoyment with a smile, and only when she had filled his mug a second time did she suggest that it might be time to start.

Spooner lifted up his briefcase and took out his notebook and pen. As he put it back down, the cat leapt onto his knee.

"You *are* honoured," Mrs Walker said. "She normally keeps a distance from strangers."

Purring loudly, Tiggy plumped paws up and down on Spooner's thighs.

"Knock her off if she annoys you," his hostess advised.

"No, no," said Spooner. "Actually, I like cats. We always had one at home. I was brought up in a bookshop and that's the last place you want to find a mouse."

"Really? What an interesting start in life that must have been."

"Aye," Spooner felt himself flush, as if she had caught a glimpse of something he didn't want her to see. "So," he broke her gaze to thumb open his notebook and take the cap off his pen, "where would you like to start?"

"The night that it happened, I suppose," she considered. "It was June's idea. As you probably know, there's a set of them go regularly to the Shadwells, but I wasn't one of them. My hours at the hospital were too long and, to be honest, I was never all that keen on the Shadwells themselves." She frowned. "I'm sure you know how superstitious us country folk can be and partly that's down to coming from somewhere so closely knit – there's no room for anyone to pretend to be something that they're not. Don't get me wrong, I'm not saying I didn't trust them because they weren't local; I just found it odd that they'd done all that travelling and never really settled any-where. You could see she'd had ambitions in show business, she was a terrific pianist and somehow that got worked into what they did. Calling it the Master Temple seemed terribly pretentious, I thought. But," she shook her head, "it kept June happy, so what was the harm in it? I was trying to keep myself busy, trying not to think about what Davey might be going through. He always used to write, you see…"

Spooner heard a wobble in her voice. She blinked and reached inside her sleeve for a handkerchief. "Sorry," she said, dabbing quickly at her eyes with it. "You'll have to forgive me. Hard as I try, I can't always control it."

Spooner thought of his grandma, having to stay strong for everyone else around her, losing her daughter and then taking over her role in bringing him up without complaint. He thought of the other parallels between his life and that of this woman sitting opposite. He was just three years older than Davey Walker would have been.

"Aye," he said. "I understand. I'd the same feeling about the place myself. There were a lot of good people there and the Shadwells do give them something they need, but…"

"Yes, a big but," Mrs Walker nodded. "The prices they charge, for a start. Anyway, I suppose me saying that makes what happened next seem all the more extraordinary. I was worried about Davey. A bad feeling, you know, that history was about to repeat itself. Now, June had seen Helen Duncan once before, up in London, and she was very impressed by her. When she heard that Gladys Shadwell had somehow managed to get her to come down to Pompey, she was adamant I should come with her."

"So you weren't actually expecting much?" asked Spooner.

"No, I don't think I was," Mrs Walker agreed. "It was more a case of humouring June and really, just not rattling round the house on my own that night."

"Fascinating," Spooner's pen could hardly keep up with his thoughts. His mind was back in the darkened parlour of the Christian Spiritualist Greater World Association, where he had awaited the Highland seer with a similar scepticism. Was this, he wondered, what he wanted to hear? That his mind hadn't being playing tricks with him that night, that someone else had the same kind of experience with Helen as he had?

"And you were the first person she picked out of the audience?" he asked.

"That's right," Mrs Walker nodded. "Well, she said there were a lot of voices all talking at once and could they please take it one at a time. It looked like she *was* listening into them, but of course, you can fake that if you're a good enough actor, and the lights were very dim. Then she pointed at me and asked if I was the one who'd been waiting two weeks to hear from someone. I went cold as she said it. I knew it was going to be Davey."

Mrs Walker's gaze refocussed. Though she continued to look in Spooner's direction, her stare went beyond his and her voice began to speed up. "You've got to remember, this wasn't what I was hoping for," she said. "To get a message from him meant he was dead, didn't it? But I got to my feet, everyone in the room staring at me, and she says: 'I've got your Davey here. You're Mrs…' and I know I shouldn't have done, but I told her my name, I said: 'Mrs Walker, yes,' and as soon as I said it, I could see him, my Davey, and I don't know how else to put this but… he was coming right through her."

Spooner's pen stopped in mid-air as he recalled the headless form that seemed to flow out of the foam of white around Helen's head in Holland Park. "I know," he said. "You could clearly see that it was him, his features were recognisable?"

"Not just his face, his voice. It was *him* speaking to me, it was *his* voice that I heard. How can she have faked that?"

Spooner got the cold chills. "That's the thing, isnae?" he said. "The voice…"

Mrs Walker didn't miss a beat. "You've seen her do it too," she said.

Spooner put down his pen. "Aye," he said, forgetting about the purpose of his visit, only wanting to know what she knew. "You're right. But it wasn't a loved one who came through to me, it was no' a person I've even met. And yet it's the voice that keeps coming back. I don't think she could have faked it either. 'Cos the thing I've learned about Helen Duncan," he admitted, "is that no one ever sees the same thing in the same room at the same time when she's the medium. When I had my experience, what I saw and heard was not the same as the people sitting each side of me."

"And how do you think that happens?" Mrs Walker stared at him intently.

"My theory," said Spooner, "and it is only a theory, is that Helen operates like a long-wave radio. She sends out a signal on a certain frequency and if there is someone else within range, someone in the audience who can pick up her wavelength, then they can turn on a kind of receive switch and her message comes through to them." He thought of Karl Kohl, tapping on his crystal set, trying to locate Clara when she had passed through any earthly range. "I think it's a gift she has, but I dunnae think she can control it."

"Which is probably why," Mrs Walker said, "she gets

accused of trickery. Why as many people love her as hate her."

Spooner nodded. "That's about the size of it, aye."

"Well, I'd like to thank her," his interviewee said, "for having that gift. Now the shock of it's passed, I realise how lucky I am. I don't have Davey no more, not here, but his words still reached me and I'll always have them for comfort. If he was there, in a room above a chemist's shop in Pompey," her eyes rolled upwards, "then he could be here now, couldn't he?"

Tiggy stirred from Spooner's lap and jumped down to the floor. She headed for Mrs Walker, rubbing her head around her ankles before leaping into her lap.

Mrs Walker rubbed a knuckle against the brindled head. "I don't know where she got it from," she said, "but June told me that Mrs Duncan's mother said she'd get burned at the stake as a witch one day. Is that what they're going to do to her?"

"I don't think they'll go quite that far," Spooner found that he could not begin to practise to deceive this woman. "But I think they mean to take her out of public circulation for as long as they possibly can."

"And you don't think that's right?"

Spooner shook his head. "I'm not sure she deserves it, no."

Mrs Walker nodded. "Then I hope I can help you to stop it," she said. "Will you tell me something in return? You must believe in it, for you to make your living writing about it, but did you go to the spiritualists because you were missing someone yourself?"

"Aye," Spooner recalled the conversation he had had with Daphne that had led him to pick up the phone to Mrs Walker. "There's someone I've been hoping to hear from for the past twenty-six years. So far," he shrugged, "no luck. But that won't stop me carrying on."

"That's a long time," Mrs Walker said. Her voice softened, along with her eyes as she did her own mental arithmetic. "Your father?" she guessed.

"My mother," Spooner told her. "She died giving birth to me. Maybe that's why she doesnae want to come back."

On the top floor of a modernist building on the Embankment, inside a panelled boardroom, the Chief, the CO and Cecil Forbes-Dixon sat around a desk. Between them lay the report on the arrest of Helen Duncan made by DI Frederick Fraser.

"I'm afraid," Forbes-Dixon was saying, "Inspector Fraser behaved against all the advice we gave him, when he charged Mrs Duncan under the Vagrancy Act. We remain of the opinion that there are serious pitfalls to proceeding with this."

"We think we may have an alternative," said the CO, nodding towards the Chief.

"Yes," said the Chief. "Witchcraft. Section 4 of the 1735 Witchcraft Act, to be precise."

26

YOU GO TO MY HEAD

Wednesday, 15 March 1944

The ringmaster stood under a spotlight. His red frock coat, top hat and curly moustache defined the traditional garb of his profession, yet the violin tucked under his chin was an unusual touch. He had not used it earlier, in his two previous acts, when he had made his assistant levitate and then sawn her in half and put her back together again. Such feats could only be followed by something still more spectacular. Facing sideways to his audience in the Birmingham Hippodrome, he looked up to the ceiling, raised his bow and plucked a silvery note from the strings.

Another spotlight swivelled from the ceiling, picking out the form of a woman standing in mid-air. Her platinum blonde, marcel-waved head was bowed and the sequins on her evening dress reflected back multiple shafts of light across the theatre. At the sound of the violin, she lifted her head and opened her eyes, as if waking from a dream.

A collective gasp, like the sound of waves breaking on the shore, rose from the crowd.

The ringmaster drew his bow a second time. A cascade of notes flew forth and the woman in the sparkling dress turned a pirouette in mid-air.

"*Oooh!*" once more, the crowd spoke as one entity, catching its collective breath in its throat as its eyes widened to take in the spectacle.

The notes from the violin formed themselves into a tune and the glittering figure followed them, dancing across the ceiling. From one side to the other she leapt and spun, a marionette keeping time to the tune. When it slowed, so did she, her body swaying, her arms outstretched like a ballerina. When it quickened, her steps became more staccato. As the fiddling reached crescendo, she turned another pirouette, then another, until her very form became a blur. The myriad beams that flashed out from her costume gave her the appearance of something from another realm, almost as if she were an angel.

In the blackness beneath, the audience gasped and moaned in a thrilling mix of fear and awe. They had never seen anything like this before.

Then, as abruptly as it had begun, the music stopped. The spell broke and the seraphim became human again, a woman suspended in mid-air, swaying and stretching her arms out to try and catch her balance. Strangled shrieks came from the seats as, for a few heart-stopping seconds, it seemed that she might tumble and fall.

The ringmaster raised his bow and brought it back down, the shivering noise mirroring the pulsation of the dancer. Then he called forth another tune, soothing this time, almost mournful. The woman above bowed her head, folded her hands in an aspect of prayer. Then she stepped off the wire.

More screams crackled through the air as stomachs plunged with the trajectory their minds had foreseen. But just as quickly their voices turned into murmurs of awe as the golden figure floated, gently as thistledown, from the ceiling to the stage. Her slippered feet touched the boards at the exact same moment that the last note from the violin dissolved and the two figures turned towards each other and bowed.

A huge cheer rose up. The Two Magicians turned to take more bows to the audience.

"Now that," said Bertie Adams, "is what I call magic."

Spooner wiped his handkerchief across his brow. "You can say that again," he agreed.

Both men rose with the crowd and put their hands together in appreciation. It was one thing knowing technically how it was done – and the Hippodrome's manager had attended rehearsals this morning in order to ascertain their uses of wires, grips and ropes – but another to see it performed, with all the elements of skill, timing, costume and music coming together to create the grand illusion.

"I doubt the Great Blondin his self could surpass that wire work," Bertie said. "I ain't seen it done quite like that before and you know I seen 'em all."

"Aye, well, for me it was the music that did it," said Spooner. The tune the ringmaster had played to make his funambulist dance was called "Death and the Lady", recorded as having being written by J. Deacon in 1700 in Anna's songbook. The one that had brought her down to earth, "My Lodging is in the Cold Ground", was by Matthew Locke, 1666.

Spooner had finally been able to return to Birmingham the previous night, eight days before Helen Duncan was due to stand trial at the Old Bailey under the new charge of Witchcraft. The legislation came from a section of a 1735 Act, originally passed by King James I over a century earlier, which defined the charge as: 'the more effectual preventing and punishing any pretences to such arts or powers whereby ignorant persons are frequently deluded and defrauded'. The Chief's idea to use it was a masterstroke.

Though the evidence against her was as flimsy as the fabric at the centre of Helen's workings – which had itself never been recovered from the Master Temple – there seemed little chance she would be able to evade such deathly wording. Her husband had managed to escape all charges, but both Shadwells would be joining her in the dock for what was shaping up to be a legal Variety bill of the prosecution's own making.

The DPP had appointed John Gonne KC as Prosecuting Counsel. As well as having a distinguished career, including a stint as Treasury Counsel, he was the son of a famous actor, which would no doubt lend him a helpful perspective. The DPP himself was to be represented by J.E. Robey, son of Britain's best-loved comedian, George, 'The Prime Minister of Mirth'. All that remained to be proved was that the accused had pretended to conjure the spirits of the dead in a manner much more crude than the spectacle Spooner had just witnessed. The testimony of the RNVR officer who had summoned DI Fraser to the Temple could be all it took to secure a conviction.

"Should we go and offer our congratulations?" asked Bertie.

Spooner was glad of the whisky that had flowed as generously as it had the first time he was here before tonight's performance. He didn't think he had ever felt so nervous as he was now, following the barrelling figure in the blue dog-tooth suit around the corridors of the Hippodrome towards the backstage area, moving quickly to avoid the crowds that would soon come spilling out of the auditorium. They went through a door marked STAFF ONLY and into a corridor where men and women hurried by, pushing rails of costumes, lengths of wire, hammers and scenery from the stage to the props department and along the rows of dressing rooms.

Bertie stopped outside one of those rooms and knocked on the door. "Management," he called. "Might I be permitted to offer my congratulations?"

Spooner held his breath as he heard the handle turn and the door swung open.

It was the funambulist who stood there, her glittering dress now covered by an equally exotic black silk kimono, decorated with swirls of gold and orange carp. Her gleaming tresses had been swept up into a black silk headscarf in readiness for her to remove her stage make-up. Her pale blue eyes regarded her visitors from under thick false eyelashes with apparent good humour.

"Ah, hello, Mr Adams." She had the husky voice of a heavy smoker but pronounced her words with care. Her eyes widened as they travelled down to the bottle of champagne that the manager proffered. "Do, please, come in."

She took a step backwards, revealing to Spooner the room behind: a mirrored wall with dressing tables, a clothes rail and a small round table beside which, sitting on a stool and smoking a cigarette, the ringmaster, *sans* top hat, looked up from a magazine and stared back at him through sea-green eyes.

Her transformation was every bit as artful as the magic she had just performed. Her hair was black now, dyed and cut into a short crop. The shading of her make-up, including the moustache and sideburns, was sufficient to disguise an already urchin-like face from any traces of being female. Dressed in trousers, braces and dress shirt, with the bow tie undone around her neck, she sat with her legs apart, cupping her cigarette inside her palm. At a glance, there was nothing to suggest anything other than a slight young man, just out of adolescence. It was only the colour and shape of her eyes that gave her away.

That, and the way she had played her fiddle.

Something passed across her face as they saw each other; her irises widened with recognition and her mouth fell open for a fraction of a second. He thought it was relief he could see there, but then her co-performer turned towards her with Bertie's offering, cooing delight and obscuring his view at the same time, so he couldn't be sure.

"What a wonderful act, Miss Anderson," Bertie went on. That was the name the tightrope walker had given when he had booked The Two Magicians. It was she who had done all the talking, both on the telephone and at the theatre. He had yet to hear her colleague, introduced to him simply as Mr Hart, speak at all.

"Where ever did you learn such skills?" he went on. "No," he put up an index finger, "I know I shouldn't arsk, we all have our secrets, don't we? Might I introduce my colleague, Ross Spooner, from the Paramount Agency in London? I think he'd like to make you an offer."

"Is that so?" Miss Anderson spun around. She put the bottle down on the table and lifted from the ashtray a cigarette in a slim ebony holder, taking a lengthy drag as she ran her eyes up and down Spooner. Her expression became a touch more sardonic as she blew out a long plume of smoke and finally extended her hand. "Well, hello, Mr Spooner," she said. Her fingers were as long as his, her grip reminding Spooner of the disembodied hand closing around his leg in his dreadful nightmare of Clara.

"Hello, Miss Anderson." Despite the urge to wince, Spooner

smiled. "And," he looked at the figure at the table, "who else do I have the pleasure of addressing?"

Sea-green eyes flashed a split-second warning. "Oh, don't mind Mr Hart." The hand that had felt like a mantrap being sprung now flapped crimson fingernails in Spooner's face. "He doesn't speak to strangers. I'll do all the talking, if you don't mind."

Of course, thought Spooner, it would be much harder for Anna to disguise her voice than anything else about herself. "As you like," he said, reaching into his pocket for his business card and smiling back as he studied the face in front of him more closely. From behind those pan-sticked features, the ringmaster tipped him a wink.

For the next twenty minutes, making small talk and drinking champagne with a man who had once put him in hospital, Spooner felt as if he was balancing on a high wire himself – if he judged any aspect of this situation wrongly, it would be him falling from a dizzy height. But he had to let go of fear and submit to trust, that the knowledge he had accrued since he was coshed to the Edgbaston pavement would render him more skilful than even such a master illusionist as the female alter ego of Nils Anders that stood before him.

"I have an idea," she said, after Spooner had described the kind of gigs he could get for them in London. "We are fully booked until the last day of April, when we are due to perform a very—" a smile twitched at the corner of her red lips, "*special* show for a private client. A performance that would enable us to demonstrate more of our talents than those you have seen this evening. Our employer that night is a generous man, I am sure he wouldn't mind us bringing a guest." She looked over her shoulder. "Would he, Mr Hart?"

The ringmaster shook his head.

Spooner's mind stared down the drop. The thirtieth of April was Walpurgisnacht, the night of the Witches' Sabbat referred to by Goethe in the grimoire once owned by Harry Price. Apart from Samhain, when Nicholas Ralphe had faced the ritual laid out in that work and been driven insane, it was the most powerful night in the Black magic calendar.

"Naturally," the magician went on, "there's plenty of room up at the Hall."

"The Hall?" said Spooner, pushing his glasses back up the bridge of his nose.

"Oh, of course, you're not based in Birmingham are you? Perhaps it would not be so convenient for you to join us," she pouted, a motion that squared her jawline, made her look altogether more masculine. "What a shame."

"No, no," countered Spooner. "It's part of my job to travel. Just give me the address and I'll be there." He opened the battered appointments book he had been supplied with for his first visit to Birmingham and began to make a note of the date.

"Take a train from here to Stourbridge on the evening of the thirtieth, one that will get you in at about ten o'clock – it is normally a regular service. We will pick you up from there. I hope you won't mind a late night."

"Sounds intriguing." Spooner wrote his instructions down.

"I can promise you," Miss Anderson said, "a night of revelation."

Spooner hadn't been able to borrow the same car that had brought him here the last time, but he'd been supplied with a very similar Rover 16. The next part of his act was to wait beside it, ostensibly smoking a cigarette but drawing attention to himself by shining a pen torch into his address book that he pretended to examine on the vehicle's roof. Bertie told him where to park. Next to the maroon Austin that The Two Magicians had arrived in.

He had not waited for long before he heard the scuffle of footsteps running towards him and a voice, like the silvery chime of a bell, said, "Mr Spooner, is that you?"

He turned, shining his torch into her face. The moustache was gone now, sponged off with the rest of her professional visage.

"Anna," he said. "It *is* you, isn't it?"

She squinted in the torch beam, turned her head sideways. "Can we go somewhere?" She sounded panicked. "Quickly, before I'm missed. There are so many things I need to explain but," she glanced backwards over her shoulder, "we must speak alone."

"Of course," said Spooner. "Get in." He opened the passenger door and she slipped inside.

As he started up the engine, she turned to him and smiled. "I knew you would get my messages," she said.

Spooner put his foot on the accelerator. "Where d'you want me to go just now?"

"Anywhere," she said, "away from here." She turned to look back out of the window as they bumped out of the car park.

"All right," said Spooner. "So, go on. What do you have to tell me?"

"I know what happened to Clara."

Spooner kept his eyes on the unlit road. "Oh," he said. "What's that?"

"She was murdered," said Anna. "Then he chopped off her hand and buried it and stuffed the rest of her into a tree. Worse than any ballad in that book I used to have." He could feel her staring at him, willing him to turn and read the meaning in her eyes. "Four little boys found her there last spring. What was left of her."

"And d'you know who it was that did this?" he asked.

"The officer," said Anna. "Ralph Nicholson, or whatever his name was. After he married her and found out she had been seeing someone else behind his back. That Professor De Vere I told you about. She was his all along. That's why she was hidden in the grounds of his estate, and that's why I left you all those messages. I knew you would realise…"

Spooner raised his left hand. "Slow down, hen. I cannae take this all in at once. Forget about Clara for a minute. What I really want to know is, what happened to you after I was left for dead on the pavement back there? It's been three years." This time he did look at her and she dropped her head, shaking it sadly.

"Of course. I'm sorry, Mr Spooner, it was dreadful what happened that day. It's the reason I didn't dare try to contact you directly." She looked back up at him. "It was Nils who did that to you. Or Miss Anderson, as you saw him tonight. He didn't realise what was going on, that I was coming with you to London. He thought you were a policeman and panicked. But he didn't mean to do you any lasting harm. I had no idea what he had got himself into, but he explained it all to me. It's shocking. Worse than you could imagine."

"D'you think we're far enough away from him now that I can pull over?" asked Spooner. "I'm not sure how much more revelation I can take without driving us into a brick wall."

"Oh!" She gave a nervous giggle and looked back over her shoulder again. "Of course."

Spooner braked at the kerb on the corner of John Bright Street, just a few feet away from the Victoria public house, stopped the engine and turned towards her. "Go on, hen," he said. "Now you can tell me."

"Clara was a spy," said Anna. "I think I realised that from the moment I saw her trunk in the back of the officer's car. I just didn't want to believe it."

"A spy?" Spooner repeated.

Anna nodded, her eyes huge in the dim light. "A German spy called Agent Belladonna. It's her fault the BSA factory got blown up that night... and a lot of other things..."

"That's incredible," said Spooner. "How do you know for sure?"

"This is the hard part." She looked down again, "Nils was helping her. But," her head came up, her gaze beseeching, "only because he had to. She was blackmailing him, Mr Spooner. She had met him before, long ago, and she knew a secret that I didn't. Something that's not his fault but could have got him deported or even killed. Nils passed himself off as Dutch, but Clara knew he really was German. And he didn't have a passport." Anna shook her head. "She had a friend who was a counterfeiter, so she fixed him up with a Dutch passport that looked as good as the real thing. But after that, he had to help her get rid of more of them and that's what the bogeys were after him for. It was a stupid thing to do – he knew it and I do too. But that's why I invented The Two Magicians, both of us pretending to be what we're not. I thought we had more of a chance of keeping him safe that way. Oh, I don't expect you to understand it at all, but Nils was my friend." She put her hand on Spooner's arm. "At times, he was my only friend in the world."

Spooner bit back the question as to why she had been hiding from him when they first met. He didn't want to interrupt the flow of her story, confession – whatever it was.

"Anyway, he didn't feel the same way. He left me in the lurch after a show in Catford on the Christmas of 1941. I thought that the bogeys had caught up with him and they might come for me next, so I kept moving on, taking any job I could get, so long as I didn't have to stay in one place too long. Then he turned up again…" she paused, staring at Spooner as if trying to convey something she dared not say aloud, "… soon after they found Clara. Persuaded me to pick things up where we'd left off. The only reason I did it was to try and find you. You're the only person who can help me."

"Did he tell you what happened? Where he'd been all that time?" Spooner asked.

She shook her head. "You don't want to know. All I can tell you is that Professor De Vere has been in Germany, working for the SS – and he's coming back on the thirtieth of April. That's who we're doing the show for and—" her voice wobbled as a single tear ran down her cheek, "I am certain he means to kill us too, once he gets us to that place. Now," she pressed her fingers into Spooner's arm. "I can't go to the police, but you can. Find the spycatcher in Birmingham and tell him if he wants to know who put Bella in the Wych Elm he's to follow you from Stourbridge that night. You'll be picked up in that car I saw Clara go into and taken to her last resting place – maybe mine too."

"But Anna," Spooner said, "you don't have to do this. Don't you see? Just don't go. Come with me to London. I've kept your songbook safe. What more do you need?"

Emotion had got the better of him, he was offering her things he had no right to promise. But however hard he tried to put up a mask, Anna had a hold on his heart.

"But I can't," a second tear emerged from the other eye and joined the first in a race down her cheeks, "none of it will work unless I go like a lamb to the slaughter. You don't understand what I'm up against and I can't tell you now…" Her hand moved to the door and she opened it with one deft movement. "I don't think you'll believe me until you see it with your own eyes. But just, please, come."

Spooner lunged towards her but she slipped through his grasp like a shadow. Her footsteps echoed up the cobbles of John Bright Street, disappearing into the night.

27

IN THE DARK

Wednesday, 29 March 1944

"I first had the pleasure of meeting Mrs Duncan in the autumn of 1932."

Swaffer looked out from the witness stand across the floor of the Old Bailey. Five days into the witch trial and nothing so far had gone as planned.

Though he had amassed plenty of notable witnesses for her defence, Helen's KC, Charles Loseby, seemed lost from the start. His opposite number, John Gonne, was a handsome, erudite man whose smooth baritone conveyed a plausibility that the older man's vocal cords, strained by the effects of a gas attack in the last war, failed to match.

The prosecution's opening evidence, from RNVR Lieutenant Stanley Worthington, went down far better than the SNU had anticipated. He amused the court with his imitation of Gladys, telling him that Helen was a "marvellous materialisation medium" complete with rolling Rhondda "r"s. Loseby's attempts to wrestle back advantage were as doomed as his witness's struggle with the material he had found on Helen's lap – another part of Stanley's testimony greeted with snorts of enthusiasm from the press bench.

The next day, when the prosecution produced DI Freddie Fraser, Loseby sought to ridicule Stanley's testimony by enquiring as to the whereabouts of this fabric. Gonne stepped in with a suggestive line about the need to have a medic to search for it. Fraser, an individual who, to Swaffer, epitomised all the worst qualities a policeman could develop, gave a knowing smile before replying to that question in the affirmative.

Because she had spent each evening of the trial being observed in test séance conditions by the SNU deputation, Loseby had hoped Helen would be allowed to demonstrate her psychic abilities to the courtroom. But the presiding Recorder of London, Sir Charles Carroll, ruled that – despite the legislation under which Helen was being tried – it would appear too much like a "medieval ordeal" for her to do so in a modern courtroom.

Swaffer filed away these words for future reference.

The only small triumph came on the fourth day, when the case was made against the Shadwells. Much to the relief of the defence, the chemist produced receipts for all the donations to charity he had made from séance profits. The main beneficiaries of the Temple's generosity were the Wireless for the Blind Fund, which put the Shadwells' pricing policies into a more positive state of illumination. The afternoon wore on with more testimonies in Helen's favour, until Carroll interrupted a cross-examination to ask Loseby how many more witnesses he intended to call.

"Let me see," said the KC, appearing bewildered, "about forty? Fifty?"

Without further comment, Carroll closed proceedings.

Swaffer knew the Recorder had an ulterior motive for this. Like his learned colleagues, Robey and Gonne, Sir Charles

Carroll also had a showbiz side. He liked to dabble in what he called humorous light musicals – and his latest offering, *The Rebel Maid*, was premiering in the West End that very night. Having been professionally obliged to sit through some of his Lordship's previous efforts in his role as a theatre critic, Swaffer felt he had enough ammunition to seize the dramatic lead when it came to his turn in the dock.

"I took with me to our initial meeting four professional stage magicians, two fully-trained doctors and two medical students," Swaffer said, his eyes travelling to the opposite side of the room, where they came to rest on the grey eyes of prosecution witness Harry Price.

"The two doctors tied Mrs Duncan with forty yards of sash-cord; she was handcuffed with regulation police handcuffs, her thumbs being tied tightly together with eight yards of thread – so tightly that it cut into the flesh. It took eight minutes to tie her up, but she was free again in less than three." Swaffer continued to stare at Harry Price until the Ghost Hunter blinked. "I doubt even Houdini himself could have managed the feat so quickly."

"And how, in the opinion of yourself and those distinguished gentlemen, did Mrs Duncan achieve this feat?" enquired Loseby.

Swaffer refocussed on the public gallery. "The spirits released her," he said, catching sight of a familiar bouffant of copper curls. "Mrs Duncan was examined before and afterwards so that I could file a thorough report for my newspaper without misleading any members of the public who were not there to witness the spectacle for themselves. I have the signed medical documents here," he tapped the sheaf of papers in front of him, turned his gaze back towards Harry

Price. "And I have also brought with me a length of butter muslin, with which I intend to demonstrate the impossibility of the prosecution's claims about regurgitation." He pulled a length of filmy fabric from his top pocket. "If I may now demonstrate?"

Gonne was on his feet in an instant. "Objection!" he barked.

"Sustained," Carroll growled. "Mr Swaffer, put that material down. There is no question of such an experiment being carried out here. I will not have the courtroom reduced to the level of an exhibition."

Swaffer waved the fabric before dropping it, so that it made a graceful plume as it drifted towards the floor. "Or a light musical drama perhaps?" he said, as he watched it fall.

A murmur of laughter rippled across the public gallery. It had not escaped anyone's attention that Carroll's play had not opened to good notices in any of today's papers.

Loseby caught the material. "You have been a dramatic critic yourself, Mr Swaffer?"

Swaffer lowered his eyes. "Unfortunately, yes," he replied.

Carroll peered darkly over his bench. "For whom?" he said.

Swaffer raised his lamps. "For the *Daily Herald*, my Lord. My employers."

Carroll's scowl deepened. "That's not what I meant. You said 'unfortunately'. For whom was it unfortunate?"

"The poor critic who had to sit through it, my Lord."

"Mr Loseby," The Recorder boomed over the sound of giggles, "I must ask you and your witness to restrict your comments to those that pertain to the case."

Swaffer took this as a cue to raise himself to his full height. His eyes travelled from the copper curls in the public gallery to the figure sat next to her in a dove-grey suit.

"The case in front of us," he said, "is of the gravest importance to those cherished ideals of freedom and democracy that we have been fighting for over the past five years. At the beginning of this week, my Lord was brave enough to say that he would not have Mrs Duncan going through the equivalent of a medieval ordeal in this room and yet this entire hearing is evidence that the orthodoxy has gone back to broomsticks. The establishment that charges this lady with the crime of witchcraft obviously cares little for the aspirations of tolerance laid down by Churchill and Roosevelt in the Atlantic Charter of 1941. Instead, it has turned to rekindling one of the great amusements of the Dark Ages – the persecution of working-class women. That is what the prosecution seek and at a time such as this they should be thoroughly ashamed of themselves."

He let his words resound around the silent Old Bailey, have time to sink into the minds of all present, before Loseby, in a rare instance of perfect timing, turned towards Carroll. "No further questions, my Lord."

Swaffer met Daphne a discreet distance away from the court, where they could avoid the throng that congregated each day on the steps to offer the accused condolences and jeers in equal measure. Her driver took them to her townhouse in Gloucester Place.

Swaffer had been invited there many times since his initial meeting with Daphne in the bitter February of 1942. All those subsequent occasions had been happy times, with like-minded souls gathered together for dining and discussion. Today's meeting would be nothing quite like those occasions, although he hoped it would prove as, or more, illuminating.

His frustration with what was transpiring in court had finally led him to ask Daphne to make an introduction for him. She was the only person who could.

After taking his coat and hat, she showed him up to the first-floor sitting room where she had told him the tragic story of her murdered friend. Waiting for him there now, standing in almost the exact spot by the fireplace where Daphne herself had that first night and smoking just as anxiously, was the mystery finally made flesh.

"Mr Swaffer," said their hostess, "Mr Spooner. Or, if you prefer, Swaff, this is Ross."

The young man that stepped towards him offering his hand was not the pale creature Swaffer's memory recalled from DCI Greenaway's office. Dressed in tweeds with a velvet waistcoat, red curls sprouting from his temples, he was every inch the bohemian, though the eyes behind his glasses held something of the sombre look of a policeman.

"Swaff," he said. "Glad to meet you at last."

"Ross," Swaffer's long fingers curled around the other man's for an instant. "I'm glad that you could come. I hope I haven't put you to too much trouble."

"Nae bother. It's no' much of a hop from here to Euston. I can get the last train back to Manchester and Ernest will be none the wiser. Well, I won't tell him if you don't."

"Gentlemen," Daphne said, "help yourselves to drinks. I'll leave you until dinner."

Both men turned towards her, placed their hands over their hearts and bowed, neither realising they did so in perfect synchronicity. Daphne smiled as she closed the door.

Swaffer moved to the drinks first. "What will you have?" he said.

Spooner lifted his empty tumbler from the mantelpiece. "Scotch," he said.

The older man smiled. "Of course." He poured their drinks, lit a cigarette and indicated the chairs by the fireplace. "Shall we?"

Spooner sat down, took a sip of his whisky and came straight to the point. "I'm thinking you want to know what happened to the statements I took for Ernest, and why they've no' been put forward as evidence?"

"Well, it does seem a trifle odd," Swaffer said, "given the way things are going. I should have thought Mrs Walker would have made a star witness for the defence."

Spooner nodded. "Aye, well she would. But let me try to explain." He put his glass down, lacing his fingers together. "Just before the arrests were made, I had a call from a reporter on the *Portsmouth Evening News*, Richard Lexy. I met him when I first went down there, in the December of '41. Back then he tried to convince me that the Shadwells were little more than a magic act. He disliked them intensely, mainly because Gladys had a friend who called himself a faith healer who'd gone down for child molesting in 1936."

"Ah," said Swaffer. "Hard not to see his point, then."

"Aye," Spooner concurred, "if they really were friends. But I'm no' sure he wasn't feeding me a line. See, Lexy was working on a story about Councillor Roberts, who, as you know, was undisputedly one of Grenville's friends. He inspected the mediums before every séance, I saw him in action myself. For Lexy, the Shadwells were a small part of a bigger picture, which turned out to be this fraud Roberts had cooked up with his ship scaler's company. Lexy's main aim when I first met him was to try and put me off writing anything about the Temple, so as I didn't do anything to blow his cover... Or, that's what I thought at the time."

Swaffer frowned. "And what did he want with you this time?" he said.

"He said he wanted to warn me about DI Fraser, which I thought was pretty rich. I can't prove it, but there was a man who looked a hell of a lot like Fraser hanging round the hotel Lexy suggested I use when I first went to Portsmouth, so I'd come to the conclusion they were in cahoots. There's also this," Spooner reached into his briefcase to present Swaffer with a copy of the paper. "Councillor Roberts on one side, Fraser dragging Gladys out of the Temple on the other. See what I mean?"

Swaffer stared at the two picture leads. It was hard not to agree with the analysis.

"Lexy admitted they'd choreographed things," Spooner went on. "Fraser helped him with his Roberts story in return for Lexy spying on the Temple and feeding him information on the Shadwells. This time, though, he said that Fraser had wanted to arrest the Shadwells years ago, at the time of the *Barham* séance, but he wasn't allowed to – someone higher up was pulling his lead."

Swaffer looked up sharply. "Did he make any suggestions as to whom?"

"Either MI5 or Naval Intelligence, he reckoned, which is why he wanted to warn me. He said Fraser would be gunning for me if this came to trial, and he'd have back-up way beyond his station. He suggested we could help each other by exchanging information and it was at that point I ended our conversation."

"Oh?" Swaffer rapidly tried to process all the angles. "And why was that?"

"Well," Spooner unlaced his fingers and spread the digits wide. "For all I knew, this could be another set-up with Fraser. It wasn't, and I got out of Portsmouth with my life, as you can see – but it gave me pause for thought. What if Lexy was telling the truth?"

The two men locked gazes. In Swaffer's, Spooner could read understandable suspicion. In Spooner's, Swaffer ascertained the qualities that had drawn his friends Daphne and Ernest towards this young man. The affable front that disguised a forensic ability to discern the real story was the hallmark of a good reporter – or a good detective. If he wasn't telling the truth, then the line he was peddling was more audacious than Lexy's.

"I had the testimonies of all these good people," Spooner went on. "These women who had faith in me and the organisation I represented. What if I was unwittingly putting them in danger by presenting their testimony in court? Because if it is true, then Helen's going down whatever we try to do for her. I mean, why else is she being hauled up to the Old Bailey and not Portsmouth Assizes? And why else have they changed the legislation she's been charged under and dug up this ancient law?"

Swaffer put his fingertips together, and closed his eyes. He couldn't argue with this thinking; it paralleled the conclusions he had drawn for himself.

"That was my dilemma," said Spooner. "So obviously, I talked it over with Ernest, laid out my fears the same way I've put it all to you. We came to the decision that it was better not to put those women at risk. We also thought it might be best for all concerned if I stayed away from the court and took care of business while Ernest came down to follow the trial."

He lifted his glass and took a sip. "Ach, but we could have been wrong. What do you think? Would you have advised differently?"

Swaffer opened his eyes. "All things considered," he said, exhaling smoke, "I think you came to the right decision. I can't see myself acting otherwise, were I in your shoes."

He saw a flicker of relief pass over the other man's face.

"And now," Swaffer raised his own glass. There was more than one reason why he had inveigled this meeting, and more than one method he could use to try and discern the truth about Spooner. "I have a question to put to you, which, in a way, comes directly from Helen."

"Oh yes?" Spooner leaned towards him, the earnest expression back in his eyes.

"What do you know about Clara?"

28

NIGHT AND DAY

Thursday, 30–Friday, 31 March 1944

Spooner sat in an otherwise empty *Two Worlds'* office, the
wireless on low in the background, a dance band rendering
of "A String of Pearls". It wasn't such a good version as Glenn
Millar's hit recording, but Spooner wasn't really listening to
the music. Nor was he studying the folder of classified information the Chief had given him to read and then destroy.
Instead, he was back in Daphne's sitting room with Swaffer.

It had been his biggest bluff yet, agreeing to see the journalist and offering up the version of events he had presented: that
it was Lexy's warnings about Secret Service involvement in the
Duncan case he was heeding in order to protect Mrs Walker,
Mrs Dowson and the rest of his Portsmouth contacts. The
Evening News reporter had unwittingly served Spooner the
most plausible line to follow in his own clandestine rendering
of events and he thought the shrewd old Fleet Street veteran
had believed him. Or at least, been convinced enough to drop
the subject and hold his peace on the matter.

What he hadn't reckoned on was what Swaffer had come
out with next. That he had received a new message from Clara,
via Helen, during a test séance the night before. Spooner was

rendered almost speechless by this. Fortunately, as it had so many times before with the people he had met along this trail, his wide-eyed response that he wasn't sure what Swaffer meant had elicited sympathy rather than suspicion.

"I believe we have both encountered this spirit before," Swaffer said, "during Helen's séances for Miss Moyes' circle in Holland Park. Or at least," he added, "Daphne told me that you had a rather disturbing experience there when you first met. Perhaps it's bold of me to assume it was the same spirit, but all the same, I should like to compare notes, if you wouldn't mind indulging me."

The journalist rose to retrieve the whisky decanter, allowing Spooner time to gather his thoughts and deduce that he could gain a valuable insight by finding out exactly what had been observed at that previous séance.

"The spirit I saw didn't give me a name," he said, as his companion refreshed their glasses. "And she wasnae someone I even knew in life. In fact, I only know it was a she because I heard her voice. The apparition was headless."

Swaffer sat back down. "Well, what I believe I saw there, on the night of the fourteenth of January 1941," he said, "was a woman about to be murdered. Strangled, I think, or choked to death. Which could explain why it was she appeared to you that way."

Spooner felt a cold breath at his neck, prickles running down his spine.

"I saw a beautiful woman," the older man went on, "with cascades of hair, like Lizzie Siddal floating in Millais' bathtub. She was singing, some kind of air, I couldn't quite make it out." Swaffer's long fingers danced in the air between them as he attempted to recreate the tune. He had written songs for the music hall back in his youth and still had perfect pitch. "*Lala lee, lala lay… You know the sort of thing I mean?*"

Spooner nodded, recognising the notes as the ones Anna had played when she was drawing her companion down from the ceiling of the Birmingham Hippodrome: "My Lodging is in the Cold Ground".

"I knew this wasn't Peggy, Helen's spirit guide," Swaffer went on, "so I asked for her name. She replied that I already knew it, and referred to me as her 'dearest'. She then said that it was a fine night for it – an echo of a thought I'd had on my way there."

"What did she sound like?" Spooner's palm tightened around his glass.

"Curious," said Swaffer. "Sort of Brummie, Black Country. Only when she said 'was' she pronounced it 'vas'. A speech impediment, perhaps?"

"Perhaps," said Spooner, not offering up the alternative: that this was how a German pretending to be English would pronounce the word. Swaffer smiled and continued.

"She went on to describe her surroundings, the moon, the snow and the woods, quite happily at first. Then abruptly, she started to sob. She glimmered for a moment and I feared she was going to fade. Then her voice came back: 'What is this?' she said. 'Why have you brought *me* here? This isn't right!' Well, I assured her that she was quite safe, we only invite those to our circle who wish to be heard. She cried out: 'No!' and there was a violent sound of choking…" Swaffer put a hand up to his throat.

"She vanished and I realised it was Helen who was in trouble. At which point, instinct took over. I dived into the cabinet and practised a manoeuvre I learned in a field hospital in Flanders. Thank God I remembered it – she would have been a gonner otherwise. She'd got something stuck in her throat. When she had recovered sufficiently, she told me she had been with this woman at the moment of her death – and that her name was Clara. Which is why I was intrigued to ask if the name meant anything to you?"

Spooner tried to swallow but found his throat was too dry. He shook his head instead.

"Strange," said Swaffer. "Because last night, this same spirit returned to me again, through Helen. I recognised her immediately. But, since her message was not one I understood, I thought that it might be for you."

"W-what was it?" Spooner put the tumbler down before his fist went through it.

"Tell he it is who seeks me," said Swaffer, "not to go back into the woods." He bent closer. "I was made all the more curious, you see, by the interview you did with Professor Melvin last month, about this mystery woman in the Midlands, Bella in the Wych Elm, as they call her. I had an inkling there were factors in common – the woodland location for one, and the fact that she was once referred to as Clarabella by the anonymous correspondent who keeps leaving messages about her," he searched the other man's face for clues, but found a flinty carapace had fallen over Spooner's eyes. "I was hoping you might be able to help me unravel the mystery," he said, leaning back in his chair. "I've searched in vain for a murder victim who might fit the bill since it happened. And if anything were to make a restless shade, then this…"

Spooner reeled himself in. If Swaffer had made this connection from the magazine rather than any ghostly communication from Clara, he could explain it away with more half-truths. Still, he needed another lubricating sip of whisky before he continued.

"Ach," he said, shaking his head. "I'm sorry to disappoint you, Swaff, but that was Ernest's idea. He was the one who first drew my attention to it, and he's had me covering that story since the messages started appearing. It's an intriguing set of coincidences, I'll grant you, and it's one of those stories the readers have been mad on. But my only real contribution to that debate was suggesting Professor Melvin might be able to explain some of the mysteries about how the body was hidden, especially that grim wee detail about the severed hand. See, my father had her books, I read them as a youth, when I first started to get interested in these subjects. I'm sure Daphne's told you a bit about my background?"

Swaffer must have sensed he would get no further with his enquiries as he seemed happy to spend the next twenty minutes chatting about their hostess, before she called them down for dinner and discussion returned to the day's events in court. They parted a couple of hours later as if happy to have made each other's acquaintance.

Spooner looked up the date in meteorological records the next morning. It coincided with the full moon on the fourteenth of January 1941. The information concurred with the findings of Professor Willis' pathologist's report about how long Clara's body had been hidden in the tree. It was a perfect fit for the night of her murder.

The music ended and a voice crackled over the radio.

"Germany calling, this is Germany calling…"

De Vere was still on the air in Berlin tonight.

*

The jury had not been at their deliberations for long. Twenty-four minutes, Swaffer calculated, looking down at his watch as the minute hand clicked to three minutes to five. He rubbed his eyes, taking in the shuffling figures. Their brevity was not an encouraging sign, considering they had sat through two hours of Loseby's closing comments. Neither was the way they all looked to the floor as they made their way back to the bench.

"Gentlemen and lady of the jury, have you come to your decision?" asked the Recorder.

The foreman stood up. "We have, my Lord."

"How do you find the accused, Helen Duncan?" Carroll asked. "Guilty or not guilty?"

"Guilty."

A great whispering swirled around the room, like the voices of disembodied spirits.

"And how do you find the accused, Grenville Shadwell? Guilty or not guilty?"

"Guilty."

At once, the voices hushed.

"And how do you find the accused, Gladys Shadwell? Guilty or not guilty?"

"Guilty."

There was silence as Helen slipped, fainting into her husband's arms.

"I shall wait in London for the sentencing," Oaten's voice down the telephone line sounded a decade older than it had the day before. "Expect to see me late on Monday. I'll come direct from the train to the office."

"I'm sorry, Ernest," said Spooner. "Is there anything I can do in the meantime?"

His editor sighed. "You know which edition to start preparing," he said. "I'll phone back with the sentences, should be just after ten or thereabouts. But leave the leader to me, will you?" Some of his old spirit seemed to crackle back at the prospect. "I'll write it on the train." Then he sighed. "There's nowt else you can do, really."

"All right," said Spooner, his eyes resting on the two mock-up covers he had been working on, "leave it to me. Safe journey home, Ernest."

He replaced the receiver, shaking his head. He took down the cover with the celebratory headline: MRS DUNCAN VINDICATED! and tucked it under his arm. Then he turned back to his desk where, from the photograph clipped to the top of the folder, stared a reproduction of an old police mugshot, taken from a 1928 German paper, that looked very much like a younger version of Nils Anders. The man in this photograph was called Otto Dieterling, an eighteen-year-old burglar from Munich. Dieterling had been jailed for stealing jewellery from the bedroom of a countess, an offence that demonstrated a dextrous ability to climb up walls and pass through tiny gaps. He served three years for it.

The first account the Chief had been able to find of Nils Anders appearing in the Goldschmidt Brothers Circus was in Hamburg, 1933, around the same time that Clara was singing at the Café Dreyer. When the circus disbanded in 1939, Anders was no longer on their books – perhaps because by then, if Anna's story was true, he was already in Birmingham. The contents of the slim dossier provided only tenuous links but the forensics from the letters and the wax from the temple joined a few more dots.

Ralphe's typewriter had not been recovered from his room

but the first letter was a match for correspondence previously provided to his CO; the second two letters indicated a different author using the same machine. The wax on the floor of the temple was made from the same substances – sulphur and pitch – as the candle in Clara's severed hand.

Spooner closed the covers of the grey folder and gathered it up with the obsolete front cover, to take down to the furnace in the cellar and offer them up to the flames. Rather, he expected, as would be his own fate, in exactly a month's time – if he were to be proved, after all, as wrong about Anna as the Chief had been about De Vere.

He left the remaining cover in place to welcome Oaten back. The headline set in bold across the page heralded the coming of THE NEW DARK AGES.

29

I DOUBLE DARE YOU

Sunday, 30 April 1944

Despite the lateness of the hour, the sun was still hanging low over the Clent Hills as Spooner stepped onto the platform of Stourbridge station at 10pm. It had been a fine day and the evening air retained its warmth, slowing the footsteps of the commuters who passed him, free now to enjoy the last half hour of daylight afforded by the clocks being put two hours' forward into Double Summer Time at the beginning of April. Watching their faces lift to the unseasonable rays, Spooner felt acutely aware of how different he was from them. How he might be gazing on the sunset for the last time.

During the course of the past month he had completed all his arrangements and said all his goodbyes. Hardest of those were the ones he had made to Oaten, Miss Josser and his life with them in Manchester, especially after the outcome of the Duncan trial.

While the jury had found all those charged guilty, both the Shadwells' charity receipts and their previous good behaviour mitigated a sentence and they were merely bound over. It was Helen who was sentenced to ten months' imprisonment and faced the ordeal of the Black Maria to Holloway prison alone.

She was bereft, Oaten reported. Behind bars, even her spirit guides had deserted her.

Spooner had prepared his own exit from *Two Worlds* as meticulously as he had been planning for tonight. So far as everyone who knew him from his work there were concerned, he was returning to Aberdeen to lend a hand to his father, who had been in ailing health of late. A cover that the Chief would allow him to take for so long as the war continued, should he be successful in this mission. If he should fail…

Spooner checked his watch. He had no doubt the instructions he had been given at the Hippodrome had been arranged precisely to render him as vulnerable as possible. There was no cover of night to cloak anyone who might be trailing him yet, in half an hour's time, with the sun finally sunk beneath those hills where he was headed, the forces of darkness would be at their most powerful.

For the past week, there had been no broadcasts from Lord Lucifer in Berlin.

There was only one car waiting on the road in front of the station. A black Rolls-Royce Phantom Mark III, the car Anna had described to him on their first meeting, its sinister tone and crouched shape suggesting a sporting version of a hearse.

As Spooner neared the vehicle, he could see the chauffeur, in black livery, sitting behind the wheel, cap pulled down so low as to obscure the face. There was someone else in the back seat too, but, as the figure behind the wheel made no move to do it for him, Spooner had to peer through the open window in order find out who had been sent to receive him.

"I'm so glad you could be punctual, Mr Spooner," the voice was familiar, even if the figure, dressed in a black suit with cropped blond hair, was not. This, Spooner realised, was Nils Anders as nature intended. Only he looked less convincing as a man. His long, sinewy form seemed ill at ease in conventional attire. His face, Spooner noted, was not entirely devoid of make-up, his cheeks had been powdered and his long lashes darkened. But, mindful of everything he had learned about hypnosis, he was careful not to look directly into the pale blue eyes that they surrounded, dropping his gaze instead onto where the other's hands rested on a malacca cane.

"My master has sent me to bring you to the party. Please, make yourself comfortable," he said, a thin humour coursing under his icy tones. "Our journey will not take long."

As Spooner closed the door with a soft thud, the chauffeur started the engine and pointed the long nose of the car away from the safety of the surrounding streets, where children like Terry Jenkins and his gang were still out kicking footballs, and into the countryside.

It wasn't long before the obelisk at the summit of Wychbury Hill became visible ahead of them, a dark silhouette against the crimson rays of the sinking sun. The road that they took snaked around it, leading directly to the gates of the De Vere estate through which he had entered last spring with the Chief. They were guarded this time by a lone figure, wearing the plus fours and Norfolk jacket of a gamekeeper, his flat cap at exactly the same angle as the chauffeur's. Without a word being spoken, he nodded them through.

"Are we going up to the house?" Spooner asked, trying to get a closer look at the man's face as they passed. The Chief had already ascertained that the Earl and Countess were not at home.

Anders chuckled softly. On the other side of the car window, the man in tweeds evaded closer scrutiny as he turned to close the gates, disappearing in the rear-view mirror as the Phantom took the same turn past the Hall and into the woods that Spooner's transport had made the last time. The sun had gone now, though the afterglow of its passing still lit up the sky above the trees in iridescent blues and mauves.

"Do you still really think it is only circus tricks you will see here tonight, Mr Spooner?"

"No," said Spooner, his eyes on the rear-view mirror. "I'm expecting some real magic."

"Then you shall not be disappointed." Anders leaned forward and tapped his cane on the partition between his seat and the chauffeur. "Here will do," he instructed and the car glided to a halt. They had not come very far, just enough to take them away from the view of the house and into the cover of the trees.

"Before we go on," Anders turned back to his fellow passenger, "it is essential for me to make a few safety checks. To ensure you are not going to try using any of the tricks of our trade against us." He lifted the end of his cane, pointing it towards Spooner's chest. "Please, show me your hands, palms outwards." His orders were an echo of Dr Bishop's instructions to Spooner on the threshold of Nicholas Ralphe's asylum cell. "And then don't make another move." With a tiny motion of the thumb, a stiletto blade was released.

Spooner did as he was told, keeping his gaze not on Anders' face but on the hands that controlled the swordstick. Beads of sweat broke out on his forehead as the blade was used to open his jacket and move deeper inside, travelling across his waistcoat to unhook the chain of his fob watch and loosen it from his pocket, dropping it onto the floor; then moving back to prod into his inside pocket and bring out his wallet, which was also allowed to fall with a thud into the space between them.

"Raise your arms," Anders went on. The blade moved over Spooner's heart. It rested there for a while, the pressure gradually increasing until he could feel it pierce the material of his waistcoat and shirt and prick against his skin.

"Oops," Anders' voice was as low as a serpent's hiss. "The blade is so sharp and one has to be so careful with these things. I'm sorry, did I hurt you?"

"No," said Spooner, sweat now running down through his eyebrows and bringing a salty sting to his eyes. "What else are you hoping to find?"

The blade moved away, taking with it the side of Spooner's jacket, so that his underarm was revealed. When Anders found no holster on the left side, he looked to the right. Then he withdrew his weapon with a smile.

"Perhaps you are less intelligent than I had anticipated," he mused. "Or," with another flick of his wrist he used the sharp end of the stick to lift the hem of the left leg of Spooner's trousers, "could it be that you think a gun is better hidden here? No?" He tried the right. "Not here, either? Well, Mr Spooner. Am I to take it that you have come unarmed?"

The blade retracted. Spooner was able to see for the first time that the silver handle on the top of the cane was fashioned in the shape of a goat's skull.

"Why should I have brought a gun, Mr...?" he began. "Oh, I never caught your name."

"I never offered it," said Anders. "But I am sure you know it, all the same."

Spooner frowned. "Is this all part of the act?" He moved his hand slowly towards his jacket pocket, from where a handkerchief protruded. Anders' blade swooped.

"Allow me," the magician's tone hardened as he lifted the silk square. He turned it around on the edge of the blade, studying it for a long minute before he conceded it was, after all, only a piece of fabric.

"Here," he tossed it towards Spooner.

Spooner wiped his brow and returned the square to his pocket with deliberately slow motions. "Finished all your checks now?" he asked.

"Mr Spooner," his companion looked pained. "You can stop pretending to be a theatrical agent. It's starting to get tiresome. Do you really think we don't know who you are?"

Spooner continued to look puzzled. "What do you mean? Who do you think I am?"

A slow smile spread across Anders' face. "Perhaps you are Houdini? Let's see, shall we? Put your arms straight out in front of you. That's right." With a flourish, Anders took from his pocket a pair of handcuffs and snapped them shut around Spooner's wrists.

"Let's see how long it takes you to get out of these," he said. "And now," he lifted Spooner's watch from the floor and made a show of studying the dial, "it's time to make our way to where the ceremony is to begin." Pocketing it, he leaned across Spooner to open the car door. "Out you go."

Beyond the claustrophobic confines of the car, the air smelled sweetly. Above Spooner's head, a dusting of stars glittered in the deep blue sky above the treetops and a crescent moon hung over Wychbury Hill. He was keenly aware of his senses heightening, none more so than where the point of the stiletto knife touched the back of his neck.

"Very good," said Anders, closing the car door behind them. "If you will now just follow the track. You can see well enough, can't you?"

Indeed, he could. Blue flames flickered ahead of them, marking their way at regular intervals along each side of the path. An old showbiz trick, rags soaked in copper chloride, Spooner reasoned. But their unearthly light brought to mind a trail made by fairies, spectral lures beckoning them deeper into the woods. An effect made more potent by the sounds he could hear around him, mirroring the dream he had of Clara with every snapping twig and scurrying of tiny feet. He wondered how many eyes were watching him; how many of them were human.

"It looks fantastic," he said. "I'm impressed."

Anders sighed. "Let me try this another way, Mr Spooner," he said. "Did you never stop to think that Anna reads that magazine that you work for from cover to cover each month? Did you not realise she was certain to see your name there?"

"Of course," said Spooner. "I was sure she would and that she'd use the magazine to get in touch with me again. Who said a theatrical agent can't have other interests? She knew mine were the same as hers."

"And what did you think those interests really were? Please don't tell me it was *volksliede*?" Anders' barked a short, humourless laugh. "Or you didn't think that she could actually be in love with you?"

"No," said Spooner. "I was pretty sure the person she really loved was Clara. That's why she wanted me to know what happened to her friend just as soon as she was sure of it. Did *you* not realise it was Anna leaving all those messages? Who put Bella in the Wych Elm? What do you reckon?"

Clapping a hand on his shoulder, Anders stopped Spooner in his tracks. The blade bit a little deeper, enough to draw blood, but the handcuffed man carried on talking.

"See, Anna thinks it was Nicholas Ralphe – Ralph Nicholson as she knew him. I actually saw the man, just before he died, and he even believed it himself. You did a good job on him, you and your Master. That's what I would call proper magic."

By now he could see it all, just as it had been in his dream. The pale columns of the temple illuminated against the dark canopy by flickering pinpoints of light. The smell of burning herbs brought to his nostrils by the gentle breeze. This time, though, it wasn't just hairs rising on the back of his neck. It was pinpricks of blood.

"It was the letters that made me certain," Spooner continued, "the ones you wrote to Professor Melvin. Ralphe sent the first one, asking her about the ritual for the Hand of Glory, once he had made up his mind what he had to do. The ones that came after were written by you on the same typewriter, which you had easy access to, since you'd had Clara copy the keys to his flat, where you'd read her reply to the first one. A great idea – except for your spelling. When you wrote to the professor, you spelled her title with two 'f's and one 's'. Clara called De Vere the professor. Was that what made the word tricky for you? A wee bit jealous, perhaps?"

Spooner could hear Anders breathing behind him becoming a little more strained. Powerless as he was to use anything as a weapon, he had to keep on using words to stop that blade from going in any deeper. Receiving no answer, he plunged on.

"See, I think you were. You had to make Anna believe Clara was blackmailing you, but I'd wager it was you set the whole thing up. You knew Clara from the thirties, back when you were with the circus in Hamburg, and you'd already established an identity for yourself in Birmingham months before she arrived. Your friendship with Anna gave Clara a professional foil while she went about seducing secrets out of Ralphe. Once you knew what he intended to do with her, you let him go right ahead. We're now on the spot where you buried the hand, so I'm guessing that once you'd seen him make his preparations, you waited here," Spooner nodded towards the portico, "to take charge of the ceremony once they got back. I also think you knew the estate a lot better than he did and that sense of humour of yours leads me to believe it was you who chose Clara's last resting place in the tree. Which leaves only one thing I'm not sure of. Did you work alone that night, or were you assisted by your Master? My understanding is that when Clara went back to Germany in the winter of 1940, it was to ensure De Vere's safe passage. But that information could be suspect. Only a Magister Templi could have successfully performed the ritual, after all."

His words hung on the air for a few moments – too hot, too prickly and smelling overpoweringly of the herbs burned in that previous ritual: rue, henbane, myrtle and belladonna. The blade dropped away from Spooner's neck.

"Not bad for a theatrical agent," said Anders. "Ninety-nine per cent of your deductions cannot be faulted. It must be your tragic obedience to your class system alone that leads you to reason that De Vere must be the head of our Order. The same deference that you show to your own superior officer, I expect."

He stepped out in front of Spooner. In the dancing blue light he looked akin to a vampire, the dark woods his natural habitat.

"Well, when you said that tonight's performance was for your Master…" Spooner began.

Anders smiled. "De Vere was useful," he said, "more useful to us than he was to the man who sent you here. It was his wish to become an adept, so his initiation was to assist us in destroying your war factory from the inside. I'm sorry if it was he you were hoping to meet this evening, but you see, Mr Spooner, I serve only one master – and as your colleague Ralphe found to his cost, his powers are much greater than any earthly lord's. Come, see for yourself how I persuaded your predecessor he had killed the great love of his life. I'm sure you will appreciate the trick of it…"

With a sharp click, Spooner heard the blade snap back into position behind his neck and he could do nothing to avoid it but walk towards the temple, trying to keep his mind ready for any eventuality he might find himself presented with.

Twelve tall black candles had been placed around the pentagram marked out on the floor, the image of Baphomet at its centre. They burned with a phosphorescent glow, emitting sulphurous notes to the smoking bowls between them. At the centre stood an empty throne, a chair made of blackened oak, the thirteenth candle placed at its base.

It wasn't the unholy setting that made Spooner's stomach turn a somersault. It was what hung above the throne, suspended from the ceiling upside down, gagged and bound from her ankles to her throat, sea-green eyes staring at him in mute horror: Anna.

"Like a lamb to the slaughter," she had said.

"You recognise the sacrifice, naturally," Anders could not conceal the delight in his voice. "As it pleased her so much to betray her sacred oaths to you, she will follow her dearest all the way down to hell. And you shall be the one to send her there."

Beneath where her body twisted in a vain attempt to loosen her shackles, across the seat of the throne was placed a scimitar, its blade a deadly crescent moon.

"Impressive, *nein*?" Anders swooped down to reach it. "This holy blade was once used by the Templars. Shedding blood with such a powerful weapon shall make the sacrifice all the more potent. Together, you and Anna shall open the door into the abyss…"

By now, Spooner had almost succeeded in pulling off the trick he had been practising so long. He had picked up two hairpins from his jacket pocket when he had returned his handkerchief, unnoticed by his host. He had them gripped between the third and fourth fingers of both hands when the handcuffs went on and had managed to slide them down in his palm by making fists as he exited the car. All the time they had been walking through the woods he had fashioned them into tools to work at the lock with, the sound of their feet and conversation disguising the noise made by each successive pin of the barrel coming loose and keeping his mind focussed on the task and not the myriad illusions he was being shown. As they entered the temple, the fifth and final pin had sprung. All he had to do now was wait for Anders to place the sacrificial knife in his hand.

"But first," Anders smiled as he turned the vicious implement around in his hand, "let me introduce you to my Master. It is in his name that all of this work is done. Hail to thee, Prince of Darkness! Hail to thee, my Lord Satan!"

As he spoke the candles shimmered, their flames guttering, while around the throne another light seemed to form out of thin air, a pale purple ball that glowed and spread lengthways and widthways, turning in front of Spooner's disbelieving eyes into the form of a massive goat. Back to Spooner came the words of the Chief: "*Ralphe said he saw the Goat of Mendes manifest in a temple in the grounds of a house on the Worcestershire borders*", and he knew he was seeing exactly what the doomed man had witnessed before him and been terrified out of his wits thereafter.

Despite the dizzying lights, smells and all the other elements Anders had working away to destroy his reason, it was this fact that assured Spooner that what he was seeing was nothing but a trick, the smoke and mirrors of the adepts of Norrie's world, not a real satanic manifestation of Triple-U will. Even if he could see every coarse black hair on the creature's body, smell the foetid aroma of its breath.

Trying not to flinch, Spooner kept his gaze on Anna, who twisted and curled above.

"Now you shall obey my Master," said Anders, "and dispatch this little traitor." He ran the curved blade around her neck with the precision with which he had wielded the swordstick, creating there a thin necklace of rubies, made from her own blood.

Everything now hinged on the timing. Catching his breath, Spooner watched Anders pass the knife through the smoke of the incense and then genuflect before the Goat, presenting the instrument of slaughter to his Master. The Beast raised its head and opened its mouth, from which emitted a cacophony of shrieks and bellows as loud as the wail of an air raid siren that seemed to be blasting up through the earth from its kingdom below.

No wonder Ralphe had cracked when faced with the same

ordeal. Poor Ralphe, who had been so unprepared; and to whom no one had ever lent a copy of *Magic for Beginners*.

Anders swept the blade under Spooner's arms, forcing him to hold them out in front of him, palms upwards, to receive the weapon.

"Take it!" Anders demanded.

Spooner felt his hand grip the handle at the same second as his handcuffs fell to the ground and, in that moment, he stepped to the side of his opponent, raising his arms in preparation to strike, forcing all his will against the sound and the fury of the performance around him into his only pure objective – to rid the world of Anders and everything he stood for.

But the moment never came.

As the knife passed between the two men, Anders' face registered first shock, then outrage and finally, disbelief. Spooner followed the other man's rolling eyeballs upwards to the perfect round hole that had appeared, as if by magic, in the centre of his forehead.

"That," said Detective Sergeant William Houlston, holding his pistol in front of him, "was for the BSA factory."

Anders gave a final gasp and fell backwards.

"And this," Houlston swivelled around, aiming now at the portico of the temple, the place Spooner suspected that a projector was hidden, "is for everyone on shift that night. Including my sister." He let off a volley of shots, drawing his finger back on the trigger until his cylinder had been spent. Wood splintered and sparks flew under the barrage and Spooner dropped to the ground to avoid the shrapnel, throwing the knife aside and putting his hands over his ears instead, until the wailing of the damned came to an abrupt and spluttering halt.

"I've waited a long time to do that," he heard Houlston say, and then: "Are you all right?"

As the DSI kneeled beside him, Spooner realised he was shaking like a leaf. He had survived, and with his reason seemingly intact, but the physical endurance it had taken had turned his body to quivering jelly. Gingerly he raised himself into a sitting position.

"I'm not sure," he admitted, raking a hand through his hair. Houlston's round blue eyes stared back at him. He had lost both his flat cap and the pencil moustache he had worn the last time Spooner saw him, part of the disguise he had used to stand in for the De Veres' gamekeeper.

"That took guts, kid," he said.

When Spooner had asked for the Birmingham spycatcher, he hadn't been entirely surprised to find himself meeting Houlston again. It seemed the feeling was mutual.

"You took your time," was the first thing he said.

But when Spooner shared the information he had gleaned at the Hippodrome, the detective's surly demeanour transformed. He swiftly ascertained that Simon De Vere had sent orders to the estate that his gamekeeper should expect Mr Anders to call at the end of the month, and to put the car, house and grounds at his disposal. The gamekeeper knew Anders by sight, but doubted the other man would have similar recall – he and Houlston looked enough alike to resemble each other from a distance, which was as close a look as Anders had ever taken at any servant of the De Veres. Houlston had been observing Anders and his chauffeur bringing in props and practising trial runs with a stopwatch while wandering the grounds with a spaniel and a pair of binoculars for the past week.

Bertie Adams had advised them on how the tricks would likely work and Spooner's library had provided further details on what to expect from this kind of ritual. They had been as forewarned as possible. Though there was one thing Spooner hadn't realised.

"I didn't know about your sister," he said.

Houlston grimaced. "We all have our reasons. I thought it might make you feel better to know what made the pleasure entirely mine."

"Is there anyone else here?" asked Spooner. "Was any of what I saw actually real?"

Houlston shook his head. "Nope. It was all a projection. Though I dread to think where that recording of the screams came from." He shook his head. "There's no one here but us chickens and no one knows that except the staff at the house… and my boss."

Houlston gave Spooner another one of his long, slow winks, as if to suggest he knew who that last person he referred to might be.

"He'll expect me to clean up," he continued, "but first, let's get you up and that other one down and we can find out who was right about her – you or me."

For the second time in their acquaintance, Houlston helped Spooner to his feet. Spooner's legs wobbled and he had to lean against the other man until he regained his balance. But it was relief now, not fear that coursed through his veins. He had survived and he had saved Anna. It was almost enough to make him laugh…

Until he turned towards the centre of the temple and saw the loose rope hanging there.

"Anna!" he called, and stumbled forward through the

smoke and the fumes. It was so hard to see anything properly. Perhaps she had managed to free herself and was crouching in the shadows waiting for him, too afraid of Houlston's presence to show herself. "Anna, you can come out now. It's all right. No one's going to hurt you…"

His voice echoed back off the walls. His lungs had become so full of the smoke that the effort of shouting made him start to cough painfully. He turned around, desperately seeking a sign of movement between the smouldering bowls and the flickering lights. All he could see was shadows and the still form of Anders, staring blankly up at the ceiling.

"I should have known…" Houlston said from behind him, all the ire returning to his voice. "He never tied her up, did he? It was all part of the trick."

"The trick?" Spooner's hand flailed towards the rope, still swinging with the momentum of its former captive's departure.

"She was in on it all along," Houlston moved beside him. "She lured you here so he could kill you, then she spent the week practising all this with him, dressed as his chauffeur. Bet you never knew she was an escapologist and all, did you?"

Spooner shook his head. "No," he said. "She believed in him once. But he let her down, disappeared on her. And she wasn't sure why until he came back, after they'd found the body in the woods. That was when she finally had to accept the truth of what he really was. That night at the Hippodrome, she asked me to fetch the spycatcher and bring you here. She knew he was trying to set me up, but she wanted this game to end with Anders dead, not me. She played along with him until the last second, but she was gambling all along that you'd get him first. That was the risk she was prepared to take, that I might actually kill her. She was still trussed up when he put the knife in my hands, wasn't she?"

Houlston grunted. "Then what's she done a runner for now?" he asked.

Spooner raised his arm to cuff away the tear that was sliding down his cheek. He hoped that, in the darkness, his companion wouldn't have noticed it. "Her work's done now," knowing as he said it that he'd never catch up with her again, not in this lifetime. All she'd ever be was a silvery trail hung upon the night air, the stardust memory of a song. "There's nothing else left for her."

Anna was gone.

EPILOGUE

Friday, 3 January 1946

Around a hundred people assembled by the gates of Wandsworth prison for the execution of the traitor, Simon De Vere. Anticipating trouble from his supporters, the police had drafted in reinforcements. But when the notice announcing the hanging was posted, just after nine o'clock that morning, only one man removed his hat and stood to attention.

The prisoner faced the rope with as cool a demeanour as he had shown the court at his trial at the Old Bailey the previous September. Perhaps he was hoping that, as had once been the case with his friend Lady Wynter, the jury would not find themselves able to pass a guilty sentence on someone of such breeding, a notion that had been dashed both then and at his subsequent appeal. Still, De Vere had gone for his appointment with the executioner Albert Pierrepoint, himself fresh from dispatching many of his lordship's former comrades at Nuremberg, dressed in his best Savile Row.

He hadn't looked so assured the last time Spooner had seen him, shortly after his capture on the Danish border the previous May. De Vere had been found lurking in an abandoned farmhouse, one of many such places in which he had sought refuge since the German surrender. Two British soldiers, part of a battalion hunting for SS and war criminals amid the defeated troops coming down from Denmark and Norway, recognised and challenged him. De Vere admitted who he was and let the soldiers in, then made a lunge for something hidden under the seat of a chair. Thinking it was a gun, one of the soldiers shot him in the buttocks.

The De Vere that Spooner met with, in the 74th British General Hospital in Lüneburg, close to the Hamburg that Clara and Kohl had once called home, rested on his iron cot with a sunken face, his dentures having been confiscated in case they contained a cyanide pill, wearing blue and white striped pyjamas. He looked much older than the man Spooner recalled from the smoky London rooms of 1939.

Their interview filled in some gaps of the story, details that would not be heard in court and which De Vere parted with unwillingly, on the sole condition that the woman he had been found with, a German redhead with an uncanny resemblance to Agent Belladonna, would be spared imprisonment herself. As he would go on to repeat at his trial, he claimed to be a patriot who had been working for the interests of his country all along.

De Vere could not remember precisely where he had first encountered the man who called himself Nils Anders, only that it was in Birmingham and, if not at a theatre or music hall, then a pub or club favoured by the city's bohemians. He found both Anders' striking looks and sophisticated patter alluring, particularly when the tightrope walker claimed to be a high-ranking Black magician. Delighted at the opportunity to sniff out a miscreant for the Chief, he began to cultivate this strange foreign creature passing himself off as a Dutchman, whom he suspected was more likely a German spy.

Anders told De Vere that he had jumped a train at the age

of twenty-one and crossed the border to the Weimar Berlin of 1933, which tallied with the date and age at which Otto Dieterling had been released from jail. In the decadent quarters of the German capital, he was initiated into a sect that worshipped Baphomet, the God of the Templars, by an adept who was also in showbusiness and helped him develop his skills both as a circus performer and as a student of the Left Hand Path. Anders believed he was part of an elite who would come to rule over the world once chaos had been unleashed from the abyss – an event that had, when the two men first met, in the October of 1939, just been set into motion.

Throughout the months of the phoney war, Anders spent a lot of time at Hagley Hall, tutoring his host in magical practices and revelling in the atmosphere of the park. De Vere reported to him the goings-on of the societies he belonged to in London, hoping to find a definitive connection. He had been attending gatherings of Mosley's Blackshirts and extolled their charismatic leader, but Anders was more interested in Captain Archibald Ramsay of the Right Club, who was telling his members to prepare for imminent invasion. De Vere duly got himself an introduction and there met a man called Ralph Nicholson, a guest of the glittering Lady Wynter, who had no idea that the handsome flight lieutenant had been sent to infiltrate the society. Neither apparently did De Vere who, reading him as a potential traitor and finding that he was stationed near to his family home, invited Nicholson up to Hagley and introduced him to Anders, who considered him suitable material for initiation.

When both men managed to avoid being scooped up in the Chief's raid on the Right Club and the subsequent prosecutions, Anders assured them that their fortune was due to the protection of Baphomet, although perhaps to test how far that luck extended, he set them a new task. He had heard there was a man in London who owned the most important grimoire in German history, a book once owned by Goethe. Knowing how well connected De Vere was, he expected it would not be beyond their powers to find it. With the help of Lady Wynter, they purchased Harry Price's folio in June 1940. Invited to the Hall to receive his prize, Anders brought with him an old friend from his circus days, who was herself now working in Birmingham, an alluring redhead called Clara Brown.

It was at this point that things started to go awry.

De Vere realised Nicholson was being set up with Clara and was alarmed at the speed with which she worked her charms – partly because she stirred up something previously dormant within him too. He had always found it easy to attract admirers of both sexes, but until then, had preferred the attentions of men. Clara awoke a desire in him that clearly still simmered. He put this down to the rituals they began practising, each one more physically and emotionally challenging than the last.

The Birmingham blitz began on the thirteenth of August, on information that, Spooner now realised, could have come from De Vere as equally as it could have from Ralphe. As he had suspected, Anders became as jealous of Clara as Anna had been of her lover, but was equally powerless to stop events from taking their course. Belladonna was doing too brilliant a job of relaying the right information back to the Abwehr.

So he turned instead to his spellbook, performing a ritual from *The High German Black Book* on Samhain six days after the last Luftwaffe raid on Birmingham. De Vere was frightened by what might occur, and so obtained a quantity of opium to dose himself with before the ceremony began. His recall of events was blurred, though his description of seeing a purple ball of light chimed with Spooner's experience. At the end of it, Anders and Clara carried Nicholson from the temple and he never saw the RAF man again.

For the next month, Clara paid frequent visits to Hagley Hall alone. She told De Vere that their Magus was making plans to receive them into his new headquarters, a castle on the Rhine. Before Christmas they took a train to London, where they spent two days in a hotel in South Kensington awaiting instructions. Early in the evening of the second day, a man called for them and drove them down to the coast. The journey took around three hours and ended at a desolate inlet, deep in the marshes, where a smack waited to take them across the Channel. The night was thick with fog, conditions they had been waiting for, and the journey made him too sick to recall much detail about either their chauffeur or the fisherman who steered their course away from the patrol vessels, except to say that Clara talked to all of them in German. Spooner wondered if Anders had used the same escape route when he disappeared from London in December of the following year.

De Vere and Clara were met by another car on the French side of the Channel and driven to Calais, from where their journey continued by air to Berlin and then finally to the Rhine Valley, where De Vere met the Magus, Heinrich Himmler, in the SS Headquarters Castle Wewelsburg. Clara stayed a couple of days longer; she was going to Amsterdam to prepare another agent for a mission. She told De Vere she had been ordered to find a mysterious cave used by the Knights Templar, that lay beneath the crossroads of two Roman roads in a town on the outskirts of Cambridge. It featured a circular recessed altar where they had carried out rites to Baphomet and also acted as a repository for their treasures, perhaps even the Grail itself. It was the cave in Royston that Anders asked Professor Melvin about. De Vere never heard from Clara again.

He was left in the very place that the Chief had hoped he would end up, the inner sanctum of the enemy, trusted with highly sensitive intelligence on the operations of Hitler's elite. Himmler decided the best use for De Vere's brand of Black Arts was in propaganda, and duly dispatched him to Berlin, where he began his broadcasts. When the German capital came under heavy Allied bombardment in 1944, he was transferred to Luxembourg and then finally Apen, near Hamburg.

De Vere denied having anything more to do with Anders once he was inside Germany. He couldn't account for the orders he had sent to open the Hall to him in the April of 1944, and why his gamekeeper had accepted them as genuine. Nor could he explain how Anders appeared to know who Spooner was really working for. The only genuine part of this conversation was the relief he showed when he learned Anders was no longer in any position to trouble him again.

Himmler ordered Wewelsburg to be destroyed on 30 March 1945. De Vere and his "wife" Gudrun – another adept within the Obergruppenführer's organisation – were issued with counterfeit British passports and turned loose. While the pair travelled, at her suggestion, towards Belgium and their eventual capture, Himmler was found hiding in a grain mill in the countryside between Hamburg and Bremen. He was taken to Security Force Headquarters in Lüneburg, whereupon the Magus escaped beyond all earthly jurisdiction, biting the suicide pill that was hidden in the back of his jaw.

The extent of the propaganda work De Vere did for him would be for another agent to ascertain, once he was recovered enough to be flown back to London. Spooner's job was to interrogate him on the subject of Belladonna, reporting to the Chief alone. Before he took his leave of the prisoner, he was shown what it was that De Vere had hidden in that abandoned house that was of such importance to him he had risked being shot.

Spooner carried it in his briefcase now, as he stood in the winter sunlight that had just started to burn through the earlier mist, illuminating the imposing Portland stone exterior of Senate House in shafts of pale yellow. Rather like himself, this building had been requisitioned for the duration of the war, housing the Ministry of Information's department of subterfuge and propaganda. It had withstood five bomb raids during the Blitz of 1940 without a soul being harmed. Now, with the peace, it had returned to its original purpose of education. The University Colleges of London had all come back, and along with them, a new department had found a home.

It was situated at the top of the tower, commanding an epic view over the capital while all around the wind shrieked and whistled like the souls of the unquiet dead – a suitable setting for Harry Price's National Laboratory of Psychical Research.

Spooner found the Ghost Hunter at his desk, surrounded by the shelves that housed his archive of magic books, bequeathed to Senate House Library for perpetuity in return for the space to run his organisation rent-free. Although their appointment had been arranged beforehand, when Spooner stepped into his domain, he still looked startled, the angry caterpillar eyebrows rearing as his grey eyes lifted from his paperwork.

"Yes?" he uttered gruffly. Then a more contemplative look stole across his features.

"Spooner," he rose to his feet with a smile. "It's you, is it?"

His civilian clothes were not so different from the outfit he had been wearing the last time they had met, though Spooner had treated himself to a new suit similar to the one that had sustained him through the war. But, seeing the older man's eyes travel upwards, he put a hand up to his hair, which now had a streak of white through the front of it.

"Aye," he confirmed. "It's me all right."

"Well," Price waved at the nearest chair. "Pull that up to the desk, then. I'm not so light on my feet as I used to be."

"But at least you've found yourself a good home now?"

"A safe haven," Price agreed. "If a little..." he wrinkled his nose, "clinical."

"Look, I'm sorry it took so long to get back to you," Spooner began. "Only I didn't want to come until I knew I had something of value to show you."

"Oh, and what could that be? Has it taken you this long to learn the secrets of that book I gave you?"

Spooner opened his briefcase. "Aye," he said, "and I've brought it back in case you want to pass it on to someone else who might need it. You may be surprised to know that I hold this partly responsible for my still being alive, so I'm very grateful to you, Mr Price."

He passed *Magic for Beginners*, a little more dog-eared now, across the desk to its rightful owner, whose eyebrows twitched speculatively as he received it.

"Is that so? Are you going to tell me why?" He flicked

through the pages, satisfying himself that this was the same tome he had lent out. "I gather you stopped working for Ernest Oaten some time ago. What have you been doing with yourself since?"

Spooner reached back into the bag. "I also found this for you," he said. "Sad to say, it has been cared for even less well, but I hope it means your collection is once more complete."

He had wrapped it in several layers of brown paper to protect it, and though its hand-tooled leather cover was battered, the pages within curled where they had travelled across the battlefields of Europe next to its carrier's ribs, it was still intact. He watched the Ghost Hunter unwrap it, his expression turning from curiosity to complete astonishment.

"*The High German Black Book*," he said, his voice rising an octave. "I never thought I'd see this again. Well, I never. Well, I never did…" his voice trailed off as he thumbed through the folio, shaking his head. Spooner watched him with satisfaction. He felt he had acquitted himself with a magician's flourish.

"I won't ask you," Price looked up, his voice becoming louder. "Indeed, I can't ask you. As a member of the Magic Circle that would be unprofessional. But I am very grateful to you, Spooner, this is quite beyond what I ever expected. Though," his eyes returned to the streak in his visitor's hair, "I did think there was something interesting about you the first time we met. Now I'm certain of it."

"Oh yes?" said Spooner. He had adjusted well enough to civilian life, finding digs in London while he mulled over what to do next. Though he'd seen enough action with the Secret Service, at the same time, he wanted to find something to do that would help keep texts such as this safe from De Vere's widow, or any other of Clara's doppelgängers. He would never forget Nicholas Ralphe's warning: "*There are always going to be more of them, using their tricks and devilry the way they used me.*"

Underneath the table, Spooner kept his fingers crossed. "What's that, then?" he said.

Harry Price smiled, showing pointed teeth. "When do you want to start?" he said.

AUTHOR'S NOTE ON SOURCES AND ACKNOWLEDGEMENTS

It was Dr Mike Dash, my erstwhile publisher at *Bizarre* magazine, who first pointed me to the story of the Hagley Woods Mystery and suggested that, if I was writing about the 1940s, I should incorporate it into my novel. For this direction, and the archive material that he shared with me, I cannot thank him enough.

This is, of course, a work of fiction, my own imaginings woven around the skeleton of a woman found by schoolboys in a tree in Hagley Woods, Worcestershire, on 18 April 1943, who has still never been formally identified. From various sources, including Brian Haughton's excellent website brian-haughton.com, the National Archives, contemporaneous police records and articles, I extrapolated on the theory that she was a German agent, an actress and singer named Clara, who was helping to orchestrate the Birmingham blitz for the Luftwaffe, as the spy Josef Jakobs claimed when he was interrogated by MI5 after being captured in farmland near Ramsey in Huntingdonshire on 1 February 1941. The spate of letters received by the Wolverhampton *Express and Star* in 1953 by the mysterious "Anna" of Claverly also claimed inside knowledge of Clara being part of a spy ring, whose number included a Dutch circus performer and a British officer who died insane in a military institution in 1942. Files relating to this latter person have still never been opened, but these strange characters, along with the hauntingly gothic settings of Hagley Park and Wychbury Hill all suggested something from the pen of Dennis Wheatley. Wheatley himself worked for the Secret Service in World War II and was a good friend of the spymaster, Maxwell Knight, whose wartime brief was to infiltrate fascist groups, many of which had occult leanings – and who first met his later recruit, William Joyce, *aka* Lord Haw Haw, at a party thrown by Wheatley. I am indebted to Paul Willetts for allowing me to use research on Knight gleaned from his own superb true-life account, *Rendezvous at the Russian Tea Rooms* (Constable, 2015), in fashioning the character of the Chief. Phil Baker's exemplary biography of Dennis Wheatley, *The Devil is a Gentleman* (Dedalus, 2009), was also very useful, as were the Black magic works of Wheatley himself, whom I feel has been an avuncular spirit guide throughout the writing of this book.

The suggestion that Clara was killed as part of a Black magic ritual called the Hand of Glory was first proposed by Professor Margaret Murray, the real Egyptologist and author of *The Witch-Cult in Western Europe* and *The God of the Witches*. The identities of the first and many subsequent authors of the WHO PUT BELLA DOWN THE WYCH ELM? graffiti remain a mystery, but there are fresh cases of it seemingly every week – the base of the obelisk on Wychbury Hill was adorned with it and placards hung around signposts and trees in Hagley Woods when I visited in September 2016. Many thanks to Suzanne Knipe for being such a brilliant local tour guide on that occasion. Suggestive though they are, I didn't make up any of the names of these locations.

I always intended to write about the case of Helen Duncan, the last British woman to be found guilty of practising witchcraft in a controversial trial at the Old Bailey in March 1944. Malcolm Gaskill's *Hellish Nell: Last of Britain's Witches* (4th Estate, 2001) provided an insightful and unprejudiced account of a case that continues to divide opinion and beg questions. It was in this book that I first came across the wonderful characters Hannen Swaffer, *aka* the Pope of Fleet Street, who defended Mrs Duncan at her trial, and Harry Price, the Ghost Hunter, who had by then spent over a decade pursuing her as a fraud. I found further press reports on the trial in the archives of the *Daily Mirror* and the *Daily Express* and my thanks to Max Décharné for hipping me to those, as well as the many other kindnesses he and Katja Klier have extended to me. I am further indebted to Harry Price's former cataloguer Christopher Josiffe for letting me run by him my theories on how Harry could perhaps connect to Clara. I would also like to thank Alan Murdie of the Ghost Club and Charles Harrowell at Senate House Library for their help and assistance, and should like to point readers towards the wonderful resource, www.harrypricewebsite.co.uk, where you can find the pictures of Mrs Duncan and her ectoplasm, as well as stunning scenes of goat-based sorcery in the Harz Mountains.

Again, the link between Price and those organisations being monitored by Maxwell Knight is purely of my own invention, though inspired by the fact that the former suffragette-turned-fascist Christabel Nicholson, who had an interest in the supernatural, also frequented the Russian Tearooms used by Nazi spies on Roland Gardens in South Kensington, which was on the same road as Harry Price's National Laboratory of Psychical Research. She was also a member of the Right Club and was tried and acquitted of being part of a Nazi spy ring in a case instigated by Knight in the summer of 1940.

I had no idea when I started writing that this story would incorporate things that happened to my own family during the war. Thanks to my granddad, Peter Unsworth, who was the spycatcher for Peterborough during the war, I did actually meet his opposite number for Huntingdonshire, DS Thomas Mills, who apprehended Josef Jakobs in the fens, though sadly I was too young when it happened to remember it now. Meanwhile, my other granddad, Horace Lawley, was working in the Spitfire factory at Castle Bromwich that was bombed by the Luftwaffe on 13 August 1941, thankfully surviving the experience and going home the same day to continue his duties as an ARP warden. So my love and thanks to my family on both sides of the Veil: my parents Phil and Brenda, who helped so much in the research of this book with their own memories of the fens and the Midlands during the war and a constant supply of inspiring reading; my grandmas Joan and Evelyn, who kept everyone safe during those dark days; my brother Matthew, sister-in-law Yvette and the next generation, Tommy, Will and Sophie-Rose. For further familial support and wartime memories, my love and thanks go to Danny Meekin, Cath Meekin, Francis Meekin, Eva Snee, Danny and Elaine Snee and Mick and Maureen Snee.

I found more about the blitzes on Birmingham and Portsmouth online, including *Remembering BSA* by Steve Hayward (https://vimeo.com/33916752, retrieved on 15.1.16); the *Birmingham Express and Star*, the *Birmingham Mail*, the *Black Country Bugle*, Warwick Library online, the BBC's *People's War* site, www.welcometoportsmouth.co.uk, Daily History blog and the *Daily Telegraph*. For history on the music halls of

Birmingham, I consulted www.its-behind-you.com, the BBC *People's War* website and www.arthurlloyd.co.uk/Birmingham.htm, through which I found the marvellous displaced Cockney, Bertram Adams of the Hippodrome. Anna's folk repertoire comes from www.contemplator.com/england/ and Spooner's favourite "Witches Reel", together with its history and an explanation for the lyrics, I found on sarahannelawless.com. Information on Rauceby hospital came from www.lincstothepast.com and the Salvation Army in Birmingham during the war from www.birminghamcitadel.co.uk.

Spooner's bookish background was inspired by Leo Marks, and his genius memoir of the SOE, *Between Silk and Cyanide* (Harper Collins, 1998).

I was further helped by the films *Millions Like Us* (Frank Launder & Sidney Gilliat, 1941), which featured the Spitfire factory, and *Love on the Dole* (John Baxter, 1941).

For continuing to support my efforts with ceaseless good cheer, sound advice and patience, I am indebted to my wonderful friend and agent Caroline Montgomery and the extended Rupert Crew Addams family of Fenris Oswin and Doreen Montgomery. It is to my intense regret that Doreen didn't get to see this book in its final form; her passing in November 2017 robbed the world of a wonderful, kind and nurturing soul and an inspiration whose memory I will always treasure.

Further felicitations for all their support to Meg Davis at Ki Agency; my editor Cecily Gayford and Hannah Westland, Anna-Marie Fitzgerald, Niamh Murray and all at Serpent's Tail; and to Pete Ayrton and John Williams. Thanks also to François Geurif, Jeanne Guyonne and all at Rivages; and Laura Meyer, Meredith Dees and all at the House of Anansi.

For further insights and help into all things esoteric across many years I would like to thank Pete Woodhead, Joe McNally and Deirdre Rusling, Benedict Newbery, Richard and Sarah Newson, Emma Murphy, Paul A. Murphy, Ruth Bayer and Dave Knight, Chris Simmons, Raphael, Lucia and Leo Abraham, Damjana and Predrag Finci, Billy Chainsaw, The Shend, Ken and Rachel Hollings, James B. Hollands and Dr Paddy, Etienne Gilfillan, Mark Pilkington, Travis Elborough, Michael Dillon, Mike Jay and Louise Burton, Lydia Lunch, David Peace, Jake Arnott, Christopher Fowler, Martin Cloake, John King and Martin Knight of London Books, Jay Clifton, Syd Moore, Mari Mansfield, Julian Ibbitson and Gerry, Jan and Jos at the Pink Shop. I owe a similar debt to Marc Glendening, David Fogarty, Jon and Caroline Glover, David Rose, Virginia Ironside and all the regulars at the Sohemian Society; and to Roger K. Burton at the Horse Hospital for keeping on keeping on against all the odds.

During the writing of this novel, I lost my job and with it the friends I worked with over thirteen years on five magazines. My deepest gratitude to Margaret Nicholls, for supporting my attempts at being a crime writer at the same time as being a sub-editor, Claudia Woodward, who got me through the door in the first place, Abby Taylor who helped so much with photo research right down to our last few days, and to my fellow members of the Miners' Social, Past and Present: Debbie Voller, Duncan Bolt, Lynn Taylor, Anna Pattenden, Kerry Sutch, Gino Tambini, Claire Ricketts, Steve Trodd, Andrew Sloan, Allinda Hardwick, Kathy Young, Suzy Prince, Rosie Evans, Saffron Fradley, Caroline Box, Rob Sekula and Alix Buscovic. Thanks also to David Ayrton of the National Union of Journalists.

Finally, all my love as always to Michael Meekin, for all his wisdom, patience, humour and ability to always find the way out of the woods.